PRAISE FOR BARBARA NICKLESS

PLAY OF SHADOWS

"A brisk and clever whodunit with chills and verve."

—*Kirkus Reviews*

"Barbara Nickless hits the ball out of the park on this one . . . This is the third in the series but can be easily read as a stand-alone."

—Midwest Book Review

"*Play of Shadows* is an artful mystery, heavily researched . . . and one that combines a contemporary serial killer with a complex of ancient myths and symbols."

—*Denver Post*

"An intense thriller that resonates with dark myth, *Play of Shadows* is another fascinating case for Dr. Evan Wilding, one of the most interesting and original protagonists in mystery fiction. I want more!"

—J. F. Penn, *New York Times* and *USA Today* bestselling author

"*Play of Shadows* is a work of mythic proportions! Once again Barbara Nickless demonstrates her masterful storytelling, and her outstanding character development. We get to see a more nuanced side of Dr. Evan Wilding (already my favorite literary character), his archaeologist brother, River, his assistant, Diana, and detectives Addie Bisset and Patrick McBrady of the Chicago police department as they delve deeply into mythology (the Minotaur of Crete) to solve this grisly crime and stop the killer's deranged game. Nickless skillfully plays with the idea of Shadow, as we see the darker side of humanity. Barbara Nickless's research is staggering, her grasp of mythology is impressive, and the story is riveting. Once I got started, I could not put it down. This is Barbara Nickless's finest work to date."

—Francesca Ferrentelli, PhD, LPC, mythologist and psychotherapist

"Featuring a truly sinister monster and one of the best chase sequences put to page, *Play of Shadows* is equal parts harrowing and intriguing. Fans of the series will be familiar with the multilayered tensions between Dr. Evan Wilding and Chicago detective Addie Bisset, but this time out Evan's brother River adds a feisty, action-oriented element to the mix. The puzzle they face is a doozy, the clues are manifold, and the trail they follow is littered with traps. *Play of Shadows* is as smart as it is captivating, right down to the last page."

—Mark Stevens, author of *The Fireballer* and the Allison Coil Mystery series

DARK OF NIGHT

"Nickless's character-driven mystery unfolds on a panoramic scale . . . Engrossing bits of scholarship tucked into a nifty procedural with amiable sleuths."

—*Kirkus Reviews*

"Evan and his immediate circle fascinate . . . Fans of religious thrillers will have fun."

—*Publishers Weekly*

"Captivating, compelling, and completely intriguing! Sherlock Holmes meets *The Da Vinci Code* in this brilliantly written and seamlessly researched adventure, where clues from the ancient past propel contemporary global intrigue. This is an immersive and atmospheric thriller, with an unforgettable main character, and I could not put it down."

—Hank Phillippi Ryan, *USA Today* bestselling author of *Her Perfect Life*

"Readers rejoice: Dr. Evan Wilding is back, and *Dark of Night* is another great vehicle for his wry brilliance. The novel is fascinating and twisty with unforgettable characters and writing that took my breath away. You'll want to clear your calendar for this one."

—Jess Lourey, Amazon Charts bestselling author

"*Dark of Night* had me at Moses papyri. Stolen antiquities, dark forces, cobra bites. What a wonderful read. What an adventure to sink into. What beautiful writing. I loved it."

—Tracy Clark, author of the Cass Raines series, winner of the 2020 and 2022 Sue Grafton Memorial Award

"Dr. Evan Wilding is absolutely my new favorite fictional human. His witty charm, his intellect—matched only by his wry humor—along with his goshawk sidekick make him exactly the kind of character who captures an audience within a few lines. Add in the talented and tough detective Addie Bisset, a death by cobra, and a collection of sketchy people all seeking the same priceless artifact, and *Dark of Night* will have you flipping pages well into the night. Barbara Nickless is a phenomenal talent, and she just gets better with every book. *Dark of Night* is her best yet. Bravo!"

—Danielle Girard, *USA Today* bestselling author of *The Ex*

"Missing artifacts? The dark underbelly of the antiquities world? Murder by . . . cobra? Count me in. *Dark of Night* is a top-notch thriller with an unforgettable lead in Dr. Evan Wilding. It's no surprise that Barbara Nickless has fast become one of my favorite authors. I tore through this novel at breakneck speed and can't wait for the next adventure."

—Hannah Mary McKinnon, internationally bestselling author of *Never Coming Home*

"*Dark of Night* is a superb novel . . . After reading the first book in the series, I was hopeful that a second book would be as good or better. I wasn't disappointed. With the new book, Barbara Nickless has solidified a great new mystery series."

—BVS Reviews

AT FIRST LIGHT

An Amazon Best Book of the Month: Mystery, Thriller & Suspense

"Well researched."

—*Kirkus Reviews*

"[In] this intense psychological thriller . . . Evan and Addie race to prevent more bloodshed. Hints of a romantic relationship between the pair enliven the story, and references to *Beowulf* and Viking history add depth. Readers will hope to see more of Addie and Evan."

—*Publishers Weekly*

"Brilliant Evan Wilding, with his goshawk and unusual friendships, will fascinate those who read for character."

—*Library Journal*

"*At First Light* is a winner."

—*Denver Post*

"A high-intensity thriller that will take your breath away . . . Barbara Nickless is an awesome talent."

—*Mysterious Book Report*

"The moment I finished this intelligent and pulse-pounding psychological thriller, I was ready for Book Two . . . Dr. Evan Wilding is one of the most interesting fictional characters I've met in some time . . . Author Nickless's prose is crisp and, at times, poetic. Her descriptions are vivid but balanced. I became immediately attached to her engaging and well-drawn characters. In some respects, *At First Light* is reminiscent of Dan Brown's *The Da Vinci Code*. I highly recommend this book to fans of fast-paced thrillers that include riddles, ancient languages, and literature."

—Claudia N. Oltean, for the *Jacksonville Florida Times-Union*

"*At First Light* is a stunner of a tale. Barbara Nickless has fashioned a deep exploration into moral depravity and the dark depths of the human soul in a fashion not seen since the brilliant David Fincher film *SE7EN*. This wholly realized tale is reminiscent of Lisa Gardner, Karin Slaughter, and Lisa Scottoline at their level best."

—Jon Land, *USA Today* bestselling author

"Barbara Nickless has crafted a dark, twisty thrill ride with a bad guy to give you nightmares, and a pair of protagonists you will want to come back to again and again. Lock your doors and curl up with this book!"

—Tami Hoag, #1 *New York Times* bestselling author of *The Boy*

"*At First Light* by Barbara Nickless is one of the best books I've read in a long, long while. With unique and unforgettable characters who match wits with a devious, sophisticated, and ritualistic serial killer, this complex and compelling story is as powerful as a Norse god and just as terrifying. I can't wait for the next book in the series featuring Detective Addie Bisset and Dr. Evan Wilding! Bravo!"

—Lisa Jackson, #1 *New York Times* bestselling author

AMBUSH

"A nail-biter with some wicked twists . . . Fast paced and nonstop . . . Sydney is fleshed out, flawed, gritty, and kick-ass and you can't help but root for her. Nickless leaves you satisfied and smiling—something that doesn't happen too often in this genre!"

—*Bookish Biker*

"*Ambush* has plenty of action and intrigue. There are shoot-outs and kidnappings. There are cover-ups and conspiracies. At the center of it all is a flawed heroine who will do whatever it takes to set things right."

—BVS Reviews

"*Ambush* takes off on page one like a Marine F/A-18 Super Hornet under full military power from the flight deck . . . and never lets the reader down."

—*Mysterious Book Report*

"*Ambush* truly kicks butt and takes names, crackling with tension from page one with a plot as sharp as broken glass. Barbara Nickless is a superb writer."

—Steve Berry, #1 internationally bestselling author

"*Ambush* is modern mystery with its foot on the gas. Barbara Nickless's writing—at turns blazing, aching, stark, and gorgeous—propels this story at a breathless pace until its sublime conclusion. In Sydney Parnell, Nickless has masterfully crafted a heroine who, with all her internal and external scars, compels the reader to simultaneously root for and forgive her. A truly standout novel."

—Carter Wilson, *USA Today* bestselling author of *Mister Tender's Girl*

"Exceptional . . . Nickless raises the stakes and expands the canvas of a blisteringly original series. A wholly satisfying roller coaster of a thriller that features one of the genre's most truly original heroes."

—Jon Land, *USA Today* bestselling author

"*Ambush* . . . makes you laugh and cry as the pages fly by."

—Tim Tigner, internationally bestselling author

DEAD STOP

"The twists and turns . . . are first rate. Barbara Nickless has brought forth a worthy heroine in Sydney Parnell."

—BVS Review

"Nothing less than epic . . . A fast-paced, action-packed, thriller-diller of a novel featuring two of the most endearing and toughest ex-jarheads you'll ever meet."

—*Mysterious Book Report*

"A story with the pace of a runaway train."

—Bruce W. Most, award-winning author of *Murder on the Tracks*

"Want a great read, here you go!"

—Books Minority

"Nickless is on my favorite-writers list now."

—Writing.com

"Riveting suspense. Nickless writes with the soul of a poet. *Dead Stop* is a dark and memorable book."

—Gayle Lynds, *New York Times* bestselling author of *The Assassins*

"A deliciously twisted plot that winds through the dark corners of the past into the present, where nothing—and nobody—is as they seem. *Dead Stop* is a first-rate, can't-put-down mystery with a momentum that never slows. I am eager to see what Barbara Nickless comes up with next—she is definitely a mystery writer to watch."

—Margaret Coel, *New York Times* bestselling author of the Wind River Mystery series

BLOOD ON THE TRACKS

A *Suspense Magazine* Best of 2016 Books Selection: Debut

"A stunner of a thriller. From the first page to the last, *Blood on the Tracks* weaves a spell that only a natural storyteller can master. And a guarantee: you'll fall in love with one of the best characters to come along in modern thriller fiction, Sydney Rose Parnell."

—Jeffery Deaver, internationally bestselling author

"Beautifully written and heartbreakingly intense, this terrific and original debut is unforgettable. Please do not miss *Blood on the Tracks*. It fearlessly explores our darkest and most vulnerable places—and is devastatingly good. Barbara Nickless is a star."

—Hank Phillippi Ryan, Anthony, Agatha, and Mary Higgins Clark Award–winning author of *Say No More*

"Both evocative and self-assured, Barbara Nickless's debut novel is an outstanding, hard-hitting story so gritty and real, you feel it in your teeth. Do yourself a favor and give this bright talent a read."

—John Hart, multiple Edgar Award winner and *New York Times* bestselling author of *Redemption Road*

"Fast paced and intense, *Blood on the Tracks* is an absorbing thriller that is both beautifully written and absolutely unique in character and setting. Barbara Nickless has written a twisting, tortured novel that speaks with brutal honesty of the lingering traumas of war, including and especially those wounds we cannot see. I fell hard for Parnell and her four-legged partner and can't wait to read more."

—Vicki Pettersson, *New York Times* and *USA Today* bestselling author of *Swerve*

"The aptly titled *Blood on the Tracks* offers a fresh and starkly original take on the mystery genre. Barbara Nickless has fashioned a beautifully drawn hero in take-charge, take-no-prisoners Sydney Parnell, former Marine and now a railway cop battling a deadly gang as she investigates their purported connection to a recent murder. Nickless proves a master of both form and function in establishing herself every bit the equal of Nevada Barr and Linda Fairstein. A major debut that is not to be missed."

—Jon Land, *USA Today* bestselling author

"*Blood on the Tracks* is a bullet train of action. It's one part mystery and two parts thriller with a compelling protagonist leading the charge toward a knockout finish. The internal demons of one Sydney Rose Parnell are as gripping as the external monster she's chasing around Colorado. You will long remember this spectacular debut novel."

—Mark Stevens, author of the award-winning Allison Coil Mystery series

"Nickless captures you from the first sentence. Her series features Sydney Rose Parnell, a young woman haunted by the ghosts of her past. In *Blood on the Tracks,* she doggedly pursues a killer, seeking truth even in the face of her own destruction—the true mark of a heroine. Skilled in evoking emotion from the reader, Nickless is a master of the craft, a writer to keep your eyes on."

—Chris Goff, author of *Dark Waters*

"Barbara Nickless's *Blood on the Tracks* is raw and authentic, plunging readers into the fascinating world of tough railroad cop Special Agent Sydney Rose Parnell and her Malinois sidekick, Clyde. Haunted by her military service in Iraq, Sydney Rose is brought in by the Denver Major Crimes unit to help solve a particularly brutal murder, leading her into a snake pit of hate and betrayal. Meticulously plotted and intelligently written, *Blood on the Tracks* is a superb debut novel."

—M. L. Rowland, author of the Search and Rescue Mystery novels

"*Blood on the Tracks* is a must-read debut. A suspenseful crime thriller with propulsive action, masterful writing, and a tough-as-nails cop, Sydney Rose Parnell. Readers will want more."

—Robert K. Tanenbaum, *New York Times* bestselling author of the Butch Karp and Marlene Ciampi legal thrillers

"Nickless's writing admirably captures the fallout from a war where even survivors are trapped, forever reliving their trauma."

—*Kirkus Reviews*

"Part mystery, part antiwar story, Nickless's engrossing first novel, a series launch, introduces Sydney Rose Parnell . . . Nickless skillfully explores the dehumanizing effects resulting from the unspeakable cruelties of wartime as well as the part played by the loyalty soldiers owe to family and each other under stressful circumstances."

—*Publishers Weekly*

"An interesting tale . . . The fast pace will leave you finished in no time. Nickless seamlessly ties everything together with a shocking ending."

—*RT Book Reviews*

"If you enjoy suspense and thrillers, then you will [want] *Blood on the Tracks* for your library. Full of the suspense that holds you on the edge of your seat, it's also replete with acts of bravery, moments of hope, and a host of feelings that keep the story's intensity level high. This would be a great work for a book club or reading group with a great deal of information that would create robust dialogue and debate."

—Blogcritics

"In *Blood on the Tracks*, Barbara Nickless delivers a thriller with the force of a speeding locomotive and the subtlety of a surgeon's knife. Sydney and Clyde are both great characters with flaws and virtues to see them through a plot thick with menace. One for contemporary thriller lovers everywhere."

—Authorlink

"*Blood on the Tracks* is a superb story that rises above the genre of mystery . . . It is a first-class read."

—*Denver Post*

THE DROWNING GAME

Also by Barbara Nickless

Sydney Rose Parnell Series

Blood on the Tracks

Dead Stop

Ambush

Gone to Darkness

Evan Wilding Series

At First Light

Dark of Night

Play of Shadows

THE DROWNING GAME

BARBARA NICKLESS

Published by Thomas & Mercer, Seattle

www.apub.com

ISBN-13: 9781662510014 (paperback)
ISBN-13: 9781662510007 (digital)

Cover design by James Iacobelli
Cover image: © beavera, © Deejpilot / Getty; © Silas Baisch / Unsplash

Printed in the United States of America

THE LEGEND OF THE MERLION

According to myth, a fourteenth-century Sumatran prince was sailing in the South China Sea when a terrible storm arose. To save his men, the prince threw his crown into the waters, a sacrifice to the gods. The gods brought the ship to an island paradise, and when the prince struggled ashore, he was greeted by a lion. He named the new land using the Sanskrit words singa *for "lion" and* pura *for "city"—Singapura.*

The merlion—with its lion head and the body of a fish—is now a beloved symbol of Singapore, where many believe it can ward off evil.

PART 1

If a kingdom be a great family, a family likewise is a little kingdom, torn with factions and exposed to revolutions.

—Samuel Johnson

1

Singapore
August 25, 6:00 p.m. SGT

Her entire life, Cassandra's father had told her: *Trust no one.*

Yet here she was. A foreigner, an *ang moh*, her life in the hands of people she hardly knew.

Another lesson from her father that she'd ignored.

She moved with deliberate slowness through Singapore's teeming streets, her skin damp in the ninety-degree heat as she drifted from one clump of tourists to another—their jostling, shouting, picture-taking enthusiasm providing cover. She'd set out from the offices of Ocean House hours ago on the route she'd planned last week—changing directions on a seeming whim, darting through traffic, ducking into couture shops and souvenir stores, pausing to light joss sticks at Buddhist and Hindu temples, her palms pressed together and her head bent in prayer. She descended into the bowels of the underground to hop on and off the metro. Virgil's words came back to her: *watch for repeat vehicles, familiar silhouettes, someone hiding their face behind a map*.

A month earlier, she'd killed most of the apps on her phone. Anything that would allow the Chinese to piece together the life of the real Cassandra Brenner. There was no avoiding the city cameras; she could only hope her disguise and a lack of Chinese sleeper agents within Singapore's Internal Security Department would protect her.

Spies would say she was running a surveillance detection route—an SDR. Cassandra understood the concept. A few years ago, one of their celebrity clients—a sheikh commissioning a three-hundred-foot luxury motor yacht—insisted she and Nadia learn how to avoid the paparazzi. He'd hired a former CIA case officer to teach the sisters how to conduct SDRs.

At the time it had seemed frivolous.

Not anymore.

She shifted her canvas tote to her left shoulder and the handle of her rolling suitcase to her right, then paused to retouch her lipstick, using a compact mirror to inspect the walkway behind her. Surely she was clear of all surveillance by now—"black" in spy lingo.

Unless she'd missed something. In the vibrant, restless, multiethnic throng swarming the city, failing to spot a tail was as easy as overlooking a spider lurking beneath the sheets.

Every spy is haunted, Virgil had said last night. *By our mistakes. By the lives we hold. By the risks we take. It goes with the territory.*

She'd shaken her head. *I'm not a spy. I'm an amateur.*

His dry laugh had sounded like fingers snapping. *Cass, listen carefully. It's critical that tomorrow you're not made before you reach the hotel. Singapore is one of the most surveilled cities in the world. But it's got nothing on Shanghai. Tomorrow is a test, but it's still dangerous.*

And here she was. She stopped at a corner, waiting for the light to change. Waiting for her sixth sense to offer up that prickle that said eyes were on her.

But her gut whispered that she was black. She crossed the street with the light, then paused in front of a restaurant to blot her face with a tissue, the paper coming away dark from sweat, the ruin of her makeup, and traces of adhesive. She was clear. She could hail a Grab taxi, be at the Marina Bay Sands resort in minutes. Wash up and order a drink.

God, she wanted a drink.

She checked the time—6:02 p.m. Right on schedule. She turned away from the heady scents of coconut curry and mango and her pretense of perusing a menu in the restaurant's window and plunged into the crowds headed toward Merlion Park.

Her blouse clung to her back, her capris to her thighs. Her bare feet squelched in rubber sandals. An hour into her SDR, the heavens had unleashed the kind of storm—sudden, savage—typical for afternoons in the tropics. Rain had lashed the streets, the sidewalks, the cars, the parks, the trees, the people until the gutters turned into rivers and the sidewalks into a brilliant bloom of umbrellas. People went undeterred about their business, as used to the storms as the heat. Only the tourists cowered under awnings or cursed and ran.

The rain had vanished as suddenly as it came, leaving the early-evening pavement gleaming. The ungodly heat pressed back in.

She paused before another restaurant. A car slowed, pulled to the curb. She prepared to run as the back door opened, then relaxed as a trio of young Chinese women spilled out, giggling, gossiping, clicking selfies.

They disappeared into the restaurant.

She was clear.

She rubbed her heel where a blister had formed, then attached herself to a different group of tourists. The last residue of rain had evaporated into the laden air, and sounds and smells burst forth with refreshed enthusiasm. She noted the hiss of tires, the mechanical cheeps and chirps of crosswalks, the tramping of thousands of pairs of feet, feet that belonged to the financial district's up-and-comers. The men wore conservative suits and ties. The women flashed an aviary of brilliantly colored skirts and dresses, blouses, and suits. The occasional whiff of perfume and cologne mingled with car exhaust and an intoxicating mix of aromas from the international lineup of eateries.

Moving faster now, she crossed through Merlion Park's well-tended grass and past the white-blossomed frangipani trees onto the jetty. She stood overlooking Marina Bay, where the Singapore River spilled into the waters of the cove and from there to the sea.

Across the bay was her destination—the three immense towers of Marina Bay Sands Hotel. Beside her was the city's iconic twenty-eight-foot-high fountain, the Merlion, boasting the head of a lion and the body of a fish. She turned around as if to take a selfie and observed the crowd, looking for faces she'd mentally categorized earlier. The Chinese man with the maroon leather briefcase and Yankees cap she'd noted outside the Takashimaya Shopping Centre. The Tamil woman in a Chanel suit and sneakers who'd boarded and exited the metro's Downtown Line when she did.

She rotated in place but saw only new faces.

She dropped her phone in her bag and forced herself to amble as she headed out of the park toward the hotel, the sun now a fiery ball slotting light between the skyscrapers. In a few more minutes, it would be night.

Operation UNDERTOW had been thrilling at first. The secret meetings, the dead drops and brush passes, the need to run SDRs whenever she met her contact. A salve to what had proved to be an unsatisfying life as a yacht designer. An answer to the emptiness inside her.

The thrill had disappeared six months ago, when she found one of their security guards dead at the shipyard, his throat cut. Virgil had told her from the beginning that it wasn't a game. The corpse had hammered it home. This was for keeps.

After finding the guard, she'd considered telling Virgil she was out. Everyone thought Cassandra Brenner was brave, mistaking bravado for courage. She was terrified.

Both she and her sister were hothouse orchids, able to flourish only in the rarefied environment of the yachting world in which they'd been raised. Voice and ballet lessons, cotillion, expensive private schools. But what remained in the void left by her former enthusiasm wasn't only fear. There was also stubbornness. Cassandra Allegra Brenner never gave up on anyone.

Her stubbornness held her in place. That, and the op itself—the work she was doing was important. The money and the perks—the outrageously priced clothes, the unimaginably expensive condo in Tanglin, fancy dinners, and elite memberships—none of that hurt, either. It gave her a chance to taste the lives of her billionaire clients. Her salary as a designer was respectable. But she and her family didn't live like their clientele.

She reached the waterfront promenade. Glass doors whooshed open. She stepped into the sublime atmosphere of Southeast Asia's largest collection of luxury goods—The Shoppes—and ducked into a bathroom to begin her metamorphosis.

In the wheelchair-accessible stall, which gave her the privacy of its sink and mirror, she slipped out of her blouse and capris, the baseball cap, the oversize sunglasses. She washed her neck and breasts and underarms with wet paper towels, then removed the prosthetic nose and jaw and scrubbed away the adhesive. She folded the clothes, sandals, hat, and prosthetics and tucked them into an inside pocket of the suitcase.

She took out the night's costume: an off-the-shoulder red sheath dress, satin heels, gold-and-ruby earrings, and a beaded purse. She applied fresh makeup in the mirror, twisted her hair into an updo, slapped a plaster on the blister, and emerged from the bathroom a different woman.

She checked her phone. Right on schedule. She strolled through the mall that lined the entryway to the hotel and paused in front of windows displaying Louis Vuitton bags and Lucchese loafers. She took her time, careful to appear like any other wealthy guest checking in for a pampered weekend in the city's former British colonial district.

Her walk through the city had been a chance for Virgil to gauge her skill at evading a tail; the stroll through The Shoppes was meant to draw out the watchers.

The Marina Bay Sands was Singapore's flashiest hotel—a casino-retail complex popular among luxury shoppers and the kind of gamblers who dropped $10,000 US on a single roll of the dice. Cassandra Brenner, yacht designer and executive vice president of the world-renowned Ocean House, was meant to appear wealthy and on the take. Where better than here?

She paused before a display of gold and gems and studied the crowd's reflection in the glittering Cartier window, her gaze roving over the throngs streaming through the mall: Malay workers, Chinese locals, European tourists, American expats.

Men looked at her appreciatively, but their gazes didn't linger. She watched for Virgil, but of course she wouldn't see him.

I'm clear. I'm good.

Breathe.

Virgil wasn't his real name. She'd chosen it for him, after the Roman poet who had served as Dante's guide through hell in the fourteenth-century epic poem *Inferno*. The choice was deliberate. She loved her family; she'd never want any harm to come to them. But she understood the risks. If she and Virgil succeeded, the resulting firestorm could engulf the Brenners and their almost mythic past and burn it to the ground.

And yet this had to be done—*needed* to be done. Then Virgil would lead her out of hell and into a clean, bright future. She hoped her family would follow. Maybe they'd even forgive her.

She rode the elevator up Tower 2 with a pair of British businessmen who eyed her in the mirrors. She felt their gazes on her as the doors opened on the fortieth floor and she glided down the hall on her $1,000 Christian Louboutin stilettos.

She glanced behind and watched until the elevator doors slid shut, leaving her alone in the long, hushed hallway.

They don't know me. They're no one.

She continued down the hall to her room and keyed herself in. Safely inside, she listened for the door to click shut. Then she kicked off the heels and leaned against a wall.

Breathe.

She dropped her purse on the couch. On the nearby table, Virgil had placed his usual bouquet of red gardenias next to a bottle of Hennessy X.O.

But one thing was missing.

The day's first scratch of alarm spread a chill through her chest. Her gut, which had been quiet all afternoon, lit a flare. Noticeably absent from the grouping was their third safety signal after the gardenias and cognac—a red-and-gold letter opener.

She retrieved a knife from her purse and—gripping the hilt the way Virgil had shown her—inspected the rooms, opened closets, checked the balcony.

Nothing was out of place; no one else was here.

Breathe.

Maybe this was another test. In which case she should abort the mission immediately. Flee the room as if her life depended on it.

But with the flowers and cognac on the table as usual, perhaps Virgil only wanted to make sure she'd noticed the missing letter opener. He would grill her about it when he arrived. Scold her for staying.

Breathe.

More likely she'd simply missed a message, a change to their routine.

She returned the knife to her purse, but her hands kept shaking.

She'd been distracted lately, busy with the build of the spectacularly over-the-top superyacht *Red Dragon*, her largest creation to date and a crowning achievement for Ocean House. Their entrée into the Asian market. Only three months until launch. Only three months to hold tight to the secrets she'd accepted almost four years ago.

She waited until the shaking stopped, then uncapped the Hennessy and poured a finger into a tumbler. She crossed to the open balcony doors, glass in hand. Night had fallen, though darkness held no sway in this city. The breeze carried a lacing of brine and fish beneath the robust perfumes of frangipani and jasmine. Far below her balcony lay the gloriously lit Gardens by the Bay and the tranquil waters of the straits, where ships floated, candles on the dark sea. Farther out, the islands of Brani, Sentosa, and St. John looked like rumpled Oriental carpets lit by a thousand tiny flames.

Traffic murmured. Closer by, cicadas whirred, and a nightjar peeped its soft *tiu tiu tiu*. She relished the languid air on her bare arms and legs.

The cognac eased into her bloodstream, and finally, she relaxed.

The scene below ignited a quiet joy in her. Singapore held promise and mystery in its colonial homes, its perfumed gardens and dense jungles, its labyrinthine markets. The heat and humidity, the exoticism, the sheer *energy* of this tiny island in the South China Sea—it was literally and figuratively a world away from the shores of Seattle, where she'd grown up.

She'd been in Singapore for nearly five years with only occasional visits home. At first, she'd worried she wouldn't find her footing. But the island had enfolded her in its diverse embrace. Singapura—the Lion City—had passed through the hands of Buddhists, Muslims, the Portuguese, the Dutch, the British, the Japanese, and finally the Singaporeans when the island became an independent state in 1965.

Perhaps, when all this was over, she would move here permanently. Become an expat like the colonial British who, after years in the Lion City, found they had no desire for the cold and fog of their homeland.

Maybe, just maybe, she'd continue the work she'd begun with Virgil.

She straightened when the door opened behind her. She returned to the room, smoothed her dress, and tucked a strand of hair back into her chignon.

It will be okay. This is the right thing to do. It will be okay.

Nadia will understand. So will Dad.

Maman and Uncle Rob, of course, will never speak to me again.

She stepped back into the room.

A tall figure stood in the darkened entryway, a silhouette of shadow.

"Ha'eem ata levad hayom?" she asked in Hebrew. A standard precaution in case they were overheard. *Are you alone today?*

It was how they always began what Virgil called their first mad minute: identification in case one of them wore a disguise, followed by a review of any safety concerns and a confirmation of when and where their next meet would be. Because in this business, interruptions came without warning.

But tonight, Virgil—usually quick to respond—said nothing. He stepped in and closed the door behind him. Now she saw there were two men. One heavyset, the other lean.

The figures moved into the light.

Neither of them was the man she knew as Virgil.

Her insides turned to liquid.

"Miss Brenner," said the lean man.

She hurled her glass at the figures, then lunged for her purse and the knife. But the men were fast. The heavy one shoved her to the floor. She cried out as her head struck the tile. The man bent, grabbed her wrists, and yanked her to her feet. He tossed her onto the bed, handcuffed her, and slapped tape over her mouth.

He leaned in. She glimpsed a tattoo of a tiger, its muscular body stretching down his neck, the tiger's red eyes burning above a snarling mouth.

He grinned. The other man snapped something in Mandarin, and—reluctantly, it seemed—the heavier man moved away. He pulled out a pack of cigarettes and walked out onto the balcony, as if he'd lost interest.

The lean man placed a small rolled cloth on the bed beside her. She watched as he unfurled the black fabric; she caught the glint of steel in the golden glow of the bedside table.

Her sob built behind the gag.

The man leaned over her. The light caught his spectacles, turning his eyes into bright hollows.

"Do not be alarmed, Miss Brenner," he said. "The knives are here only as an inducement for your cooperation. We just need a little information. Then you will be free to go."

She fought to hold the sob.

"If I take away the gag, do you promise not to scream?"

She nodded.

"If you scream, everything will end here. Do you understand?"

Another nod, more frantic.

He removed the tape from her mouth.

"Tell me about the boat," he said. "About *Red Dragon*."

She stared up at this stranger with his lean, handsome face and glacier smile, his eyes now glittering like black agates behind the lenses. He would be from the Guóānbù, she guessed. China's foreign intelligence service. He would have come to Singapore to stop the CIA's China Mission Center from acquiring RenAI: the artificial intelligence created by George Mèng.

Obtaining the AI from Mèng had been deemed critical for the security of the US. It was why Cassandra was involved. But UNDERTOW had another purpose, one she must never reveal.

No matter what men from the Guóānbù did to her.

"What do you want to know?" Her voice was a whisper, breathy and weak.

"Everything." The man touched his fingers to her cheek. His surprising tenderness almost made her weep. "About your client, Mr.

Mèng. And, of course, his yacht, *Red Dragon*. Everything. Do you understand?"

She nodded and closed her eyes and began the lie she and Virgil had created. The story they were to use if either of them was captured.

Lies mixed with truth. She hoped it was enough.

2

Seattle, Washington
One Day Earlier
August 24, 6:00 a.m. PDT

On that warm August morning, I woke early, roused by gulls screeching along the shore. Beside me, Matthew was still asleep, sprawled on his back, snoring faintly. I showered and dressed for the day's work in a white linen suit, slingback pumps, and a sleeveless taupe blouse. *The uniform*, as I thought of it. Last night, my father had called a 7:00 a.m. council meeting.

Family only.

Something was up.

Matthew's eyes opened as I was buttoning my jacket.

"Nadia," he whispered.

But he was asleep again before I could answer.

I tucked the sheet around him. Matthew—a commodities trader—was due to return to Florida today. It would likely be weeks before I saw him again. Our relationship was exclusive but casual: careers first, love a distant second.

My phone pinged as I was walking to my car. My sister, Cass.

What's up with the meeting? she texted. Past my bedtime here.

Singapore, where Cass was overseeing the build of *Red Dragon*, a boat she and I had designed together, was fifteen hours ahead of Seattle, making it after nine at night in Southeast Asia.

Her text was followed by a yawn emoji. Then: You know I'm up early. Is the family trying to kill me?

I laughed, relieved that she sounded like herself. Cass had been moody lately. Secretive. I texted back: No idea what the meeting is about. Turn off the camera and sleep. I'll fill you in later.

Her reply was quick: And miss Guy and Uncle Rob fight? Ha!

That was Cassandra through and through. I was miserable when the family argued, always the first to beg for peace. But Cass rolled up her sleeves and jumped right in.

My sister and I were opposites in almost every way. She was outgoing, indifferent to rules and propriety, a woman with the skill and charisma to convince our ultra-high-net-worth clients—people with hundreds of millions to spend on a toy—that her ideas for their yachts were better than their own.

I was solitary by nature, reclusive, happiest when I was designing yachts in the isolation of my own thoughts.

Still, we were best friends. And despite our differences, someday—hopefully in the far future—she and I would run Ocean House together.

I got into my car. About to drive. See you on video in a few.

Nadia wait, came her reply. There's something we should talk about.

Three dots indicated she was still typing. I stowed my briefcase and took my sunglasses out of the console. After another moment, Cassandra's message appeared.

Never mind. We'll talk later. Luv u sis.

Love you back.

—

Robert Eugene Brenner—my urbane, Ivy League–educated uncle—waited for me outside the steel-and-white-plank seven-story headquarters of Ocean House Yacht Design & Naval Architecture. Rob was six foot two, silver haired, with the athletic grace of a Baryshnikov and a tanned face refined into well-worn leather. A halo of cigar smoke circled above his head like a Churchillian prop; the sun winked off his Bentley aviator sunglasses.

"Thank god you're here," he said as I approached the front door. "It's going to be a bloodbath. Tigers at the Colosseum. Roadside bombs. Someone's going to be required to commit hara-kiri."

"You know I hate it when you mix your metaphors." I accepted Rob's tobacco-laden kiss. "What is this council meeting about?"

"We're being pilloried."

I pulled back. "Pilloried?" Ocean House was yacht royalty. Unassailable. The trade rags sang our praises. Our builds won top awards. Clients convinced friends to get on the waiting list for one of our bespoke boats. Admittedly, our bottom line had been dipping in and out of the red for a year, but still. "Pilloried for what?"

Rob smashed out his cigar on a concrete ash receptacle. "Oh, don't let me spoil the fun. Come find out for yourself."

He opened the door and ushered me inside. Once through the door, I paused as I did every morning to take in the sights and sounds of the place that had been Cass's and my home away from home since we were children.

Ocean House was eighty years old. Young by European standards, but we'd grown fast, expanding into the yacht market with the cowboy enthusiasm of our adopted country. We employed three thousand people around the world: designers, engineers, skilled workers, and apprentices. Here at headquarters were the admin offices as well as R&D, exterior and interior design, and the brains behind our shipyards in Seattle, London, and now Singapore. Men and women moved purposefully through the lobby and in and around the sea of cubicles beyond. The bank of elevators dinged, landlines rang, doors to the walled offices opened and closed. Conversations rose and fell in a Doppler shift as people swirled past in suits and dresses. No Pacific Northwest athleisure wear in these offices.

Rob took my elbow and steered me through the lobby to the elevators. He stabbed the button for the seventh floor and said, "Your father, as you can well imagine, is the spark that will set our boat on fire if we don't manage him. As soon as Guy starts railing at journalists that Ocean House will always be king while stating we're considering semicustom builds, we'll look desperate. We can't afford desperate." He adjusted the lapels of my jacket. "You've got to talk him off the ledge."

Rob, the perennial optimist.

Guy had set the meeting on the family's private top floor in a corner office with a view of Puget Sound. We'd laid out a huge sum of money for this waterfront building with its luxurious office suites, private dining room for executives, gym, and a host of other amenities. In the yacht-building world, image was everything.

I waved Rob ahead and stopped in the kitchen for coffee. I was surprised to see my hand trembling as I poured. I scolded myself. Rob was big on drama—whatever Guy had to share was probably minor. A tempest in a teapot, to borrow one of Rob's expressions.

I carried my coffee and briefcase down the hall and paused outside the conference room to observe my family.

Robert and Guy Brenner were cochairs and co-CEOs of Ocean House. Guy handled the marketing and administrative side of the business. Rob, who had a background in marine architecture, served as creative director. My mother, Isabeth Brenner, with her Harvard MBA, filled the role of chief financial officer.

Somehow Rob and Guy made it work, even though they were as unlike each other as a tugboat and a racing yacht.

Rob was a man of sartorial splendor. He dressed like our clientele, in elegant suits or yachting clothes, and was always ready to talk fine wines, fine whiskys, rare books, and the latest offerings at Sotheby's. He tended to drop dollops of philosophy and Shakespeare into his conversation. Clients loved his ability to sound like a bon vivant while he cheerfully kissed ass.

Few discerned the wolf beneath the lapdog.

My father was Rob's dark doppelgänger. Guy Brenner was compact and pugnacious, a man of elbows and teeth whose presence took up half of any room he was in, along with most of the oxygen.

My mother, petite, French, and—Cass and I speculated—beloved by both men, oversaw all of it from the inner sanctum of her small office. She was the cajoler, the one who smoothed ruffled feathers and drew the brothers back together whenever they argued, which was daily.

My family. Apex predators. I loved them, admired them, sometimes resented them for their talk of family nobility and honor and their whispered secrets. Secrets to which Cassandra and I had never been privy. Maybe we'd get the secret handshake when we took over the company.

At the moment, Rob stood frowning out the window at the sound, where banking clouds glowed scarlet in the western sky. Cassandra, attending remotely from Singapore, appeared on the large monitor that hung on the far wall, cupping a coffee mug and yawning.

Guy and Isabeth—they'd dropped "Dad" and "Maman" as soon as Cassandra and I hit our teens—sat at the table, flipping through paperwork, their shoulders hunched.

Over their heads, gazing austerely down, hung a photograph of my great-grandfather Josef Brenner, the founder of Ocean House. Family lore said Josef carried the blood of Austrian nobility through his father. His mother, according to legend, had secretly married a nobleman, who was hastily sent away when the marriage was discovered. The marriage was annulled, and all records destroyed. Only a diamond-and-emerald brooch, the rumor of nobility, and baby Josef bore testament to the union.

I blew Josef's photo a kiss, then squared my shoulders and strode in. Isabeth glanced up and smiled. Guy didn't bother. I could almost see the storm cloud over his head.

I chose an empty chair across from them and set my briefcase and coffee on the table. From the screen, Cassandra gave me a small wave.

Guy finally looked up.

"About time," he growled. His pugilist demeanor turned the room into an arena. "Let's get started. Isabeth?"

My mother handed me the latest issue of one of the industry's trade magazines, *Showboats International*.

"It's hitting the newsstands this morning," she said. "Cassandra, I emailed a copy to you."

I took a seat and began reading.

Will Newcomer Paxton Become the Next Yacht King?

When the rich buy Mercedes, the ultrarich buy Bentleys. For years, this has meant a full-custom motor yacht from Ocean House. The House's boats have carried emirs and oligarchs, kings and princes, around the world for eighty years.

But newcomer Paxton Yachts, the eponymous company of CEO Brandon Paxton, is setting itself up as some seriously stiff competition. With in-house design led by two of Ocean House's former top creatives and an R&D department boasting some of the best "boat minds" in Europe, Paxton is taking a run at the monarchy.

Headquartered in Germany's Bremen-Vegesack, the indisputable heart of shipbuilding, Paxton has been garnering praise and awards for its elegant designs and

> German craftsmanship. It's also getting huge props for its innovative processes and a new semicustom line built on a proven naval platform, all of which reduces build time for clients eager to launch. Some of their semicustom interiors are clearly designed with the Asian market in mind. Paxton boasts a wait list with—our sources tell us—some very impressive names, including members of several prestigious East Asian dynasties.
>
> Has the American firm run its course? Is it time to return royalty to Europe, where royalty began?
>
> Only time will tell if Brandon Paxton is the new king.

I sucked in a breath and read the article again. I stole a glance at Cass on the video screen. Our eyes met. We would be up against Paxton for a slew of design awards at next month's ritzy yacht show in Monaco. Suddenly, the show became something more than a friendly competition. Whether we won or lost could decide our future.

"Paxton is going to fuck us over," Guy said.

Rob turned from the windows. "Let's not get ahead of ourselves. A snippy piece in an industry rag isn't going to sink the ship."

"No?" Guy glared up at his brother. "They took two of our best designers, in case you—our lead designer—hadn't noticed. They've got a wait list—"

"An alleged wait list," Rob interjected.

"Oh, they've got a goddamn wait list. Tell them, Isabeth."

Isabeth glanced up from her papers for the first time since she'd nodded at me. Still a beauty at fifty-nine with her honey-blond hair and graceful figure, this morning she looked pale, her blue eyes muted.

She sighed and removed her reading glasses.

"I had lunch with a close friend from my undergraduate days in Paris," she said. "Celine was in Seattle for a few days, chasing a lead on Native American art for a client. She's working sales for Paxton Yachts. After two bottles of a rare Riesling, courtesy of Ocean House, Celine told me that Paxton has signed YBAs with the head of one of the world's biggest social media platforms. And with a prince from Bavaria's abolished monarchy."

I tilted back in my chair. YBAs were yacht-building agreements. These weren't signed until everything for a build was ready, from design to safety, timelines to budget. Once an owner committed to a YBA, it was showtime.

"So what?" Rob said. "They've signed a would-be and a has-been."

"Unfortunately, no," Isabeth said. "A social media hero and a man whose name still carries a great deal of cachet. It's a triumph, Rob. Worse, Celine thinks they have a member of the king of Thailand's family on the hook. And that cuts right into our growth trajectory into Asia."

Rob folded his arms. "Snobbery. Elitism. There is no way Paxton is building the kind of quality we are. Not with the speed they're moving at."

Pink rose in Cass's face. She picked up her phone and thumbed through the screen as if bored by the conversation. I noted her elaborate manicure—unusual for her.

"We have our own wait list," I said. "There are more than enough clients for Paxton *and* for us. We'll simply do what we've always done—stick with full-custom boats and then design and build better than anyone else. I don't see reason to be alarmed."

The room fell silent, as if cleaved by an axe.

"You didn't tell her, did you?" Guy said to Rob.

My stomach arced through a delicate flip. "Tell me what?"

A vein throbbed in Guy's forehead. Rob studied his hands.

I tapped my foot. "Tell me."

On the screen, Cass still hadn't looked up. Was everyone crazy today?

"Yes, Rob," Guy said. "Tell your niece about *Rambler*."

I looked back and forth between Guy and Rob. *Rambler* was a 240-foot build for a wealthy developer from Montana. Thirty seconds ago, I would have expected a glowing report about the maiden voyage of Rob's most recent launch. But the look on my uncle's face said the news wasn't good.

"Rob?" I prompted.

"Catastrophic engine failure," he said in a flat voice. "*Rambler* suffered a cascade of electrical and hydraulic failures on her maiden voyage. We're still investigating, but we suspect defective parts."

Cass finally lifted her eyes.

Guy said, "They got stuck in the middle of the Mediterranean, not to put too fine a point on it. The Italian coast guard had to disembark the passengers while mechanics were flown in to fix the problem. Which they couldn't. Damn thing had to be towed. We're lucky it didn't sink."

On the screen Cass squeezed a blue stress ball.

I breathed. In through the nose, out through the mouth. "How could a failure like that happen?"

"Sabotage," Guy said.

But Rob shook his head. "Nothing so dramatic. It was almost certainly a supply chain failure. With shortages, suppliers are rushing diagnostics. This is the result."

"That doesn't matter," I said. "Any problems should have been caught during sea trials."

Rob's expression turned stubborn. "We're looking into it."

Guy stabbed a forefinger at the papers on the table in front of him. "My vote still goes to sabotage. Could be some eco freak doesn't like it that an asshat from Texas is pillaging Montana's wilderness. Maybe he managed to get himself involved with the build. But for the moment, it's a mystery. A mystery that has taken a lot of the shine off our name.

We won't keep our clients with this kind of bullshit. Especially with the *Showboats* article. Nadia, do we still have *Sovereign II*?"

I held up a folder from my briefcase. "Matthew signed an LOI last night." A letter of intent was the first stage in the building process and one reason Matthew had flown to Seattle. Our shared love of yachts was what had first brought us together: I'd designed *Sovereign I* for him. Now Matthew wanted a bigger boat. "We also have Warren and Leanne Korda. I spoke with them yesterday. I'm flying to Florida next week to show them my preliminary designs for *Lovely Lady*."

"An LOI is more of a moral agreement than a legal one," Guy went on. "Still, first-rate work, Nadia. Congratulations. But if the Kordas expressed interest, I expect them to bail as soon as they hear about *Rambler*."

Rob held out his arms, palms open. "Bad things happen. People understand that. We roll up our sleeves, stay on top of our current builds, and prove to the world that we're still Ocean House. Our name—our family name—is worth more than that of some upstart in Europe. The brand is everything."

Steel flashed in Guy's eyes. "Since when did you corner the market on naivete?"

"Ever since you lost whatever mettle you used to have," Rob snarled. "What the hell is the matter with you, Guy? You didn't even want to expand into Asia, where the real money is. *Audentes Fortuna Iuvat.* Or to put it in words you'll understand: fortune smiles on the brave, and frowns upon the coward. Have you lost the obscenely small pair you were born with?"

Guy pushed to his feet. The brothers locked eyes across the table.

Isabeth's silk-over-wire voice slid into the gap. "Gentlemen. Do I need to put you in separate corners?"

Rob yanked out a chair and sat. "What's our reputation worth to you?" he asked Guy. "Do we stay with full-custom boats? Or cheapen ourselves doing semicustom and refits?"

It was the same argument they'd had for the past year, ever since rising expenses, cost overruns, and worried millionaires had slowed our growth and hurt our bottom line.

"Making payroll is what matters." Guy pushed back his chair and stood. "First things first, we make sure we don't slip further into the red. If that means opening a line of semicustom builds or doing refits, I'm for it. Maybe we even outsource the builds and focus on design, which is the girls' strength. Now all of you out. I need to talk to Nadia."

On the screen, Cass waved and blew a kiss before exiting the meeting.

My argumentative sister had been uncharacteristically quiet. But I pushed aside my worry. For now, there were more pressing concerns.

Always the one to fire the final arrow, Rob paused at the door. "We can't get back into the black unless we're aggressive. We expand into new markets. Hire more people. And stick with what we do best. Ocean House is custom. No compromises."

He stormed out. Isabeth rolled her eyes and followed him.

After I closed the door behind them, I turned to face my father. What I saw made me take a step back.

Guy's pallor had turned gray, his sunken cheeks like caverns carved out of bone. Now that the wave of anger had passed, he had aged ten years in ten seconds.

"Guy?"

He sank back in his chair. "Have a seat, Nadia."

I came around the table and took the chair next to him.

"I'm sending you to Singapore," he said.

"What?" I glanced up at the now-dark screen. "Why?"

"I'm sick, Naughty."

Naughty. My nickname. Rarely used. A nauseating panic filled me. "How sick?"

"I've got one foot in the grave," he said. "Which . . . okay. It is what it is. But now the other foot is losing ground fast."

My hands flew to my chest.

"Naughty," he said. There was a warning in his voice: *Don't you dare break down.*

I sucked in a shaky breath and lowered my hands. When something went wrong at sea, the absolute first thing you had to do was not panic.

Think first, act second. Panic only when it was all over. The Brenner mantra.

"Be specific," I said.

He didn't meet my eyes. "I've got a few months."

I shoved my hands into the pockets of my blazer to keep them from leaping toward my heart again.

"Cancer?"

He nodded. "Mesothelioma. Cancer of the thin tissues. From asbestos exposure in the shipyards, back in the day."

"Okay." I nodded. "We've got this. There are treatments. Chemo. Infusions. Trials. You can go to—"

Guy raised a hand. "I'm not doing any of that bullshit."

Alarm tongued the base of my spine, an ice-cold rasp against my vertebrae. But I held my voice steady.

"Dad, you have to fight. You've always been a fighter. You're sixty-one. You have years ahead of you."

"No. I don't."

He turned away and straightened the papers in front of him. Through a film of tears, I watched as he closed each folder and lined up the corners. On the back of one of his hands was a tacky white substance—residue of medical tape. And a bruise, blue under his translucent skin.

"Dad, please—"

"It isn't what I want. Not for you and not for Cass. Not even for Rob. And certainly not for your mother. But it's time to wave the white flag. I don't want to go out weak and frail, clinging to life." Guy gave an emphatic headshake. "I'm dying on my own terms."

My heart battered against my sternum. I sometimes didn't know where my family ended and I began. We were a collective organism, the whole dependent on the parts. What was I without my father?

"We need you," I said. Meaning, *I* need you.

"You'll manage. Cassandra is strong-minded. Willful. Which is both good and bad. But she's also an excellent project manager. And you're the best damn designer on God's green earth. Better than Rob, even if you don't know it yet. Plus, you can read a room better than anyone else. That's a useful skill in our line of work." He patted my hand, the gesture awkward for its rarity. "The two of you will do just fine. You'll have your uncle and mother. You don't give Isabeth enough credit. She'll be here for you and Cass."

The chill climbed up my spine. "What do Rob and Isabeth say about your decision to not get treatment?"

"They don't know I'm sick."

I closed my eyes. Pictured my parents in their separate bedrooms with their parallel social lives. Isabeth busy with our sinking fortunes, Guy snarling off any intrusion. Rob oblivious, as usual. No doubt Guy was leaning on his secretary, Tyler Jacobs, to help him erect a smoke screen: lying about appointments, managing medications, covering for Guy when he was tired.

When I opened my eyes again, Guy was back to rearranging the files.

"Why not tell them?" I asked.

"Loose lips sink ships," he quipped. But his laugh was hollow. "And you're not to tell them, either. Not yet. I'm filling you in because Ocean House is going to come crashing down on your shoulders and Cass's. You need to be ready."

I nodded, even though the idea of moving into a true leadership role felt like stepping off a cliff. "But why not—"

"If you rat me out, your mother will collapse, and Rob will go on a bender. People will realize something is wrong beyond *Rambler*'s failure. We can't afford to let the world know that I'm not still at the helm. If this gets leaked before I'm on my deathbed, then Paxton will win. Brandon Paxton will bleed off all our talent and steal our clients. But if we keep this tight, then we have a chance to turn things around before I go to meet the devil. What we're going to do is start moving you and Cass into position."

I'd thought we had years. "We aren't ready."

"Bullshit. You and Cass have been preparing for this since you were weaned off your mother's tit." He splayed his knotty, sunspotted hands on the table. "I need you in East Asia. First because I want you to tell your sister in person. She shouldn't learn this from a phone call, and I can't travel. But also because something is—as Rob would say—rotten in the state of Singapore."

Something inside me fell away. "*Red Dragon* is only seven weeks from sea trials."

"That's right. If the schedule slips, it will be another black mark against us."

A headache bloomed. I pinched the bridge of my nose. "What do you mean, something is rotten?"

He pushed the folders around. "I've never been much on gut instinct. But I can smell 'fishy' from half a world away. There's something off with Cassandra. Or with the build. Or both. I need you there." He paused, seemed about to add something. But all he said was, "I've made the arrangements. You fly out early tomorrow morning."

"Of course," I agreed, even as I wondered how I'd manage it with everything else. "But I've read her reports. And we've talked. Some, anyway. She's been quiet. But everything is fine."

"Cassandra quiet?" Guy raised a thick eyebrow. "And you're not worried?"

"Point taken. I'll check things out in person. On one condition."

"I'm not much in the mood for bargaining."

"By the time I return," I pressed, "you will have told Isabeth and Rob. You can't expect Cass and me to carry this by ourselves."

He rubbed his unshaven chin. "How about we wait until you report back? Then we'll tell them together. Deal?"

"You promise?"

"I promise."

"Then it's a deal."

He eased my hands from my pockets and gripped my cold fingers. He peered into my eyes. I lowered my gaze as I felt him take my measure.

With one knuckle, he tipped up my chin. "Do you remember the drowning game?"

My fingers turned colder. I hadn't thought about the game in years. Cass and I would take turns "drowning"—first in the family swimming pool, later in a lake, and finally the ocean. One sister would have to rescue the other. As Cass and I grew older, we vied for more-elaborate scenarios involving sunken ships or unfeigned drunkenness or shark-infested reefs.

After one close call, Guy ended the game. The point, he'd told us, was not to get ourselves killed. It was to realize we must always be there for each other.

"Find out what's wrong with the *Red Dragon* build, Naughty," he said. "Find out what's going on with Cass. Then get into the trenches and fix it."

3

Singapore
August 25, 8:57 p.m. SGT

Eight thousand miles away, on the other side of the Pacific Ocean, Han Chenglong, who called himself Charlie Han, stepped into an elevator at the Marina Bay Sands in Singapore.

He rode the elevator down from the fortieth floor to the garishly lit Shoppes, his hand rubbing the back of his neck. In the middle of drawing out information from the girl, a weariness had descended on him with the force of one of Singapore's monsoon thunderstorms, bringing with it a headache and the need for fresh air.

Interrogation, no matter how subtle or crude, was hard work. Even a Guóānbù professional like Charlie sometimes required a break. He hoped he could trust Dai Shujun not to touch the girl while he was away. Dai was a brute.

He went out through glass doors into a velvet night. Heat and humidity enveloped him. He followed a sign to a designated smoking area and removed a Marlboro from a gold case.

The cigarette case was the only thing of value his parents had given him. That, and the wisdom that forgiveness is more easily obtained than permission.

And, often, forgiveness didn't matter.

As the tobacco hit his lungs, his shoulders came down. The headache lifted. He tilted his head back and watched insects dance in the streetlight.

The interrogation of the girl was going well. For a pampered *ang moh*—a Caucasian—Cassandra Brenner was tough. Even so, she had already told him much about *Red Dragon*. Never mind that he already knew everything she'd so far offered. The details he sought would come before morning.

But getting those details might necessitate a higher degree of force. He walked a tightrope. The splashy locale his boss had insisted on. The bribes he might have to pay. Being saddled with a beast for a partner. And the risk that the girl could die. If she did, it would be a slap to the CIA. But her death could not, must not, come back on him or the Guóānbù.

He tipped his head back farther, searching all the way up to where the hotel belled out, concealing the upper floors. While he would have preferred to grab the girl off the street, a public operation was too risky, given Singapore's surveillance and Cassandra Brenner's status as an American businesswoman. Fortunately, she'd fallen for his ruse—helped along by her own assistant—to meet at the hotel. Once she'd arrived, everything had clicked into place.

Charlie and his men had tracked her through the hotel lobby and watched as she'd boarded an elevator under the lewd gazes of two British businessmen.

Earlier, Charlie's contact inside the hotel had made sure the cameras observing the fortieth and forty-first floors had gone offline at 5:32 p.m. A few minutes after that, Charlie had ridden an elevator to the forty-first floor, where he'd booked a room ostensibly for a business client and a girl Charlie had procured for him. Hiring a prostitute for an associate was a not-uncommon arrangement among Chinese financiers. But in this case, the businessman had been one of his men, the girl a nobody from the red-light district in Geylang.

Once their target was in her room, Charlie and another of his men had taken the stairs down to the fortieth floor, still without cameras tracking their movements. A key from his contact had gotten them inside Cassandra Brenner's room.

Tonight, once Charlie finished with the *ang moh*, the prostitute would disguise herself as the American girl and walk out of the hotel for the benefit of the surveillance cameras.

Oh, so easy.

It was good fortune for him that the American CIA was still weak. In 2010, Guóānbù had gutted CIA operations in China, killing or imprisoning twenty of their sources. After that, the Americans became timid, pulling in like a sea anemone while the Chinese dragon found its voice and breathed fire. These days, an occasional CIA operative might be brilliant. The Texan running the woman—Virgil, she'd called him—had been decent. He'd even tried to recruit Charlie, and it hadn't been a bad pitch. But it had proved fatal for the Texan, who, as the Westerners liked to say, now swam with the fishes.

Charlie swatted away a mosquito and puffed out a satisfied ring of smoke. George Mèng—aristocrat, entrepreneur, owner of *Red Dragon*—would soon be his. This was the best way for a poor farmer's son to prove his worth to those at the highest echelon of the Chinese Communist Party: expose the treachery of one of their own. As Sun Tzu said, "In the midst of turmoil, there is opportunity." The Chinese Communist Party was in chaos. And Charlie was superb at seizing opportunity.

He stubbed out his cigarette in the ashtray, careful not to let ash fall to the ground. The Singaporean police were bastards about litter. He pocketed the cigarette butt in case there was an investigation. Cameras were one thing. DNA another.

And there *would* be an investigation if the girl stopped cooperating.

4

Changi Airport / Block 9, Singapore General Hospital
August 26, 3:05 p.m. SGT

I landed at Changi Airport in Singapore with eyes heavy with fatigue. Despite the alprazolam I'd taken to calm my nerves, sleep had been fitful. Every bit of turbulence had shot me upright in my seat, wondering whether *this* was when the plane would go down.

I sent a text to Cass that I'd landed but got no response. I cleared customs, then looked for her familiar figure, which was so like my own: long brunette hair and a tall, willowy form—to quote the industry mags.

But if Cass was here, she was doing a good job of hiding.

I checked my phone. Nothing. Fatigue washed over me. It was after midnight, Seattle time. I groaned.

"Damn it, Cass."

Someone spoke my name. I turned.

"You must be Nadia," a Chinese woman said. The trace of a smile appeared on her lips. "You look so much like your sister."

In the bright lights and tropical greenery of the airport, the woman stood out like a rare bird of rich plumage. Petite and slim, she wore an elegant yellow sheath dress, drop earrings of gold and pearl, and a cool expression. She held out her hand.

"My name is Tan Mei Ling, but in Singapore I am called Emily Tan. I'm your sister's assistant."

I smiled. "Of course. Cass has mentioned you."

As we shook hands, a thin gold bracelet glittered on Emily Tan's slender wrist. Her skin was like silk. I caught a whiff of her perfume—something exotic and flowery.

As I towered over her, *tall and willowy* felt suddenly more like *gangly and awkward.*

I picked up my briefcase and grabbed the handle of my carry-on. "Where *is* my sister?"

The faintest break appeared in Emily Tan's porcelain veneer, then vanished as she slid on a pair of sunglasses.

"If you will come with me," she said, "I'll explain everything."

She's in a meeting, I thought. Or there was an issue with the build.

I trailed after Emily through the automatic glass doors and out onto the sidewalk. The light was dazzling, the tropical heat a blade that pinned every living thing to the earth. In the short stretch of pavement that we crossed toward a waiting SUV, sweat gathered under my breasts and along my ribs.

"I'd forgotten the heat," I said.

Emily didn't look back. "It is severe. But you will adjust. Most everyone does."

A driver took my case and loaded it into the back of the white SUV, then held the passenger door open for us. Inside, the interior was cool and dry. I leaned back in my seat.

Emily turned toward me, as if in preparation for an intimate conversation. But instead of meeting my eyes, she stared down, perhaps at her hands, which were folded in her lap.

"I did not wish to tell you in public," she said as the driver pulled away from the curb and joined a stream of cars heading toward the exit. "But I am afraid I have terrible news."

My breath caught. I glanced away, out the window. Emily said nothing more, perhaps waiting for me. The thought flashed through my mind that this was my last normal moment. The instant before everything changed.

I shook off my doomsday thinking and pulled my gaze back to the SUV's interior. My eyes were still dazzled by sunlight, so that Emily and the driver were mere shadows.

Think first. Act second. Panic only when it's all over. "Is Cass okay?"

"I am so sorry, Nadia. There was a terrible accident." Emily made a small sound in her throat like a faint cough. She pushed her sunglasses up on top of her head. Her gaze was on the floor. "Your sister fell to her death. Please accept my condolences."

My pulse throbbed in my neck, a metronome cranked up to prestissimo. "There's been a mistake."

"No mistake. I am so very sorry."

I pressed the tips of two fingers to a spot just above the bridge of my nose, as if forcing Emily's news into my skull.

Cass, dead.

It wasn't possible. I'd just seen Cass on the video screen twenty-four hours ago. Spoken with her. She'd sent me texts.

And miss Guy and Uncle Rob fight? she'd typed. *Ha!*

I heard Guy's voice in my mind. *Think, Nadia. Assess.*

Then act.

I hugged myself. "What happened?"

"Her body was found on the grounds of the Marina Bay Sands Hotel. I have been told only a little about the circumstances."

I felt myself falling, too, as if the seat had vanished. The SUV, the road, the ground beneath the road, the entire island. I was sinking into the sea. Distantly, I picked up a few words spoken in Emily's soft voice.

Fortieth floor. Marina Bay Sands. Possible suicide.

"She'd never," I said. "It's a mistake. Maybe she had to go somewhere. Out of town. They found a body, and for some reason they think it's her."

Emily's voice was gentle. "There is no mistake, Nadia. Her body was found last night. The police took fingerprints and positively identified her from the prints taken for her entry into Singapore. DNA will confirm it."

The police? DNA? Oh my god.

Outside, traffic rushed by on the expressway, the tropical sun winking on mirrors and hoods. Everything was suddenly moving too quickly, like a black hole sucking us into its depths.

The driver signaled and took an off-ramp.

I pinched myself. Hard. *Focus.* "Where are we going?"

"Your Seattle office booked a room for you at the Raffles. Isn't that where you stayed on your previous trip? I thought you'd want to go to the hotel to rest and recover a little. Tomorrow we will go to pay our respects and collect Cassandra's belongings."

I shook my head. "Now."

"Now what?" Emily asked.

"To the morgue. We'll go now." I leaned forward and touched the driver's shoulder. "Please."

The look Emily gave me was filled with pity. "Nadia, you do not want to see your sister. It was a long fall. The . . . injuries are extensive. It's not how you want to remember her."

It took a moment to process Emily's words. I filled my lungs and breathed out as I spoke. "I understand. But I still want to go."

"They close in an hour," Emily said. "And I do not yet have Cassandra's papers. The state coroner requires her passport and work visa for their reports and for . . . processing the body. It is better if we go tomorrow. The authorities will expect us then. They will phone when they're ready for us."

"We'll go now," I said again, trying not to think what a fall from the fortieth floor would do to a human body. "I don't care what the authorities expect. If you don't want to take me, I'll get a taxi."

"It is not how things are done here. We don't have—"

I held up a hand. The pulse in my neck had slowed. Visible composure was my superpower, learned at an early age. Never let them see you sweat. Or cry. Or yell.

Or grieve.

I was back in control.

I said, "We can go back tomorrow with whatever the state requires. But I need to be with Cass."

Emily gripped the handles of her purse and stared at me. Perhaps she saw my determination. Perhaps she pitied me. After a time, she said, "If that is your wish."

She spoke to the driver, who nodded and accelerated through traffic.

The morgue of the Health Sciences Authority was tucked inside Block 9 of Singapore General Hospital in the southern part of the city. A young man with spiked hair and a lab coat greeted us in a waiting room where the air-conditioning had been set to polar. *Forensic Medicine Division* was embroidered on his coat in English and Chinese. Emily told him our names. In heavily accented English, he told us to leave, that our presence was against protocol. He tried to shoo us toward the door.

"Go, go, come back with appointment," he said. "Not okay to have you here."

But when it became obvious that it would take a natural disaster to force me out the door, he relented. He jotted our names on a clipboard and indicated we should remain in the waiting area—someone would be with us shortly.

We perched on chairs like two mourning doves, soft and still. Ten minutes later, another man appeared from the back. As the door opened, then closed behind him, the pungent whiff of chemicals washed through the room.

This man was middle aged and heavyset, with deep golden skin, a bald head, and the mournful manner of a priest who had just heard a cruel confession. He shuffled toward us, shoulders bowed, favoring his left knee. He wore a baggy blue suit and a wrinkled button-down shirt that was patterned on the front with small brown stains.

I blinked. Tea. It was just tea.

The man homed in on me. "Nadia Brenner?"

Emily and I stood. "I'm Nadia."

He held out his hand. "I'm Investigations Officer Huang Lee with the Criminal Investigations Department of the Singapore Police Force. You may call me Inspector Lee."

At the litany of official names, bile rose in my throat. I swallowed and accepted the investigator's hand. His grip was warm and firm, slightly damp. He clasped my fingers for a moment, then released me and turned toward Emily Tan, who introduced herself as Cassandra's assistant.

"We spoke on the phone," she said.

"Of course." Lee gestured for us to resume our seats. "I was about to return to the office when I learned of your arrival at the morgue. It is unfortunate we are brought together under these circumstances, but fortunate for us to be able to speak in person."

I lowered myself into the chair as if the world might again vanish beneath me, leaving me drowning in open water. "What happened?"

I waited for Inspector Lee to tell me that there had been a mistake. Cassandra was fine. An unfortunate case of the wrong identity.

"I am very sorry to tell you that your sister jumped or fell or—and this is unlikely—was pushed from a fortieth-floor balcony at the Marina Bay Sands resort."

Grief folded into horror. "Did you say 'pushed'?"

"It is doubtful. Another client at the hotel, a reputable German businessman, signed a statement that he witnessed your sister jump. We're looking at her death as most probably a suicide."

"Jumped," I whispered.

"Terrible news, *lah*," Inspector Lee said.

The room turned sideways. Every bone in my body dissolved as if grief were a bath of acid. Distantly, I felt Emily's cool hand on mine.

My eyes skipped past the inspector's concerned expression to the room's mint-green walls and functional furniture. Without my wishing it, my mind raced through the math: forty floors came to more than four hundred feet.

I tucked my chin and focused on a square of linoleum. Black specks on green, like tiny rowboats on an artificial lake. I forced my gaze up. "Suicide."

"I am only a few hours into my investigation, *lah*. But it appears so. Sadly, we have many suicides in our country among the young. Academic pressure. Relationship problems." He produced a notebook and pen from a jacket pocket. "Was your sister troubled? Financial difficulties perhaps? A love gone wrong?"

"No. No. Cass was fine. She was good. She was working on the most important project of her life. It made her happy . . ."

My voice trailed off as I recalled Cassandra's text from the day before.

There's something we should talk about.

I dropped my eyes. The square of linoleum wavered as my tears rose. Emily pressed a tissue into my hand.

"What project was your sister working on?" the investigator asked.

I wiped my eyes and lifted my chin to the level of the coffee table in front of us. Spread across the surface were copies of *Tatler* and *Vogue Singapore*. As if the grieving would seek solace in photos of wealthy homes and haute couture.

I cleared my throat. "Cass is managing the build of a superyacht called *Red Dragon*. Our family designs and builds yachts. *Red Dragon* is—was—to be Cass's greatest accomplishment."

"Perhaps this 'build,' as you call it, was not going so well?" Inspector Lee suggested. His voice had turned even more gentle. The mournful priest now offering absolution. "Perhaps there were problems."

"It's going exactly as it should," I snapped, turning away from the glossy magazines. "I read her project reports just last night. Today, rather. On the plane. Tell him, Emily. The build is going fine."

Emily's porcelain face remained impassive. Her eyes, I now saw, were golden brown with flecks of jade around the irises. She removed her fingers from mine and folded both hands in her lap.

"No build goes perfectly," she said.

"Of course not," I said. "There are always hurdles."

"Sometimes these hurdles are minor. Sometimes more."

My cheeks grew hot, as if I'd been slapped. "Are you suggesting there are serious problems with *Red Dragon*?"

Inspector Lee tugged on his ear.

"I do not know." Emily gave me an apologetic nod and said to Lee, "Cassandra had become distracted. Often absent from the office and shipyard. When I asked if she was depressed, she told me not to worry. But I grew concerned after she began to disappear for hours and the build schedule slipped."

"The schedule has slipped?" I stared. "Why haven't I heard about this?"

Emily's gaze met mine. "Cassandra was very specific. This was a private matter. It was not my place to share my concerns. Not with anyone."

My mouth fell open. I struggled to regain my composure. "Our build supervisor. He must know."

"Mr. Ewing believes Mr. Mèng requested additional security measures which have impacted the schedule. He does not know that the delays were due to Cassandra's inactions."

George Mèng, the wealthy Chinese man who had commissioned *Red Dragon*. An entrepreneur who specialized in the development of AIs—artificial intelligence software.

Inspector Lee scratched the side of his nose. "How long ago did Miss Brenner become"—he glanced down at his notes—"distracted?"

"I remember the date well," Emily said, "because the first time she disappeared from the office without explanation was on the day of my mother's birthday. Almost five weeks ago."

My breath vanished. Five weeks?

A yacht build involved hundreds of contractors and millions of hours of hard work and talent. It was—essentially—a series of crises, one problem after another. Delays were inevitable. But five weeks? If this was true, then Cassandra had been lying in her reports. Lying to her family.

There's something we should talk about.

No wonder Guy was concerned. He'd clearly sensed something about Cassandra that I had missed.

Or Emily Tan was lying. Which made no sense, either.

But Lee nodded as if her words confirmed a private suspicion. He jotted a few lines in his notebook. "Miss Tan, what do you think Miss Brenner was doing during these times she was away from the office?"

Emily's dress rustled as she shifted in her chair. "Cassandra did not confide in me, other than to mention she was consulting an astrologist. But those meetings would not explain all her absences."

"That's absurd." My voice rang like the slap of a metal ruler. "Cassandra was as superstitious as . . . as a fish. She doesn't buy that nonsense."

"It is my belief that she went to an astrologist on the wishes of Mr. Mèng," Emily said. "To ensure an auspicious build and a fortunate launch."

"Conferring with an astrologist is common in Singapore," Lee pointed out. "Everyone does it, whether or not they believe. It's more like a social event."

"But Cass went alone to see the astrologer," I said. "Right?"

"I do not know," Emily said softly. "She might have been accompanied by Mr. Mèng. Or someone else."

"Was she seeing someone?" Lee asked. "A secret lover would explain a lot. Perhaps she threatened to leave him. Or to make their relationship public. Sometimes with government officials, they get entangled with women they shouldn't and . . ." His voice trailed off.

"And the women get murdered?" I said.

"No, no. But it can be shameful for the woman to be rejected. Sometimes she does not take it well."

Emily ran her palm along the surface of one of the magazines. A handsome model stared back. "It is possible. But if I am completely truthful—"

"Please," Lee interjected.

"Then the truth is that Cassandra never acted like a woman in love. She was not happy. Although she was often energetic when I saw her at work or the occasional dinner. Overexcited. Almost . . . frenzied. As if she were, I do not know, maybe taking something." She glanced at me, and I was surprised to see the shimmer of tears.

"Drugs?" Lee asked.

"Perhaps."

This time I saw the words Lee wrote in his notebook in English: *Vic into drugs.*

He didn't add a question mark.

Lee cleared his throat. "Miss Tan, Miss Brenner, do you know *why* the deceased might have checked into a luxury resort? If she wasn't meeting a lover, I mean. Is it possible she had taken up gambling?"

Emily looked at her folded hands. "Anything is possible. As I said, she did not confide in me."

I snapped my fingers. "Cameras. Singapore has cameras everywhere. They will show us what happened. Who came and went from her room."

Lee pulled out a sweat-stained handkerchief and patted his broad face. "Unfortunately, the cameras on the fortieth floor, where your sister was staying, were not functional at the time of her death. But we will be able to track her in the lobby and elsewhere. The casino, if that is where she went. And we will discover if anyone was with her. I have people working on it."

"Don't you think that's odd?" I asked. "For the cameras to be conveniently broken on her floor?"

"It happens." Lee shrugged. "The forty-first floor was also affected. These particular cameras were nearing their maximum number of usage hours and were on a list to be replaced. *Ah so suey.* Bad luck. It is all too common in Singapore. But, of course, I will investigate the possibility that the cameras were tampered with."

"Cass wouldn't jump," I persisted.

Yet even as I spoke, I recalled a time when we were in university together—Cass had fallen into a depression after her boyfriend left her. It had taken counseling, antidepressants, and equine therapy to bring her back.

"It can be very hard to hear this kind of news," Lee said. He reached a hand toward me, and I swatted it away, along with my doubts.

"It's not that it's hard," I said. "It's false. Someone did this to her."

Lee stared down at the hand I had struck. "Miss Brenner. We have that witness. According to him, your sister deliberately climbed over the railing and stepped off the balcony."

"It was dark, wasn't it?" I pointed out. "How well could this witness see?"

"The tragedy occurred just after midnight. But there are many, many lights in Singapore. True darkness doesn't exist in our city."

"It seems like it does."

Lee hitched up his pants. "If the state coroner finds anything unusual during the autopsy, if I see something suspicious on the cameras, or if guests on the fortieth floor heard or saw anything out of the ordinary, then I will conduct an investigation. If not . . ." He spread his arms. "Then I will close the case, *lah*."

I absorbed this news.

"And now, Miss Brenner. Would you be kind enough to look at your sister's belongings, see if anything surprises you? I am sorry to ask. It will make you *buay song*."

"*Buay song* means unhappy," Emily explained.

"I am already *buay song*. Of course I'll look."

Inspector Lee's face crumpled into creases like a well-worn pillow. *"Okay lor."* He stood. "Please wait here."

5

Block 9, Singapore General Hospital
August 26, 5:00 p.m. SGT

A few minutes later, the same man who had greeted us earlier emerged through a door from the back, trailed by Inspector Lee. The man carried a large metal tray.

He placed the tray atop the magazines and took a nearby chair.

Inspector Lee sat down and leaned in.

"This is everything," he confirmed, presumably for my benefit.

"Except her clothes," the younger man answered. "Dress, bra, and panties."

I flinched at his matter-of-fact voice.

"In the room was a bouquet of red gardenias," Lee told me. "We are working to see who delivered them. Also, a bottle of expensive cognac."

I pulled my expression into neutral and said nothing.

Each of Cassandra's possessions had been placed in a separate plastic bag. Clipped to the side of the tray was a typewritten inventory. Lee unclipped it and set it in front of me.

Possessions: Brenner, Cassandra Allegra
Case #1384-FN-19

- Jewelry: Ruby and gold drop earrings, brand unknown
- Shoes: Christian Louboutin red satin pumps with peep toe
- Purse: Jimmy Choo Honey Gold Suede Clutch Bag with Crystals
- Contents of purse:
- Lipstick: Rouge Orange Hermès matte lipstick (#53)
- Compact mirror: gold
- Credit card: American Express Platinum
- Business cards: Cassandra Brenner, Designer, Ocean House (12)
- Plastic bag with 1.21 grams of unknown white powder
- Plastic straw cut at an angle on each end
- Yin and yang necklace, black and white, on gold chain, brand unknown
- Hotel key: Marina Bay Sands, Room 4015

Unknown substance? I lifted my eyes to Lee's. "What is this powder?"

"We cannot be sure until the lab has analyzed the substance. We will also run a toxicology screen."

"It's not cocaine," I said. "Cass has never used street drugs."

Lee remained silent.

"Maybe a friend . . ." I let the thought trail off. What friend? Why would Cass be carrying someone else's drugs as she plunged to her death? Indeed, why had she been carrying her purse?

"Maybe," Lee agreed in a neutral voice.

I put aside the implications of the powder for the moment and examined the two larger items. The shoes and the gold evening purse.

A red smear marred the crystals on the clutch.

I shuddered. "Is that—"

"The bag, like the shoes, was found near the deceased," Lee said. "Separated during the fall."

My stomach flipped. At the same time, my methodical mind whispered: *Who climbs over a balcony railing in stilettos?*

"Where is her phone?" I asked. "And keys? Cassandra didn't have a car, but she has a condo in Tanglin. Ardmore Park."

Lee looked again at the morgue employee, who said, "This is everything."

"Someone took her phone," I said. "They planted the drugs and took her phone."

"Why would someone do that?" Lee asked.

I had no answer.

After a moment, Lee cleared his throat. "Does the purse look familiar to you?" he asked, including Emily in his gaze.

"No," I said.

Emily shook her head.

"My sister wasn't much for fancy clothes unless there was a big yacht event," I said. "She's never owned expensive things like these."

My eyes skimmed over the drop earrings, their gold-and-ruby luster still visible through the plastic bag. Everything on the tray was a far cry from Cassandra's usual flats, linen pants, and canvas totes. Cass enjoyed bright colors but rarely wore jewelry. She was practical. Efficient. Economical with her appearance as well as her life. At most she'd don a black cocktail dress and wear Grandmama's paste jewelry.

"Perhaps," Emily ventured, "she became someone else in this country."

Lee lowered his eyebrows. He scratched under his chin. "Singapore does change people," he said after a moment. "For good and for bad."

Was it possible for a person to change so much?

If Cassandra *had* changed, were the changes merely skin deep? Or had the shift gone deeper?

I reached for the bag holding Cass's yin-and-yang necklace. Lee's immense hand gently interceded. "For now," he said, "look only."

I fished out my own necklace from where it hung around my neck and held it up for Lee.

"She was Yang and I Yin," I said. "That's what she told me when she bought these necklaces. I'm the thinker. She was the doer."

Yin and Yang. Soft and bright. Earthy and airy.

I brought my hands to my throat.

Alive and dead.

"I'm ready to see her," I said.

—

A woman in blue scrubs met us at an industrial-looking elevator, a paper mask tucked under her chin, her hair covered by a surgical cap. She smelled of chemicals and cleaning agents and a vague hint of something I couldn't define and didn't want to. The three of us—Emily had chosen to remain behind—rode down in silence.

Lee and Emily had tried to convince me to forgo the viewing. It was unnecessary and would make me greatly *buay song*. I'd explained that seeing Cass was imperative and that Lee would be *buay song* if he refused to allow it.

But as we rode the elevator down, my pulse returned to prestissimo.

"This way," said the woman, exiting the elevator.

I hung back. Lee gave me a kindly look.

"Would you prefer to return upstairs?" he asked. "This viewing will only make your loss harder."

But I stepped into the hallway. I was done with the thinking part. We were on to acting.

Panic would come when I was finally alone.

—

Five minutes later, I sat in a chair as directed and peered through a window at a tiled room with metal drawers and a single body on display.

The sheet-covered shape on the metal embalming table was clearly not in one piece and bore only the faintest outline of a human body. When the tech folded down the sheet, Cass's face was unrecognizable. It wasn't at all like looking at her. Except for the wavy fall of dark, blood-soaked hair, it could have been anyone.

It could have been me.

"She has a tattoo," the morgue technician said. "Would it help for you to see it?"

I nodded. The tech covered Cass's face and tucked the sheet back from her shoulder. The skin was bruised and split, but the yang tattoo and the surrounding words—*light*, *sun*, *active*, *strong*—were visible.

I'd forgotten about the tattoo. Cass had gotten it five years ago, just before she moved out of our shared apartment and flew across the world to take up her position in Singapore. I was supposed to get a matching tattoo on my right shoulder. But I was busy, and I hated needles, and—conveniently—I forgot about it.

"Have you seen enough?" Lee asked.

I nodded, understanding with lightning-bolt clarity why the tech had insisted I sit down.

"It's Cass," I said before the room went dark.

Sometime later, I followed Emily through the morgue's door and into the cool white hallway. I gripped a bottle of a sports drink Lee had rustled up from somewhere, and a plastic package with two pain-reliever tablets.

Emily stopped. "You are okay now?"

My stomach seethed. "Sure."

"Then please excuse me. I need to use the restroom. I will meet you by the front doors."

I nodded. I wanted to wash my mascara-smeared face, but it felt intrusive to follow Emily into the bathroom. Instead, I found a shallow alcove with a water fountain. I turned my back to the handful of pedestrians in the hallway and cleaned the black goop from beneath my eyes using a damp tissue and a compact.

I was about to close the mirror when I caught the reflection of a man in the glass. He had stopped just outside the alcove.

I lowered the mirror and turned.

The man was lean, of average height, with close-cropped black hair and eyes hidden by steel-rimmed spectacles that reflected the hallway lights like silver coins over the eyes of the dead. He wore black pants and a black trench coat over a gray tee. His hands—I noticed his hands even though they were motionless—were slender but sturdy looking, the fingers strong, the knuckles calloused. The nails on his left index and middle fingers were gone.

His smile was merely a simulacrum of pleasantry. "You are Nadia Brenner."

"Have we met?"

"Not officially."

"But . . . at a yachting event, perhaps? Or . . ." My voice fell flat under the analytical precision of his gaze. "Or perhaps you knew my sister?" I took a step forward. "Cassandra?"

He continued to stare at me, his eyes like fingers picking at my flesh. Goose bumps rose on my arms.

"Who are you?" I asked.

Abruptly, he turned on his heel and strode away, leaving behind only the whiff of nicotine. I stepped out of the alcove and watched as he disappeared through the same door Emily and I had just exited.

I shoved my compact in my purse and hurried after him.

Emily's voice sounded behind me. "Nadia! We should go."

I stopped. "There was a man here who knew me. He knew my name." I hugged myself. "The way he stared at me . . ."

Her heels clicked on the tiles as she came toward me. "Someone working with the inspector, no doubt. Probably your beauty gave him a momentary distraction." She touched my arm. "Come. I'm sure it was nothing more than that."

6

Block 9, Singapore General Hospital
August 26, 6:00 p.m. SGT

Charlie Han had not expected to find the sister compelling.

From her polished hair and smooth skin to the elegance of her clothes, she looked very much the white, pampered American his men had tailed in Seattle. A lily-white orchid thriving in the fertile shade of the well-heeled yachting world.

Yet what he felt toward Nadia Brenner wasn't disgust, but pity.

After he'd hammered the mystery around in his skull, understanding came. He recognized the unfiltered grief and horror in the girl's expression—he'd seen it on his parents' faces when they learned that Xiao—their daughter, his sister—had been arrested for treason.

He'd seen it on his own face that same night in the aluminum mirror at the boys' dorm.

Charlie had killed more than a few people. Some he'd murdered with his bare hands, others with a knife, a few through the expedient and recently deployed method of defenestration—tossing someone out a window. He would carry their lives forever. But it appalled him to realize that if it came to killing Nadia Brenner, he would do so with some regret.

Having robbed her of her sister, he was oddly reluctant to rob her of her life.

7

Block 9, Singapore General Hospital / Keppel Shipyard
August 26, 6:00 p.m. SGT

The sun hung in the western sky as we emerged from Block 9 and into an evening heavy with moisture. A light wind blew inland from the Singapore Strait, stirring the trees and blowing loose strands of hair across my face.

Traffic whizzed by on the other side of a low fence.

I turned my face toward the sinking sun. From deep inside I felt a sharp snap. Something breaking that could not be repaired.

Cass was gone.

"I've called the car," Emily said, stopping at the curb.

I took my grief and horror and locked them momentarily away. I had to think of Ocean House. "I need to see *Red Dragon*."

"Do you not wish for some privacy to call your family?"

I shook my head. "It's three in the morning in Seattle. I'll let them have a final peaceful night."

Or as peaceful as it could be while Guy faced his illness and Robert worked to discover what had caused *Rambler* to implode.

"You are strong willed," Emily said.

I didn't feel strong willed. I felt like tissue paper flattened on a wet sidewalk. But I lifted my chin. "We don't have time to waste, do we? Not if the build is five weeks behind."

At a port north and west of where the container ships docked, Emily directed the driver to pull up to a pair of high steel gates. I recognized this as Keppel Shipyard, where Ocean House had rented space for *Red Dragon* to be outfitted and commissioned—the final stages before the sea trials. I'd been in both this yard and the build yard on my previous visit, touring the facilities during the weeks while the hull and the superstructure were joined together.

We checked in with the security guard, and he opened the gates remotely for the car to drive through. Around us laborers toiled on refits and repairs. Emily told the driver to drop us off in front of a sprawling office building and to wait there until we'd finished.

She gestured toward the building. "The on-site offices of Ocean House. I checked in with our build supervisor, Mr. Ewing, but he has left for the day."

I followed Emily down a path toward the water as the sun began its plunge into the ocean. Security lights flared on. The concrete path gave way to gravel and then mud, which Emily negotiated gracefully. I worked to match the smaller woman's pace and poise.

We rounded a bend, and there was *Red Dragon*.

The boat rose high above us, floating serenely in the bay. The port lights reflected on the water and on the ship's red-and-onyx dragon-etched hull. Emily led me up a steep staircase to a viewing platform. From there it was possible to see that *Red Dragon* was more than a luxury ship. More than a research vessel. More, even, than a wealthy man's ego forged out of teak, aluminum, and steel.

She was art.

The boat, officially known as OH M/Y 243 until she was commissioned, was 336 feet long with a 47-foot beam. Her internal volume boasted a gross tonnage of 2,999 GT. She was an ultrafast displacement boat with a hull tunneled for reduced draft while in shallow waters. She had a maximum range of five thousand nautical miles at cruising speed.

With a full-service crew of twenty, she could carry up to eighteen guests in nine staterooms. Her tender garage boasted a sailing dinghy, support tenders, Seabobs, sea scooters, Windsurfers, and, most impressive, a Triton submersible that would allow Mr. Mèng to indulge in underwater exploration.

But the statistics said little to anyone outside the industry. What would matter to yachting magazines, future clients, and the media was that *Red Dragon* was the embodiment of elegance and strength. A tribute to man's determination to navigate the world and a promise that he could. It was a structure built to close the gap between continents and prove that man dominated nature.

I leaned against the railing, reaching out a hand as if I could touch *Red Dragon*'s gleaming hull, with its elegant bow, graceful stern, and—most unusual—metallic red paint and the serpentine dragon that curled along her length.

Inside *Red Dragon*, lamps glowed, revealing tantalizing glimpses of the luxurious interior draped in golds and creams and vivid reds, all accented with metalwork of shimmering bronze.

Although I'd been part of her design from the beginning and reviewed sketches and photographs during the process, I was stunned.

"She's magnificent," I murmured.

Emily moved to stand beside me. "Glorious," the other woman agreed. "George Mèng is a very lucky man."

"George Mèng and his family," I said. I'd read a description of the billionaire's wife and children in Cassandra's notes.

"Not his family." Emily shook her head. "They cannot sail with him."

"What do you mean?"

"George Mèng is an important man to the Chinese Communist Party," Emily said. "The brilliance of his work in artificial intelligence makes him irreplaceable."

I was confused. "Meaning what? Don't they want George and his family to enjoy this yacht he's commissioned?"

"*Red Dragon* will serve Mr. Mèng well as he hosts business associates and fellow researchers from around the world on her glorious decks. That is why he was allowed to commission the boat and why the party insisted on her grandeur instead of frowning on a display of wealth they normally consider vulgar—*Red Dragon* will impress scientists and investors from America and Europe and help advance Mr. Mèng's research. But it is forbidden for him to take his family on board."

The Chinese were infamous for stealing trade secrets. Would Mr. Mèng be sharing research or appropriating it? But I focused on the family. "Forbidden because . . ."

"Because if he has his wife and children with him, the party worries he might not come home."

It took a moment for Emily's words to make sense.

"You mean he might defect?"

"That is the government's concern. It is not, I believe, a reasonable worry for a man like Mr. Mèng, who is well placed within the party, has his own wealth, and work he loves. There is no reason for him to leave a country that has given him so much. But this is how the party thinks."

"How sad for his family, that they can't enjoy the yacht."

Emily's earrings danced as she shrugged. "Mr. Mèng's family does not suffer. They have a beautiful home in Shanghai. High-rise apartments in New York and Paris. A country home in Lijiang. There is much for them to enjoy in the world. They are loyal to the party and happy to do their part for the glory of their country. Additionally, it is my understanding that Mrs. Mèng is susceptible to seasickness. She has told me she is secretly relieved at not having to go on an ocean voyage."

I turned so that I faced the shorter woman and parked an elbow on the railing. "You know so much about Mr. Mèng's family from working for Cass?"

Emily's face was unreadable in the semidark. A single band of light fell across her jaw, as if she were an actor in a film noir.

"I am not Singaporean," Emily said. "I am a Chinese national, which means I understand how my country works. Cass thought of me as her assistant, and I acted in that capacity. But I am employed by Mr. Mèng to facilitate communication between his staff and Cassandra's. In America, I believe I would be called chief of staff." The band of light moved to the center of her face as she shifted, highlighting her cheekbones. "Or, rather, chief of staff *was* my job. I do not know what will happen now."

With Emily's words, the weight of Cass's work crashed onto my shoulders. I would not be able to leave Singapore anytime soon, save for a brief trip to fly Cass home. I would have to take her place here until *Red Dragon* had finished sea trials and was ready to be delivered to George Mèng.

Ocean House and the family came before my grief or my personal wishes.

A sudden longing for Seattle and its comfortable familiarity swept through me with the forlorn simplicity of a foghorn. I longed for my office and staff. My apartment. My handful of friends.

And my family. My soon-to-be miserably broken family.

More than my longing for home, I so desired Cass's presence beside me that her loss fell like a physical blow. I staggered and gripped the railing, glad that the coming night covered my weakness.

After a moment I said, "Then I guess that means you are now my assistant."

"You will take your sister's place?"

I drew a deep breath. "*Red Dragon* is my ship until Mr. Mèng takes possession. I'd like to board her now."

The shadows had crept across the viewing platform. They swallowed Emily's face and form.

"As you wish," she said from the darkness.

We went down the stairs, walked to the passerelle, and boarded Ocean House's most magnificent yacht.

8

***Aboard* Red Dragon**
August 26, 7:00 p.m. SGT (4:00 a.m. PDT)

Red Dragon's interior was as magnificent as her glorious hull and decks. Elegant, stylish, distinctive.

But it was also *wrong* in a way only a designer or architect would notice.

Until we'd walked into the master suite, I'd been impressed with the yacht, even as I worried about what remained to be done before she was ready for her sea trials. Cass had modified the boat from my original design, which I had created four and a half years earlier. This was normal—design changes inevitably occurred during a build due to architectural or safety issues and requests made by the owner.

But until now I hadn't found fault with my sister's work. The flow through the living and crew quarters was streamlined and inviting. The living areas were comfortable and spacious, a fusion of modern and classic, East and West, and the engineering rooms and bridge boasted the latest technology. The tender garage, which was outfitted with lockers and changing rooms, was ready for *Red Dragon*'s vessels and toys. Mr. Mèng's master stateroom offered privacy and luxury—he could go days without seeing anyone, even as he roamed his isolated corridors or sunbathed on his cloistered deck.

There was plenty that remained to be done. Openings for recently rerouted piping still awaited finishing work. In other places, bare metal remained to be cleaned and painted. On the exterior, the fairing and painting of the hull's superstructure were complete, but some of the railing and portions of the deck had yet to be installed. Cassandra was following an outwardly chaotic system, which happened when there were delays in one area while something else surged ahead.

Cause for concern, but not alarm.

But in George Mèng's circular, ten-thousand-square-foot stateroom, something was off.

I trailed behind Emily while she pointed out some of the suite's notable features: an immense skylight surrounded by a gold mosaic dragon, a lighted niche containing a bronze replica of one of China's terra-cotta warriors, a bowl-shaped copper bathtub sized for a crowd.

"Mr. Mèng wanted the best," she said. "Your sister and I worked with—"

Abruptly she broke off and glanced at her phone.

"Forgive me," she said with a small bow. "I must take this. I will just be a moment."

After Emily left, I wandered around the suite in the nonslip canvas slippers that Emily and I had each donned before stepping onto the teak deck. I gaped at the display of opulence that only Mr. Mèng would ever enjoy. I wondered how it would be to live in such lonely splendor.

I stopped in the middle of the bedroom, which was centered on a king berth across from a Chinese brush painting of needle-thin pines, misted hills, and a single man, who trudged up a mountain path carrying on his back an immense load of firewood.

A metaphor for Mr. Mèng?

The wood tile mosaic of a dragon surrounded the berth itself. The dragon probably indicated protection, but it struck me as threatening.

I frowned and walked around the suite again—bedroom, bathroom, lounge and study area, a small spa and gym, an extendable balcony, cavernous wardrobes.

The dimensions didn't add up. The room, though large, was too small to match the measurements designated for this space that I'd originally created and had seen in Cass's electronic files.

Unease tiptoed down my spine.

The most logical explanation for the missing square footage was a hidden panic room—a concealed space where the owners and members of the crew could hide. These days panic rooms were an essential aspect of global yachting. If you planned to voyage through areas that harbored pirates—the Strait of Malacca, say, or off the eastern coast of Africa and up into the Arabian Sea—then a panic room gave you a safe place to wait out an attack until help arrived.

Panic rooms were typically located in the crew mess, where everything needed to support human life and to communicate with the outside world was already in place. And, in fact, there *was* a panic room on *Red Dragon*. It was near the crew's mess, right where I'd placed it in my original design. I'd given the area a cursory glance as Emily and I walked by.

So where—and what—was the missing space?

I might not have known Cass as well as I'd thought. But I knew the twelve-square-foot discrepancy wasn't due to a mistake.

My mind returned to the contents of her purse.

Plastic bag with 1.21 grams of unknown white powder

Plastic straw cut at an angle on each end

Drugs? I shook my head. The idea of smuggling made no sense. Not for a billionaire. And not for my sister. And not on a boat being built in Singapore, where dealing illegal drugs carried a mandatory death sentence.

I could not imagine anything that would make Cass that desperate. Not even the sinking bottom line of Ocean House.

And even if, by some unfathomable turn of events, it *was* true, there were plenty of places to hide illicit items on a yacht this size. The master stateroom wasn't one of them.

I went out into the passageway to look for another door, perhaps a steward's supply closet. Nothing. I returned to the room and made a final circuit. Probably the reason for the missing footage was benign. A second panic room with a concealed door. But I needed to know.

This was my ship now.

My thoughts scattered at the sound of Emily's voice as she returned.

"It is magnificent, is it not?" she asked.

I faced her with the question on my lips. *There's missing space. Where is it?*

But something in her dispassionate expression stopped me.

I didn't know Tan Mei Ling a.k.a. Emily Tan. My sister had presumably trusted her. But since I could no longer talk to Cass, Emily would have to earn my confidence. There were other ways to figure out what was going on.

I'd work it out without her help.

Emily bade me good night when the driver dropped me at the hotel.

Raffles Singapore was an opulent colonial hotel first built by the British in the early 1830s as a bungalow-style beach house and later converted to today's luxury hotel. It was named after the English statesman Sir Thomas Stamford Bingley Raffles, who took control of Singapore in 1819. The hotel has served such notable guests as Queen Elizabeth II and the Duke and Duchess of Cambridge, as well as Rudyard Kipling, Elizabeth Taylor, John Wayne, Michael Jackson, Joseph Conrad, Pablo Neruda, Somerset Maugham, and my personal favorite—Charlie Chaplin.

It was also the original home of the famous cocktail the Singapore Sling, invented by a Raffles bartender in 1915.

But tonight the hotel's grandeur and its history—both good and bad—were lost on me as I followed the bellhop past potted palms, bouquets of orchids, and the lobby's ancient grandfather clock up to my room on the third floor.

Alone at last, I sat in front of the mirror and removed my makeup—stripping off the elegant, composed version of myself to reveal the grieving woman underneath. I took a shower, wrapped myself up in the hotel-provided robe, ordered a late dinner, and tried to appreciate the comfortable elegance of my room, with its four-poster bed and large seating area.

When the food arrived, I sat at the table in the window nook and picked at the chicken satay and cucumber-chili relish while I waited for the hands on the clock to reach ten o'clock, which would be 7:00 a.m. in Seattle.

The image of Cass on the morgue table battered me.

I pushed away the food and went to gaze out at the red-tiled courtyard, where tourists strolled the gardens—ghostly figures moving between the glow of lights and the tropical darkness.

Today had upended my once-solid sense that I knew Cass every bit as well as I knew myself.

The fact that she'd booked a room at the city's most expensive hotel complex.

The fancy clothes and jewelry she'd died in.

The white powder in her purse; I couldn't be coy with myself—it was almost certainly cocaine.

The horrifying possibility that she had taken her own life.

Or, worse, had gotten involved with the kind of men who would convince her to jump.

Or help her off the balcony.

I picked up my phone. Called home. When Isabeth picked up, I burst into tears.

"Maman," I whispered. "Something terrible has happened."

9

Singapore Financial District
August 27, 8:00 a.m. SGT

The next morning I stood yawning in the marble-and-steel lobby of Sixty-One Robinson in Singapore's financial district. Emily was at the lobby desk, requesting a key card so that I could access Ocean House's administrative offices on the fourteenth floor.

She wouldn't kill herself, Isabeth had said as we spoke through the long night.

But Guy's voice, broken and hoarse, came across the miles: *She was troubled, Isa. Something was wrong. Our Cass was hurting again.*

I'll arrive in Singapore as soon as I can, Rob had assured me. *Two days.*

My early-morning conversation with my beloved Matthew had lasted less than five minutes. *Come home,* he'd said. *Let me take care of you.*

I wish I could. But I'm staying to finish Cass's build.

A brief silence, then: *I understand.*

The obligation of work was the language we both spoke.

—

On the fourteenth floor, Emily stopped at a door with a brass plate that read Ocean House, Singapore. Inside was a neutral-palette reception area with a love seat, two chairs, and a receptionist's desk, all empty. A hallway led off each side of the lobby. The doors I could see were closed, the rooms silent.

"Most of our staff are at the shipyard today," Emily said. "A few, like the design team, work primarily from home. Mr. Mèng and all but three members of his SFO team are in Shanghai."

SFO—single family office. Ultra-high-net-worth individuals, UHNWIs, typically have an SFO to administer not only their financial assets and personnel but also certain physical properties such as planes and boats. Yacht specialists from Mr. Mèng's personal SFO handled *Red Dragon*'s employment contracts, payroll, insurance, and other responsibilities, including overseeing the build and paying Ocean House as each stage of construction was completed.

Emily turned down the right-hand hallway and unlocked the door to the first room, stepping in ahead of me to flip on the lights.

"This is Cassandra's office," she called from within. "Mine is located next door."

I remained near the gold-and-beige love seat, unwilling to cross the threshold. A clock on a side table ticked in a syrupy voice. Far away, in another world, the elevator dinged.

Emily reappeared from inside Cass's office. "Nadia? Would you rather wait?"

Would I? I shook my head and moved into the doorway. The room smelled like Cassandra—her perfume, her shampoo. I caught the woodsy tang from a recently burned candle. It was the scent of sea and pine.

Just like home.

I braced myself against the doorjamb.

Emily straightened something on Cassandra's desk.

"You are tired," she said.

I nodded.

"I will get you coffee." Her voice was brisk. "How do you prefer it?"

Grateful that she would give me time alone with my thoughts, I scraped up a thin smile. "Cream, please."

I listened until the outer door closed behind her, then forced myself to enter the room. I removed my jacket and purse and set my briefcase on the floor next to the desk.

The office was in the state of casual disarray that was a hallmark of Cassandra's work and personal life. On a drafting table sprawled open notebooks, rolled-up blueprints, and a scattering of pencils and rolls of drafting tape along with a magnifier and a couple of architectural symbol templates. Her desk held a calendar, an assortment of drafting tools, and a marine design engineering book. A raincoat had been tossed over the desk chair, and an umbrella leaned in the corner. Two bookcases dominated one wall at a right angle to the immense windows. The shelves held only a handful of books, a few local souvenirs, and a row of framed photos.

Near the windows, with their magnificent view of the district's skyscrapers, a sago palm turned brown. Dust motes floated in the air.

The photographs drew me. I crossed the room.

Cass had arranged the pictures in chronological order. The first was of our great-grandparents Josef and Hedy Brenner—Pop and Nana—standing on the porch of their home in Austria sometime in the years leading up to World War II. Next came a few shots of our grandparents Erich and Clara, followed by our parents' wedding picture on Bainbridge Island—Isabeth glowing in a beaded Parisian gown, Guy in a tuxedo and rare good humor.

Finally came a photo of all of us—Isabeth and Guy, Rob, and Cass and me. We stood next to the sign marking the entrance to our Seattle shipyard. All of us were smiling. Cass had her arm around my shoulders.

I picked up the photo of my family, the one with Cass's arm around me. A stab of pain caused me to blink back tears.

"What happened, sis?" I whispered.

Cass had been quiet lately, it was true. And Guy had sensed something was wrong. Now I had the indisputable fact that *Red Dragon* was behind schedule and Emily's word that the fault lay with Cass. There were also the strange facts surrounding her death. The fancy hotel and fancy clothes and the white powder.

The man who'd witnessed her fall.

When Cass had plunged into depression in college, I'd been the one she'd turned to. Why not this time? What had she been keeping from me and why?

The outer door opened and closed, and Emily entered Cass's office, balancing two cups of coffee and her key card. Her gaze went from my face to the photos and back.

"Your sister loved all of you very much," she said, looking at the photo as she handed one of the coffees to me.

I replaced the photo. She'd loved all of us. But maybe not enough to stay.

Emily moved toward the desk. "Are you ready to start going through everything for *Red Dragon*?"

"Almost. But can you first give me a little more time? Say, an hour? That will make sure the coffee hits my nervous system and gets me moving."

I tried on a wan smile.

Emily's expression fell just short of a frown, but she was clearly displeased. I understood. She must be tired of passing all the delays on to George Mèng.

"Last night you were anxious to get started," she said.

"I only need an hour."

Her expression turned neutral. "Of course."

After Emily left again, I didn't waste any more time thinking about the past. The hour I wanted was not to reminisce or to allow space for my grief but to see if I could figure out why *Red Dragon* was late and where the stateroom's missing dimensions were without Emily looking over my shoulder.

The woman remained a black box. *Trust, but verify*—a strategy Guy told me had guided American politicians during the Cold War. Of course, he also liked to say, *Trust no one.*

Since I couldn't verify, I wasn't prepared to trust.

The first thing I focused on was the large whiteboard behind Cassandra's desk, which showed a high-level timeline for *Red Dragon*'s final weeks: the outfitting and launching of the boat, followed by two sea trials. On the first trial, we would travel north and east through the South China and Philippine Seas to Shanghai, where Mèng's personal belongings would be stowed and *Red Dragon* would be provisioned for the second leg of the sea trial. The second, shorter journey was to Apo Island, a marine sanctuary in the Philippines.

The last, glorious date—November 10—was for the commissioning of OH M/Y 243, when she would be christened *Red Dragon*. Someone had drawn a line through the date with a red dry-erase marker and written a question mark above it.

I stepped back to take in the full board. All through the earlier phases—planning, engineering, creating the hull and superstructure—everything had gone according to schedule. This much I knew from Cass's reports and my previous night's tour of the boat.

As proof, Cass had taped up photos of the yacht in various stages of completion.

Things had started to go haywire after *Red Dragon* was moved from the construction yard to the outfitting facility, where she now waited. It was clear from the residue of dry-erase marker visible on the whiteboard that the dates had changed and changed again.

I turned away. I'd find no answers here. Only signs of trouble.

Next, I opened the safe next to her desk using our shared set of codes. It was empty save for *Red Dragon*'s general arrangement plan—the GAP. Essentially, details of the boat's floor plan. During a build, the customer gets a simplified version of the GAP while the designer maintains the technical version, which includes details of the electronics, plumbing, and wiring as well as the layout.

This GAP was stamped DRAFT in red letters. Odd that Cass had locked it away. Was it so no one got confused and worked off an old version? That would suggest a shoddily run office, which was not Cass's style.

But maybe the GAP held the secret to the missing space.

I carried the bound GAP to the drafting table, cleared a space, and laid it out. I began flipping through pages.

Everywhere—in the margins, sometimes scrawled in ink over the drawings—were Cass's notes, her tight, angular penmanship so different from my own loopy style. She'd made design enhancements, written in requests from George Mèng, even added whimsical sketches, like a guest diving off the swim platform and a shark swimming near the hull. Some of her notes were specific in detail, with bullet points and dates. Others, like a rectangular outline in the hull—perhaps space for an additional trimming tank—were vague. Doodles without commitment.

Now I understood why she'd kept it. She'd used the general arrangement plan as her working pad, a place to capture ideas before jettisoning some and committing others to the current digital plan. She'd likely locked it away because it was personal. A private physical design board.

I turned to the section detailing the master stateroom.

There I found a black twelve-by-twelve square labeled "tech," located behind the wall that held Mèng's berth. In yacht design, black areas were a way to designate space for computer-related technical items—routers, switches, servers, peripheral devices. These were primarily associated with the bridge; I'd never seen a tech area next to a master stateroom, or a tech room that couldn't be readily accessed. Maybe it had to do with Mèng's work as an AI designer.

On my laptop, I opened the specs Cass had uploaded to our Ocean House shared cloud account. The most recent updates were from two weeks ago. The black tech area had vanished from the schematics, replaced by an enlarged lounge area.

Cass had simply erased the void.

A chill settled on my shoulders. I made an immediate decision. Tonight, late, I would go alone to *Red Dragon* to find this missing space and determine its true function. If all I found were slots for switches and conduits for coaxial and fiber-optic cables, I would figure the room had to do with Mèng's AI work and move on.

If it held something more sinister, maybe it would be time to panic.

I returned the GAP to the safe.

I walked to Cass's desk, sat down, and hunted through the deep drawers for a laptop. No luck. Perhaps it had vanished, like her phone and her keys. Or maybe she'd taken it home—I'd check when I went to her condo.

I opened her leather-bound calendar. It was an old-style planner with two pages allotted to each day. Many of her appointments, I suspected, would be in her phone's calendar app. But maybe there would be something. Cassandra had always enjoyed the visceral feel of old-fashioned paper and pen. And some part of her had never entirely trusted technology. *The curse of man,* she'd sometimes called it.

Emily had said that Cassandra's mysterious absences from the office—and her equally odd visits to an astrologist—had started five weeks ago. I flipped back two months, looking for a snapshot of her life before things had begun to change in July.

I found appointments with vendors, shipyard staff, team members from Mr. Mèng's SFO, and what I guessed were social meetups or possibly romantic dates; most of these were at two of the city's expat hubs—the American Club and the Tanglin. Cass had been living the life.

I pushed away the day planner and squeezed my eyes shut for a moment against the pain I felt at her familiar writing, her self-chiding notes like, "If I don't get my hair cut soon, they'll need a Weedwacker." Or, "Makeup or nose job? Ha!"

I toed off my shoes and gave myself a moment, curling into a fetal ball on the chair until the worst of the pain had passed. It was like riding a ship in a storm, waiting for calmer seas.

After a time, I straightened and pulled the calendar back toward me. Knowing how Cassandra liked to tuck away reminders and note cards, I picked up the calendar and gently shook it. A single business card fell out and floated to the floor. I snatched it up.

Dr. Sayuri Saravanan
Professional Vedic Astrologer
Baboo Lane, Little India

Cass's mysterious astrologist. Maybe Dr. Saravanan could offer a few answers. I was looking on my phone for Baboo Lane when I heard Emily return. I palmed the card and slipped it into my purse as she appeared in the doorway. She looked flushed, as if she'd hurried. She carried an umbrella, from which she shook a mist of silver drops.

She unbuttoned her raincoat. "Did I give you enough time, Nadia?"

"For now, thank you."

"Key staff will arrive in the early afternoon. We need to eat, so I thought we would have a quick lunch first. Also, Mr. McGrath from NeXt Level, the firm Cassandra hired to handle security on board *Red Dragon*, is hoping to meet you for dinner at the Tanglin Club. Would you like me to tell him yes?"

I had no appetite, but I agreed to both lunch and dinner. I had to eat to keep up my strength; plus I wanted to see the Tanglin, where Cass had gone for dinner at least a few times. And I needed to get the details from McGrath of what sort of security measures had been installed on the boat.

Details about which Cass—in her reports—had been unusually vague.

I hadn't thought too much about that before.

Now the issue of security felt paramount.

10

Lau Pa Sat
August 27, 11:00 a.m. SGT

"If you haven't experienced a hawker center, you must do so while you are here," Emily said, hailing a taxi. "It's a must-do for everyone who comes to the island. The market I will take you to is in the middle of the financial district. Lau Pa Sat was one of Cassandra's favorites." She opened the door. "We are only half a block away, but shall we take a small tour of the area first? Perhaps this will allow you to see Singapore through her eyes."

I pushed aside the now-familiar twist of the knife as I followed Emily into the cab. I wondered how I'd be able to stomach *any* food, no matter how good.

But to be with Ocean House meant leveling up. The client is God, and valued employees are demigods. Their needs dictate yours. Stay out to all hours, smoke if the client does, drink if the client wishes—but nurse that cocktail and swallow the yawn. Bestow carefully crafted compliments, lay out free theater tickets, and visit employees in the hospital or maternity ward.

Throughout, never lose your poise.

"What are hawker centers, exactly?" I asked, although I barely cared.

She smiled. "They are the culinary soul of Singapore."

The taxi driver turned down a tree-lined avenue. His comparatively leisurely pace would have infuriated customers in America, but I was grateful for the air-conditioned respite, a gentle glide through a shimmering concrete canyon as Emily pointed out landmarks. Architecturally grand skyscrapers towered over small restaurants on well-marked corners. Ornate temples, crowded with worshippers, came and went with startling regularity. Pedestrians strolled—or occasionally ran—along wide sidewalks and stopped obediently at intersections under signs that offered paternal advice to watch for traffic. Not a single stray bit of graffiti or so much as a wisp of trash marred Singapore's reputation as a clean, wholesome place to live and conduct business. Even the people looked flawless in their suits and sheath dresses and chic haircuts.

The driver let us off at the corner of Boon Tat Street in front of an octagonal, open-sided building with iron pillars, a red-tiled roof, and a clock tower rising from the center. Even before we walked up the steps and into the building, smells washed over us through the open doorways and three-quarter-high walls. Frying bread, spicy curries, roasting meat, and the homey aroma of rich broths. Despite my sorrow, my stomach growled.

Inside, the heat pounced, unmoved by the fans whirling overhead.

Aisles lined with food stalls marched toward the center. I blinked against the cacophony: the roar of voices, metal spoons striking serving dishes, forks scraping the melamine serving ware, the hiss of meat sizzling, and phones chirping and squawking and beeping. Everything was clean and modern and of a high gloss—a blur of light and people and the kind of food I'd seen only in magazine spreads.

Emily urged me forward, leading me down one of the aisles. "Something you should know before you order your food is a simple truth about Singaporeans."

"And what is that?"

"They love their chilies. The hotter the better."

My eyebrows shot up. “Cass detested spicy food. How could this be one of her favorite places?”

“Oh, not so. Cassandra adored the food. She used to beg the chefs: hot, hotter, hottest.”

I was skeptical. My sister, who’d refused to eat Isabeth’s one attempt at green chili sauce. Or even a dish with paprika.

Had she changed so much?

I let Emily steer me to a table, where she placed her umbrella to mark our territory while we shopped.

“Do you believe Singapore changed Cass?” I asked.

Emily slid through the crowd. “It is true that she had fallen in love with the country. And to fall in love means you must change.” Her voice held a plaintive note.

“Singapore hasn’t worked the same magic on you?”

She looked away. “It is not my place to fall in love with this country. It does not belong to me. Nor I to it. Now”—she glanced at her watch—“we should order. We do not have a lot of time.”

Minutes later I stared down at a bright-red bowl of bee hoon noodles floating in a vivid orange broth.

Laksa, Emily called the dish. Cassandra’s favorite. She had ordered a version for me that was topped with shelled prawns and tiny cockles. Now she pushed a small bowl containing what looked like freshly ground red chilies. She looked at me sideways, from under her eyelashes.

“Cassandra liked her food with much heat,” she said.

I heard the challenge in her voice and nodded. If hot was how my sister preferred her food, then I would do the same. After all, I’d loved Isabeth’s green chili. I used my chopsticks to scoop some of the chilies into my bowl, stirred them into the laksa, then lifted a prawn from atop the steaming noodles.

I popped the prawn in my mouth.

Two seconds later, my head exploded.

Emily covered her mouth with her hand to hide her grin, but I saw the glee in her eyes. She pushed a bottle of water toward me as tears sprang to my eyes and my cheeks caught fire.

I swallowed the prawn; the searing heat left a smoldering trail down my throat and spread across my chest. I guzzled the water. The men at the next table over lifted their own bottles and cheered me.

I dried my eyes with a napkin.

"Cass really ate this?" I asked when I could speak.

Emily had regained her composure. "Not at first. I should have encouraged you to go more slowly. But perhaps it is like diving into the work required for *Red Dragon*: There will be much pain at first. But then will come the joy."

My mouth was in flames. "This was a test."

"Maybe a little. Now let me get you something less lethal. I know what you will like. Wait just a moment, please."

She headed briskly away.

A breeze rushed through the open doors, and a sudden rain fell, drumming on the high roof and splashing the sidewalks outside. The temperature dropped a degree or two. People chatted around me in a smattering of foreign tongues.

I was putting away my sunglasses when a familiar figure standing in a nearby queue caught my attention. The man flashed briefly into view and vanished again as the crowd shifted.

A moment later, he reappeared.

I sat up. The man was lean, with short-cropped black hair, wire spectacles, and a black trench coat.

It was the man who'd been watching me at the morgue. The man who'd called me by name. He stood on the other side of the alleyway, waiting in line near a stall advertising Malay food.

At that moment, Emily returned bearing a bright-blue plate piled with rice and chicken and naan. She placed it in front of me with a small flourish.

"Hainanese chicken rice," she said as she took her seat. "Singapore's national dish. Not hot."

"Emily," I said.

She looked over at me, and I leaned across the table.

"Remember the man I told you about yesterday?" I said, keeping my voice soft. "The one who was watching me after we spoke with Inspector Lee? He's here now. At the Malay stand across the alley. Second in line."

Emily picked up her water bottle and nonchalantly looked around as she drank. She froze when she saw him. She gave a faint gasp, and the water bottle slipped from her hand and hit the tile with a thwack.

Alarmed, I said, "Who is he?"

Her wide eyes came back to me. She'd gone as pale as the orchids in the Raffles lobby. Her hands shook as she picked up her half-empty bottle.

"You know him!" I whisper-shouted through the melee around us. "Who is he?"

"No, no," she protested. "I do not know him."

"Then why are you afraid?"

"It is just—"

I glanced over at the food stand and back to Emily. "He's coming."

In seconds, a kaleidoscope of emotions flickered across my assistant's face: anger, fear, panic, and finally resignation.

Then the man was at our table.

"Miss Brenner. Miss Tan." His eyes lingered on Emily. "Are you enjoying your lunch?"

Emily looked down, firmly dropping the ball in my lap.

"I don't believe we've met, Mr. . . ."

"My name is Charlie Han."

Automatically, I offered my hand, and we shook even as gooseflesh rose on my arms. What was Emily so afraid of?

She kept her eyes downcast, offering no clues.

Han was slim and compact, a man who held his body tightly, the way a snake might coil before striking. His up-tipped chin suggested arrogance. I noticed again the missing nails on his left hand.

He said, "I am sorry about your sister, Miss Brenner. It is a tragedy."

Sudden sweat beaded at my hairline. "How did you know Cass?"

"Your sister and I had occasion to work together."

"You're in the yachting business?"

He peeled back his lips in the likeness of a smile. "Ah, no. Other business."

My heart lurched. "And what business is that?"

He glanced at his watch. "I'm afraid I must go, Miss Brenner. I hope we have the chance to speak again. Miss Tan, do take care."

He bowed to me and slid away through the crowd.

Emily stood abruptly and removed a folded tote from her purse. "We should pack up our food and take it back to the office. The staff will be arriving soon. I will get containers. Please, Nadia, remain at our table."

I watched her go. Across the alley, a worker at the Malay stall handed the man a paper bag. The man crooked it in his left arm as if it were heavy and strode toward the door. At the entrance, he paused and popped open an umbrella. Just before he walked out into the storm, he glanced back.

The coiled energy of his body, the manner in which he leaned forward that suggested a threat, made me shrink into my seat.

Our eyes met briefly before he turned and vanished into the rain.

"Who is Charlie Han?" I asked Emily as we stood on the steps while our driver approached and pulled to the curb. The rain had stopped, and already the sun burned down.

Emily held up a finger to the driver that he should wait, then glanced around. She had regained her composure—perhaps her superpower, like mine, was her ability to feign calm. Casually, she opened her purse as if searching for something.

"I do not know Mr. Han," she said softly. "But I know his kind. China has citizen spies everywhere. They are like grains of sand, each adding their small piece to the picture China creates of everything within and outside its borders. It is the price of doing business with the Chinese."

"Han is a spy?"

"Spy. Informant." She kept digging in her purse. "I do not know. Perhaps he is a wolf warrior—diplomats known for being aggressive and combative. It is common for them to approach civilians."

"But he said he knew Cass."

"Likely a lie meant to gain your confidence. Do not trust him, Nadia. He and his kind are dangerous."

Trust no one.

But another thought pushed at me, turning me cold in the heat of Singapore's sun. "Could he have something to do with Cass's death? He was at the morgue."

Emily removed her sunglasses from their pocket within her purse and closed the bag—her search had been a tactic. Her face slid from a veneer of composure into sadness.

"I think, Nadia, only Cass had anything to do with her death."

Emily pasted on a cheerful expression as we walked into the offices of Ocean House, where a tall man stood in the lobby. She introduced me to Mr. Mèng's broker, Andrew Declough.

I banished my irritation, summoned a gracious smile from the depths, and offered my hand to Andrew.

"A pleasure," I said as we shook.

"All mine," he answered, his accent Liverpool Scouse.

Emily gave a small bow and peeled off to her own office.

"I'm so sorry about Cassandra," Andrew said. He was a rumpled man in his fifties with a creased face, a forehead high as the Cliffs of Dover, and a head of graying hair that flowed to his shoulders. "She spoke highly of you."

My smile flagged. "Thank you, Andrew. Is management here?"

"In the conference room and eager to meet our new lead. You *are* our new executive admin, right?"

I hoisted my smile, injecting confidence that—no matter what—Ocean House carried on.

"Absolutely," I said.

To complete the logistical nightmare of outfitting *Red Dragon*, Ocean House employed 150 workers in the yard, plus management staff. Outfitting is a tremendously expensive and complex process during which a variety of systems and equipment are installed and integrated. The process involves teams for electrical, mechanical, plumbing, interior, security, an on-site project manager, and the build supervisor.

Today I was meeting with the team leads from each department except security—I would see Connor McGrath of NeXt Level Security at dinner. Our team consisted of a multiethnic mix of two women and five men. Clearly mourning Cassandra's death, they nonetheless made me welcome and spent the afternoon updating me on their specific areas of the project. They were smart, enthusiastic, and ambitious. But it was obvious the constant schedule changes had damaged morale. The build supervisor—whose job required him to spend every day in the trenches—looked especially morose.

I would have to get on top of things quickly.

"We're going to get back on schedule," I promised them after listening to their reports and suggesting ways we could tighten and accelerate the timing. "We're going to finish *Red Dragon*."

They actually cheered.

At five I sent the managers to a local bar, promising I'd join them shortly, food and drinks on the House's tab. The last thing I wanted was to sip cocktails and make small talk with a group of relative strangers. But these were *our* strangers, and this was about rebuilding the team, making myself accessible, and cheering up the lot of them.

"Did it go well?" Emily asked as she entered Cass's office, where I was reviewing reports.

"They're a good group." I made a final note from the meetings today and slid the papers into my briefcase. "They're eager to get back on schedule."

"Cassandra was a good recruiter."

"She was good at a lot of things."

Emily trailed a finger along one of the bookcases, straightened a few of the books so that their spines lined up like good soldiers. "I spoke with Inspector Lee this afternoon."

I felt a moment of whiplash as I swerved from *Red Dragon* to my sister. I zipped my briefcase closed and turned to face her. "What did he say?"

"Nadia, you will not like this. But"—she met my gaze—"they have decided not to do an autopsy. The investigation is complete."

I recoiled as if she'd struck me. "It's been twenty-four hours."

"Inspector Lee has ruled Cassandra's death a suicide. He will still run a toxicology report to be thorough. But the witness who saw her jump is unimpeachable. And her neighbors mentioned that she had seemed distraught. Most importantly . . ." She came toward me until we were almost touching. "They found a note."

"A note." I sank into my chair. Cass's chair.

"The inspector found it at her condo. A postcard. Addressed to you, but never mailed."

She'd been *planning* this? For how long?

I bit down on my pain before I hurled myself out my own window—*her* window.

Why, Cass? Why would you do this to all of us? We always said, where there's life, there's hope.

The word *condo* hit a moment later. I needed to visit Cass's place. Go through her things. Feel her presence. That thought had been slipping in and out of my consciousness all day like a cobra winding through tall grass—I was afraid to go. Afraid that I would carry what I'd seen in the morgue into her home and taint her memory.

Step up, Nadia.

I rose and moved away from Emily's hovering warmth, the exotic scent of her perfume.

"What does the postcard say?"

She held out a blank #10 envelope.

"Inside is a photocopy of the postcard," she told me. "I do not know what it says. I hope it offers some comfort."

I took the envelope but didn't open it. It seemed to glow in the light from the lamp even as, outside, evening encroached with the stealth of a spy.

"I won't stop searching for answers," I murmured.

Emily reached out and grasped my fingers.

"It is a mistake to chase illusions, Nadia. To look for tigers in an empty jungle. Cass took her own life. Would you throw yours after? You are a stranger to this land, but I know that Singapore holds invisible currents and riptides. If you are not mindful of where you go, of whose path you cross, you could be swept away."

I shook my head derisively. "This is Singapore, not Moscow."

Emily tightened her grip on my fingers, then released them. "But men," she said. "Men are the same everywhere."

11

Elephant Room / Churchill Room—Tanglin Club
August 27, 7:00 p.m. SGT

The Elephant Room on Tanjong Pagar Road was a fusion of the old Singapore and the new—modern, brash, and bright, with British pub-style leather booths and a wall of whiskys that would rouse envy in any enthusiast.

I found the Ocean House staff upstairs at a corner booth near a window, some of them boisterous, some weepy. When they spotted me, they waved me over, making room at a table littered with half-empty glasses and the detritus of food. To a man—and woman—they were three sheets to the wind.

I didn't waste any time trying to catch up.

I'm not much of a drinker. Dinners and parties with clients had taught me the art of the sip. Tonight, though, I went straight for the throat.

"Glenlivet single malt," I said when the waitress came around. It was Guy's anesthesia of choice. It might as well be mine.

I drank the first whisky in three burning swallows and ordered another.

The group raised their glasses. Nothing like a boss who is willing to get sloshed with the troops.

"To *Red Dragon*!" cried our electronics manager, Colin Chua.

We raised and clinked our glasses.

"To *Red Dragon*!" Colin shouted again.

"To Cassandra!" offered one of the women, a plumbing expert named Cheryl Vittachi.

The crowd sobered, and for a moment, a respectable silence reigned.

Then another man, Eddie Lim, shouted, "To Ocean House!"

"Ocean House," I said, "always delivers."

"To Nadia!" from all of them.

"They love you," Andrew Declough rumbled. His high forehead shone with sweat in the ever-present humidity.

We clinked and tossed back our poison of choice.

An hour later Declough and my managers, stuffed with appetizers of coconut sambal and chicken curry, were beginning to sober up, or at least make a good run at it. They departed for the Tanjong Pagar MRT stop and then on to dinner with their families.

I remained at the table, ignoring my third whisky and watching the team through the window as they sauntered in a zigzag fashion down the sidewalk. They turned and waved. I waved back.

After they disappeared, my eyes went to my briefcase, which I'd leaned into a corner of the booth. Even out of sight, the envelope holding Cass's final note seemed to burn within.

I pressed the heel of my hand to my forehead. Open the letter and have my worst fears confirmed? Or leave it untouched and keep the sliver of hope that she hadn't died because she was too filled with despair to go on.

Was murder worse than suicide? Suicide worse than a crazy accident?

Did I want to know?

And with that, the woman who always had a plan suddenly didn't.

I picked up the whisky, swirled the ice. Scattered about the table was an army of dead soldiers: beer and wine bottles mixed with empty glasses, the ice melting into amber-tinted sludge.

I had more than an hour until my dinner with the representative from the security firm, Connor McGrath. I should go back to my room. Make a schedule for tomorrow, which included visiting Cass's condo, giving Inspector Lee my unvarnished thoughts concerning the end of the investigation, and, of course, diving into the hours and hours of work required to bring *Red Dragon* back on schedule. This last item was critical—once we'd completed the boat's outfitting, Mr. Mèng's financial officer would write Ocean House another check. Said check would be enough to give our bottom line some buoyancy.

But at the moment, I hadn't the heart for it. I took a healthy swallow of the Glenlivet and opened my briefcase. My fingers found the smooth paper of the envelope and pulled it free. I tore open the sealed flap.

Inside was a photocopy of the front and back of the postcard. The front showed a temple, identified with English lettering as Thian Hock Keng in Singapore's Chinatown.

On what would be the back of the postcard were lines of photocopied text in Cassandra's unmistakable handwriting.

Dear Nadia,

If you are reading this, it means that I am in trouble. Dear sister, I didn't want to cause you or our family worry. But I have been struggling for a long time. Know that what I did will ultimately be the right thing for everyone. And that I love you very much.

You will have decisions to make about Red Dragon. Remember, you can be both yin and yang. Bright and quiet. Your feet on the earth and head in the stars. Be wise, my darling sister. Be watchful. Remember what Guy used to tell us about trust? His favorite saying? And how we'd roll our eyes? Ha!

The only thing our parents got right is that family is the most important thing, and for that reason we owe ourselves the truth.

You are my own Mazu.

xoxo

Cass

I blinked through my tears, then read and reread the message. After the third reading, her words still didn't make sense.

What truth was she talking about? And who or what was Mazu? I did a Google search. Mazu was a sea goddess.

A goddess. I dropped my phone on the table. *Oh, Cass. What do I do with that?*

I took a sip of the Glenlivet and pondered Guy's favorite saying: *Trust no one.*

Cass was telling me to scrutinize everyone and everything. *Be watchful,* she'd written. *Be wise.* She must have feared or suspected someone. Yet she hadn't felt she could simply pick up the phone and tell me.

My hands turned cold. I looked down to see them trembling and clasped my fingers together. My mind replayed the recent family meeting and Cass's image on the video screen. Her uncharacteristic disinterest in the breakdown of *Rambler*. Her fancy nails. Why would Cass get a manicure before hurling herself out a window?

Tears flowed again, and I reached for a napkin.

Movement at a nearby table broke my miserable reverie.

Two men—one Caucasian, one Chinese—were seating themselves at another booth. They wore polo shirts and shorts and smelled of grass and sweat. The Caucasian was red across his nose and cheeks. They must have ordered downstairs, because soon after they sat, a waitress brought them beer and plates of satay.

I returned to Cassandra's note. After a few more reads, I slipped it back in the envelope and into the briefcase. Then I stared out the window at the steady stream of pedestrian traffic.

After Cassandra would come our father's death. Ultimately, presumably, it would be only me. How would I manage? And if I couldn't, what would become of Ocean House?

A voice came at my elbow. "Anything else, miss?"

It was the waitress from downstairs. I shook my head and told her to close out the tab. She cleared the table and—at my request—removed the mostly untouched Glenlivet.

After she left, I downed a glass of water, hoping to dilute the whisky in my stomach. I glanced around. Noise filtered up from the floor below, but the upstairs had emptied out. The Caucasian man had already left, and only his Chinese friend remained.

Our gazes locked.

He was large, muscular, motionless—a slab of granite squeezed into the booth. The white polo shirt and shorts sat on him like a costume. A tattoo of a tiger rippled on the side of his neck, the beast extending from behind his left ear toward his shoulder, where it disappeared beneath his collar.

I blinked first. I returned my eyes to the window and the jangling, busy world outside. When I glanced over again, the man was tapping on his phone.

It could be that Tiger Man was a reporter looking for a scoop on *Red Dragon*. The details of Mèng's ship were a legally bound secret—normal in the world of superyachts, where the wealthy want to keep the specifics of their assets private and the hoi polloi want the inside dirt. Maybe he'd been tipped off that members of our staff were gathering here.

But Cass's warning to be watchful and Emily's reaction to Charlie Han at the hawker center—along with her talk of wolf warriors and spies—had leached into me like a toxin.

I wasn't merely sad now. I was frightened.

I checked the time. I was due to meet Connor McGrath in the Churchill Room at the Tanglin Club in twenty minutes. I glanced again at the man. He'd stashed his phone and now stared at me through narrowed eyes as if I were a problem he needed to solve.

I didn't fancy having Tiger Man follow me, if that was his intent. I'd call a Grab car to get to Tanglin, but first I wanted to know if he really was a threat. I checked the map of my location for nearby restaurants, then talked loudly through a fake phone call as I gathered my belongings, pretending that my date was picking me up downstairs and we were walking to a nearby restaurant called Pasta Bar.

Still on the phone, I hurried past the man; I felt his eyes on me as if I carried a target on my back.

Downstairs, I ducked into an alcove and watched the room. Less than a minute later, Tiger Man appeared. He stepped out onto the sidewalk and looked up and down. He turned right, in the direction of Pasta Bar, and strode away.

Shaking, I waited inside until my Grab driver pulled up.

When I arrived at the Tanglin, the doorman at the top of the wide marble steps ushered me into the club's elegant lobby and directed me across the expanse to the Churchill Room. Inside the restaurant, I gave my name to the hostess. While she checked her list, I scanned the room, which was raucous, crowded with post-workday Singaporeans—mostly ethnic Chinese and the occasional white face ruddy with sun or alcohol. Snatches of conversation filled the air, much of it a babble of Chinese dialects—Hokkien, Mandarin, Cantonese. From a nearby table, an American voice declaimed on Singapore's recent purchase of F-35 jets.

"We need 'em to fight the Chinese," he told his companions. "China's military has doubled the number of cruise and ballistic missiles it's got. Been building up their navy. The South China Sea is where the next war is going to start. Not Russia. Not Korea. Not Ukraine. You ask me, it'll be in the Philippine Sea. With a nice side dump on Taiwan."

"How delightful, Bill," a woman commented in a dry voice. "A little preview of how we're all going to get blown to bits. Where's the waiter? I need another drink."

"Good thing no one asked him," someone else said. Laughter followed.

I turned away. Cass was our Asia expert, but I knew enough to realize that the man spoke the truth, however much his dinner mates didn't want to hear it. The geopolitics of America's relationship with China danced along an ever-shifting wall; someday the wall seemed likely to collapse.

The Churchill Room consisted of old-world-style dark wood trim, high ceilings, brass accents, and plush carpeting. It had once been prized by the British as a home away from home—thus the name, which was bestowed on the bar in 1957, long after the Japanese were routed at the end of the war and the Brits had reestablished themselves. Twenty years ago, according to what Cass had told me, the place had still been a white holdout. Now the club was almost exclusively Han Chinese. I was conscious of being an outsider.

The hostess smiled at me. "This way, ma'am."

As we crossed the room, I spotted a man I recognized from a photo in Cass's files as Connor McGrath. He stood when he saw me.

McGrath was about my age—early thirties. He had thick brown hair cut short, gray eyes, an angular jaw and narrow nose, and the lean, sculpted build of a runner. He wore pressed gray slacks and a white shirt that he'd unbuttoned at the collar. The folded-back cuffs revealed tanned forearms, with a Bremont diving watch on his left wrist and a leather-and-silver bracelet on his right.

The intended message, I supposed, was professional and successful but still hip. He stepped around the table as I approached, and we shook hands. His grip was firm. No wedding ring. Neatly trimmed nails, light calluses, maybe from taking up tennis or racquetball.

Observations like these were a habit drilled into Ocean House employees: note the details. It was as automatic to me as breathing.

"Connor McGrath," he said.

"Nadia Brenner."

"I am so sorry to hear about Cass." His voice was deep, with a faint rasp.

I held my poise as he pulled out my chair. "Thank you."

A waiter approached and we ordered drinks. A beer for McGrath, club soda for me.

"Cass talked a lot about you," he said as he resumed his seat.

I glanced away and blinked. "Don't believe half of it."

His laugh was soft. "She adored you. Among your many virtues, she said you were the most honest person she knew."

It seemed an odd observation to make, but I went along. "I'm a devotee of Thomas Jefferson. He wrote that honesty is the first chapter in the book of wisdom. Not that he himself was always honest."

"And you want to be wise."

I met his gaze. "There are worse things to aspire to."

"Certainly. Plus, to paraphrase another wise American and professional liar, if you always tell the truth, you don't have to remember your lies."

Surprised, I laughed. "Mark Twain! Well, there's an advantage. I've never tripped over my own words."

A waiter brought our drinks and took our order—a starter of Wagyu beef tataki to share. When we were alone again, Connor rested his elbows on the table, hands fisted beneath his chin, while around us the international babel surged and retreated in waves.

"Forgive me for getting right to the point," he said. "But what is going to happen now?"

"I'll remain in Singapore and take over the build. And don't apologize, Mr. McGrath. It's why we're here."

"Connor, please." He adjusted the flatware in front of him. "It's more than business to me. George Mèng is a longtime friend—we were in a PhD program together at MIT, and we've stayed in touch. *Red Dragon* is important to him."

I could have commented that every wealthy man's yacht was important to him. But Connor's jaw had tightened. Beneath his friendly words, another note sounded. A thread I could hear but not understand. Maybe it was nothing more than concern.

"You don't want him to be disappointed," I ventured.

Connor relinquished the flatware. "George inspires loyalty. You'll learn that when you meet him."

There was something disarming about Connor, and I found myself wanting to smile back. But we weren't through the bad news. "I assume you know that *Red Dragon* is behind schedule. Mr. Mèng must be upset over the delays."

We fell silent while the server deposited our tataki and glided away.

"Actually, no," Connor said. "George has requested additional security, and many of the delays come from my department. A piece of software he requested was still in beta. And there have been equipment holdups."

I kept my poise as I dished a slice of tataki onto my plate. But my brain lit up with the oddity of Connor's words. There was nothing in Cass's notes to indicate *Red Dragon*'s security was the reason for the slipped schedule.

And Emily had said the delays were Cass's fault.

"Why don't my build supervisor and chief of staff know about this?"

"Mr. Mèng prefers to keep the additional security measures confidential, at least as much as possible. Cass was willing to cover for us."

I sliced into the tender tataki. "And you would like me to do the same. Is that why you asked about my penchant for honesty?"

"You're an astute woman."

"Facts without the flattery is fine, Connor." But I smiled even as my mind conjured up the mysterious black space in the master stateroom and unease coiled like a wire in my stomach. Briefly I considered asking Connor about the missing space.

Trust no one.

I held my silence.

Connor said, "What else can I tell you?"

I dropped my napkin in my lap. "Why the need for extra security? It's almost as if Mr. Mèng is expecting a war, not the potential for pirates." I was thinking of wolf warriors and citizen spies. Was Mr. Mèng keeping his security measures hidden from his own government?

"It's personal for him. A few years back, when he was a guest on a friend's yacht, George was abducted at gunpoint and held captive with a demanded ransom of three million US. The kidnappers were a hacking group who held George for twenty-four hours before the Chinese Communist Party managed a rescue. None of the kidnappers survived."

"The CCP killed them?"

"Execution-style."

I pushed away the image Connor's words conjured. "What makes Mr. Mèng so important to the CCP?"

"George is president and CEO of RenAI—China's leading AI research firm—and their most talented specialist. Breakthroughs in AI come from having a sufficiency of three things: data, computing power, and talent. China has the data and is improving on tech, but they're hurting for skilled AI people. Losing George would take away their greatest asset just as his research is approaching a breakthrough."

I should know this. But none of it had been in Cass's files on Mèng. Which was another odd discrepancy. Knowing everything about the client was key to designing the perfect boat.

"Who were these hackers?"

"A small-time group out of Belarus. Most of those interested in George's AI work are rogue states and terrorist groups hoping to engineer biological weapons or create automated weapons systems. It's an AI arms race, and whoever gets the biggest, baddest AI first will have a shot at ruling the world."

He finished his beer. Instantly the waiter appeared at our table. Connor asked if I wanted anything else to eat. But my stomach roiled. When I demurred, he suggested brandies. I nodded and the waiter vanished.

"Thanks for filling me in," I said. "Shall we get down to the details?"

For the next hour, over snifters of Hennessy, we reviewed Connor's plans to protect *Red Dragon*, should the need arise. The list of protective features included security film on the bridge and stateroom windows, strobe lights, and near-military-grade lasers for blinding attackers. Barbed wire could be rolled out as necessary. And the swim platform—called a beach club on a yacht—could be raised quickly using a hydraulic arm. This would prevent easy boarding.

"Of course," Connor said, "my men and I will be on guard with weapons visible. I've learned a show of arms is the greatest deterrent to would-be boarders."

"And what happens to these guns when we're in port, Connor? Most countries won't allow them. We could be arrested on the spot."

"We'll off-load to one of the tenders if necessary. And there are other arrangements I can make. We will be clear in the eyes of the authorities, I promise."

"And in my eyes?"

"You might have to follow your sister's lead and trust me."

I thought of the warning in Cass's letter. *Be watchful. Trust no one.* "I don't want to go to prison."

"Nor do I."

I frowned at him. His gray gaze held steady. Finally, I said, "We'll call it a détente for now. I need to get *Red Dragon* back on schedule."

"There won't be any more delays from NeXt Level Security."

"Can I have that in writing?"

He laughed. "It will be in your inbox first thing."

Outside the restaurant, Connor opened the door to the Grab car I'd ordered.

"I look forward to working together, Nadia."

We shook hands again. I reminded myself that Cass had recruited NeXt Level Security and vetted Connor—the founder and CEO. Connor McGrath had to be on the up-and-up.

He closed the car door behind me, and I watched him stride away into the purple dusk. I knew his company had a healthy bottom line, but outside of that, I'd been able to find little about them. Connor himself remained a riddle.

Maybe that was how the heads of security companies liked it. But despite Connor's friendliness and ease, I sensed I was still on the outside struggling to understand details contained in shadows.

Everything about *Red Dragon* was turning into an enigma.

And at the middle of all of it was my dead and possibly murdered sister.

12

Raffles Hotel
August 27, 10:00 p.m. SGT

My head was spinning from the brandy and the implications of Connor's words when I walked into the regal lobby of Raffles.

"Miss Brenner!" called the receptionist. "Good evening, ma'am. I have a message for you."

She smiled as I approached the desk and handed me a sealed envelope. "A gentleman left this for you an hour ago."

The envelope was blank. Someone had attached a yellow sticky note with my name neatly printed on it. "Did he give a name?"

"I am sorry, no, Miss Brenner. He said very little. He was middle aged and Chinese. That is all the information I have." She glanced at her computer screen. "I understand your uncle is arriving in two days. I have put him in a room near yours on the third floor. Will that be acceptable?"

"Perfect," I said. "Thank you."

I moved away from her obvious curiosity about the note and tore open the flap. Inside was a single folded sheet of paper.

> Dear Ms. Brenner,
> We must talk. Please meet me tomorrow morning at
> 7 at the Lian Shan Shuang Lin Monastery in Central

> Singapore. I will be alone. I ask that you, also, come alone.
>
> I have two children who are much the same age as you and your sister. They are attending university in America. Like you, they live on the far side of the globe from their lonely father.
>
> No father should lose a child. Especially, no one should lose two.
>
> Respectfully,
>
> Huang Lee

My thoughts swirled. I steadied myself against one of the lobby's pillars and reread the note.

No father should lose a child. Especially, no one should lose two.

Lee's request to meet at daybreak, and in such a strange locale, implied our meeting would be off the record, a private conversation. Would that prove to be a good thing, or bad?

I fished his business card from my purse and dialed the number. It rang on and on without going over to voicemail. I disconnected.

Should I even go? Something was clearly, as Guy had told me, rotten in the state of Singapore. But I was desperate for answers. Maybe Lee would provide them.

I folded the note and returned it to the envelope. I hugged myself and stared at the gleaming white tiles of the lobby floor.

Footsteps approached. "Are you all right, miss?"

I straightened, then took a step back in surprise. It was the man I'd seen earlier sitting with Tiger Man at the Elephant Room. Early fifties, tall and tanned and fit. A sweep of silver hair. He'd changed from the golf clothes into chinos and a button-down.

Intelligence shone in the alert eyes watching me from beneath arched brows.

"Did you receive bad news?" His voice rumbled like tires over gravel.

"What?"

He gestured toward my hand, which clutched Lee's note. "The envelope. Does it contain bad news? You turned so pale I worried you might faint."

"Oh. No. Thank you for your concern." I lifted my chin and smoothed my features to show nothing more than mild interest. "Didn't I see you earlier at the Elephant Room?"

He smiled, but the alertness in his blue eyes didn't change. "Guilty as charged."

"The man you were with, the one with the tiger tattoo. He's a friend?"

His eyes narrowed, emphasizing a fan of crow's-feet. "You mean Dai Shujun. Hardly a friend. I suppose you could call him a business associate."

"Your business associate tried to follow me."

Something rippled across the man's face.

"I'm sorry," he said, "although I can't say I'm surprised. Dai can't resist a beautiful woman. I'll warn him away. He isn't the kind of man you want dogging your steps."

"He's dangerous?"

"Let's just say he hangs out with rough company."

"Like you?"

He laughed, revealing oversize canines. "I'm the exception that proves the rule. We suspect Dai is affiliated with one of China's crime syndicates. You've heard of the triads? Gangs that specialize in extortion, prostitution, drugs. Gambling. Much of it with the blessing of the Communist Chinese Party. I keep an eye on men like Dai Shujun. I don't consort with them."

Cass's belongings on the metal tray flashed before me. The white powder. I winced.

"I've alarmed you needlessly. Please don't worry. I'll deal with Dai. I just wanted you to be aware." He touched my shoulder, a tap of reassurance. "I'm Phil Weber, with the US Foreign Service. Watching out for my fellow Americans from the lobby of the Raffles." He grinned, and the laugh lines bracketing his mouth deepened. "This place is infinitely better than the stuffy confines of the embassy. Plus, the air-conditioning works. Now, can I get you anything? A bottle of water perhaps?"

His attention was almost fatherly, and for a moment the desire to confide in this agent of my own government filled me with a need like hunger. What a relief it would be to hand over my problems to someone who might be able to help. Who could perhaps determine what, exactly, had happened in Cass's room at Marina Bay Sands.

Unless, of course, Cass had been involved in something that would destroy her reputation and that of Ocean House.

Triads. Citizen spies. A plastic bag with 1.21 grams of unknown white powder.

I held my tongue.

Weber whisked a card from his wallet and presented it to me with a slight bow, holding the card in both hands. "This is the way to offer someone your card in the East. Etiquette requires that you accept it with both hands and look at it for at least a moment or two before tucking it away."

I took the card in the manner instructed.

PHILLIP WEBER
UNITED STATES EMBASSY
CENTRAL INTELLIGENCE AGENCY
27 NAPIER ROAD
SINGAPORE 258507

"You're CIA?" My mind conjured up images of cigarette-smoking men in black fedoras. And Emily's voice as she spoke of Charlie Han—*spy, informant, perhaps a wolf warrior*. "Aren't you supposed to be incognito?"

"I'm what's known as a declared officer. What people don't realize is that a lot of CIA's work is straightforward. We liaise with the locals.

Get the lay of the land. Find out where we might be helpful. We aren't all spies engaging in cloak-and-dagger stuff."

"Are there cloak-and-dagger operations in Singapore?"

"Not much," he said. "It's a rather dull posting. And now it's your turn, if you would be so kind. You are . . . ?"

"Nadia Brenner. With Ocean House."

"Nadia Brenner and Ocean House." His eyebrows shot toward his hairline. "You're Cassandra's sister. I should have realized. You look so much like her."

"You knew her?"

"Oh, yes. Our paths crossed rather often. Dear god, Miss Brenner—Nadia—I am so sorry." He gestured toward a pair of wingback chairs. "Can you sit for a moment?"

We walked across the atrium. On a small table between two chairs lay a copy of the *Straits Times*. Next to the newspaper was a crystal tumbler half-filled with whisky. The ice cubes were melting, the glass sweating.

He waited until I'd taken a seat, then gazed at me with sympathy. "Now tell me. What can I do to help? Would you like a drink?"

I waved away his offer. "Please tell me first what you know about my sister's death."

"Embassy personnel were notified almost as soon as the police identified her. The legat—the FBI's legal attaché—went to the scene." He palmed his head. "It's hard to understand what causes someone to make a decision like that."

"I was told there will be neither an autopsy nor an investigation."

"Oh, but there was an investigation. The legat spoke with Inspector Lee, the detective in charge of your sister's case. Lee talked to witnesses at the hotel. Examined your sister's room there and her home."

"He spent a few hours." I allowed my bitterness to show. "What can he learn from that?"

"It seems hasty to you. I understand. If this were Russia, say, or a backwater like Somalia, I'd agree. But the authorities here are honest and efficient. Inspector Lee will follow through on toxicology. If he finds anything suspicious, he'll reopen your sister's case. As well, of course, we're monitoring everything in case there's the least indication that it wasn't suicide." He leaned toward me. The not-unpleasant smells of sweat and deodorant rose from his skin, unavoidable in a climate like Singapore's. "Are you aware of the note found by the police?"

Briefly, I considered sharing the other note—the one from Inspector Lee. *Maybe things aren't as honest and efficient as you think,* I wanted to tell him. Instead, I said, "Don't you think it's odd that she wrote a supposed suicide note but didn't take it with her to her suicide?"

"Maybe she'd been thinking about it for a long time. Perhaps her night took a wrong turn and she decided to use an opportunity when it presented itself."

"Do you really believe that, Mr. Weber? Do you believe that a young, successful businesswoman working on the most important project in her life would check herself into the most expensive hotel in the world's most expensive city and then decide to leap from the balcony?"

He leaned back. His eyes narrowed until the irises became half-moons. "Do *you* have reason to think otherwise, Miss Brenner?"

Again, I considered sharing my fears with this man. And again, I stayed quiet. I was intimately familiar with how powerful men think, and Mr. Weber was a powerful man. But spies and secret diplomacy were out of my bailiwick.

Weber softened. "I'm not trying to offer an explanation, Miss Brenner. Only my bewildered sympathy. Cassandra was a bright soul. Cheerful and kind."

"You said your paths crossed often?"

"I don't want to give you the wrong idea—I didn't know her well. I chatted with her here and there at parties thrown by the American expat community. Often these were events at the American Club. It's my job to make the rounds, and occasionally I saw her there. We spoke now and again, but only briefly. We'd complain about the heat or trade restaurant recommendations. Idle chitchat."

"She was a member of the American Club?"

"I imagine. She might have been invited by a member, but most Americans working here join. I also saw her at Tanglin and at the Republic of Singapore Yacht Club once or twice."

"Was she usually alone?"

He knuckled his chin. "Sometimes. And sometimes with her assistant."

"Emily Tan?"

"I believe that is her name."

"Never anyone else?"

"I don't recall."

"You shared this with Inspector Lee?"

"Of course."

I pictured Cassandra at the American Club. She would have been laughing and chatting. Flirting harmlessly with the men and befriending their wives. It was how Cassandra and I had learned to behave long ago, taught by our parents to recognize that every wealthy person we met had the potential to become a client. Maybe the expat crowd was what made Cassandra decide to invest in fancy clothes. Maybe they had pulled her into gambling. Even into drugs.

Perhaps, Emily had said, *she became someone else in this country.*

Weber's voice rode over my thoughts. "I'm acquainted with another member of your family. Robert Brenner."

I blinked. "My debonair uncle. How do you know him?"

"Rob and I met eons ago. Tennis club. His grandparents knew mine decades back in Austria." His gaze had turned inward, and briefly his lips pulled tight, as if he'd tasted something sour. "Now I'm sitting here with his niece. Small world."

Something perverse compelled me to say, "He's never mentioned you."

Weber's upper lip rose, revealing the large canines. "Like I said, it was eons ago. And we've followed very different paths."

But something glinted in his eyes. Disdain? Dislike? Even, perhaps, unease?

Everywhere I turned, I faced a thicket of unanswered questions. Exhaustion swept over me. I found my way to my feet.

"It was a pleasure to meet you, Mr. Weber."

He rose as well. "Please let me know if I can do anything for you, Miss Brenner. My office is always open."

His eyes stayed on me as I made my way slowly up the central staircase. When I reached the first floor, I glanced back. Mr. Weber had vanished. The receptionist had momentarily disappeared. The lobby was empty, its colonial elegance undisturbed by human warmth.

In my room, I made myself a lukewarm cup of coffee, gulped it down, and changed into leggings and a T-shirt, grateful that everything was black, even my sneakers.

I snugged a ball cap over my hair, ordered a Grab car using the app, then placed my phone in the safe in case someone like Tiger Man—Dai Shujun—had found a way to track my movements. My credit card, passport, and room key went into the waterproof pouch I used when traveling. I slid the pouch into a zippered pocket of my leggings. I took the hotel's flashlight from the nightstand and shoved it into another pocket, its rounded end protruding. Five minutes later I let myself out of the room to wait at the curb for my ride.

It was time to learn whether *Red Dragon* would yield any answers.

13

Red Dragon
August 27, 11:00 p.m. SGT

Keppel Shipyard was quiet this late at night. As the taxi drove me along the road skirting the fenced yard, the empty parking lots inside stretched beneath the stars. The skeletal frames of massive boom cranes cut geometric figures against the gray-black sky while below hulked the behemoths of oceangoing vessels—commercial ships, pleasure yachts, and military cruisers—all at various stages of assembly or refit. Some ships floated serenely in the bay; others were in dry dock.

Only a few security lights shone.

I had the driver drop me off at the west gate. I showed the guard my passport, and he verified my name against a list on his computer.

"It's a long way to your build, Miss Brenner," he said. "You want me to find someone to give you a lift?"

"That won't be necessary. I want to walk around and get a feel for the place."

"At night?"

"I like the ambiance."

He stared at me, surely convinced I'd lost my mind. But I didn't want anyone hovering over my shoulder. I smiled to make my words convincing. He shrugged and rummaged around in the shelves behind him, returning with a flashlight and a folded glossy. "Hard to see much of anything in the dark," he said as he handed the items to me. "That's a map of the yard."

"Thank you." I'd already memorized where I needed to go, but the Maglite would serve much better than my flimsy hotel flashlight. "I'll return the torch when I'm done."

"Be safe."

He gestured me toward a pedestrian entry. A buzzer sounded and the gate clicked open.

I followed the road and moved at a fast clip. It felt good to stretch my legs and let the night air clear my head. The guard's shack and the main gate faded to pinpoints of light as I approached the water and turned west, heading past a series of platform supply ships fallen silent without their masters. I'd never realized how eerie a shipyard could be at night after the workers have left and darkness turns the boats into lurking dragons, the cranes into pterodactyls. At every creak and scrape, I found myself glancing over my shoulder for pursuit. I narrowed the beam on the Maglite and blocked part of the glass with my fingers, making myself less conspicuous.

After a mile, I could make out the concrete-block office and the viewing platform Emily had taken me to the night before. Fifteen minutes later, I stood at the edge of the wharf, surprised by the metallic taste of fear in my mouth.

Fear of what I might find, I supposed. Fear that if I kicked over a rock, I wouldn't be able to hide from whatever crouched beneath it.

My sister's choice to conceal something on *Red Dragon* ate at me. Had she been ensnared in a world impossible to escape? Was the hidden space linked to her supposed suicide? Or to China's interest in her?

"Damn it, Cassandra," I whispered as I stared up at her yacht. "What were you doing? Why didn't you tell me?"

You'll figure it out, sis, came Cassandra's imagined voice. *You always do.*

"Maybe not this time," I answered out loud. "Give me a clue."

Far off, a night bird called. Wind ruffled nearby flags.

Workers had doused the interior lights, but in the security lights, *Red Dragon*'s hull glowed. I stepped onto the aluminum-and-steel passerelle—the gangplank—which was mounted near the aft of the ship and bridged the gap between the wharf and the boat. It swayed beneath me as I climbed, and the chain railing clanked. Below, black water obscured the hull.

My heart pounded in rhythm with my footsteps as I hurried up the passerelle's stairs.

At the top I stumbled, my feet betraying my unease. I steadied myself, slipped out of my dirty street shoes and into deck slippers, and tucked my sneakers out of sight in case someone came by.

Red Dragon boasted five decks—lower, main, wheelhouse, upper deck, and the sundeck. The owner's suite was on the main forward deck. Aft of the master stateroom were the guest cabins and a salon—the marine equivalent of the living room. On the deck above were a library; a second, smaller salon; and a gym. Crew resided in the lower deck along with Mr. Mèng's marine science lab, the panic room or citadel, and the engineering space.

I hurried up the curving flight of stairs to the main deck. There I punched in the access code Emily had provided for the yacht's living quarters. I raised the Maglite. Its bright beam cut through the darkness, sparking off copper trim and glittering glass. I passed through the immense salon, with its gravity-defying chandelier and the comfortable groupings of sofas and chairs and tables, slowing despite myself to admire an immense library table carved from the rare wood of the yellow pear tree, the grains flowing beneath my light. Past the table was a wet bar carved from what I knew to be Brazilian kingwood, backed by a copper-framed mirror as large as a king bed.

Everything spoke of opulence and comfort—no expense had been spared, no possible luxury overlooked.

I strode down the wide passageway past the guest cabins. A second code gave me access to a private section of corridor leading to

Mr. Mèng's stateroom. As I reached for the room's door handle, a faint scraping sounded from a distant place on the boat. I froze.

I strained my ears, but the noise faded, then stopped. I pushed the door open and stepped inside the stateroom, once again gaping at the opulence of a place that rivaled any penthouse suite in a five-star New York City apartment.

I paced the length and breadth of the suite, confirming what I already knew—the space was indeed smaller than the floor plans in Cass's safe had indicated. Cassandra's black space was here. Somewhere.

I called up a mental image of the general arrangement plan Cassandra had locked away in her office. According to the GAP, the hidden area would be behind the wall against which the king berth was placed.

I approached the duvet-covered, many-pillowed bed.

Bracketing the low ebony headboard and rising on the wall above it was the intricate mosaic of a dragon, a twin to the beast encircling the skylight that I'd noticed on yesterday's walk-through with Emily. Formed out of thousands of tiny wood tiles selected from different trees—black to rich browns to red—the dragon shimmered in the Maglite's beam, almost as if it were alive. It was a stunning piece of art. And, if I was right, the gateway to Cassandra's secret: a passage to her phantom room.

Beginning on the left side of the mattress, I slowly moved my hands up and down over the tiled surface, feeling with my fingertips for anything that yielded beneath my touch. When I'd searched as high as I could reach, I climbed onto the berth and continued my exploration of the wall.

A subtle inconsistency in texture, an unexpected roughness that would allow someone to find the location even in the dark, guided me to a square of four tiles.

I gently pressed each tile, then tried pressing all four at once.

A faint click sounded to my left, and the outline of a door appeared on the wall next to the berth.

For a moment I merely gawked at it, my heart racing as I pondered the implications of such careful concealment and the intricacy of the engineering. Then, afraid of what I might find, I hopped off the berth, slid into the narrow gap behind the built-in nightstand, and pushed open the door.

My flashlight revealed a ten-by-ten space. On my right, two large metal boxes took up almost half the floor space. I propped the hotel flashlight on the floor to keep the door from swinging shut and possibly trapping me inside. Then I opened the lid of one box.

It was filled with Tasers—illegal in Singapore but not unusual on superyachts due to the ever-present risk of piracy. I checked the second box; it contained stun grenades, often called flash-bangs. Also illegal. And a dazzle gun—a nonlethal weapon that uses an intense blast of green light to disorient and temporarily blind a person.

I returned to the first box—I'd glimpsed something beneath the Tasers. My flashlight picked out the glint of gold. I propped the torch on the corner of the box, removed some of the Tasers, and reached down. My fingers curled around one of the gold objects, and I eased it free.

It was a one-kilo gold bar roughly the size of a smartphone and weighing maybe two pounds. Given current gold prices, I knew its worth approached $70,000 US.

Holy damn.

I removed a handful of Tasers; there were a lot more bars. I did a calculation—maybe a million and a half dollars' worth of gold hiding in Cass's black area.

A flush of adrenaline burned through my body like a lit fuse.

If someone wanted to launder money—say, money made smuggling weapons or art or drugs—gold was one of the best ways to do it. Preferred by crime syndicates around the world.

The hell, Cass?

That thought was quickly followed by another: *Who knows about this? Charlie Han?*

Feeling sick, I closed the boxes. I shined the light around the room to see if I'd missed anything, hating to think of what else I might find. I spotted another door, its outline nearly invisible in the textured wood. It was on the wall opposite the door I'd entered through.

It took me a minute to open this second door, which also had a concealed pressure latch, although nothing as elaborate as the mosaic dragon on the outer door.

A wave of warm air greeted me. A steep set of stairs led down into darkness. The Maglite picked out only a handrail and a bend in the stairs.

Go on, sis, said Cassandra's voice in my mind. *What are you waiting for?*

But I was frozen.

Was this room a second access leading to the panic room on the lower deck? That would explain the contents of the boxes: weapons for protection, gold for bribes if worse came to worst.

Certainly, if terrorists and state actors had an interest in Mr. Mèng, then a door that was nearly impossible to find made sense. For garden-variety pirates, a heavy lock would have sufficed. Or a door hidden in the back of a wardrobe. Even a simple trapdoor concealed beneath built-in seats or in the floor. Pirates were usually in a hurry, grabbing the most visible goods and anxious to flee before the authorities arrived.

The sophistication of the concealment suggested fear of an equally sophisticated attack.

I stepped onto the first stair. The stairwell, unlike the open areas of the ship, was crude and unfinished. The air smelled faintly of oil, as if the stairwell led to the technical area of the ship—the engine, the heating and cooling systems, everything required to keep the yacht running.

Maybe it didn't lead to the panic room.

I'd descended two more steps when, from far away, a thump and the sound of voices warned me that I wasn't alone on the boat. My first thought was to pull both doors closed and flee down the stairs. But for all I knew, I'd be trapped.

Instead, I retreated, pulling the second door closed and hurrying to the first one. I grabbed the hotel flashlight, closed the door, and turned to face the doorway.

No one was there. Acting on instinct, I darted into one of the built-in wardrobes and pulled the door almost closed. I turned off the Maglite.

Seconds later the overhead lights came on, and I watched through a crack in the door as Emily Tan strode into the room. Trailing close behind her was a hulking cinder block of a man dressed in black trousers, a dark tee, a black ball cap, and sporting a tiger tattoo. Dai Shujun. Phil Weber's so-called business associate.

He isn't the kind of man you want dogging your steps, Weber had said. *We suspect Dai is affiliated with one of China's crime syndicates.*

And now here he was. With Emily.

When he turned sideways, hands on his hips while he surveyed the room, I glimpsed the handle of a gun tucked into his waistband.

What the hell was Emily and Dai's connection? I sensed link chaining into link, pulling tight.

"Nadia?" Emily said. "Are you here?"

I held still, breathing through my mouth.

Emily turned to Shujun. "I'll search here. You check the guest cabins."

After the man left, Emily went to the berth. I saw the bent outline of her head as she took in the disturbed duvet and the pillows I'd scattered during my search for the hidden compartment. She stood there a long moment. Then she smoothed the duvet, straightened the pillows, and turned.

"Nadia?"

Now I didn't breathe at all. I could almost imagine her eyes meeting mine through the narrow slit in the wardrobe door. But then she moved away.

"Nadia, if you are here, there is something you should know," she said. "Few things with *Red Dragon* are as they appear. Charlie Han is only one manifestation of the dangers that threaten you. These dangers grew too great for Cassandra to manage, and she chose death over what men might do to her. I do not want you to die as she did, alone and afraid."

I squeezed the Maglite to keep my hands from shaking.

"Finish *Red Dragon*," Emily said. "Turn it over to Mr. Mèng and leave Singapore. Do this as quickly as you can. If you pry, if you ask questions, if you behave in any way other than as a professional yacht builder come to finish a big project, you put yourself in terrible danger. Do you understand? The man accompanying me tonight . . . he is dangerous. And he and others are watching you, waiting for you to make a mistake. To pry. To ask the wrong questions."

I willed myself not to move even as my heart pounded hard enough to send blood roaring through my ears.

Emily cocked her head as if listening, then said, "There is an expression that comes from imperial China. The phrase is, 'Chu songs on all sides.' It concerns a great war between two men who would be emperor, and how one was tricked into fleeing when he heard the enemy singing songs from his homeland and thought his own troops had deserted him. What it means now is for someone to be besieged and hopelessly alone. That is you, Nadia. You are surrounded."

She leaned toward the wardrobe as if she knew I was there.

"Do not trust anyone," she said in a whisper.

After a moment Emily's retreating steps echoed back to me. She'd gone into the passageway. I heard her voice and—presumably—Shujun's deeper rumble. Their voices rose and fell, occasionally vanishing, as they moved around the yacht. Forty-five minutes later, their steps sounded on the gangway.

I waited another half hour, then crept out of the wardrobe.

I stood in the doorway for fifteen more minutes. There came only the normal sounds of a yacht in its shipyard. The creak of metal. The faint swinging of the chain railing of the passerelle.

I left the owner's suite, hurried back down the passageway, let myself out the door, then jerked to a stop as a shadowy form appeared next to the passerelle.

Lifting my chin, I forced a bravado I didn't feel. "Who are you?"

The figure stepped forward. The form of a man took shape, but I could make out no details.

"Dai Shujun?" I worked to make my voice firm. "I'm a friend of your friend. Phil Weber."

The man raised his arm. Even in the gloom I saw that he held something. A gun? A knife?

I didn't wait to find out. Without time to punch in the code and return inside, I spun and raced along the exterior walkway. Steps echoed my own. Heavy, insistent.

Predatory.

Halfway down the length of the boat, I darted up an external staircase to the upper deck. At the top, I glanced behind just long enough to see a shadow ascending the stairs after me. I burst into a second salon—a cozy space where crew would serve evening cocktails to the guests. My feet barely touched the floor.

Surprised to find the door to the captain's bridge standing open, I sprinted through the room, my gaze flitting over the controls that governed the vessel, the blank screens that would spring to life when *Red Dragon* launched. I considered locking myself in the bridge or the captain's quarters and calling for help. But I didn't know if the communications systems were online. Trapping myself here was a temporary solution at best.

I climbed the spiral staircase to the sundeck, realizing I was only delaying the inevitable. I should have gone down instead of up and buried myself in the crew quarters or inside the yacht's technical area.

But even there a persistent hunter would find his prey.

I stood in open air. Lights glittered on the horizon. Closer by, the shipyard's security lights glowed with a fierce irony—they couldn't help me. The sundeck offered nothing but deck chairs, an empty infinity pool, and a wet bar. Feeble barriers. It was a dead end. I looked wildly about for a hiding place.

The man's footsteps closed in. I approached the railing and shined my light down the curved side of the ship.

Forty feet below, the dark waters of the harbor sloshed against the ship, disturbed by movement somewhere else in the bay.

I raised the Maglite, holding it like a weapon.

My pursuer appeared in the doorway, a mere shadow. I cried out as a brilliant green light exploded in my field of vision, blinding me.

A laser gun.

I turned and scrambled blindly for the railing, dropping the Maglite. My hands found the rail, the cool metal grounding me. Although I was temporarily blinded, I knew the harbor's waters, black and still, waited below.

Another flare of light behind me. I clambered over the railing. I would have to hurl my body far into empty space to avoid smashing into the lower decks.

The image of my sister's face during her fall from the hotel balcony flashed before my laser-dazzled eyes. Her fear, her desperation, perhaps resignation at the inevitability of the descent.

I leaped into the void.

14

Keppel Shipyard / Lian Shan Shuang Lin Monastery
August 28, 2:00 a.m. SGT

The sensation of falling was a rush of terror and freedom, lit only by the green afterimage from the dazzle gun.

I arched my back to keep from rolling forward and, when I judged the water was near, straightened and pulled in my arms.

I struck the depths and plunged into the bathwater-warm blackness as the bay's brackish water swallowed me with violent force. Immediately I spread my arms and legs to slow my descent, then let buoyancy pop me back to the surface.

Green rings pulsed in my stunned field of vision. Another burst of green light flared overhead. I dived and groped my way toward *Red Dragon*'s hull, then pulled to the right, still underwater, heading for the next quay and a place where I could haul myself out of the bay and run for cover.

Once clear of *Red Dragon*, I surfaced for air. I strained my ears for sounds of movement on the boat, but the slosh of water against the hull—generated by my own dive—drowned out everything else.

There were no more laser bursts.

I paddled and blinked in the dark water, relieved when the blinding green rings began to fade. After a few minutes, as the afterimages continued to dim, I dived again. When I next surfaced for air, I could see that a smaller yacht, 120 feet or so, occupied Number 3 Quay next to *Red Dragon*. It looked quaint beside the superyacht. I dived a final time and swam to the smaller yacht. Hoping the boat's alarm system didn't blare out news of my presence, I hauled myself up onto the dive platform and ran along the length of the yacht to the gangway.

I'd lost my slippers in the dive. With a murmured apology, I helped myself to a pair of deck shoes and ran down the passerelle to shore. Without pausing, I darted to the nearest set of buildings. A peek through a lighted window revealed a hull-fabrication area.

I crouched and waited for my furious heartbeat to slow enough to allow sounds to trickle in.

Crickets. The buzz of nearby security lights. A huff of wind in the still-oppressive heat.

I pushed my wet hair from my eyes and peered around the corner. I made out *Red Dragon* on the far side of the nearer yacht. From my vantage *Red Dragon* appeared dark and empty, brooding, suddenly sinister.

I ducked back down and did a quick self-survey: I had a sore jaw, a painful back, and a headache from hitting the water. I still had my waterproof pouch with my room key and passport. My half of Cassandra's yin-and-yang necklace was still tucked inside my sports bra. The hotel flashlight had fallen out of my pocket and would be at the bottom of the bay.

I hurt. But I was in one piece. At least so far.

I pulled up my mental map of the shipyard and plotted a course back to the gate that would leave me hidden from view for most of the time.

I ran.

When I arrived at the security guard's booth, he took in my wet hair and sopping clothes.

"Get lost?" he asked wryly.

I was still breathing heavily. I gripped my side where a painful stitch had formed. I should never have given up my morning runs. Or the push-ups, crunches, lunges, and everything else that had once been part of my daily routine.

"Took a wrong turn," I said. "Short pier."

He chewed his lip for a moment. Settled on, "I suppose my Maglite is gone."

"It's on *Red Dragon*. I'll return it to you tomorrow."

"I see."

I tugged back my wet hair. "I was supposed to meet Emily Tan on the boat, but she didn't show. Did she come in?"

A slow nod. "She and her security guy. Forty minutes or so after you did. They're still in the yard. Want me to call them?"

"Did you tell them I was here?"

He scratched a grizzled jaw. "I don't remember saying anything. They didn't ask."

So how had they known that I was on *Red Dragon*? The location finder on my phone would indicate I was still at the hotel. Had Dai Shujun been watching for me at Raffles, then followed me here and called Emily?

"Then I'd rather they didn't hear about my little accident," I said. "It's embarrassing." I leaned in and lowered my voice. "To be honest, I'd really appreciate it if you didn't mention that you saw me tonight."

"Saving face?"

"Trying to."

Another nod. "I'd rather they not know about it, either. Me letting a young woman roam around the yard by herself, and she didn't even bring a flashlight. I've got my own face to think about."

His words were hard, but he grinned at me. I grinned back, although God alone knew how I managed to summon the energy.

"I'll bring a flashlight next time," I said.

"And pack a dry suit."

He winked.

I winked back.

"Want me to call you a taxi?" he asked.

"Please."

While I waited, steam rising off my clothes, one thought claimed my mind.

These men Emily spoke of had killed my sister. Whether they'd pushed her or she'd jumped, they'd killed her.

After an hour of nightmare-shattered sleep, during which Emily shouted for me to run, I rose—grateful to be alive—at 4:30 a.m. for my meeting with Inspector Lee. Other than a bruise along my jaw, I'd survived my plunge into the bay intact.

I made coffee and downed a protein bar, dressed in casual clothes and my second pair of sneakers, then crept along the hotel's groomed grounds, watching for Dai Shujun or one of his comrades. Spotting only hotel staff, I headed for the metro, my eyes scanning the quiet world around me as I zigged and zagged and periodically changed directions. A few early-morning joggers appeared out of the dark and fell away without giving me a second glance. The neighborhood of Raffles still slept.

When I reached the City Hall MRT station, it was empty save for a pair of security guards, who nodded at the tourist seemingly eager to start her day.

I purchased an EZ-Link card at an automated kiosk, walked across a floor so immaculate it gleamed, and followed the bright-white arrows and well-marked signs to the escalators and the belowground platform for the North–South Line. One thing I had to give the Singapore government credit for—they had cleanliness and signage down like no other place I'd been.

A young Chinese woman dressed in a white lace blouse and jeans waited for the train along with her infant, who was snugged comfortably in a stroller. I offered a smile while we waited behind the taped lines; her return smile was subdued. The baby cooed. When we boarded, there was no one else in our car or in the cars on either side. A sign on the wall warned against smoking, eating, or drinking on the train and listed fines and jail time.

One sign briefly lifted my spirits. No durians—the beloved and uniquely stinky fruit of Singapore—were allowed. The sign suggested no fines or jail time. Maybe the transit police merely threw you—and your smelly durians—off the train.

Safe for the moment, I relaxed into my seat and contemplated the day.

First was this morning's 7:00 a.m. meeting with Inspector Lee. I couldn't imagine what he intended to tell me. But a Buddhist monastery seemed as safe a place to meet as almost anywhere.

Afterward, I would go to Cassandra's condo at Ardmore Park in Tanglin to learn what I could about the stranger my sister had become and to hunt for any evidence of the pressures Emily claimed Cass had been under.

In the afternoon I'd go into the office and work with our build supervisor and Andrew Declough to get *Red Dragon* back on track now that Connor McGrath's security upgrades weren't delaying us.

Of course, my plan for the day depended, in part, on what Inspector Lee wanted to tell me. And what I'd do with that information.

Do not trust anyone.

I stared down at my sneakered feet. It was hard admitting to myself that all I wanted was to take Cass back to Seattle and stay there forever. I knew what she would do for me: She would fight against every lie. She would fight to give me voice.

She wouldn't stop until she'd uncovered the truth.

I touched the yin-and-yang necklace beneath my shirt.

I had neither Cass's courage nor—perhaps—her desperation.

—

The predawn sky had been clear when I entered the City Hall station. When I emerged from the station at Toa Payoh, clouds had moved in, and the dawning day had turned close and muggy. The scent of approaching rain rode the air.

It was a twenty-minute walk to the monastery. Taking a bus would have shaved the time down to a handful of minutes. But I wanted to get a sense of the area and approach the temple grounds undetected.

I turned right into a residential area lined with apartment buildings.

Toa Payoh, like every other part of Singapore I'd been to, was clean and well kept. The pig and poultry farms that—according to my online research—had once surrounded the monastery had long ago been replaced by bright-blue public housing apartments and postage-stamp squares of grass boasting exercise equipment and playgrounds. Small signs advertised classes in English. I passed a few closed American restaurants—McDonald's, KFC, Starbucks.

A cluster of trees amid the asphalt and high-rise condos suggested the monastery was nearby. I slowed. Lights shone in a few of the flats, but the neighborhood was otherwise quiet. A single car dawdled past.

A few minutes later, I stood across the street from the Lian Shan Shuang Lin Monastery.

The vast temple grounds—partially visible from the road—were walled and dark. What I could glimpse through the gate looked like something from *Mulan* or *Crouching Tiger, Hidden Dragon*. A sea of red-roofed Buddhist temples with a courtyard that stretched beyond the gate. Elegantly trimmed bushes marched along the paved entryway, and immense white pillars held up a blue-and-clay-red arch bedecked with Chinese characters in gold. Eight stone lions guarded the entrance. On the far side of the monastery rose a many-storied pagoda. Its elegant carvings and gold *chatra*—the spire at the top—were incongruous against the backdrop of a high-rise apartment building.

A young woman pushing a stroller walked past the monastery's driveway. I gave her a sharp glance, but she wore different clothes from the woman on the metro and pushed a different kind of stroller.

I'm getting paranoid.

To which Cassandra responded in my mind: *Just because you're paranoid doesn't mean they're not out to get you.*

I checked the time—6:50 a.m. The gate remained closed. The monastery's small parking lot was empty.

At 6:58, I crossed the street and approached the pedestrian entrance.

A robed monk appeared, his head shaved, his saffron garment neatly draped around his slim form, one shoulder left bare. I expected him to tell me that I would have to come back at eight, but instead he smiled and unlocked the gate. He opened it just enough for me to slip through, then closed and locked it behind me.

"I'm here to meet Inspector Lee," I said.

He beckoned for me to follow.

We walked through a second gate, past a jade-green pool where stone dragons spouted water, then across an intricately mosaiced courtyard and through a third gate. The monk moved like a ghost in front of me, his bare feet making no sound. The lowering clouds and heavily leafed trees obscured the surrounding city.

A mystical quiet lay upon the temple complex. I felt I'd gone back centuries in time.

I followed the monk up a set of stone stairs; he let me linger long enough to read the sign and realize we stood at the monastery's main entrance, the Mountain Gate. Buddhist guardians—including the giant Four Indestructible Warriors—gazed down on us from the painted doors, their bearded faces fierce, their heavy armor intricately patterned.

The monk gestured for me to remove my shoes. I stepped over the raised threshold and followed him inside, where a gold Buddha sat atop an altar. On either side were other gold statues—deities, I assumed. Or assistants of the Buddha.

The air smelled of burning joss sticks and the offerings of ripe oranges and melons that filled the copper bowls. From somewhere music played, a low chanting.

The monk smiled at me again and held up a hand, indicating I should wait. Then he bowed and left. I stood in front of the altar and looked at the low, padded stool where worshippers would kneel before the Buddha. The vinyl covering was cracked and peeling, testimony to the weight of many prayers. A part of me wanted to kneel as well, to beg Buddha—since I was in his temple—to help me understand what had happened to my sister.

I took a step closer to the altar.

The chanting stopped, and a hush grew until it was a held breath.

A voice shattered the stillness.

"Welcome to the Lian Shan Shuang Lin Monastery," said a man from behind me.

I turned, expecting Inspector Lee. But it was the man from the morgue. The man whom Emily had warned me against at the hawker center.

Charlie Han.

I took a step back, stumbling against the worship stool.

Han moved into the temple. The reflection of dozens of lit candles danced in the glass of his wire spectacles. He tapped his umbrella against the open palm of his hand.

"I am glad you came, Miss Brenner. We have much to discuss."

15

Lian Shan Shuang Lin Monastery
August 28, 7:05 a.m. SGT

I stared at Charlie Han with horror.

"Where is Inspector Lee?" I asked.

Han leaned his umbrella against the wall inside the entryway and slipped off his shoes. "The good inspector decided that meeting with you was not in his best interest."

Gooseflesh prickled my arms. "What have you done with him?"

"I assure you, no harm has befallen Huang Lee."

"The way no harm befell Cassandra?"

Han strode past me and stopped before one of the gold statues flanking the Buddha.

"What do you know of Buddhism, Miss Brenner?"

I said nothing.

"We are standing in Tian Wang Dian, the Hall of the Celestial King," he said. "This warrior I stand before is the Skanda bodhisattva, one of eight divine protectors of the Buddha's relics. He protects the teachings of Buddhism, and for this I honor him."

"You're a Buddhist?" I scoffed.

The faint ripple across his shoulders suggested a shrug. "I am Chinese. That means I am many things. I have studied the philosophers Confucius and Mencius and the Buddhist leader Nan Huai-Chin.

The *I Ching* and the *Romance of the Three Kingdoms*, and Mao's *Little Red Book*. Most importantly, I follow the wise words of our paramount leader, the general secretary of the People's Republic of China."

"Is this litany meant to impress me?"

"Whether or not you are impressed, Miss Brenner, is immaterial to me. Although I believe it would serve you to become familiar with the culture of most of the people who live in Singapore. That is merely good business."

Understanding the people of Singapore had been Cass's job. All I had was the story I'd read in a guidebook about the merlion and a prince who sacrificed his crown to an ocean deity in the hope of getting his men to shore alive.

If only I, too, had a crown. I would gladly toss it overboard for help, divine or otherwise.

I stared up at the Buddha's benevolent gaze. "You told me at the hawker center that you and Cass worked together."

"It is true. She talked to people. Heard things. Now and then she would pass along information."

Charlie Han. Spy. Informant.

"Cass a spy?" I tried a laugh, coughed when it remained in my throat. "I don't believe you."

He tipped his face toward me, his expression unreadable. "Your sister's fall from that balcony was both unfortunate and unnecessary."

My heart clenched, but I held myself still in imitation of the serene Buddha towering over us. "What do you know about my sister's death, Mr. Han?"

I watched from the corner of my eye as he stepped closer to the statue of the Skanda bodhisattva and tilted back his head. The statue's eyes gazed past him. "I know that you suspect your sister did not kill herself. Would it comfort you to know that I share your doubts?"

I kept my eyes locked on the Buddha. "I'm listening."

"Your sister meant well. At least in the beginning. She was desperate to help your company manage their financial setbacks. But Cassandra was too easily swayed by stronger forces. And too fragile to balance her yin-yang." He pressed his palms together and gave the statue a small bow. "She was persuaded to take the dark path. I believe the price she paid for this decision was her life."

The smell of wax and incense thickened. From outside, far away, came the flutter of bird wings. But I was thinking—again—of that white powder. Of a hotel room that cost more than a month's earnings.

I was also thinking that Cass was neither easily swayed nor fragile.

"Were you my sister's confidant, Mr. Han?"

"Now and then."

He turned his gaze from the calm face of the Skanda bodhisattva and studied me. Although Charlie Han was twenty years younger than my father, his hard stare reminded me of the way Guy had regarded me before he sent me to Singapore. As if my flesh were translucent and revealed every weakness within.

I pressed my damp palms to my pants. The day's rising heat made my skin long to slip from my bones.

"No words?" Han said. "Perhaps you would like to see more of the monastery. Lian Shan Shuang Lin was established by a wealthy merchant in the late nineteenth century. I believe his generous act shows that one can be both a good businessman and an honest man."

"Is that what you are?"

"I am not a businessman. But I am honest when it serves me. And it serves me for you to know the truth." He gestured toward a hallway. "Shall we?"

Without waiting for an answer, he strode, sock-footed, toward the hall that opened on our right. I hurried after him. We passed through another temple, this one larger than the first, then through a doorway into a tree-lined courtyard. The rising sun sulked behind the clouds, its diffuse glow warming the gold-enameled decorations on the eaves and the Chinese characters emblazoned on the walls. Our presence felt like an affront to this peaceful place.

My long hair against my neck brought unwelcome warmth. Sweat beaded. I found a clip in my purse and twisted the strands atop my head.

Han gestured toward a stone bench beneath a pair of trees. The leaves were the soft color of unripe olives.

"Please, sit, Miss Brenner."

I did as he suggested. He sat beside me and removed his eyeglasses. Without the reflective glass shielding his eyes, he looked younger than I'd taken him for. Younger and almost vulnerable.

He said, "I imagine you know a great deal about your client, Mr. Mèng."

Sudden sunlight stabbed through a wider break in the clouds and flared in my eyes. I pulled back into the thin shade. "Of course. Understanding a client's needs and wishes is the first step in creating a yacht."

"Then you are aware of his taste for opulence, which is displayed so dazzlingly aboard *Red Dragon*. Presumably you also know that his family is part of what is referred to in China as the red aristocracy."

"Members of the Chinese Communist Party?"

"Much more than that. They are descendants of those who fought with and defended Chairman Mao Zedong in his revolt against Chiang Kai-shek in 1949. They are royalty, Miss Brenner. But, sadly, that doesn't always make them virtuous men and women."

I kept my gaze on the temple on the far side of the courtyard. A monk walked past a doorway. Candles flickered within the gloom. The pit that had opened in my stomach suggested I knew where Han was heading: illegally concealed weapons and a stash of gold bars didn't coexist with virtue. I closed my eyes.

Han went on, his voice a wasp in my ear. "Mr. Mèng had the kind of education and opportunities afforded only the highest members of the CCP and their families. The best schools. Private tutors in mathematics and the arts. Trips abroad and education at the most renowned universities in the world. And to his credit, Mr. Mèng—unlike many members of the red aristocracy—is not only brilliant but hardworking. He was born, as you Americans say, with a silver spoon in his mouth. But he did not waste his opportunities. He worked hard at elite schools in China, then obtained his PhD in computation science and engineering at MIT in Massachusetts. He studied neural networks and artificial intelligence with some of the biggest names in the field. When he finished his studies, he brought his knowledge back to China."

I opened my eyes. "He stole our secrets."

Han looked at me, a strange twist to his lips. Like bitterness. "He brought home his education."

"I would expect you to be appreciative of that, Mr. Han. But you're cross."

Sudden anger simmered like steam in a closed pot. "He also brought home his new American ways."

"You don't approve."

"My feelings in the matter are of no concern. I am here at the request of the Central Commission for Discipline Inspection. They have their own worries about the Americanization of Mr. Mèng."

"Discipline inspection?"

He heard something in my tone. "I assure you, there is nothing charming or antiquated about the commission. We are the highest anti-corruption agency in China. We have eyes everywhere. And we are quick to act." He returned his spectacles to his face, and his eyes vanished behind reflected daylight.

I was confident my own expression betrayed nothing. "What does this *discipline* commission have to do with Cass?"

"Please." He held up a hand. "Allow me to explain."

Once again I noticed his hands. They were not the hands of a bureaucrat, soft and manicured. Han's palms were calloused, the remaining nails ragged, the knuckles overlarge, as if from long labor. Or a lot of bar fights.

I fished in my purse for my sunglasses, as if hiding my eyes would hide my thoughts. "I'm listening."

"China is a difficult place these days for billionaires," Han said. "Our leader recognizes that it is wrong for the desires of the few to be raised above the needs of the many. Some men and women—those who are too American, too greedy to be true patriots—they flee our great country. And in doing so, they steal their wealth away from the people to whom it rightfully belongs."

The glittering opulence of *Red Dragon*. Her powerful engines, her sophisticated technology. The submarine. The helipad. Even the astonishingly beautiful yellow pear tree table that had caught my eye when I'd walked through the salon. "You believe Mr. Mèng has put his wealth into *Red Dragon* and will sail away with it."

"Someday, perhaps, that is his intention. But we believe that first he has other work in mind. What is the oldest business in the world, Miss Brenner?"

I played his game. "Prostitution."

His tongue clicked against his teeth in a tsking sound. "You Americans and your obsession with sex. I am speaking of trade. Even before warfare or prostitution, there was the exchange of goods. And the dark side of that worthwhile enterprise is smuggling."

My hand twitched, the smallest betrayal.

Han caught it. "Perhaps you know more than you allow, Miss Brenner."

"Is everyone at your discipline commission so imaginative, Mr. Han?"

He continued. "Once it was opium that flooded our ports. Now it is cigarettes. Cars. Beer. Oil. Genuine Moutai instead of the fake swill being touted to the gullible wealthy. And, of course, it goes both ways. Smugglers not only import goods to China but export our commodities to other countries. The wealthy have realized that if they can no longer overtly transfer their millions out of the country, they can steal away art and gold and precious relics. Illegal drugs. Unwilling women. All that is required is a place on a ship where this cargo can be hidden and protected."

Cass's black space. I wanted to close my eyes. "Singapore as a smuggling base? The government wouldn't tolerate it."

"Singapore is a city of mandated virtue. But men don't take well to mandates. Not when there is profit to be made."

"You could say the same of communism. How strong is the socialist ideal when politics runs up against profit? Or freedom?"

His smile was cold. "Those of us who work for the discipline commission are patriots. We care more for China than for personal wealth. Even more than for our lives."

A lizard, a tiny emerald jewel, darted from under the bench and disappeared into the shadows that hugged the temple walls.

"Did someone from your commission kill my sister, Mr. Han?"

"We had no reason to want her dead. Cassandra was useful to us. She worked for Mr. Mèng. But she also worked for us."

"You're lying. Cass would never risk our standing by spying on a client. Reputation is everything to Ocean House. Without it, we don't have a business."

"Perhaps Cassandra felt there was nothing left to save, given that Ocean House was built on the bones of a questionable—even immoral—past."

"What?" I was bewildered.

"You are surprised, Miss Brenner. Didn't your sister share what she'd learned about your family? Or did she keep that quiet as well?"

I laughed, forcing the sound through my throat. We had secrets, but I had always known they were small ones. Cass and I used to giggle that our kindly pop had been a serial killer or a bank robber. Still, Han's words triggered a memory: a fight between our parents and Uncle Rob that Cass and I had witnessed from a doorway when we were little. The furious shouts had caused Cass and me to burst into tears. Isabeth had rushed out and scooped us up, kicking the door closed behind her. The last thing I'd heard Rob say was, "We can't change what we are. No one can know."

Isabeth had taken us to the kitchen for ice cream and assured us that we were the descendants of aristocracy, even if my great-great-grandfather's family had annulled the marriage. No shame in that.

The emerald lizard reappeared. With a strike like a snake's, Han snatched the creature and held it in his palm, closing his hand.

"You are familiar with Paxton Yachts," he said as the lizard flailed frantically, trying to escape the cage of Han's fingers.

Still reeling from the idea that Cass might have known a secret I didn't, my mind shot back to the family meeting in Seattle. The article in *Showboats* suggesting that Paxton Yachts was poised to dethrone Ocean House. And Rob's fear that my father would become cautious enough to let Paxton win in the custom market.

Han said, "Paxton is determined to control the yacht market in Asia. For this reason, they have established bases in Singapore and southern China. They are partially financed by the Second Department—China's military intelligence group. Not that Paxton is aware that they are—in effect—working for my government. They believe they are accepting investment funds from private financiers."

"Military intelligence?" My voice was a whisper. "What are you talking about? What does any of this have to do with Cass? Or with you and your organization? Or even Mr. Mèng?"

The lizard's head appeared between Han's thumb and forefinger. Gently, Han steered it back into its cage.

"Mr. Mèng was encouraged by his superiors to work with Paxton. By choosing instead to have *Red Dragon* built by Ocean House, Mr. Mèng revealed himself to be less than loyal to his country. His actions have upset factions within China's military."

The questions that had swirled in my mind since learning of Cass's death now coalesced into a dark and ugly picture.

"The Second Department wants to stop Mr. Mèng," I said. "Keep him from finishing his yacht. From smuggling his wealth out of the country. If he had commissioned the yacht with Paxton, you could have controlled him from the beginning. But he broke rank."

Han opened his hand. The lizard paused and blinked as if unaware it was free. When it finally fled, I let go a breath.

Han said, "My group and the Second Department don't see eye to eye on the governance of our people. It is terrible, but just as in your country, there is a rivalry between different government groups. Likely, the Second Department would have persuaded Paxton through financial means to delay *Red Dragon* indefinitely. My organization, on the other hand, is happy to let Ocean House build Mr. Mèng's yacht. It is what the higher-ups in my government want. We are not, however, agreeable to letting him smuggle out his wealth. Which is where your sister came in."

Han leaned forward, elbows on knees. "To ensure Cassandra's loyalty, Mèng bought her expensive baubles, paid for her condominium in an exclusive neighborhood, promised to convince his friends to turn away from Paxton and commission their builds with Ocean House. In return, she agreed to help him smuggle his wealth. But all the time she was pretending to help Mèng, she was reporting to me. Your sister was astute, cashing in on both sides of the struggle. Her mistake was in ignoring the risk from the Second Department."

Han was lying. I sensed deception in his barely perceptible fidgeting, the distraction he had created with the lizard. But I also detected truth. That Paxton might be unwittingly funded by the Chinese government. That the Second Department was trying to control Mèng's wealth. That Cass had been caught between George Mèng, the Second Department, and Charlie Han.

"By accepting Mèng's bribes," Han said, "Cassandra offended the Second Department."

Truth? Or lie? Han gave away nothing. I looked away, up into the trees. "And they killed her?"

"I am not privy to the Second Department's decisions. But I suspect that is what happened."

"And now you want me to take her place."

"I will protect you."

"From men like Dai Shujun?"

Han made a clicking sound with his tongue. "Dai is one of mine, Miss Brenner. Clumsy and brutal. But effective."

I recalled the words of the CIA-declared officer Phil Weber. "Doesn't Dai work with one of the triads?"

"His position allows him flexibility."

I went as still as a deer hiding from the hunting gaze of a tiger. The calm part of my brain spoke softly: *Think, Nadia. Think very carefully. You are in a bad spot.*

Would Cass really help George Mèng smuggle his wealth out of China? If I were honest, the answer was yes. Cass was a compassionate capitalist who believed a man should be able to keep his hard-earned wealth so long as he paid his taxes and held a strong philanthropic bent. If Mr. Mèng's wealth was as substantial as Han suggested, then the temptation to help him, and thus our family's bottom line, would be irresistible. A win-win for Mèng and the Brenners and America—and a poke in the eye to the communists.

But she would not sanction smuggling drugs or weapons or women. Nor would she agree to work with the Chinese government. If Cass had done anything illegal, it wouldn't have been something that violated her personal code of ethics.

At least, that was true of the Cass I thought I knew.

An image of her shattered body floated behind my eyes, and I hated myself for the thought.

"Miss Brenner." Han's voice broke into my ruminations. "You are taking the news of your sister's likely murder remarkably calmly."

I turned my gaze to his—my oversize sunglasses against his reflective spectacles.

Let him believe I was calm. That was my gift. *Sprezzatura*, my grandmama had called it, borrowing the word from an Italian friend.

To be nonchalant without apparent effort, even as one was torn apart inside.

I said, "Why are you telling me about the Second Department? Assuming it's true, why would you betray elements within your own country to an *ang moh*?"

Han's face gave away nothing. "*Ang moh.* A Caucasian. You learn quickly. As I said, inside China, there isn't complete agreement among the party's ministries and commissions. Some men and women work for the party. Others work for themselves." He clasped his hands. "Help us trap the men who led your sister to her death. Simply that, Miss Brenner. There is no need for you to become involved in Chinese internal affairs. But neither should you let elements within the Singaporean government whitewash your sister's death under pressure from the Second Department."

Inspector Lee's note—his *alleged* note—appeared like a photograph in my mind.

We must talk . . . No father should lose a child. Especially, no one should lose two.

Had Lee—if he'd really written the note—intended to tell me that his hands were tied by forces he didn't dare defy? Had someone in his own department stopped him from meeting me?

I said, "Did you leave the note for me at Raffles or did the inspector?"

"The note was not my doing. But whatever the inspector told you, you should know that he now understands there are many currents surging around your sister's death. Some are strong enough to drown a man. Inspector Lee has sufficient experience as a detective to realize when he should let higher authorities handle a case."

Whatever internal machinations were going on within Singapore's Major Crimes Division, I couldn't hope to understand. But I wouldn't help Han or spy on Mr. Mèng. My job was to finish the boat and make sure nothing came back on Ocean House. I would tell Mèng to remove any illicit items from the boat immediately. And if he wanted to smuggle anything, he could do so after the sea trials and after *Red Dragon* had been formally commissioned. For now I would finish the boat, collect our final payments, and get the hell out of Singapore, just as Emily had advised.

Firm words. A good plan.

But inside I was miserable. Walking away meant allowing Cass's murderers to also walk away. I would sacrifice justice for Cass on the altar of Ocean House.

I placed my hands in my lap, forcing stillness. "You clearly have power in Singapore, Mr. Han. Why don't we arrange for you to board *Red Dragon*? You can look for smuggled goods and secret rooms to your heart's content. That should assure you that Ocean House has never and will never assist in illegal activities."

"Ah, if only it could be so easy. Mr. Mèng has refused, and he has ultimate say. And he has many friends. Unless we catch him in the act of smuggling goods to or from China, unless we have irrefutable proof of his crimes, these friends will protect him." He shifted to face me. "Mr. Mèng has spent years divesting his real estate holdings and stockpiling cash. He has turned some of that cash into art, some of it into gold bullion. He owns millions in US dollars in jewelry and uncut diamonds. It is almost unfathomable for someone like you and me to understand the extent of his wealth."

Perhaps for Han. I'd been around this kind of wealth my entire adult life. After a while I'd almost gotten numb to it.

Han continued, "We have learned that *Red Dragon*'s first sea trial will take her from Singapore to Shanghai. We believe Mèng has agreed to smuggle contraband from Singapore to authorities in Shanghai in exchange for their agreement to look the other way when he sails off with millions. We also know that, as is customary for the yacht's designer, you will be with him during the voyage to Shanghai and again when he departs for the second sea trial. All you need to do is keep your eyes and ears open. Tell us what you see. Doing so will entrap an evil man, help avenge your sister's death, and prove that Ocean House has a reputation worth upholding."

"It's all very clear to you, isn't it?"

"The right path is always well marked."

I wished that were true. "And what of the Second Department? Don't they want to be part of this plan to prove Mr. Mèng disloyal?"

"They will be caught flat-footed, as you Yanks say, when *Red Dragon* arrives in Shanghai, and it is the Central Commission for Discipline Inspection and not the Second Department who exposes George Mèng. We will have shown that loyalty to the party preempts loyalty to one's peers."

"Congratulations, Mr. Han. Yanks also talk about killing two birds with one stone. You would destroy Mèng and shame the Second Department in one blow."

"We believe in efficiency."

"So it seems." I stood. "But Ocean House is not political. My answer is no."

"Then you will cause the same problem for the Second Department as did your sister."

"Is that a threat?"

His face turned as flat and blank as a new sheet of paper. "It is. But it does not come from me."

The clouds closed in. A light wind lifted off the branches, the air tightened, and a few drops spattered my arms. Thunder cracked.

I said, "My job is to protect my family."

"And tell me, Miss Brenner, how your parents will feel at losing two daughters? I can give you forty-eight hours to consider my request. After that, men in the Second Department will make up their own minds about you. I suspect they will find you an impediment. Neither Dai Shujun nor I will be able to protect you."

Han stood. He gave me a curt bow and strode away across the courtyard. His smooth gait, the confidence of his bearing, rendered his human form tigerlike. Hunter and stalker. Eater of men.

I waited until he disappeared, then stepped out from beneath the shelter of the trees.

Cass. Oh God, help me. What do I do?

Lightning flashed. The heavens opened with a deluge that flattened the world to a single shade of gray.

16

Lian Shan Shuang Lin Monastery / Singapore City
August 28, 8:30 a.m. SGT

From the back seat of his car, Charlie Han smoked and watched the woman.

This *ang moh* was nothing like her sister. Where the older girl had been bold in her determination to help Mèng, this one was cautious. Careful. He didn't know if she'd believed his mix of lies and truths about her sister, or his story that he worked for the Central Commission for Discipline Inspection. In the end, it wouldn't matter.

He needed her, so he would find a way to convince her. As Sun Tzu wrote, "The victorious strategist only seeks battle after the war has been won."

Once he turned Nadia Brenner, he would at last hold his enemies in his fist, much as he'd held the green crested lizard. A single flex of his muscles and Mèng and his enemies in the Second Department would be crushed.

Yet the thought didn't bring the pleasure it once had. Because the destruction of his enemies wouldn't give him what he most deeply wanted.

Charlie stubbed out his cigarette. *"Zǒu ba,"* he said to the driver. "Let's go."

He pulled off his spectacles and rubbed his eyes.

How had he gotten here, so far from the rutted lanes and crumbling concrete homes of his village in Qinghai Province? The one-room school dormitory he'd shared with the other boys. The filth and scarcity and grinding poverty. Now he was a respected officer of the Guóānbù. So different. So strange. Sometimes it was hard to believe both places existed in the same country. Despite the tenets of communism, China was a patchwork of the haves and the have-nots.

His family had been moved to Qinghai as part of the CCP's push to occupy former Tibetan territories. Built on the Tibetan Plateau, their village was cold, racked by earthquakes and landslides, sandstorms and heavy winds. Populated with unhappy Tibetans and descendants of the Mongols.

Charlie had despised Qinghai. His family and the families of the other farmers were essentially prisoners. The work was hard and unrewarding, the schools poor, and the chances for escape to a better life close to zero. But Charlie had escaped, and sometimes—rarely—he thought that he should be content with that escape. Let his obsession with Mèng go.

But then he would remember his sister, Xiao. She had not escaped.

He closed his eyes. Xiao had been beautiful. Smart. But also foolish. She had allowed herself to be influenced by the locals. She'd begun by bringing up her crazy ideas to her family. *Free Tibet,* she'd said. *We have no right to be here.*

Their father had beaten her, but Xiao persisted. She began to speak out at school. She joined a demonstration staged in front of the local party headquarters.

Yes, Xiao had been stupid. And bad things happen to stupid people. But she'd been young. Impetuous. It was George Mèng's father—then governor of Qinghai Province—who had issued the command that led to Xiao's arrest and disappearance. Her likely death.

The injustice of it had first broken Charlie's heart, then enraged him.

While Mèng earned scholarships, elite jobs, and prestigious positions reserved for the party's elite, Charlie was left to search for his sister.

Quietly proffering questions, secretly searching files. Because of the party's blunt determination to expunge traitors, he suspected authorities of blocking his efforts. Yet he refused to accept that Xiao had gone to a place he couldn't reach.

Despite his background, Charlie had done well within the Guóānbù, the Ministry of State Security. But he wanted more. And to satisfy both ambition and revenge, he was risking everything to prove what he knew: Mèng was a traitor. Not merely a would-be defector but also an asset to the CIA. Charlie was sure that Mèng was supplying the Americans with information about China's AI program. He just couldn't prove it.

The vise around Charlie's neck was tightening. The wrong people were watching, and his position in Singapore had become precarious. It had taken months for him to convince his boss to let him trail Mèng. *Watch and do nothing,* his boss had told him. *See what the man is up to. Look for signs of defection. Nothing else. Mèng's wealth? Pah. Let the Second Department worry about that.*

It is Mèng's AI and his knowledge that we can't risk losing.

Chinese AI experts entered and left the country all the time. But even Charlie's boss understood that RenAI was unique. Special. Dangerous.

Charlie dropped his glasses as the driver hit the brakes. He fumbled blindly until his fingers closed on wire and glass.

The car exited the expressway and turned onto a surface road. Rain sluiced down the windows and banged on the roof like gravel falling.

Sun Tzu had also said that when facing a larger foe, taking them directly is foolish. This was where Charlie had made his mistake. His weakness was the fierceness of his emotions. The desire to destroy Mèng was an itch buried deep in a place he couldn't scratch. In his desperation to relieve that itch, he had become hasty. People had died, including the guard at the shipyard he'd killed weeks earlier.

Charlie's boss had been reprimanded.

The ice was cracking beneath his feet. Destroying a traitor to the Chinese Communist Party would be a coup and a springboard to Charlie's rise to the upper echelons of MSS.

But tearing apart an innocent member of the red aristocracy would mean death.

The car sloshed through puddles collected beneath the overpass. A tidal wave of rainwater washed down the windows.

"Turn here," he said to the driver. He would go to Geylang, take relief as a man sometimes must.

That thought, too, brought him little pleasure.

He pulled out the gold cigarette case his parents had given him. Gold for him, jade for his sister. Treasures passed down through the generations and clung to through famine and want. The heirlooms had remained in the family through Mao's Great Leap Forward, the Four Pests Campaign, the Cultural Revolution. They had survived and now belonged to Han. Someday he would find Xiao. When he did, he would take the small jade dragon that sat on the mantel at his home in Guangdong. He would place the jade dragon in her palms and restore her to his family. He would see his parents smile again. He would use his own placement in the party to protect her.

But first, first he would annihilate George Mèng's life, as Mèng's father had destroyed Xiao's life.

And his own.

17

Ardmore Park
August 28, 8:30 a.m. SGT

Rain pounded the sidewalk while I waited beneath the shelter of a kapok tree for my ride to appear. I dialed Emily. She answered by asking me whether I was still at the hotel and when I was coming into work. I explained I had to take care of a few things and would be in the office that afternoon.

Neither of us mentioned the previous night.

"I need to meet with George Mèng right away," I told her. "In person."

"What you ask is not possible. Mr. Mèng is in Shanghai."

I wouldn't discuss anything with my client over the phone. "Tell him it's urgent. It's a five-hour plane ride. He can fly here for lunch and be home for dinner."

"Mr. Mèng is a very busy man. He will not be able to—"

"Tell him if he wants his boat, he needs to meet with me tomorrow. Or tonight if he'd prefer." I ended the call.

Emily dialed back, but I blocked her calls. I was angry, scared, unwilling to be dissuaded from my path of confronting George Mèng. I needed to vent my fury at him for dragging Cass into his activities. And to warn him that Ocean House would not be involved in anything illegal.

My Grab ride pulled to the curb. "Ardmore Park," I confirmed.

As we pulled into traffic, I watched out the back window for a tail. But in the rain, all the cars looked the same.

"You okay, miss?" asked the driver.

"I'm fine. Thank you."

But I was shaking so hard that I thought my bones would rattle into pieces.

—

Cass's condominium was in the Tanglin district of Singapore, a stone's throw from the American Club and the members-only facility where I'd met Connor McGrath for dinner—the appropriately named Tanglin. Nearby were the embassies for China, Japan, the US, Australia, and the UK. A short walk in the other direction would get you to Orchard Road, the world-renowned shoppers' paradise.

I knew all this from the maps app on my phone. Cass had not lived in Ardmore when I visited her two years earlier. Then, she'd been in a reasonably priced flat far north of here, in the residential town of Sembawang.

I directed the Grab driver to turn into the entry for the Ardmore Park condominiums. The driver stopped at the security checkpoint, and a smiling man in a navy rain jacket, hood pulled up, stepped into the downpour to peer into the car. I pushed a button to roll the window partway down, bracing myself to convince this man to let me into Cassandra's flat.

Rain splashed inside.

The guard leaned closer, and his smile vanished. "You're Cassandra's sister," he said.

"I'm Nadia Brenner."

"I'm so sorry about Cassandra," he said. "I assume you want to get into her place."

"Yes. But I haven't found her keys."

"Not a problem, Miss Brenner. I'll have someone meet you in the lobby—you need a key to access the elevator. Uma will go up with you. Cassandra's condo is in the second tower on the thirtieth floor."

I flinched. *If you were going to kill yourself, Cass, why not do it here? Thirty floors is high enough.*

But she hadn't killed herself. Or not willingly. I was now convinced of that.

—

A few minutes later, a petite Tamil woman in a pale-pink suit stood with me in the hallway outside Cassandra's condo. She unlocked and opened the door.

"The door will lock behind you when you leave," she said. "Stop by my office, and I will provide you with a key. Cassandra's lease does not expire for two more years. Will you want to assume the lease? Properties here can be difficult to come by."

"I don't know yet." It was a lie. Even if Ocean House managed to breach the Asian market, none of us would be residing in Ardmore Park.

We stepped into the entryway. Our heels echoed on the wood veneer. The air was pleasantly cool—the air conditioner was on, but not cranked. I set my purse on a nearby table.

"The police have been here?"

"Yes, madam. I let them in myself and waited while they looked around."

I met her gaze in the mirror that ran the length of the foyer. "Did they take anything?"

She frowned.

"Please. She's my sister."

Uma hesitated, then nodded. "The inspector took what looked like a postcard from this table and placed it in an envelope. I also heard them say they needed a DNA sample."

"Anything else?"

"No, madam. I am sorry."

After she left, closing the door behind her, I stood for a moment, breathing in the mix of aromas. There came the faint hint of Cass's favorite perfume. And an unfamiliar muskier scent. A man's cologne?

"Cass," I whispered. "What were you and George Mèng doing?"

It was like the old game, where we'd taken turns hiding, then rescuing each other from the depths. Except this time, even as I looked for her, she'd already drowned.

I took a single step forward. My own reflection in the mirror made me jump.

In the glass, I appeared aloof—even bored. My expression was tranquil, my eyes revealed nothing. I stood with my usual upright carriage—a carryover from the years of ballet my mother had insisted on. Sometime this morning I'd lost one of my earrings. I removed the other and dropped it in my pocket.

"Charlie Han told me today that I might be murdered," I said to Cassandra's silent condo.

From somewhere in my memory, I caught the trill of her laughter. The two of us standing over a cage holding Cass's new pet—a tarantula.

Pick it up, she'd said.

I can't.

It won't hurt you. I promise. You have to try. Otherwise I'll think you're a chicken.

I am *a chicken.*

I turned away from the mirror. I hung my jacket over a chairback and gave myself the tour.

Cass had spared no expense. Wide-planked floors, marble counters, warm teakwood cabinets. The two-story condo featured a gourmet kitchen, which had probably gone unused during Cass's stay, since she hated cooking. The dining room boasted a table for ten and a sideboard topped with what looked like ancient ceramics. Quality knockoffs, surely.

On the balcony were pots of bonsai—a surprise since I hadn't known Cassandra to have a green thumb.

With each step I took through her condo, my sister slid away from me, falling into depths I couldn't plumb. This was the home of a stranger.

I stopped before the floor-to-ceiling windows that ran the length of the living room. The view presented lush acres of trees and gardens backdropped by condo towers and Singapore's skyline. How often had Cassandra stood here with a glass of sauvignon blanc—her favorite as well as mine—and contemplated life's usual questions? Was there a man in her life whom she hadn't told me about? Was she excited for the future of Ocean House and her eventual position as co-CEO? Did she truly relish her new life in Singapore?

Or was she scared, pressured, facing an abyss only she and George Mèng knew of?

Make that Mèng and Emily Tan. And perhaps Charlie Han. Even Dai Shujun. I suspected all of them knew more about my sister's life in Singapore than I did.

I went up the stairs to her workplace. A plain black desk and matching chair centered the room; an empty built-in filing cabinet took up half of one wall. Another wall carried shelves filled with nonfiction books on Singapore and China, along with artifacts from Cassandra's travels to Malaysia and the Philippines. At least this I understood: she had always loved art from other cultures.

An unconnected power cord and a laptop stand indicated where Cass's computer would normally be. Had it been stolen? Lost?

Open on the desk were a utility bill for the condo and an American Express statement showing more than $5,000 US in charges. I picked it up and scanned the expenses: restaurants, Grab fees, a monthly charge for the Tanglin and American clubs. Several charges to the Singapore Yacht Club. It was a high bill, but there was nothing unusual listed. Membership to the private clubs was a business expense in our line of work. There was no indication of any personal shopping—no clothing or jewelry stores.

I opened the desk's center drawer.

Inside was an air and hotel itinerary that showed Cass had traveled to Austria in July—in the middle of the installation of freshwater and sewage systems on *Red Dragon*, a critical time. She'd spent three days in Salzburg at the Hotel Goldener Hirsch, then returned to Singapore. Scrawled at the bottom of the itinerary were the words *Salzburger Landesarchiv*.

Presumably Cass had gone to meet with a potential client. But she hadn't reported any business expenses; Isabeth would have mentioned it at our regular meetings.

Late July was also when, according to Emily, Cass had begun disappearing from the office and *Red Dragon*'s schedule had slipped. And when she'd become unhappy.

Salzburger Landesarchiv. I looked it up. It was the name of the archives in Salzburg.

The buzzing wasp of Han's voice sounded in my ear. *Didn't your sister share what she'd learned about your family? Or did she keep that quiet as well?*

Our great-grandparents Pop and Nana were from Austria.

I rolled out the desk chair and sat.

Under the paper, inside a cardboard box, I found a beaten-up elongated copper rectangle roughly seven inches long and less than an inch wide. Three embossed Hebrew characters graced the top of the rectangle. Flat decorative triangles at each end suggested nail holes.

From my work with Jewish clients, I recognized the copper piece as a holder for the scroll that Jews hang on their doorposts. I turned the copper box this way and that in the sunlight making its way through the blinds and casting the room gray.

An old memory scratched. Years ago, I'd seen this mezuzah—or one just like it—at our house on Bainbridge Island, even if I hadn't known what it was. I closed my eyes and probed my memories.

An image flooded in. I'd gone into Pop's study. I'd been nine or ten, which would have made him a still-robust octogenarian. His book-crammed room, with its musty scents of paper and pipe tobacco, the framed photographs of boats built by Ocean House, the immense globe and forbidden wet bar—Pop's den was my favorite room in the house.

He'd turned when he heard me bounce in on a quest for the treats he kept in his desk. I'd glimpsed a copper mezuzah in his hand and—shockingly—tears in his eyes.

The dust in here is bad, he'd said as he placed the mezuzah in a drawer. *Now what are you here for, Naughty? A Mozart-Bonbon, I'll wager.*

I snapped back into the present. Maybe Cass had taken the mezuzah case from our home because of her fondness for old relics. But its presence with an Austrian trip itinerary suggested something more complex.

A fragment of a conversation echoed in my mind. Cass saying, *Hey, Naughty, maybe the good Catholic Brenners are actually Christ killers.* I'd been appalled by her language and tried to hush her, but Cass's eyes had glinted with mischief. *Did you think of that? Plenty of Jews converted—at least outwardly—when they fled Europe.* She'd puffed up her chest in imitation of Josef. *Maybe Pop wasn't a bank robber. Maybe he was a rabbi.*

Her suggestion had shocked me—we'd grown up in a devout Catholic family who attended services and Mass and honored the saints. What if our real identity was something else entirely? But for all the momentary fission I'd experienced, I'd soon forgotten about it. I thought she had, too.

The presence of the mezuzah and the last lines on the postcard she'd left me suggested otherwise:

The only thing our parents got right is that family is the most important thing, and for that reason we owe ourselves the truth.

I slid the mezuzah in a canvas tote hooked over the back of the chair and continued my search. I found nothing else of note. And nowhere on the desk or in the drawer or in the filing cabinet was there any mention of Charlie Han.

The only other item on the desk was a gold letter opener. Chinese characters marched down one side; on the other was written *Red Dragon* in English. I tested the point and found it razor sharp.

It wasn't uncommon for wealthy yacht owners to create tokens like this for guests to take with them. But this letter opener—with its sharp point and solid heft—felt like a weapon. I dropped it next to the mezuzah in the canvas tote.

Finding nothing more in the study, I went into her bedroom and searched through her closet and the dresser. Finally, there were all Cass's familiar things—linen shirts, crop pants, several suits. A simple black dress and a handful of flashy scarves. Her worn Louis Vuitton purse, a close twin to mine. Nothing over-the-top extravagant. And no jewelry.

If George Mèng had been buying her "baubles," as Charlie Han had put it, where were they?

I walked through the rest of the two-thousand-square-foot place. A well-stocked bar, an empty fridge, neutral decor that looked nothing like Cass—perhaps she'd hired a designer. The trash cans were almost empty, and the sinks devoid of water spots. Her condo was more like a place to entertain guests than a real home.

Now it felt like her tomb.

I returned to the bedroom and looked in the medicine cabinet. There were birth control pills. A bottle of Ambien, half-full. Band-Aids, an inexpensive face cream, cotton balls, and a nail file. Toothbrush, toothpaste, and floss. A nearly empty bottle of her perfume. In a drawer I found a hairbrush and comb and a hair dryer. A few cosmetics. Cass's natural beauty had needed nothing else.

I walked back through the condo, looking for places where she might stash drugs: the freezer, the toilet tank, behind furniture and inside cabinets. I peered inside a ceramic jar labeled "Rice" and found what was clearly rice. Dutifully I dug through and found only more rice.

But my sense of relief felt false; if she were helping Mèng smuggle drugs, she wouldn't hide them here.

I returned to the windows and watched a phalanx of gardeners descend on the grounds.

"I'm scared, Cass," I said. "Talk to me."

The carpets and plush furnishings swallowed my voice.

An image rose of Cass standing in our shared room. As teens, we'd often hidden things from our parents behind the headboards of our twin beds. Initially we'd stashed love notes and photo booth snapshots. Later, a wine opener. Then birth control. We'd felt clever with our choice of hiding spots, although I don't think Guy or Isabeth ever bothered to search our rooms. They had trusted us. More than that, they'd fallen into the comfortable trap of many parents—if you figured your child was behaving herself, you didn't need to spend time monitoring her. There were plenty of other things needing your attention.

But if Cass wanted me and only me to find something . . .

I hurried back into the bedroom. I pulled aside the nightstand, with its iPhone charger and yet another book on Singapore, and slid my hand between the king-size headboard and the wall. I felt only smooth wood. I pulled back my hand, removed my suit jacket, and reached in again, almost up to my shoulder.

My fingers brushed something soft and smooth like paper, held in place by tape. Gently, I tugged the item free.

It was a padded manila envelope, five by seven, sealed shut.

I reached behind the headboard again but found nothing else. I sat on the bed and used the letter opener from Cassandra's desk to open the envelope. I shook the contents out on the bed.

There were three photos. I laid them out in a row, then picked up the first one, a family picture.

Centered in the photo was an Asian man I recognized as George Mèng. He stood with his wife and two children, a girl and boy, aged around ten and twelve. The family was at the seashore, the girl holding up a large conch shell with open delight. Mèng had his arms around her, while his wife hugged their son. Nearby was a heap of wet suits and fins. Everyone looked thrilled to be there, to be together. Perhaps unfairly, a burn filled my chest that this man should have what Cass was forever denied: a family. A life.

The second photo was of Mèng by himself, unposed and candid, perhaps unaware someone had taken his picture.

He stood in a park or forest. Behind him rose an immense tree with multiple trunks and a roped barrier. Unlike the family picture, in this shot Mèng looked melancholy. More than that, he appeared haunted.

"What are you up to, Mr. Mèng?" I asked, the anger simmering. "Is that a look of guilt? What would your beautiful wife and children think of you, if what Charlie Han said is true?"

Finally, I picked up the third picture. This one I studied for a long time.

It was Cass and Emily Tan standing in front of a fish tank at a sea aquarium. They wore shorts and tank tops, their arms around each other. Their smiles were huge. Cass was tanned, her hair tousled, her sunglasses propped on her head.

Emily's head rested on Cass's shoulder.

It was a gesture I recognized from a thousand photos of Cass and me throughout our girlhood and teens. Besties, fellow adventurers, goofy pranksters. Joyous to be with each other and sure that life—and our love for each other—would last forever.

And here was Emily, standing in my place, her head nestled against Cass's shoulder in a way I so often had. Someone who didn't know Cass might think she and Emily were lovers. But they weren't. They were friends. Besties.

Tears sprang to my eyes. Had Emily betrayed their friendship? Had she helped lead Cass astray? Emily worked for George Mèng. She was his liaison with Cass. If Mèng had asked Cass to do things that led to her death, it seemed likely Emily knew about it. Perhaps, even, had facilitated it.

Do not trust anyone.

I dropped the photo as the weight of grief crashed down on me with a fist of cold iron. I stood and ran to the bathroom and vomited into the toilet. I vomited until nothing was left but bile. Then I vomited that. When my heaving stopped, I sank to the floor and curled against the wall and—finally—let loose the great sobbing cries I'd been holding back since I'd seen Cass's lifeless body at the morgue.

—

After, I rinsed my mouth at Cass's marble sink, splashed water on my face, and used her brush to smooth my hair. I returned to her bed and slid the items back into the envelope, then went out to the foyer and put the envelope, the mezuzah, and the letter opener in my purse, leaving the tote. I retrieved my phone. Still not wanting to talk to Emily, I calmly checked in with the broker, Andrew Declough. He and I reviewed some key items for the day, and I told him I'd be in the office before long.

After we hung up, I returned to the bedroom. I kicked off my shoes and lay down in Cass's unmade bed, gathering the silken warmth of the covers around me and curling into a ball. I breathed in her scent, knowing this was all I would have for the rest of my life. A fading fragrance and memories.

And questions. So many questions.

—

An hour later, downstairs in the administration building, I collected a key to Cassandra's front door and copies of the paperwork she'd signed when she leased the condo.

I showed Uma, the woman who'd unlocked Cass's door, the photo of George Mèng standing in front of the immense tree.

"Do you know where this is?" I asked her. "Is it a park?"

Her face lit. "Of course! The barrier fence gives it away. That is the fig tree at the summit of Bukit Timah Nature Reserve. I have been there many times. It is our country's highest peak." She studied the photo. "He's a handsome man, isn't he?"

"Did you ever see him here?"

But now her face closed. "It is not my business to watch our guests."

"Of course. I understand. It's just that I'm afraid I haven't met any of my sister's friends here. I want to hear their stories." I let my pain shine in my eyes. "With her gone, these stories are all I have."

Her face softened. She glanced over her shoulder at the other woman in the office, then ushered me into the hallway.

"I don't know his name, but I have seen that man twice," she admitted. "Both times in the evening. He was carrying a bottle of wine. And once flowers."

I pictured George Mèng at the seashore with his family. Then in my sister's bed. I shook the image away. Emily had been certain that Cass wasn't seeing anyone. And if she was Cass's new bestie, she would know.

Then again, Emily was prominent on the long list of people I couldn't trust.

"Wine and flowers, how lovely," I heard myself say. "Did he stay long?"

She flushed. "Both times he was still here when I left for the evening. You might check with the guard at the front, but I very much doubt Desi will tell you anything. He and the other guards feel strongly about protecting the privacy of our tenants."

I thanked her and walked outside. The rain had stopped, and the sun was dazzling.

The light was a mockery.

18

Little India
August 28, 11:30 a.m. SGT

The woman was right—the guard at the booth was friendly, but I could get nothing from him about who had visited Cass. Maybe Inspector Lee had enjoyed better luck. If he'd even asked during his quickly curtailed investigation.

Han had indicated that the Chinese Communist Party might be putting pressure on Singaporean officials to cover up Cass's death. Was that really possible? Had Lee intended to tell me things that would undermine his own government?

I walked out of the gated community and stood on Ardmore Road in the shade of a pair of palms gyrating in the breeze and watched steam lift from the road. All around, birds sang and called, a liquid counterpart to the purr of passing Ferraris and Lamborghinis. Going into the office was next on my agenda, and I decided it would do me good to walk to the metro station, even in the heat. Even with Dai Shujun and the Second Department presumably on my tail. Last night's impromptu swim and run had proved that I'd fallen out of shape.

As I reached into my wallet for the EZ-Link card, my hand brushed against a business card. I pulled it out.

Dr. Sayuri Saravanan
Professional Vedic Astrologer
Baboo Lane, Little India

The astrologer. With everything else, I'd almost forgotten. Emily had suggested that the visits were due to Mr. Mèng's superstitious desire for a safe voyage. And that the change in Cassandra coincided with her visits there.

I found Dr. Saravanan on a social media app and dialed his number. A warm male voice answered. I explained that I was Cassandra Brenner's sister and that I needed to meet with him.

If Cassandra's name meant anything to him, he gave no indication. "My fee is seventy Singapore dollars cash for a reading. I'll send you the information. Do you use WhatsApp?"

The messaging service. "I do." And if the man wanted to give me a reading, whatever that entailed, I wasn't going to argue. Maybe he would tell me my future. Hopefully I had one.

"I will send my address to you," he said. "Be here in two hours. I close after that."

He disconnected. I opened WhatsApp. A few seconds later I received an address on Baboo Lane—the same one that appeared on the business card.

Google Maps showed me I could walk to the Newton metro station and catch the Downtown Line to Little India. I saw no sign of Tiger Man—Dai Shujun—or anyone else who appeared to take note of me. And I was only a few hours into Charlie Han's promised forty-eight before the Second Department came after me.

But did I really want to trust Han's word?

Given everything that had happened during my short time in Singapore, I decided to take a roundabout path. Run an SDR the way Cass and I had been trained. If I were being tailed, maybe this would shake the cockroaches out of the walls.

I turned off location tracking on my phone and switched it to airplane mode, then pulled on my sunglasses and started out, feigning nonchalance.

Inside me, the deer crouched, shaking.

Terrified.

Dr. Sayuri Saravanan's office turned out to be his top-floor flat in a government-built apartment building. When I arrived, hot and sweaty from running an SDR, the front door was propped open, letting in the light breeze. I glanced through the screen. A man in his fifties stood in the kitchen, lighting a cigarette. He was short and lean and dark skinned, dressed in a T-shirt and sweatpants.

"Come in," he said when he saw me.

Inside, I tugged off my sneakers. I followed the astrologer through the small, drab living room and into the kitchen. He gestured for me to sit at the laminate-topped table. There were no velvet curtains, no Tarot cards, no crystal ball. Just a man with a keen gaze and a pyramid of packs of Pall Mall cigarettes large enough to stock the local market.

He peered at me, then smiled. "So. You are Cassandra's sister. I was saddened to learn from Mr. Mèng of her death. She spoke often of you."

"I don't mean to be rude, Dr. Saravanan. But why did she come to you? Cass was . . ."

"A skeptic?" The smile held. "She was worried. Sometimes scared. She didn't understand that life on the path of the Tao is difficult. Each of us must learn to accept the river's flow. Fighting it only brings misery. Now"—he propped his cigarette in a ceramic bowl and held out his hands—"which is your dominant hand?"

"I'm not here for a reading, Dr. Saravanan. I want to talk about Cass. What was she scared of? Why did she come to you?"

"Allow yourself to be in the river, Nadia." His voice was gentle. "The answers to your questions and Cassandra's fears lie inside you. We will get to one through the other."

I bit down on my impatience. "I'm right-handed."

He picked up his cigarette and watched me through a haze of smoke. "Place your right hand on the table, palm up."

Reluctantly, I did as he ordered.

He again propped his cigarette in the bowl and picked up my right hand, cupping it in his left.

"You care a great deal about your family."

"Dr. Saravanan—"

"It is good and right for a daughter to love her parents. Her uncle. But this love can become a prison if the fledgling doesn't leave the nest when the time has come."

My hand twitched in his grasp.

"Of more concern are the bad men who pursue you," he said. "I see two life lines, Nadia Brenner. Both spring from a choice in your life. One path allows a long life. The other . . . the other gives you very little time."

That's ridiculous, I wanted to say. But no words came out.

"We must try to understand this," he said. "In order for you to make the right choice."

"Wouldn't the right choice be the one that keeps me alive?"

"Perhaps. Perhaps not. There are times when doing the right thing is dangerous. This is something Cassandra knew."

A bloom of heat spread through my chest, a burn of anguish. "What do you mean? What right thing?"

Before Saravanan could speak, a sound near the front door made me cry out.

"Hush, hush," the astrologist said. "It is only my beautiful Abyssinian. You see?"

An immense tawny-colored cat with oversize ears was struggling to push her way through a cat door cut into the screen. It was a battle—the cat was fine boned but muscular, too large for the door. She forced her way inside, rattling the door in its frame, and gave me a baleful stare before stalking off down the hallway.

I gave a weak laugh. "You need a bigger door."

"That is what everyone thinks. But the struggle is what makes her strong. Now, please, feel safe here. Cassandra did."

"You just told me that I might die soon. How can I feel safe anywhere?"

He finished his cigarette, contemplating me through the smoke, then returned to studying my palm. A sudden wind rattled the screens on the window and front door, followed by a burst of rain pounding the roof.

"Both paths have costs," he said. "The question we must consider is this: Which costs are you willing to pay? You've read about our merlion? The lion appeared before Prince Sang Nila Utama after he sacrificed his crown to save his ship and crew."

"I've heard the story."

Saravanan's expression was grave. "The crown is a symbol. Of a prince's right to rule. Of his place in society. And, in the case of Prince Sang Nila Utama, of the price he was willing to pay to save his men."

He released me. He sat back in his chair and shook out another smoke from the nearest pack of Pall Malls.

"You don't believe, but I can read the truth in your palm, Nadia Brenner. I can read that your life is in danger. And also your soul. But I know other things, too. Things I don't need your palm to understand."

I narrowed my eyes. "Like what?"

"By now I suspect you've been approached by a man calling himself Charlie Han. He no doubt told you many lies. He would have told you that George Mèng is a bad man who convinced your sister to do bad things."

A shiver walked my spine. I realized I was "it" in a game of blindman's buff. "How do you know about Charlie Han?"

"From Cassandra."

"She knew him?"

"Not his name. Not the particulars of his mission. She was only aware that someone watched her."

"But you know his name."

"I learned it yesterday."

"From whom?"

"From your security chief, Connor McGrath."

The small room became smaller, as if the walls were squeezing in. I stood. "Connor knew about Han and didn't warn me?"

The Abyssinian cat appeared in the living room and regarded me with the eyes of a sphinx.

"Nadia. Please sit."

The world was spinning. "How do you know Connor? What's your interest in *Red Dragon*?"

"I shared my interest in the boat's fate with Connor. Just as I shared it with Cassandra. I am on your side."

Suddenly I couldn't listen to anything more. I couldn't process Saravanan's words. I knew only that I needed to get away.

"Stop." I pushed past the table and stumbled toward the door.

"Where will you go?" Saravanan asked me. "Connor and I can help you."

"Stay away from me."

A figure appeared in the doorway. I staggered back as a man jerked the door open. Tall and rough looking, his jeans ripped and oily, his gray hoodie stained and spotted with rain. Sunglasses concealed his eyes. Unkempt blond hair stuck out in spikes; his matted beard gleamed with moisture.

He came inside and shut both the screen and door behind him, turning the lock.

19

Little India
August 28, 3:00 p.m. SGT

I grabbed my purse, groping for Cass's letter opener.

"Nadia, it's me," said a familiar voice.

The man pulled off a blond wig and stuffed it in the pocket of his hoodie. He tugged at the beard and mustache, wincing, until they, too, vanished. Glasses followed. Only the oily stench of his jeans remained.

"Sorry to frighten you," said Connor McGrath. "I couldn't risk being recognized coming here."

My fear flipped to rage. "You lied to me. You're my security chief, but you told me nothing about Charlie Han. Or what Mèng is up to."

Connor spread his hands in a gesture of appeasement. "I'd hoped not to involve you. I wanted to let you finish *Red Dragon* in peace and return to Seattle none the wiser. But then Charlie Han made his move." His eyes darted to the letter opener in my hand. "Again, I'm sorry. I know you've been through a lot."

"I trusted you."

Connor said, "Cass gave me a message to pass on to you. She said to tell you that if you got dragged into the subterfuge, you should know that people like me—people who work for the CIA—are like that tarantula she convinced you to hold when you were kids. Hairy and ugly perhaps"—he flashed a smile that didn't reach his eyes—"but we would never hurt a friend."

CIA? Two CIA agents—two *alleged* CIA agents—in two days. Was Phil Weber's presence in the lobby at Raffles coincidental, or was he part of whatever was happening?

I glanced down at the letter opener in my hand. It shimmered in the dim light. Would I really have used it?

Connor kept his feet planted. He was talking fast now. "Charlie Han is a different matter, Nadia. He *will* hurt you. Just like we suspect he hurt Cassandra. Yes, I'm CIA. I'm with the China Mission Center. Cass was helping us arrange for George Mèng and his family to flee China when she was murdered."

"Murdered." The word sat like thorns on my tongue. I felt sick. But also less alone.

"Mèng has good reason to defect," Connor said. "And we have an interest in seeing him succeed."

"Why does the CIA care about one Chinese family?"

"George has pioneered the use of generative artificial intelligence in predictive diplomacy. Or, as George calls it, chaos-theory peacekeeping. At its simplest, his AI applies game strategy to prevent war. With RenAI in the wrong hands, though, things could go badly awry."

"You're saying Cass died for a fancy piece of software."

"I'm saying she died to help preserve peace. What did Han tell you? That George is smuggling art and gold and, good lord, cigarettes?"

"I found gold," I said, then clamped my mouth shut.

"George *is* taking some of his wealth with him, mostly for bribes. But this operation is about his family. That's why Cass agreed to work with us—to help George's wife and children escape a repressive society. The technology was secondary to her."

Of course Cass agreed to help. Not Cass the smuggler. Cass the rescuer. I wrenched myself away from the grief that tried to swallow me.

"What about NeXt Level Security? Is it a front?"

"We were hired by Ocean House to manage *Red Dragon*'s security," Connor said. "But we're what's known as a CIA proprietary, meaning NeXt Level is owned and operated by the CIA. Not on paper, of course. I *am* a valid security expert. We really are installing the security measures George wants and needs. But I'm also an NOC—an operative acting under nonofficial cover."

Without realizing it, I'd backed up against the wall of Dr. Saravanan's living room.

Connor's voice pressed on. "I'm here because my predecessor, Cassandra's handler, was fished out of Singapore River, his throat slit. A few hours after that, we got word about Cassandra's death."

"Her handler?"

Connor shrugged out of his hoodie to reveal a tattered Grateful Dead T-shirt. "Your sister wasn't just helping behind the scenes with design elements for *Red Dragon*. She was following Chinese nationals we believe are part of Charlie Han's group. She eavesdropped on them at private clubs and took note of who went in and out of the Chinese embassy."

My head spun. "Cass was a spy?"

"It's why we got her the condo in Tanglin. It made her presence in the shops and restaurants there normal. Living in the neighborhood, she'd naturally stop by Tanglin Club for a glass of wine after work. Sometimes stay for dinner. Chat up other members. To anyone watching, it made sense for Ocean House to trawl for potential clients there. But Cass was watching the Chinese expats and visiting nationals."

I gathered my thoughts, which were skirting away like sunlight chased by nightfall.

Everything in the room had turned sharp. Vivid. The rain spitting on the window. The musky smell of Saravanan's cat and his Pall Malls. The heft of the letter opener slick in my sweaty palm. In another apartment, a child wailed and was hushed.

I said, "Cass wasn't looking for clients. She wasn't trying to help Ocean House expand into Asia."

“No,” he said. “Your sister was an asset of the CIA.”

—

A short time later, the three of us sat at the table in Saravanan’s kitchen, the letter opener glittering on the Formica tabletop. The cat took a place on the counter near the window and coolly groomed herself.

“She wasn’t followed?” Saravanan asked McGrath.

“No one made her at the station, which is where I came in.”

“Sloppy work on their part,” Saravanan said.

“We got lucky.”

“It wasn’t luck,” I said. “I ran an SDR before I took the metro.”

Connor looked impressed. “I knew Cass had training. I should have realized you would as well.”

“I’m rusty,” I admitted. I glanced at Saravanan. “And you’re, what, a recruiter? Did you pull Cass into this?”

He shook his head. “I’m a support asset. I merely offer a safe place for spies to rest.”

I considered that. “I’d like a cigarette.”

Saravanan gave his gentle smile. “I already told you that your life is in danger. Why rush things?”

“You also told me I don’t have long to live.” I nodded toward the pile of Pall Malls and held out my hand. “I’m a stress smoker. And right now I’m stressed.”

He offered a pack. I tapped out a cigarette, and he lit it for me.

McGrath followed suit with a cancer stick of his own. “I’m still cutting back,” he said.

Soon we sat in a wreath of blue-gray smoke. Saravanan rose, bowed to each of us, and said, “I will leave you to it. Nadia, it was a pleasure. I hope whichever path you choose is the one that most comforts your soul.”

He disappeared down the hall.

I looked at Connor. Think first. Act second. If you're still alive at the end of the game, *then* you can panic.

"Let's start with Charlie Han," I said, my voice becalmed between rage and sorrow. "You think he murdered Cass."

"He's our top suspect, although he's never before risked such a dramatic setting. He's usually a back-alley guy."

"Usually?"

"Han isn't squeamish about wet work."

I pictured the glittering lenses of Han's spectacles. His cold smile and calloused hands. And the odd vulnerability I'd noted when he removed his glasses. I aimed my cigarette at Connor. "Are you responsible for leaving my sister unprotected?"

"I wasn't in Singapore that night. But it's true that CIA failed her."

I sucked in nicotine until my head whirled. My beloved Cass. The terror she would have felt staring down forty floors. The horror just before she reached the pavement.

Instantly I was back in the drowning game. It was almost the last time we played. Cass had swum out until she had exhausted herself. *Why did you do that?* I had asked her later. *You could have died.* But she'd been exhilarated. *It was the freest thing I've ever done,* she'd told me. *Free because I didn't have to count on myself. I knew you would come.*

I dug the fingernails of my free hand into my palm. "Han told me he works for the Central Commission for Discipline Inspection."

Connor held his cigarette between his thumb and forefinger, like a European. He tapped ash into the bowl. "Maybe that's his cover. But Han and his partner, a man named Dai Shujun, are employees of Guóānbù, the Ministry of State Security, which is China's CIA."

"I know Dai Shujun. He's been tailing me." I said nothing about meeting Phil Weber at Raffles. I didn't have many cards, but I would keep close the few I had.

Connor eyed me through the smoke. His hair was damp with sweat from the wig. "Dai is on our radar. He's a better criminal than intelligence man. Has his fingers in a lot of pies. He's a bit of a wild card."

Adrenaline ticked in my pulse. "What about the Second Department?"

"China's military intelligence?" A deft flick of Connor's wrist and ash rose in the bowl. "What about them?"

"Han accused the Second Department of killing Cass. He asked me to watch Mr. Mèng for him and said that if I refused, then he could no longer protect me, and the Second Department would kill me as well. He gave me two days."

Connor mashed out his cigarette and leaned in. "Nadia, listen. The Second Department and MSS have been in a turf war for years. Each wants to impress those at the highest level of power—the Standing Committee and China's paramount leader. But none of our intelligence suggests the military is involved with Han's operation or that you are in any danger from them. Han is trying to coerce you through fear."

I blew smoke from the corner of my mouth. "He's effective."

"We won't let you get hurt."

I envisioned Cass's body at the morgue. I looked away until I could rearrange my expression into a surface of calm.

"Nadia?" Connor said. "Have you considered going home to Seattle?"

I swiveled back. "Of course I have. But whoever takes my place would also be in danger."

"Not in the same way. The Guóānbù undoubtedly has spies in the shipyard. But you, like Cass, offer something unique. Partly because you are female—the Chinese believe women make better spies. But also because you are the future of Ocean House. And that makes you vulnerable, more so even than other members of your family. Vulnerable to bribes if your company isn't doing well. To blackmail, if there's any secret dirt. To the desire to expand into Asia if that's what you hope to do. The Guóānbù can lean on you for all or any of these reasons."

At Connor's words, I was ashamed of the relief that filled me. I could go. Leave *Red Dragon* to Emily and Andrew and the rest of the staff. Oversee the outfitting and launch from the other side of the ocean.

"But." Connor leaned forward and peered into my eyes. "If you decide to stay, we could use your help. The first sea trial will take *Red Dragon* from Singapore to Shanghai. In Shanghai, the Chinese authorities will inspect the boat. George's wife, Li-Mei, and their children will also be in the city. Their only chance to board is while *Red Dragon* is docked for the inspection. We've arranged a rather elaborate journey for them from their house in Shanghai to the dock, even as it appears—thanks to our operators—that they are instead headed for their country home. Because of the intense scrutiny in China—both human and digital—this has been a massive undertaking. And dangerous.

"Once they reach *Red Dragon*, they must get into hiding. And stay hidden throughout the next leg of the journey until they're smuggled off. That's where you would come in."

Cass's black space. The room behind the dragon.

I pictured a woman and two frightened children dodging cameras and eluding spies and police in the streets of Shanghai to reach *Red Dragon*. "The boat is the only way?"

"Given China's surveillance and how closely authorities monitor its borders, yes. George can't leave if Li-Mei is out of the country. She can't leave if he is gone. *Red Dragon* is their only chance for a free life."

"And what happens when the Chinese authorities realize the family has fled?"

"We have a plan for that."

"I hope it's a good one." I helped myself to another cigarette and used Saravanan's plastic lighter. "The fallout will be colossal."

"You would be their best cover to prevent that fallout," Connor said softly. "Able to move freely about the boat, expected to interact with staff and actively look for issues that need to be addressed during the trials. Your presence would make everything appear normal."

I looked up at the ceiling, spotted an immense muddy-brown spider in one corner. I pitied whatever walked into its web.

Connor added, "We would also provide a monthly CIA consulting retainer."

I lowered my gaze and pulled away. "Do you know what you're asking? I don't mean my personal safety. I'm talking about my family. If word got out that Ocean House had anything to do with Mr. Mèng's defection, no one would trust us. My actions would close off Asia to us forever. We need Asia, Connor. Ocean House won't survive without it."

"Your sister didn't see it that way. She believed she was doing the right thing by opposing China's dictatorship and brutal men like Charlie Han. She believed that, in the end, her actions would help Ocean House."

"Cass was an idealist."

"Aren't you?"

He pulled a sheet of paper from his shirt pocket, unfolded it, and pushed it across the table to me. "Here's everything we know about Han."

1. SUBJ 42-YEAR-OLD CHINESE NATIONAL. BORN IN QINGHAI PROVINCE TO FARMERS HAN HUAN AND HAN MIÀO.
2. SUBJ HOLDS UNDERGRADUATE DEGREE IN INTERNATIONAL RELATIONS FROM PEKING UNIVERSITY (2001). MSc IN SECURITY STUDIES FROM LONDON SCHOOL OF ECONOMICS (2003).
3. CURRENT JOB SR OPERATIVE IN MINISTRY OF STATE SECURITY (MSS), PEOPLE'S REPUBLIC OF CHINA. LIKELY CAPACITY: RECRUITMENT OF INTERNATIONAL ASSETS W/FOCUS ON WESTERN TARGETS. CURRENT STATION SINGAPORE. PREV FOUR YRS LONDON.
4. PREV JOB CYBERSECURITY FOR RenAI. PARTY-BUILDING ADVISER IN CHARGE OF CCP UNITS

W/IN PRIVATE BUSINESSES. SUBJ CLASHED WITH CEO OF RenAI. REF INF. COLL. WAS DEMOTED AND TRANSFERRED.

5. WIDOWER (HAN JING DECEASED—2007).
6. ONE SISTER HAN XIAO. XIAO ARRESTED BY CCP FOR INVOLVEMENT W/PRO-TIBETAN INDEPENDENCE PROTESTS IN QINGHAI (2006). WHEREABOUTS UNKNOWN. DECEASED? PARENTS TRFD TO BEIJING FOR SECURITY REASONS.

I read the dossier twice, then smoked for a minute or two, processing the information the way I would the profile of a potential client. Maybe I was intrigued by this peek into the spy world. Maybe I was playing a game with myself that I might step into Cass's very expensive shoes.

I said, "RenAI is the name of George Mèng's company. What does it mean that Han oversaw a party unit there?"

"In China, even private companies must adhere to party authority. It's common practice for every business to have a chapter of the party on the inside, keeping an eye on things. Bringing the party into George's company would have been a way for Han to prove his loyalty to the CCP. We don't know what caused his disagreement with Mèng." Connor parked his elbows on the table. "Any other questions about him?"

I shook my head, and Connor picked up the paper and used the lighter to set it on fire. He let the flaking pieces fall into the ceramic bowl. Then his eyes caught mine. "What else do you want to know?"

The room had turned close and hot despite the rain splashing against the window. I held my cigarette in my mouth and shrugged out of my linen jacket.

"You mentioned the condo," I said when I'd resettled. "Did the CIA also pay for Cass's clothes? All the charges on her card?"

"The luxury items were part of the deceit. If the Guóānbù started looking too closely at George and *Red Dragon*—which is exactly what happened—we wanted it to seem as if George's interest was purely material. He might get a slap on the wrist for stashing some wealth outside the country and lavishing gifts on a beautiful woman. But his connections within the party protect him. What we couldn't afford was for anyone to suspect his actions had to do with his family."

"Cass and George weren't lovers?"

McGrath's laugh was short. "It didn't hurt for people to think so. But no. That, too, was part of the act."

"And the cocaine in her purse?"

"Part of the disguise."

I was on a roll with the questions, and so far, Connor was cooperative.

"What about Emily Tan?" I asked.

"Unfortunately, we don't have much information on Miss Tan. She's from mainland China, and her family is still there, which potentially gives the MSS a hold over her. We know she has met with Han. Whether or not you agree to work with me, tell Emily as little as you can. I've already warned Mèng."

I grunted and drew on my cigarette. I blew smoke toward the spider. "Do you have a dossier on George Mèng?"

"Tell me what you want to know."

"It's pretty simple. I want to understand why Cass cared enough about him and Li-Mei to risk her life for them. And why it's so vital for Mèng to leave China that he's okay if people die to help him escape. Is this RenAI that important?"

"It's critical. China has five hundred nuclear warheads. In a few more years, it will have double that number. The CCP wants George's AI to control those warheads. The other issue is the ocean. Numerically, China has the world's largest navy and is fast catching up in other metrics, such as advanced technology and ship capability. And despite warnings from the United Nations, the dragon is pushing its territorial reach into the South China Sea and coming into constant conflict with the US Navy. RenAI will allow the Chinese to predict and counter our every move with little risk to themselves. We have nothing that's equivalent. Not yet."

"And Mèng loves America so much he'll betray his country? Is he also a spy for CIA?"

Connor's gaze held steady. "George is not a spy. And he loves his country, but not the dictator who runs it. He doesn't want his children to be raised on party propaganda and to live in a surveillance state that disappears its own citizens when they disagree with the party. He wants what we all want for our children. For them to be free to choose their own lives."

I finished my cigarette. Was it my imagination, or had Connor's jaw tightened when I asked if George was a spy? Did it matter?

My throat was parched. I stood and searched Saravanan's cabinets for glasses. I filled two at the sink, gave one to Connor, and drank gratefully.

The rain slowed, then stopped, and sunlight streamed through the kitchen window. Saravanan's cat curled up on the counter and closed her eyes.

"If Mèng is such a golden boy," I said, "then why is Guóānbù suspicious of him?"

"When RenAI began to perform tasks it hadn't been programmed to do, it became clear that the AI had gone beyond what George had expected, with unknown consequences. George tried to shut down that development before the CCP became aware of his AI's capabilities. He had promised himself his work would never be used for military purposes. But word of the advancement leaked, and the CCP ordered George to double down on his original research. So far, George says, he's managed to keep RenAI confined. But he can't carry the bluff for much longer. Now that CIA has finished incorporating certain features into *Red Dragon*'s security, it's urgent we get him out as soon as possible."

"Mèng came to Ocean House five years ago. If that's when he panicked, then surely by now the CCP has already taken over RenAI."

"George conceived of *Red Dragon* as a way to leave China with his family long before his breakthrough with RenAI. Once he realized he was running out of time, he came to us. Both SIGINT and HUMINT—our communications interceptions and word from our people on the ground—revealed that Guóānbù was watching George. That's when we knew that hiding the family would require structural changes to *Red Dragon*. Stashing the family in the crew's quarters or tucking them into extra space in the technical area wasn't going to be sufficient. Our man pulled in Cassandra."

"And threw her to the wolves," I said bitterly.

"That wasn't the plan."

I said, "If China gets wind of the fact that American agents are helping George Mèng escape and even arming him against the MSS, you're going to start a war."

"Not if we're careful."

"Careful? Jesus, Connor, look where that got my sister. I'm sure George Mèng and his wife are wonderful people, and his kids are adorable. But are you willing to start a war for the sake of one family?"

"That's why we have to move fast to get George and his family out. Then make them disappear." He ran a hand through his clipped hair. "Nadia, I must ask. Are you willing to help George's family in Shanghai and on the second sea trial? And to tell Charlie Han that you will do as he asks? With Han, all you would need to do is pass along the false information we supply to you. We would be nearby every time you meet. Watching. Ready to move should he become a threat."

But I already had my answer.

I stubbed out my cigarette, slid Cass's letter opener into my purse, and stood. My hands were shaking; I gripped the chair in an effort to make them stop. I was through with my questions for Connor. I had questions for only myself. How had Cass said yes to these men, knowing what it could cost our family and Ocean House? How had she gone through her days aware that at any moment she might be made by someone and silenced? Where had she found the courage? Why hadn't she told me?

What would I have done if she had?

Know that what I did will ultimately be the right thing for everyone, she'd written on the postcard. The card wasn't a suicide note. Her words had been meant to reach me if she was killed.

And what she'd done had most definitely not been the right thing.

I peeled my hands off the chair. They were still shaking. "What you're asking is nowhere inside my wheelhouse. Believe me, I am very good at knowing when I'm in over my head. Cass"—my voice hitched—"Cass was brave. I'm not. I never did touch that tarantula she told you about. I'm not going to start now."

Connor got to his feet. "'The only thing necessary for the triumph of evil is for good men to do nothing.'"

"A quote often wrongly attributed to Edmund Burke. But you can't guilt me into this. I *can't*, Connor. Don't you understand? I'm too scared." I held up my hands as proof. "And I'm a terrible liar. Absolutely awful at subterfuge. You know that. You were interviewing me about honesty during our dinner. And I failed. What more proof do you need? Charlie Han would see right through me. Assuming I didn't just crumble right out the gate and confess everything."

As my voice rose, the cat stood and hissed.

"More than that, I'm not willing to risk my family for George's. Nor will I jeopardize Ocean House for what his AI might—in theory—someday wreak upon the world."

Saravanan appeared suddenly. He took in my face and Connor's, then scooped up the distressed cat, which melted into his arms and began to purr. "What will you sacrifice, Nadia, to save your sister's memory and to help George Mèng? That is the question you must ask yourself. Will you choose a long life? Or a virtuous one?"

I grabbed my purse and stalked to the door. I yanked on my shoes. I was crying. Angrily I dashed away the tears with the back of my hand and jerked the door open.

"My family," I said. "I choose Ocean House."

20

Little India / Singapore Financial District / Raffles Hotel
August 28, 4:00 p.m. SGT

I hurled myself down the stairs and down the sidewalk toward the metro. A block from the station, I slowed to a walk and glanced behind.

Connor hadn't followed me. Not that I could tell, anyway. The entire world felt filled with invisible watchers. The elderly woman with a shopping cart. A young man on a bicycle. The Malay woman with a backpack.

Weary, afraid, Cass a ghost walking beside me, I strode past the metro station and turned down a side street, entering a maze of 1920s-era shophouses. Since the rain had stopped, a relentless heat pressed down. I was soon drenched in sweat. Vendors called out from the shadowy interiors of their shops, offering henna tattoos, gold bangles, souvenirs, sweets. The smells of curry and chilies floated on the air from mom-and-pop restaurants. Across the street, pilgrims removed their shoes and entered a Hindu temple, hands clasped in prayer.

My heartbeat slowed. The burn in my chest faded.

In place of my terror and rage, I became numb.

From the shade of an awning, as rows of gold Buddhas winked behind me, I called Emily and told her to send a driver.

—

Emily greeted me when I walked into Ocean House's suite of rooms. She held a stack of papers in her arms. I heard the rest of the staff talking in their offices. The door to the suite of offices belonging to George Mèng's single family office—where members of his staff managed their parts of the build—remained closed.

"You have been busy," Emily said.

Our eyes locked. I imagined we were both thinking of what she'd said to me while I hid on board *Red Dragon*.

Had Emily been Cass's friend? Or her betrayer? I scowled. Damn the torpedoes. "Emily, Charlie Han—"

The papers slid from Emily's grasp, plunging to the floor and scattering.

She dropped to her knees. "I am sorry. So clumsy."

I joined her on the floor. We collected the papers. She wouldn't meet my eyes. I decided I didn't want to talk about Charlie Han after all. Or anything else. I'd determined on the ride over that my next task was to handle the most immediate requirements for *Red Dragon*, then get Cass home. After that . . . after that was a giant question mark. Could I help Mr. Mèng's family without endangering myself or my family? As well, thoughts of justice for Cass pinwheeled through my mind. But how can you get justice for your dead sister when the authorities refuse to investigate, and her likely murderer is a foreign intelligence agent?

A voice slithered into my mind: *By taking up her work.*

I ignored it.

"I spoke with Mr. Mèng," Emily said. "He will come first thing tomorrow."

I gave her the papers I'd gathered and stood. "Cancel that. I'll meet with him another time." The last thing I needed was to look Mèng in the eyes and inform him that I was a coward.

She rose as well and trailed after me into Cass's office. "I don't understand. Mr. Mèng wants to speak with you. You need to meet face-to-face."

I rounded on her. "What I need is to get my sister home and get *Red Dragon* back on schedule. I don't require Mèng for either of those things. If the authorities agree, in two days I'm taking Cass's body home to Seattle, and I will stay there at least until her funeral. After that, I'll reevaluate where we are with *Red Dragon* and decide on my next steps."

Her eyes widened. "But we need you here, Nadia. To finish the boat. To do it quickly. *Then* you can go home."

"You and the staff and Mr. Declough can manage without me until I return."

And maybe forever.

Life would go on. I would be bent and battered but still intact. Wasn't that what Cass would want?

Emily interrupted my thoughts. "What about me?"

I stepped into her space. I stood a full head over her. "Yes, Emily. What about you? What will you do while I'm gone?"

She backed away. "Nadia, what has happened? You are angry."

"Angry? Imagine that." I forced myself to lower my voice even as my hands curled into fists. *She trusted you, Emily,* I thought. *She cared about you. And maybe you gave her to Han. Or to the Second Department. God alone knows.*

Emily watched me with wide eyes. She looked like a deer herself.

To her credit, she'd tried to warn me on *Red Dragon*.

I forced my hands to relax. I stepped back and made my voice soft. "'Chu songs on all sides,'" I said, quoting her own words back to her, the words she'd spoken on the yacht. *Besieged on all sides.* "I heard you. And now I understand. It will be good for me to get away for a short time. Then I'll return to—quickly—finish *Red Dragon*."

She watched me, her face neutral. "That is good," she said after a moment.

"You still have a job, Emily. I need you here. George Mèng needs you. I just hope you're doing what is right. I hope your loyalty is where it should be."

She blinked at me, then went to the windows, a slim figure silhouetted against the light. She looked as frail as I felt.

I hoped for a confession. A revelation. But all she said was, "Would you like me to bring you some tea? Perhaps some lemon balm to ease your mind?"

The metaphorical door between us—barely opened—slammed shut.

"Lemon balm tea would be lovely." I settled myself behind Cassandra's desk. "Maybe in an hour. Right now, I need to be alone with my thoughts."

She retreated, closing the door behind her. I sent Uncle Rob a text telling him that he should take the train from the airport or arrange for a car. He had a room near mine at Raffles, and I would meet him in the lobby or somewhere on the grounds.

He didn't answer. He always paid for Wi-Fi when he flew, but by now he was probably asleep. His plane wouldn't land in Singapore until tomorrow morning.

I locked the door, put my phone in "Do Not Disturb" mode, and got down to the business of *Red Dragon*. Ocean House would deliver the boat. That would end our obligation to Mr. Mèng.

No other Brenner would die for his family. I'd made my choice: finish *Red Dragon* without involving ourselves with Guóānbù or the CIA.

Then move on.

The next morning, leery of the office and Emily and of being followed, I decided to work from my laptop at the hotel. I dressed in lightweight flowing pants, a sleeveless blouse, and an equally lightweight jacket, then twisted my hair into a chignon and applied makeup with a light touch. After adding gold earrings and heels, I took a final check in the mirror and drew on lipstick with a steady hand, completing my uniform as if it were a normal day.

Pretending darkness didn't lurk in the shadows carved by Singapore's sunshine.

Downstairs, I did a quick scan for Charlie Han and Dai Shujun. Seeing neither, I settled at a table in the courtyard, ordered breakfast, and handled emails and phone calls from the staff while I waited in the shade for Uncle Rob to arrive.

An hour in, I paused and poured more coffee. I needed to decide what to tell Uncle Rob about my planned stay in Seattle. I tried out a few conversational scenarios in my mind and finally determined I would tell him nothing except that I needed to remain in Seattle for a time to complete some tasks. Connor had spoken in confidence, and to share what he'd said—even with Rob—was inviting trouble. Plus, Rob would find the idea of spying romantic. Smuggling hapless dissidents! Saving the world! It wouldn't harm Ocean House. It would make us mysterious. Valuable. Even glorious.

He'd want to jump in with both feet.

I had to keep him safe and blissfully unaware only until tomorrow, when—with the blessing of the authorities—we'd board a plane for Seattle with Cass and leave all this behind.

The waiter took away my barely touched breakfast and brought a fresh pot of coffee and a warm-from-the-oven croissant with coconut jam. I removed my jacket and returned to my work. Everything required to finish the boat was in place. Now that NeXt Level Security was no longer creating a delay, the build just needed a few nudges, a little oversight, and some overtime to haul it back on schedule.

When Rob hadn't appeared or called by noon, a cold unease filtered through the day's heat. I confirmed that his plane had landed on time, then sent him another text, telling him where I was.

Fifteen minutes later I phoned him.

"I'll be on my way soon, Naughty," he said when he answered. "I hope so, anyway. Bit of a mix-up with the luggage. We'll see how quickly they can get this sorted out. How do you lose a man's luggage on a flight with no layovers?"

"Sorry, Rob," I said, swept with relief at the sound of his voice. "God forbid you should have to wear the same set of clothes two days in a row."

"With the length of the flight, I already have been. And a man needs to be at his best."

I managed a small laugh. "Let me know when they get it figured out."

I scanned the courtyard, as I'd done every half hour all morning. The tourists had vanished into the day's activities, or at least into the air-conditioning of the shops and restaurants. But I'd been joined by a member of the Guóānbù. A wall of human flesh, Dai Shujun sat on a bench in a ball cap and button-down, the collar turned up. He sat in profile to me, watching the fountain, or pretending to. The courtyard's fountain was lovely but likely didn't warrant much notice from a man like Dai.

Charlie Han's promised forty-eight hours weren't up. In theory, Dai was here to protect rather than harm. But gooseflesh rose on my arms even in the heat.

One more day. Two at the most. Then I could stop looking over my shoulder.

It was three o'clock before Rob arrived, trailing his oversize suitcase. I stood to greet him, happier than I'd ever been to see his aristocratic mien and graceful posing.

"Planning on staying a few months?" I teased, gesturing toward his bag.

"I'm a true Boy Scout—I like to be prepared." He kissed my cheek. He looked rumpled and pale. Haggard. Still aristocratic, but not his usual debonair self. "Nadia, my sweet child. I'm so glad to see you. How are you holding up? What a horror this has all been."

We hugged, and I waved him to a chair. "Sit down. Are you hungry?"

"I devoured everything they put in front of me on the plane. Trying to build up my strength." He shuddered. "I'm not even entirely sure what they served me. What I need now is a cocktail."

A waiter appeared at his elbow with that almost magical sixth sense they have at Raffles.

"A Singapore Sling, of course," Rob told the man. "When in Rome, and all that."

"Of course, sir. Would you like the original Singapore? Or perhaps the Maldives version?"

Rob feigned horror. "Only the original will do."

The waiter vanished. Rob picked up my glass of water with a rhetorical "Do you mind?" and downed it.

"Now. About Cassandra." Sudden tears stood in his eyes, and he blinked. "Guy and Isabeth have provided electronic signatures on everything that needs to be signed. They've released the body to a funeral company, which will perform a cremation. Not what we would wish for, but otherwise everything is delayed. The director is seeing to the paperwork and working with the consulate to arrange for Cassandra to fly home with us. She'll be ready as soon as we are." He blew his nose. "I'm a foolish old Catholic who wants her to have a coffin even though she's only . . . only ashes now. If you don't like the casket I selected, we'll get another in Seattle."

"Oh, Rob," was all I managed.

He reached across the table. His hand was liver spotted, the veins like swollen rivers. I raised my eyes to his face, startled to see how the skin had shrunk around the bones. Uncle Rob had always been bigger than life to me. But now I saw him for what he was—a sixty-three-year-old man who'd just lost someone he deeply loved.

"Well," he said. He eased his hand free of mine and pulled a cigar from an inside pocket of his travel jacket. He looked at it ruefully. "Once, Raffles offered its customers Davidoff Dominicana cigars. Now?" He glanced around as if surveying just how far Raffles had fallen. "This hotel is as overregulated as the rest of the city. I miss the old days."

"When were you last at Raffles?"

He sighed and tucked away the cigar. "I was twenty-six. Pop and Nana brought Guy and me to stay here. They came through Singapore when they fled Europe after the war, and they wanted us to see the place. Not that they could afford to stay at Raffles their first time through." His smile was sweet, his gaze far away. "Pop and I spent delightful evenings smoking and drinking in the billiard room."

I retrieved the mezuzah from my purse and placed it on the table in front of him. "I found this at Cass's condo."

For a moment Rob didn't move. Then he pressed his index finger against the inscribed Hebrew letters, his chin tucked toward his chest.

"Rob, were Pop and Nana Jewish?"

He jolted as if my words startled him, then picked up the mezuzah and slid it into a pocket. "This should be at home on Bainbridge. You don't mind if I return it, do you? Cass had no right to take our mezuzah."

Charlie Han's words came like the whine of a mosquito: *Perhaps Cassandra felt there was nothing left to save, given that Ocean House was built on the bones of a questionable—even immoral—past.*

I said, "I'd like to know the truth about our family."

He lifted his eyes. "A lot of people changed their identities when they came to Singapore. Pop and Nana made that choice, and I respect it. Let sleeping dogs lie, Nadia."

I considered fighting him. But now wasn't the time. And it didn't seem terribly important with everything else that had happened. I intended to rouse the dog at some point—Cass had all but ordered me to. But I'd wait until the immediate crisis was over.

Rob twisted in his chair. "Where is that drink?"

A waiter entered the courtyard holding aloft a tray with a tall glass filled with bright-red spirits and garnished with slices of pineapple. He set the cocktail in front of Rob with a flourish.

"Excellent," Rob said. "Bring another, please. My niece is going to want one."

I shook my head. "It's too early for me."

"Nadia, trust me. You're going to want it. I did a lot of thinking on the flight over."

I took in the grim expression on his face and nodded my agreement to the waiter.

"Go light on the gin," I told him. "And add lots of ice."

Rob barked a sound that might have been a laugh. "She doesn't mean it. Bring me a second while you're at it. Heavy on the gin for both of us."

21

Raffles Hotel
August 29, 3:30 p.m. SGT

The afternoon sun became a blast furnace. Rob and I retreated farther into the shade. Fans beneath the eaves morosely pushed the air, cooling off nothing but the giant banana spiders hulking in the corners.

It was just us and Dai Shujun, sweltering.

Rob cleared his throat. "Naughty, I need you to hold your horses, button your lips, and ride the tide of what I'm about to tell you."

Unease hammered at my temples. "You're mixing your metaphors."

"There are worse crimes." He sighed, and the sadness in his eyes deepened. "I'm responsible for Cass's death."

"Oh, Rob, you're not. She—" I paused. What could I say to him? Not the truth.

"There's a lot going on that you don't know about," he said. "I'd hoped to talk to you before Guy sent you here, but I didn't get the chance. Still, better late than never. Ocean House will be yours one day, and I want you to go in with your eyes open."

A warm puff of air from the fan stirred my hair. A chorus of cicadas sounded from the greenery near the fountain, and a bird gave a loud *uwu* whistle.

"Go on." I braced myself.

Rob took a healthy swallow of his Singapore Sling, then set the glass down. A bee buzzed around the sweetness, and he waved it away.

"Cass and I—" He stopped, then restarted. "Ocean House is in worse straits than you think."

I don't know what, exactly, I'd been expecting. For Rob to tell me that he knew Cass was working with the CIA? That he understood the danger she'd been in? My mind was still with Connor in Saravanan's apartment; I hadn't given Ocean House's bottom line much thought other than that we couldn't risk losing the market in Asia.

I pivoted. "How bad is it?"

Rob dabbed the moisture from a drink coaster and fanned himself with it. "We're in the red. Deep."

I gaped at him. "Isabeth—that's not what her reports have said."

"We were wrong to hide the full extent of our troubles from you and Cassandra. It was Goebbels, I believe, who said that a lie told often enough becomes the truth. If that were the case, we'd have no worries at all."

I growled. "Rob."

"Wait. There's more." He swallowed more of his drink. "On top of our financial concerns, Paxton Yachts has bled off more of our talent than we let on. And I agree with your father—I think they had a hand in sabotaging *Rambler*."

As if Cass's death hadn't been enough, Rob's admission confirmed my cloak-and-dagger fears. At the monastery, Charlie Han had said that Paxton's funding came from the Chinese. Now I was struck by the weight of what that meant. The danger wasn't just to me; it was also to my family and Ocean House.

"Sabotage," I echoed. "Do we have proof?"

His sigh was almost a sob. "Cass was helping me troubleshoot *Rambler*." He looked away, fanning himself hard enough to stir his thick silver hair. "She knew what was at risk for us. And still I leaned on her. 'Finish *Red Dragon* ahead of schedule,' I told her as things went from bad to worse. 'Find more clients. We're *desperate*,' I said. 'It's on your shoulders.'"

"Rob, stop. Please. Cass was stronger than that. Whatever drove her to—to take her own life, it wasn't anything you did. But if Paxton is guilty as you say, then they must be held accountable."

"My Nadia." He patted his eyes with a cocktail napkin. "We've already lost one Brenner to this struggle; we can't risk losing another. After we take Cass home, I want you to remain in Seattle and focus all your energy on our domestic market. Build *Sovereign II* for Matthew. And while you're at it, maybe marry the guy—you've been stringing him along for years. I'll finish *Red Dragon*. And let me worry about Paxton and Asia. I'm not as young as I used to be, but I can still give as good as I get."

"Rob . . ." My voice trailed off into a thicket of things I couldn't say. I ignored his gibe about Matthew. "Let's get Cass home, and then we can think about the future. Maybe Asia isn't right for us just yet."

He reached over and squeezed my hand hard enough to hurt. "Don't tell me you've bought into your father's timidity."

Before I could respond, a vaguely familiar voice boomed, "I'll be damned! Rob Brenner!"

We both turned. Phil Weber was plowing toward us from across the courtyard. He wore tennis whites; as he approached, the childhood scent of coconut suntan lotion reached my nose.

Rob's face had gone the color of sea-foam. He pressed a hand to his chest, and I worried about his heart. But he stood as Weber approached and pasted on a smile. "Phil!" he cried. "My old tennis buddy. What a surprise."

Weber grasped Rob's hand in one of his and gripped Rob's elbow with the other. "It's very good to see you." He nodded at me. "And Nadia. A pleasure."

Rob waved Weber toward a chair. "Join us?"

I sneaked a glance toward Dai Shujun. He had abandoned the fountain and disappeared. Maybe he preferred I not point him out to Weber.

"I'll join you for a moment," Weber said. "Then I must be off. Tennis match with the British attaché, which is always humbling. The man has a wicked serve. I'm deeply sorry about your niece, Rob." He brought me into his gaze. "Nadia and I made our acquaintance recently. How are the two of you holding up?"

"We're doing as well as we can," Rob answered. "But it's good to see you, Phil. It's been, what, ten years?"

A note of warning sharpened Rob's voice, and a crease appeared between Weber's eyes—there and then gone. The ten years was a lie. What was that about?

Weber nodded. "Ten, at least," he agreed. "You still get out on the court?"

"No more tennis," Rob said. "I'm entirely too lazy. And work keeps me busy."

"You and Guy have done wonderful work with your grandfather's company. Congratulations on your success."

"You haven't done half-bad yourself."

Weber gave a half smile. "It's been a good run."

"You give up the old work?"

"Not at all." Weber's smile widened, revealing the large canines, but his eyes darkened. "Never stopped." He glanced at his watch and stood. "Good to chat with you both. Sorry I can't stay. I'd love to catch up. Maybe dinner?"

"We're flying out tomorrow," I said. "To take care of my sister."

"Of course." He clasped Rob's shoulder. "Your family is in my prayers. Don't hesitate to call me if you need anything. Anything at all."

Rob and I watched Weber walk the path toward the front drive. Rob picked up his drink and downed half of it.

"Son of a bitch," he said.

"What was that about the old work?"

"Phil used to be in law enforcement," he said shortly.

"And the lie about how long it's been since you saw each other?"

"Sometimes, my dear, you overread the room." He drained his glass and stood. "I'm going to check in and unpack. Probably take a short nap. Shall we meet in the lobby for dinner?"

"Let's make it six o'clock. We can eat here at the hotel and have an early night."

After Rob left, I checked in with our build supervisor, Owen Ewing. I explained that I'd be accompanying my uncle back to Seattle in the morning to take Cassandra's ashes, and that I trusted him and Andrew Declough to manage things while I was gone.

"When do you expect to return?" Ewing asked after expressing his condolences.

"It might be as long as a few weeks." I said this even as I knew that I was almost certainly not coming back. Nor was Rob, if I could prevent it. "I'll be in daily contact via video chat. And I can be back in Singapore within twenty-four hours if need be."

I ended the call, then phoned each of the managers on Cass's staff with the same news. Finished, I headed upstairs to shower and change, my heart constricted by guilt.

I could never tell my family the truth about Cass's death. Not without exposing Connor McGrath and risking Mr. Mèng's family.

Forgive me, Cass, for hiding the truth. And for not taking your place.

Again, I sensed her ghost dogging my footsteps as I mounted the stairs.

You're the one who must live with yourself, Nadia. Her voice seemed to echo down the hallway.

You're the one who said family is the most important thing, I shot back.

As I opened the door to my room, air-conditioning blasted me. I shivered in the sudden cold.

I drowned, Cass's ethereal voice murmured. *And you weren't there for me.*

22

Changi Airport
August 30, 5:30 a.m. SGT

Rob and I arrived at Changi Airport three hours before our 8:45 a.m. departure. Dawn was still an hour and a half away, the coming day's heat only a promise in the soft air. Faint stars shone in a milky sky as we disembarked with our luggage and headed inside.

We were met at customs by a woman from the funeral home, who assured us that Cassandra would be well cared for during the flight. We signed additional paperwork with a customs official, then watched as airport attendants rolled away her casket.

Rob put his arm around my shoulders. He didn't look as if he'd slept any better than I had. He was still on Seattle time, which meant the night was just starting for him. We settled in the United Airlines lounge, ordered breakfast, and watched the sky grow light. While Rob was pouring coffee, I opened my laptop and typed "Phillip Weber" in the search field and then narrowed my query down to "Phillip Weber of the CIA in Singapore." I wasn't looking for anything in particular, just operating on a hunch—something about Weber antagonized Rob. And Rob had lied about how long it had been since they'd seen each other.

I hoped information would pop up since Weber was a declared officer. But there wasn't anything, not even a photo on the embassy website.

There was also very little information about Weber's most recent years, which made sense given he worked for one of the most secretive intelligence agencies in the world. But according to a variety of articles and profiles, he had spent the first twenty years of his adulthood hunting Nazis, with a focus on Austrians who had been involved in the Final Solution. This wasn't an insignificant number; according to websites, 70 percent of those heading up concentration camps were Austrian. And most Austrians had welcomed the Nazi invasion of Austria.

The skin on my shoulders tingled, as if someone had opened a door to a cold Austrian winter. My great-grandparents had lived out the war in the town of Mattsee before immigrating to America. Josef Brenner had been a master craftsman and operations manager for a successful shipbuilding firm—there were a great many lakes and rivers in landlocked Austria.

What if the great family secret wasn't that Pop and Nana were Jews hiding behind a protective mask of Catholicism? What if instead of the hunted, they were the hunters? It would certainly explain Rob's antagonism toward Weber. On the other hand, if Pop had been a Nazi collaborator, why hadn't Weber exposed him?

I told myself I was overreacting. Making mountains out of molehills, as Rob often said. But I couldn't shake off my unease. *The only thing our parents got right is that family is the most important thing,* Cass had written, *and for that reason we owe ourselves the truth.*

Frantically, like a squirrel looking for its lost stash of nuts and acorns, I started entering search queries, using Boolean operators to be as specific as possible:

Josef Brenner AND Nazi Party AND Austria

Josef Brenner AND Nazis

Phillip Weber AND Josef Brenner OR Robert Brenner

The last query—Phillip Weber and Robert Brenner—led me to an article in the *Yale Alumni Magazine* that featured both men. A Yale journalism student had tracked down the former top players on the Bulldogs tennis team to get their thoughts on how their years as tennis aces had impacted their careers. Weber and Rob had been the stars on a team from the top-ranked Ivy League school. They had alternated as captain for their first three undergraduate years, and both claimed to have learned teamwork and leadership skills that had served them well in their careers.

Before their fourth year, Uncle Rob had dropped off the team.

In the interview, Weber spoke about his remarkable time as a Nazi hunter, saying, "The Webers suffered terribly during the war. Most of my grandmother's family in Austria were murdered. I decided to set myself up as a lone crusader for justice. Of course, I had some help." Here, according to the journalist, Weber had winked.

I looked up from my laptop. "Rob? What kind of law enforcement was Phil Weber in?"

Rob didn't look up from his phone. "Not sure. Interpol, maybe?"

Rob didn't know. I took that as a good sign and returned to my screen.

Weber had certainly had success. Over the twenty years he'd spent tracking down former SS members, Nazi officers, and collaborators, he'd assisted local authorities in South Africa, Canada, and Venezuela in arresting and detaining six of the Nazi Party's cruelest instruments of the Final Solution. A seventh had died under mysterious circumstances, and Weber was briefly questioned by the police in Rio.

I bookmarked the article and kept probing, moving from one search engine to another.

Forty minutes later, I sat back with relief. For a moment I'd been terrified that my great-grandfather had been on the wrong side in the modern world's greatest moral battle. But I'd found nothing to suggest Josef should be on Weber's list of former Nazis and collaborators.

Maybe Cass's theory was right: Pop and Nana were Jews who'd decided to conceal their identities.

I looked up at Rob again. "How did you and Weber meet?"

Rob sipped his coffee and held the ceramic mug in both hands. "What's the fascination with Weber?" His voice had taken on the rasp of burred metal.

I turned my laptop to show him the screen with the article on the Yale tennis team.

Rob rolled his eyes. "Yes, yes, we both attended Yale. And we played tennis together. What about it?"

"Articles about Weber say his family was originally from Austria. You two must have talked about the old country and your families."

"Weber talked. His family was important. Wealthy. Politically connected until the war and then again, years later. My grandfather was a mere boatman, far beneath the notice of people like the Webers."

A bitter note undergirded Rob's usually smooth demeanor. "Is that why you left the team?" I asked.

"I left because of a torn ACL. I had surgery two weeks before the start of the season."

"I'm sorry."

He set down his coffee and waved a dismissive hand. "It's ancient history. Look, my dear, we need to focus. I can't stay in Seattle for more than a week. Two at the most. Our delivery date is coming up fast. The first sea trial is scheduled for October eighteenth. That's seven weeks away."

I drew in my breath. Time for my pitch. "I need you to stay in Seattle with me, Rob. The family should be together. Owen Ewing and Andrew Declough are first rate—having them in Singapore allows us to manage *Red Dragon* from Seattle."

"You really are turning into your father." The burr had sharpened.

"I have my reasons. Please, Rob. Promise me you'll at least consider it."

He narrowed his eyes. "What if Mèng gets cold feet because we've run away and decides to hire Paxton to finish *Red Dragon*?"

"This late in the game? He won't." I couldn't tell Rob the truth: that by going to Paxton, Mèng knew he would be walking into a trap. "But even if he does, we'll get paid for our work, and we'll get credit for the design. Then we move on to other billionaires, starting with Matthew Hoffman. We will land on our feet. But I need you with me. Guy is . . ."

Dying, I almost said. Maybe it was time to break my deal with my father and tell Rob that in a matter of months—already shorn of Cass—we would go from four to three. Time to batten down the hatches.

But Rob's gaze had turned inward; he didn't seem to be listening.

My phone pinged. A message from United Airlines.

"It's almost time to board," I said. I would tell Rob about Guy on the plane.

We stood, gathered our belongings, then walked to the gate. As we waited for the announcement for priority boarding, Rob touched my sleeve.

"Old man's bladder. I'll be right back."

"I'll watch your carry-on." Rob had left most of his belongings in storage at Raffles for his planned return.

He shook his head. "I need something in there. Go ahead and board and order a scotch on the rocks for me. I won't be a minute."

I boarded and settled in and watched the stream of passengers moving toward the economy section. I felt bad for these travelers—I'd done enough international travel in economy to know how miserable it could be.

I pulled my laptop out of my carry-on and slid it into the seat pocket. Then I dug through my purse for my phone and checked my messages. I answered two from Emily and another from Owen Ewing.

By the time I was finished, Rob still hadn't reappeared. But the plane would be boarding for at least another half hour. I opened my laptop and forced myself to focus on *Red Dragon*'s scheduling details. I shot off an email to Andrew, requesting that he close a task and asking him to keep me apprised.

I looked up when the pilot introduced himself over the speaker and said that we'd be departing shortly. I dialed Rob but got no answer. When a flight attendant walked past, I stopped him.

"I'm concerned," I said. "My uncle hasn't boarded."

The attendant checked his iPad. "Robert Brenner? We've made an announcement for him at the gate."

"Thank you. I'll keep trying to reach him."

"I'll speak with the pilot," the attendant said. "But we can't give him more than ten minutes."

"I understand." But my heart pounded. I recalled the way he'd grabbed his chest when Weber appeared at our table. What if he'd collapsed in the bathroom? I unbuckled my seat belt, grabbed my belongings, and headed toward the exit.

And ran headlong into Dai Shujun.

Our eyes met; the tiger tattoo on his neck rippled as Dai looked down at me.

A wild card, Connor had called Dai. *Brutal,* Charlie Han had said. *Affiliated with crime syndicates,* according to Phil Weber.

I didn't think Dai was here to protect me from the Second Department.

The flight attendant returned. "I'm sorry, Ms. Brenner. No word from your uncle, but we can't wait any longer. I need you to return to your seat." He glanced at Dai. "You as well, sir."

I pointed at Dai. "This man has been stalking me. Can you please tell him that after we land, I'm going to report him to the authorities if I see him again outside baggage claim?"

The attendant's expression grew stern. He turned to Dai and spoke rapidly in what I presumed was Mandarin. Dai replied, and the attendant turned back to me.

"He says he is so sorry to alarm you. It is a misunderstanding. He has business and family in San Jose. But I'll mention him to airport personnel on the ground in San Francisco. For now, please return to your seat."

But I leaned toward Dai. "I'd better find out that you're on this flight because your beloved granny lives in San Francisco. If you follow me to my hometown, I'll report you to the FBI. Am I clear?"

Dai's expression didn't change. I held his gaze. My hands were shaking.

"Ms. Brenner," the flight attendant said.

Dai squeezed past me and headed toward the back of the plane.

"I'm getting off," I said.

Just then my phone pinged. I glanced down.

I am sorry to abandon you, my darling Nadia. But we must see Red Dragon through. I will be with you in spirit as you and your parents bury our Cassandra. Home soon. DON'T WORRY!

Sudden pain sliced through me. It wasn't like Rob to abandon both of his nieces.

"Damn it, Rob." I hovered, undecided. I couldn't leave Cassandra. Nor could I let Robert face whatever was happening in Singapore alone.

The attendant said, "The door is closing, Ms. Brenner. Are you staying or going?"

Reluctantly, I returned to my seat.

You're in danger, I texted Rob. Talk to Connor McGrath. Tell him you need protection.

I have Weber. The old bastard will protect me.

Weber???

Yes. Three dots floated on my screen, indicating Rob was still typing. Then, It's on the Q.T. darling. Forgive my evasiveness but I know the score. Weber has got my back. No worries. I'll explain all later.

I stabbed at the keyboard. Explain now.

C in on it. We made a deal. We need this for OH. Don't tell Guy.
I love you.

You made a deal with Phil? What deal?

I stared at the green rectangles on my screen. The three dots had disappeared. Rob had gone silent on me.

The plane's exterior door closed. The flight attendant appeared at my shoulder. "Ms. Brenner, I need you to stow your laptop."

I tucked the computer in my briefcase and nudged it under the seat. I switched my phone to airplane mode. Around me, passengers donned headsets and began scrolling through the movie options. I swallowed a pill for my usual flight anxiety and watched out the window as the island of Singapore dropped away and the waters of the South China Sea spread below, its rippling blue surface hummocked with distant islands.

Cass and Rob had made a deal with Phil Weber. Weber worked for the CIA. Which meant Rob had known all along the danger Cass was in. And he'd let her face it without him.

I'm responsible for Cass's death, he'd told me.

Cass had written on her postcard: *Remember what Guy used to tell us about trust?*

To the vanishing island of Singapore I whispered, "Trust no one."

PART 2

One life is all we have and we live it as we believe in living it. But to sacrifice what you are and to live without belief, that is a fate more terrible than dying.

—Joan of Arc

23

Seattle, Washington
September 21, 1:30 p.m. PDT

We buried Cass on a gray and windy Sunday afternoon on a hillside that gave her a view of her beloved Lake Washington, the city of Seattle, and the distant cranes of our shipyard.

Guy, Isabeth, and I sat in the front row in white folding chairs, close to Cass's coffin and the open grave. The news of my father's dying had yet to break—our fellow mourners would ascribe his ashen complexion and sunken cheeks to grief. Until the media got the scoop, my parents and I were very good at pretending that—other than the coffin containing Cass's ashes—we were fine.

While the priest spoke and the chairs of the mourners creaked and birdsong spilled from the trees, I turned inward, my thoughts churning through the past days.

—

Every day since my return, I'd been on video calls with Rob and the managers in Singapore as we worked to finalize *Red Dragon*. Rob and I never spoke of Phil Weber or whatever deal he and Cass had cut with the CIA officer. Sorrow and fury simmered beneath my surface, but I did what I was masterful at—I compartmentalized my feelings enough that I could remain civil toward Rob, and we could work efficiently with each other and the team. Rob assured me that he was safe and well, and I left it at that. But I wondered whether I could ever feel close to him again.

On two separate occasions after my return home, I picked up my phone, intending to dial Connor. Unsure what it was I wanted—forgiveness for running, absolution for being a coward, the assurance that the Mèng family's defection would move forward—I never placed the call. With Rob now handling our contract with NeXt Level Security, my relationship with Connor was over.

From Inspector Lee, I received Cass's Confirmation of Death number and a digital link with which we could download her death certificate. He included a handwritten letter informing me that Cass's case had been officially ruled a suicide and was now closed and that he was deeply sorry for my family's loss. In the last line of his note, he wrote that he was glad I had returned to Seattle.

I busied myself with the work for Matthew's *Sovereign II* and took the next steps in designing a yacht for his friends Warren and Leanne Korda, who—despite the loss of *Rambler*—had signed a letter of intent. When I received word that two more of our designers had decamped to Paxton Yachts, I rolled up my sleeves and—because it was both my job and a distraction—began scrutinizing Paxton: I read about them in the news and the yachting rags, tracked them through their social media, tried to lift the hood on their financial postings. I discovered a gleaming, wholesome surface and knew it would take more skills than I had to uncover any link to the Chinese-based funding that Charlie Han had alluded to. I picked up the phone and put one of our financial wizards on it. "Nothing illegal," I said. "Nothing that will tarnish our name." He promised to get back to me with whatever he found.

The incident with the failed yacht, *Rambler*, still loomed. Rob had leaned hard into the suppliers, and several errors concealed by falsified reports had been uncovered in an audit. It was enough to allow us to suggest, although not prove, that *Rambler* hadn't failed due to any lack of engineering or oversight from Ocean House.

But I wanted proof, not media speculation or panicked accusations from Rob and Guy. A week after my return and another week before Cass's service, I picked up the phone and called Matthew.

"Welcome home," he said. "It's good to hear your voice."

"And yours."

I gave him the date for Cass's funeral, and he promised to do his best to attend despite a conflict in his schedule.

I stared at the disorganized mess of papers on my desk. "I need a favor. You've heard about *Rambler*?"

"It made the news. And nearly scared off the Kordas."

"Guy and Rob suspect sabotage."

Matthew's disbelief showed in his laugh. "Why would anyone sabotage your build?"

"That was my reaction, too. At first. But"—I took my phone off speaker and held it to my ear—"now I've got a hunch they might be right. Do you have someone among your thousands of employees who could investigate? Outside the normal channels, I mean."

A pause. "Are you asking for a hacker?"

"It would be a quick in and out, wouldn't it? Not risky."

"Hacking is always risky. And I can't believe I'm hearing this from my law-abiding, nonconfrontational Nadia."

"Are those the reasons you're fond of me? For my conformity?"

"That along with your beauty and brilliance. Send me what you've got on *Rambler*. No promises."

"I owe you."

"Never say that to a commodities trader."

After we hung up, I leaned back in my office chair and stared at the ceiling, surprised and quietly pleased by my own audacity.

Yet, even as I buried myself in the joy of designing *Sovereign II* and the necessity of my other work, I remained fearful that my departure from Singapore hadn't removed the threat of the Second Department or the Guóānbù—Charlie Han's Ministry of State Security. And what of Dai Shujun and his ties to Chinese gangs? With a fascination that was at first morbid and then horrified, I read articles on the immensity of the Chinese triads' operations inside America's borders—drugs, human trafficking, money laundering, fraud. Twice I thought I spotted Dai Shujun at Seattle's Pike Place Market; he melted into the crowd before I could be sure. Another man, an Asian whom I called Smoking Man, stopped daily outside our office building, standing on the pier with his cigarettes, smoking and watching before strolling south. I sent one of our security guards out to have a chat with him. The man offered Tom one of his cigarettes, and they smoked and shared a laugh. "He loves boats," Tom informed me when he returned. "No worries. Just a man on a walk."

Maybe. But maybe not.

I installed an additional lock on my apartment door and placed a camera at the top of the stairs that led to my residence. I bought a Taser and kept it near me. I began running and lifting weights again, working to get back into the fighting shape of my twenties. In addition to training my body, I trained my mind. I hired an online tutor and studied Mandarin, read up on Confucianism, and dipped into Sun Tzu's *Art of War*.

When I committed, I committed.

Three days before Cass's service, after I'd drunk two fingers' worth of Glenlivet single malt, I got a tattoo—my matching yin to Cass's yang.

I approached the graveside as a hawk shrieked overhead. The wind had fallen quiet, the afternoon darker. Mist filled the air and a chill had crept in. The priest nodded at me. I tossed earth onto Cass's coffin.

I'm sorry that you died and that you were probably terrified and that I wasn't there for you. I'm sorry I didn't visit more often. And I'm sorry that I'm not brave like you, Cass. Nor honorable. You were always the best of us.

I turned and walked away from her grave, slipping through the crowd so that I didn't have to watch the gravediggers move in as the ceremony ended. At the edge of the knot of people, I stared out over the cemetery, which was wet and gloomy, olive green and marble gray in the dull light. Trees stood in clumps, a few of their leaves already yellow and orange, bright against the wrought iron fence. My gaze fixed on a stone mausoleum with an open doorway, and I thought that I would sit there whenever I came to visit Cass, safe from rain and sun and curious eyes.

A figure moved in the mausoleum's shadows.

I stared.

Dai Shujun.

My knees buckled. Someone nearby caught me.

I couldn't live with fear like this. A day-to-day grind of watching over my shoulder, sprinting from my car to my apartment door, ordering groceries for pickup, and constantly wondering why a man might be watching me.

"It will get better," murmured the woman who'd caught me. She helped me straighten before nodding at my thanks and rejoining her companions.

I looked again toward Dai Shujun.

And now, as the man stepped clear of the doorway, I saw that I was wrong. It wasn't Dai, but another man I recognized. I'd seen his picture in our company files. In photos taped to the back of Cass's headboard. Early forties, slim and handsome, today he was dressed in a black suit and tan trench coat.

George Mèng, manifesting in the cemetery like a ghost from the other side of the world.

24

Seattle, Washington
September 21, 3:00 p.m. PDT

I pushed my way to the edge of the throng of mourners.

Around me, people stopped to give my arm a squeeze or to offer a quick hug before merging into the stream of attendees heading downhill toward their cars—umbrellas up, wet grass clinging to their shoes, tiptoeing around goose droppings. With the conclusion of the funeral rites, friends scattered like startled crows, eager to escape the weather and our palpable grief. They would reflock at the reception, far away from the coffin and its gaping hole.

I told Isabeth and Guy I needed a little time with Cass, and that I would see them soon. I stood in the rain until the last of the mourners disappeared down the hill. Car doors slammed, engines roared to life. Two employees began folding and stacking the chairs.

The gravediggers moved in.

In person, George Mèng was gracious, a slim figure with a vaguely distracted demeanor. After we shook hands, we seated ourselves across from each other on a pair of stone benches.

"I am deeply sorry about Cassandra," he said. "She was not only creating and building *Red Dragon*. She was a friend to me and my family."

Mèng's voice was crisp and clear with a faint New England accent. From studying at MIT, I recalled Connor saying.

I didn't mince words. "I'm of no use to you, Mr. Mèng. I'm not going back to Singapore. If you came all this way to ask for my help, I'm sorry."

"That's not why I'm here."

His words surprised me. "Then why?"

"I came to apologize to you and pay my respects to Cassandra. I also came to warn you."

"Dai Shujun," I said. "I know. Is he here as an agent of MSS, or does he have another agenda?"

Mèng looked surprised. "MSS, as far as I know. And there are others." He removed a pack of cigarettes and turned them in his hand. "It's brutally simple. You cannot escape what is happening in Singapore by running away."

"I didn't run away," I snapped, as if it mattered. "I came home with"—my voice broke—"my dead sister."

Mèng's hands stilled on the pack. "My words were harsh. I apologize. But you need to understand why returning to Seattle won't help you. Your name, unlike your uncle's, is on a list held by the MSS—the Guóānbù. And by the Second Department."

"A list?"

"Names of people suspected of spying against China."

I huddled into my raincoat and choked out a laugh. "That's ludicrous. I never spied for anyone." I rubbed my palms against the bench. "Why me but not my uncle?"

"I believe Phil Weber has managed to shield Robert. Plus, their focus is on you as the future of Ocean House in Asia."

The rain came harder, pounding on the stones of the mausoleum and splashing through the doorway, sheeting across the floor, and spattering our shoes. Outside, the gravediggers had closed Cass's grave and were laying down fresh sod.

In the dull light Mèng tapped out a cigarette and offered the pack to me. I shook my head.

He said, "Dai Shujun's only job is to observe you. To watch, listen, and follow, then report back to the Guóānbù. Wherever you are, Dai will also be. Wherever you go, Dai and others will follow."

Smoking man. I hunched into the shadows. "Are they here now?"

"Dai has been lured to a coffee shop by one of my associates. We have a few minutes."

I glanced through the arched doorway; the gravediggers were packing down the sod. "You've made a long trip across the Pacific to offer condolences and a warning."

He tapped his cigarette on the pack but made no move to light it. "I believe it every person's duty to do the right thing when and as they can. My government would tell me that meeting you is not correct. But what do I know? I'm only a scientist who tries to follow the tenets of Confucianism because I believe those principles teach us how to live a virtuous life. Loyalty. Justice. Respect. Harmony. I'm not made for this world of shadow play."

"And yet you're an asset for the CIA."

His glance was sharp. "I'm not."

I shrugged. Likely I'd never know the truth. But I felt an unexpected rush of camaraderie with this near stranger. If he were a spy, he probably wouldn't be happy about it.

"I'm not cut out for it, either," I said.

"And you shouldn't be." Mèng pocketed the cigarette pack, then leaned forward and rested his elbows on his knees, balancing the unlit cigarette between his fingers. "You and I are civilians, each with our own passions and the desire to pursue them without interference. All we know of tradecraft is that it is dangerous and sometimes immoral. I hope spies will save my family. Perhaps even the world. But I don't pretend to understand them."

The rain turned back into mist. I rose and went to the doorway, leaning against the damp stones of the arch, where I could watch both Mèng and the graveyard.

"If I'm on a list of names, how do I get off of it?"

"You don't. But soon the list won't matter. Dai will follow you until *Red Dragon* is delivered, then disappear like smoke along with other watchers. All you must do for now is stay away from Singapore and China. Maybe stay away from China forever."

"Not a problem. There are other yacht markets in Asia." I toed a puddle of water. "The first time I saw Dai Shujun, he was having dinner with an employee of the CIA, Phil Weber."

"Dai is probably providing false information to CIA. I'm sure Weber knows he can't be trusted. But for CIA to check in with Dai now and again gives Weber an excuse to watch him."

"Weber pulled Rob and Cass into this."

Mèng nodded. "He has some hold over your family. Cassandra wouldn't tell me."

A hold. From Weber the Nazi hunter. "As in blackmail?"

"I'm sorry, I don't know."

Our family. I hadn't given the mezuzah or Cass's trip to Austria much thought since I'd been home. "Charlie Han implied there is something questionable in my family's past. Cass once theorized that our great-grandparents were Jewish. A shock for this Catholic girl, but neither terrible nor a crime. But maybe it's worse. Maybe they were Nazis."

Mèng's face shone pale in the gloom. "Is there any family untouched by hatred? In my family and Charlie Han's are ancestors who joined China's Cultural Revolution. They participated in massacres. Desecrations. As many as two million people died. As for Charlie Han . . ." Mèng stuck the unlit cigarette in the corner of his mouth and patted his pockets for a lighter. "Han is pursuing his own vendetta against me under the guise of an MSS operation. He wants to destroy my family the way he believes my father destroyed his."

It seemed we all had our family troubles. "*Did* your father destroy his?"

Mèng's headshake was faint. And sad. "Many years ago, my father was the governor of Qinghai Province on the Tibetan Plateau, where Han's family lived. Han's sister was caught up in a sweep of anti-government protesters and imprisoned. It was my father's duty to oversee the sentencing, and the sentences he handed down were harsh. He was not given a choice. The party spoke, and he had to obey. To go against the party would have led to his own imprisonment and endangered our family."

"Han must know this."

Mèng gave a soft shrug as he removed a lighter from an inside pocket. "Revenge is easier than forgiveness. Han knows only that he cannot blame the party to which he's sworn allegiance. Doing so would create an internal battle he cannot face. He must blame my father, not the CCP. He will stand by his duty."

"As your father's duty was to hand down sentences to the protesters."

"Yes."

"Duty," I echoed. Duty to family, to community, to the state. I'd always seen responsibility as a virtue. But the choice to obey laws and follow orders was showing me its gray side.

"Do you mind if I smoke?" Mèng asked. "It's become a nervous habit."

"A common one, apparently." I was thinking of myself and Connor in Dr. Saravanan's kitchen. "Go ahead."

"Thank you."

I hugged myself in my coat as the sharp odor of tobacco floated toward me. "Truthfully, Mr. Mèng, I don't know what I should do with your apology. My sister is dead. Your regret won't bring her back or keep me safe."

"I understand." He released a cloud of gray smoke. "Cassandra adored you."

The same words Connor had used.

"I would have protected you if I'd been able. Told you to leave immediately. I was in China and unaware either of your arrival in Singapore or that Cassandra and her handler had been murdered. On the day I got the news of their deaths, I was called before the party in Beijing. One does not allow a summons from the Chinese Communist Party to go unanswered. I asked Emily to warn you in my stead."

I glanced through the open doorway. A sparrow huddled on the branch of a nearby pine. Water dripped from the needles. "Emily did warn me, although not right away. But I don't trust her."

"Emily—like so many of my countrymen—is trying to protect herself and her family. It isn't easy to be a good person in Communist China. Emily's family was threatened. Her brother briefly arrested under charges of sedition. Due to great pressure, Emily was—as your intelligence services would say—compromised. She took tremendous risk in warning you."

I rounded on him. "Yet you let her work with Cass, *knowing* she was compromised."

"Cassandra also knew. But she understood that Emily was trapped and trusted that although she might be under the thumb of her government, their friendship meant she wouldn't betray Cassandra. I had no choice but to keep Emily in my employ—it was part of our pretense that everything was normal. Cassandra felt she should do the same. We kept information strictly compartmentalized, and Emily's presence, ironically, helped us maintain appearances."

"Keep your friends close and your enemies closer?"

"In a way. Under the guise of a typical build, Cassandra fed Emily misinformation about *Red Dragon*. Misinformation that would ensure Guóānbù didn't learn what we were doing."

The floor plan I'd found in Cassandra's locked safe on my second day in Singapore. The specs with the phantom room. Had Emily seen them?

"But Emily must have told the Guóānbù something. Why else was Cass killed?"

"We don't yet know what happened that night."

"I know too many people are dying."

"Please believe me, Miss Brenner. I will carry the deaths of Cassandra, Virgil, and the security guard forever."

I stared. "What guard?"

"A man was murdered in the shipyard near *Red Dragon* six months ago. We suspect Charlie Han."

I pictured Han's rough hands and shuddered. "I didn't know."

Mèng stubbed out his cigarette and rubbed his eyes with his palms. When he lowered his hands, pain showed plainly on his face. At this, something inside me eased. I began to understand why Cassandra had liked Mèng. He'd said it was hard to be a good person in China. And yet he had tried.

Tears filled my eyes. I turned my back to Mèng and stared out the doorway.

A solitary figure in black was climbing the hill. He carried white roses.

"We have company," I said.

Mèng came to stand beside me. "Do you know him?"

Warmth filled my chest as I realized I did. "It's okay. He's a friend. Matthew Hoffman."

We both watched as Matthew laid the roses at the base of Cassandra's headstone, his head bent as if in prayer.

"You should go," Mèng said. "We cannot risk being seen together. Not even by a friend. I will wait here until you are safely away."

I held out my hand. "I wish you luck, Mr. Mèng. I'm sorry that I'm not courageous like my sister."

We shook, and a soft smile lifted his features. "We each find courage in our own ways, Miss Brenner. Design your beautiful boats. Create a future. Find a way to be happy."

I stepped free of the mausoleum. Matthew had straightened and was already heading back down the hill.

"Nadia," Mèng said.

I turned.

"I want you to know that Cassandra died for something important. Not only my family, but RenAI. My AI has the potential to be as deadly as Oppenheimer's bomb. And before she died, Cass went a long way in keeping it out of the wrong hands. Knowing this about her won't bring her back. But maybe it will offer comfort."

I thought about the nuclear arms race. The Cold War. Mutually assured destruction. Since my return home, I'd read predictions from experts that AI was as dangerous to humans as global pandemics and nuclear war. That, ultimately, AI would drive humans extinct.

If the Chinese managed to keep RenAI, how could the technology be countered? What would balance the scales?

Mèng seemed to understand my thoughts. "Unlike chess, there is no winning move. I chose in my ignorance to create Ren, unaware the technology has no limits. You chose, in your wisdom about yourself, to acknowledge your limits. You are wiser than I."

From behind me came the flutter of wings as the sparrow fled. "How do we live with these choices, Mr. Mèng?"

But he shook his head. "For that, I have no answer."

25

Seattle, Washington
September 21, 4:00 p.m. PDT

I caught up with Matthew at the bottom of the hill. Wordlessly, he opened his arms, and I walked into them.

"I'm sorry," he said. "I'm so sorry."

I collapsed against his chest and wept.

We sat in the front seat of my Porsche. Matthew had picked up a local sauvignon blanc, and we passed the chilled bottle back and forth.

He lifted a strand of my hair, let it fall between his fingers. "Was it rough in Singapore?"

I closed my eyes as his hand moved to massage the back of my neck.

"It was," I said. "Singapore killed Cassandra. It nearly killed me."

His hand froze. "What?"

I'd spoken without thinking. I moved my neck beneath his palm. "Don't stop."

His fingers found the back of my skull and gently rubbed. "Nadia?"

I opened my eyes.

He removed his hand and regarded me with an expression caught between surprise and confusion. "What are you talking about?"

I'd always leaned on Matthew for advice. He was twenty years my senior, a brilliant businessman and strategist, with rumored connections to the inner sanctums of the major powers—the US, China, Russia, France, and the UK. His intelligence had lured me into his bed, but also guaranteed I'd never allow our relationship to deepen. I didn't want to run in his circles.

If I told him the truth of what was happening now, he would take it on himself to intercede. And that would put him at risk.

"I was being metaphorical," I said. "The work was hard. Cassandra and I both struggled. That's all."

The Porsche's cabin was becoming overly warm. I turned down the fan. In the quiet, the sound of rain filtered in. Rainwater gushed along the curb.

"Something more happened than Cass dying," he said. "You're spooked."

"I *am* spooked. Cass took her life, and I insisted on seeing her body. I will live with that. But also, men are watching George Mèng, and they were watching me as well. It rattled me. But I'm home now. And in a matter of weeks, Rob will commission the boat to Mèng. We'll be out of Singapore."

Matthew pulled back. Unless I planned to bring him into my confidence—and I didn't—I was playing with fire. Matthew was a master at reading people. And he hated being lied to as much as I did.

His frown wrinkled his entire face. "Has this build gotten you tangled up with China's Guóānbù? They're bad news, Nadia."

Leave it to Matthew to know about China's Ministry of Secret Services. But I was pretty good with my own poker face.

"Never heard of them. But if so, it's over now. I swear, Matthew. I'm okay."

His face softened. "Whatever you want from me, you know you only need ask. If you want an army of bodyguards, I'll have them delivered to your door." He caught my hand and kissed the palm. His lips were warm.

I ran my fingers through his hair.

"Marry me," he said.

Now I was the one to laugh. But he didn't join me.

My laughter died. "You're serious," I said.

I expected a quip, but he said: "Marry me. I'll travel the world with you. Wherever your work takes you."

"Matthew. I care very much for you. But you move in circles that are light-years beyond where I want to be. I love what we have. Why ruin it?"

"Stop there," he said. The lightness vanished from his face. "Just don't say no. Not right away. I have terrible timing. You're mourning your sister. Just know that the offer stands for a year."

"Only a year?" I teased.

"With an automatic renewal for five." He leaned across the console and kissed me. "If you need me, and I mean for anything, call me. I'd love nothing better than to be your knight in shining armor."

"I could use one right now."

"Yeah?"

I touched the empty wine bottle. My head was floating. "I need a ride to my parents'."

Later, after the reception at my parents' home on Bainbridge Island, after Matthew left to board his private plane to return to his conference, I went searching for my father.

The house Cassandra and I had grown up in was a rambling rancher with six bedrooms, a library and den, a gourmet-size kitchen, all surrounded by tall pines. The best features were the wraparound deck and—across the yard—a long stairway down to the dock and the fifty-foot family yacht, *Redemption*.

I'd stayed away from Bainbridge when I first returned from Singapore, worried about Dai Shujun and Smoking Man. But Guy and Isabeth's address wasn't a secret; my absence didn't keep them safe. I began to come often to have dinner and to sit in the bedroom I'd once shared with Cass. Sitting on my old bed, I gazed at pictures from our childhood and teen years and pretended that the last month hadn't happened.

This evening, when I couldn't find Guy, I changed my clothes, gave up on the house, and went out the front door. My father half rose from the porch steps when he heard me coming.

"Hiding?" I asked.

"Nadia. Come sit with me."

I lowered myself onto the stairs. "You holding up?"

"No. But at least with everyone gone I don't have to pretend."

I longed to lean against him, find comfort in his warmth. But that wasn't Guy's way.

I zipped my hoodie. "I can't believe Rob didn't come back for the service."

Guy patted my knee. "Remember, he's doing Cass's work. Completing her masterpiece. What better way for him to help me and honor her?"

I heard the implied criticism: Rob had to go in and finish what I couldn't.

But I had no fight in me. "I miss her."

"Me too." He nudged his shoulder against mine—Guy's version of a hug. "Let's take *Redemption* out."

"You sure?"

He grasped the railing and pulled himself to his feet, waving away my help. "If you think I'm too sick to handle a fifty-foot boat, then shoot me now."

"I'll get a gun," I said. But I was smiling as I put my arm around his newly thin shoulders and gave him a brief squeeze. "Let me grab our windbreakers."

We motored out of the small cove as the clouds lifted and the setting sun's reflection lit our way across the water. I stood at the helm while Guy sat on a stool next to me. We cruised past the lower part of Whidbey Island on a heading toward Port Townsend. When no dangerous men materialized in speedboats, I relaxed and let the peace of the water seep into my skin.

I shifted the engine's gears—*Redemption* purred as I opened the throttle, and we headed north.

"Penny for your thoughts," Guy said.

I glanced over in surprise. "You've never said that to me."

"Death has a way of encouraging a man to rectify past mistakes."

"You mean Cass's death."

"And my own."

"Don't be morbid," I snapped, having had enough thoughts of death for one day.

But he grinned. "Getting sentimental about your old man?"

"You flatter yourself."

He laughed.

I looked out again toward the water and the billowing gold of cumulus clouds near the horizon. A brief haze of tears blurred my vision. It was hard watching this man—who had been a giant throughout my life—turn frail. Bowed, his belly gone, the gauntness of his face only partially concealed behind a new beard.

For both our sakes, I changed the subject. Feigning nonchalance, I said, "Why did Pop name this boat *Redemption*?"

He shot me a look. "What makes you ask?"

"Seems like something I should know. Maybe tell my kids someday."

Guy sucked in a deep breath and let it go. "Two months ago, I would have given you a pat answer about how the Brenners redeemed themselves from a life of manual labor and became the kings of the luxury boat business."

"And now?"

He stared westward, past me, his blue eyes still vivid, the setting sun giving his face a false vitality.

"You are the sole heir to Ocean House," he said. "Which means you are also the sole heir to the family skeletons."

I slowed the boat until we bobbed on the swells pushing their way into Puget Sound. I motored toward a small island and dropped anchor in a quiet cove surrounded by high rock walls and wind-twisted pines. I shut off the engine and released the anchor. The lonely cry of a loon echoed around us.

"Then I guess it's time I knew," I said.

26

Puget Sound
September 21, 6:30 p.m. PDT

Guy and I sat on the sundeck. I switched on *Redemption*'s string of fairy lights, dug out a bottle of Glenlivet, and collected cheese and crackers from the galley. I poured a finger of whisky for each of us, then took the cushioned sunbed next to his, kicking off my deck shoes and tucking my feet beneath me. I spread a blanket over our laps as a damp chill filled the evening.

"Goddamned miserable day." Guy swallowed half his Glenlivet, glanced sidelong at me, and cleared his throat. "I hate this."

I felt a childish lick of satisfaction. "Suck it up, buttercup." Words I'd heard often enough as a kid, whether it was a skinned knee or a broken heart.

Guy set down his glass and smacked my thigh. It felt like the brush of a bird's wing. "Buttercup, my ass. I don't know where to start."

"Why don't I make it easy for you." I fixed him with a grave stare. "Are we Jewish?"

He looked at me from beneath thinning eyebrows. "What makes you think that?"

"Pop's mezuzah. I saw him with it when I was little. Then I found it in Cass's condo."

Guy shook his head. "No, Naughty. We're not Jewish. We're . . ."

He paused. Reluctantly, the idea like lead in my stomach, I moved to the next conclusion. "We're Nazis."

"Seems like you've already got the story."

The weight morphed into burning coals in my gut. *Nazis.* Was this what Charlie Han had been alluding to when he talked about our immoral past? And if so, how had he learned about it?

I stared down at my glass. "Did Cass know?"

"I never talked to her. And Rob would sooner shoot himself than tell anyone. He's haunted by the idea that any surviving Kleins might come after us for reparation. How'd you guess?"

"I followed breadcrumbs. But I'd like to hear the full story."

"I don't think I know the full story. Rob might. Our past always mattered more to him."

Guy reached into his pants pocket and pulled out a small velvet pouch and tossed it to me.

I snatched it out of the air. "What is this?"

"Your inheritance."

I untied the thin blue ribbon and upended the contents of the pouch into my palm. I gasped. Shining in the fairy lights, a painting of a woman's face gazed up at me. She wore a crown and necklace and a half smile. Her eyes were kind. The painting was set in a brooch of gold adorned with tiny emeralds and diamonds.

"Is she family?"

"Maybe. That's Sisi, also known as Empress Elisabeth of Austria, who died under an assassin's knife. Family legend says that Sisi gifted the brooch to a distant cousin, a young man, who passed it along to a beautiful servingwoman whom he wooed, married, and impregnated. Not necessarily in that order."

I nodded. This much of the story I knew, although I'd never seen the brooch. "The servingwoman was Josef's mother. The family forced an annulment."

"And the young man fled for distant parts. Here's the thing, Naughty. I don't know if the story is true, or if Josef stole that brooch. I don't suppose we'll ever know."

"There are DNA tests."

He shrugged. "That's up to you. To me, whether we have royalty in our background or Nazis, or both, doesn't matter. What matters is who we are now."

I slid the glittering brooch back into the pouch. When Guy gestured for me to keep it, I dropped it inside a zippered pocket.

"You're unraveling my identity," I said. "Gone are the aristocratic Brenners. In their place, monsters."

"But I'm not, little lion," he said, using my other childhood nickname. "Your identity doesn't depend on your family."

"Rob would say Ocean House is built on a lie."

"He's wrong. Ocean House is built on hard work and talent."

I pulled my knees up to my chest and wrapped my arms around my shins. "Tell me what you know about our Nazi past."

"You're sure you want the gory details?" I nodded, and he settled himself against the cushions. "Fine. You know the first part of the story. Your great-grandfather Josef, whom all of us called Pop, was a carpenter for Klein Marine in the Austrian town of Mattsee. Klein specialized in yachts for the gilded crowd. Any given day, you could spot a flotilla of Klein yachts on Mattsee Lake, sails rippling, a white wake behind them—the most beautiful sight in the world, my father said."

I relaxed into the story. I'd listened to Pop talk about the lake's teal-blue waters, its grassy shores studded with trees, the red-roofed village homes, the Benedictine abbey's Gothic steeple.

And, of course, the boats.

"It was good work, a solid paycheck," Guy went on. "But although your great-grandfather put himself through night school and worked harder than anyone else in the shipyard, the Klein family didn't promote him. The engineering positions he longed for were reserved for members of the family. A peasant like Josef Brenner was not welcome into their exalted ranks."

"Josef didn't tell them about his aristocratic past?"

Guy shrugged. "We'll never know. If he had, they probably would have laughed. Josef was hired in 1932, when he was only seventeen. This was the year before Adolf Hitler became chancellor of Germany. In Austria, the National Socialist German Workers' Party was illegal, but it carried huge appeal for working-class men like Josef. People whose ambitions were thwarted by the wartime economy and who found themselves unable to get ahead."

"Were the Kleins Jewish?"

"As Jewish as Mother Mary and Joseph."

I took a hefty swallow of the whisky, then set my glass aside. I was tonight's designated driver. Guy could drink for the both of us.

"When the government weakened under hyperinflation," my father continued, "the Austrian middle class, including Josef and Hedy, struggled to obtain basic goods. While Josef labored for the Kleins, my young grandmother began bartering for daily necessities—milk, eggs, flour. She turned bitter at the family's loss of economic security and their former standing in the community. When a German immigrant whispered to Josef that it was the Jews holding him back, Josef resisted. But as the economy bottomed out and people said it was the fault of the Jews, Josef had a change of heart. He joined the National Socialist German Workers' Party, otherwise known as—"

"The Nazi Party. He was—"

"Card carrying."

The wake from a passing coast guard vessel lifted *Redemption* and gently resettled her. Guy nodded toward the bottle of Glenlivet. "Pour. And this time, be generous."

I poured.

Guy continued, "The Workers' Party was, as I said, illegal. But it offered Josef what he wanted—the assurance that he was superior to the very men keeping him down. After Austria was annexed into the German Reich, the government seized Klein Marine, which they considered vital to the war effort. Officials sent the family's women and children to Ravensbrück, most of the men to Mauthausen, and turned the entire enterprise over to an Aryan businessman. That businessman anointed the top-ranking Nazi Party employee to manage the factory and shipyard."

"Josef."

"It's ugly, Nadia. But what else could he do?" Guy's voice was oddly gentle. "My grandfather accepted the position, but in doing so, he managed to save three members of the family and a handful of Jewish workers. As Klein Marine was retooled to build marine engines for the war effort, Josef convinced the party to let him retain Asher Klein and his sons, Ethan and Elias, along with a few others. He risked his own standing by going before the state inspector—the Landesinspekteur—to argue that the Nazi Party needed these men's expertise."

"A real Oskar Schindler," I said. I'd meant it to sound snarky. But my voice was only sad.

Guy leaned in, his eyes dark. "People do what they must to survive. He could have buried those men."

"And they agreed to work, even as their wives and daughters went to the gas chambers?"

Guy held my gaze another moment, then turned away. "They wouldn't have known the true purpose of the camps. Not then. I imagine Asher Klein and his sons thought they'd be reunited with their families after the war ended. Eventually, though, when Josef could no longer protect them, the Klein men were also sent to their deaths."

"An entire family." For a moment, I couldn't find air. "Simply . . . wiped out."

"Possibly there are other Kleins, perhaps in Israel or America. But of Asher's extended family in Mattsee . . . as far as I know, all of them perished."

Speechless, I stared into the gloaming. Another loon, or perhaps the same one, cried from the water. Stars fanned overhead, a spray of diamonds like the ones on Sisi's brooch. Water lapped at the *Redemption*'s hull, a soothing sound that had rocked me to sleep many a night when I was a child, but which offered no solace now.

After a time I said, "Ocean House is built on the blood and bones of people we helped kill."

"We didn't help kill them."

"Neither did we help them escape."

"I know, Naughty. It's a horrible story. Now you understand why Rob has worked so hard to hide it from both competitors and clients. He's afraid it will destroy us."

"It *is* a horrible story." I turned to face him. "But you and Rob weren't born. *Your* father was a baby. How can anyone blame you for the actions of your grandfather? Pop is long dead. And some might even argue that he was a mere cog in a cruel machine, condemned to accept that cruelty to save himself and his family."

"Ah, my little lion. Now you're being naive." Guy's cynical laugh cut the air. "You know what they'll say. That no one held a gun to Josef's head and forced him to be one of the first Austrians to join the party. As it says in the Bible, the sins of the father will be visited upon the children and their children's children. If word of this gets out, the trolls and social justice fundamentalists will tear us apart. Not a single one of our well-heeled clients will risk having their name associated with Nazis."

Unnerved, queasy, I tossed the blanket aside and stood. I paced the deck, scanning the pink-stained horizon as the last of the light faded. I pulled my hood up over my beanie and resumed my seat. Gnats swarmed the fairy lights.

"Do you know Phil Weber?"

Guy palmed his head. "The Nazi hunter? That's going back years. What makes you ask about him?"

"I read an article."

Guy grunted. "Phil came sniffing after Josef decades ago. Because of Phil's relationship with Rob, he let our grandfather's past remain in the shadows. But men like Phil Weber don't give away anything for free. I've always wondered when that bill will come due."

"Phil works for the CIA now." I tucked my hands in my pockets, felt the lump of the brooch. "Rob and Cass made an agreement with him to also work with the CIA. Or, at least, I think that's what happened."

Guy had sunk into the cushions as we spoke, but now he bolted upright. "That son of a bitch. It finally came time to pay the piper, and he did it with my *daughter*."

"You know Cass wouldn't do anything she didn't want to do. As for Phil . . . Rob didn't say much. Almost nothing, really. A few texts he sent after I boarded the plane in Singapore." I was babbling.

Guy watched me, his eyes glued to mine, waiting for me to sort it out. But I couldn't tell him the truth. There was George Mèng and his family to protect. And perhaps it was better for Guy to think that Cass—in the end—had chosen her own way out.

I settled on, "It's complicated."

"Working with the CIA usually is."

"You can ask Rob about that. I'm not working with them."

"Right." He clicked his tongue. "You can leave out the details, little lion. But can you tell me some of what happened in Singapore that has you so jumpy? I've been watching you, and I know there's something more than Cass's death. If Rob dragged you into his business, I might finally kill the son of a bitch."

"Rob didn't drag me into anything. I'm not involved with the CIA."

He took my arm. "Your entire life and Cass's, I've worried about plane accidents or car accidents or—God—that you'll drop your hair dryer in the bath. I've worried about date rape and salmonella poisoning. All the usual things that give a father nightmares. But I never worried that you or your sister would get swept up in a geopolitical fight."

It would have been funny if it weren't true. With superhuman effort I dug a laugh up from the coals burning my belly. "I'd worry more about salmonella."

He smiled, too, even if there was no mirth in his eyes. Then he sighed, a sound that echoed through the quiet air like surrender. He tapped his glass. "It's a full-bottle night."

I reached for the Glenlivet. In the distance, a single light off our starboard side emerged from the sound, the first vessel I'd seen since the coast guard cutter had zipped by an hour earlier. The boat was dark save for its stern light. It wasn't illegal to fish in Puget Sound at night, so long as you weren't hunting sturgeon. But it was illegal—and risky—to do so without sidelights and a masthead light.

The boat motored until it was less than a mile off *Redemption*'s starboard side. From inside the bridge came a soft beep—an alert telling me that a moving object had entered the one-half-nautical-mile safety zone I'd set. I stood and walked onto the bridge and checked the radar. A blip on the screen showed a vessel four-tenths of a mile away, with a "trail" suggesting the boat had followed the same path as *Redemption*. The boat had turned off their AIS transponder—the automatic identification system.

I watched for a moment to verify that the vessel was no longer moving, then grabbed the binoculars and returned to the sundeck. I braced my arms on the railing.

"What is it?" Guy asked.

"Maybe nothing." I glassed the horizon until I found the boat. It was a familiar type of speedboat—a thirty-nine-foot Nor-Tech Sport with top speeds over one hundred miles per hour—faster than we could manage. Two men sat in the front.

It was hard to be sure, but based on the man's bulk, I thought one of them was Dai Shujun.

The hair rose on the back of my neck.

There was no time to wonder about Dai's motive. Whether he'd come only to observe or he had something worse in mind, out here, we were sitting ducks. I lowered the binoculars and pulled Guy to his feet. "Dad, we need to go."

He shook me off. He grabbed the binoculars and scanned the horizon until he found the Nor-Tech. “Those men are Asian,” he said. “Is this about Singapore?”

“Yes.” I headed into the bridge, and he followed.

“Do they want to kill you or capture you?” His voice was eerily calm.

“It’s a guess.”

I turned the display lights on the console to red so they wouldn’t be as visible. Not that it helped in the moment since Dai likely had military-grade night vision goggles. But if I played this well, it would matter soon enough. I entered the Port Townsend Yacht Club as my destination on the chartplotter and turned off our own AIS.

“That’s a fast boat they’ve got,” he said. “You going to try and outrun it? Or hide?”

“Both. We don’t need to go far.”

Guy glanced at the radar. Then, while I went fore to bring in the electric anchor, he disappeared below. He returned with a rifle and came to stand next to me at the helm station. He didn’t force the helm away from me, but he stayed close, the rifle leaning nearby, one hand gripping the console’s grab rail.

“I know this island,” he said. “There’s a deep draft all the way around. The cliffs drop straight into the water. You can launch from the other side.”

I nodded and started the engines, then took a final glance through the binoculars. Dai had motored closer; he was little more than a quarter mile away. He had confirmed my guess by lifting night vision goggles. NVGs kill depth perception, but even so it felt as if Dai were looking straight at me from only a few yards away.

As I watched, he drew the flat blade of his hand across his throat.

I killed our lights and watched the radar and sonar screens as I pulled out.

“Wait.” Guy’s voice stopped me. “He’s moving again.”

My pulse fluttered. “Where?”

"Away."

I idled the boat and glanced at the radar screen. Guy was right. Dai had turned the speedboat around and was heading southwest. Perhaps back to Seattle or Bainbridge. I turned the radar to long range, but Dai vanished behind a curve in Whidbey Island, his message delivered.

I slumped into the helm seat and stared at the empty horizon as my blood pulsed behind my eyes. Dai's presence was a warning. Only that.

But it could have been much worse.

"The hell was that about?" Guy asked.

I stirred and grabbed my phone. I dialed the private security company we used for protection at yacht shows and when working with high-profile clients and their accompanying paparazzi. I asked the person who picked up to send two men to our home immediately, make sure Isabeth was fine, and post the men on the property until I said otherwise.

When I hung up, Guy's face had collapsed, as if his skull had turned to sand.

His eyes glittered. "Did those bastards kill Cass?"

I hesitated, then said, "I think so."

The deck chair scraped on teak as he fell against it. I gripped him, easing him into the chair. He grasped my arms.

"Promise me, Nadia." His voice was cotton. "Promise me you won't go back to Singapore."

I snugged a pillow behind his head. His grip on me tightened until it hurt.

People who knew my father only a little thought his personality consisted of a switch that toggled between mean and meaner. But it was simply that Guy went all in. When he loved, he grabbed hold with the strength of a python. When he loathed, he sank his fangs into the object of his ire.

"I won't go back, Guy."

A high-pitched wailing came from him, a sound that turned my blood to ice. Guy was scared and he was dying and he couldn't protect his children. I held him tight, finding my own python strength.

After a time, he turned into my hug and quieted. We sat like that for a long while as I stared into the deepening night, watching the stars burn brighter.

27

Seattle, Washington / Salzburg, Austria
September 22, 1:00 a.m. PDT

After midnight, while Guy and Isabeth slept, I pulled on a coat and boots and went outside. The night was dark and filled with stars, the prickly silhouettes of western hemlocks swaying in the salt-laden breeze. I seated myself on the porch stairs where I'd found Guy earlier.

I thought for a time about Singapore and Dai Shujun's threat on the boat. George had told me that Dai would disappear like smoke once *Red Dragon* was delivered. I was sure he believed it. But after seeing the Guóānbù agent tonight, I realized that if Ocean House expanded into Asia, Dai Shujun and men like him would always be there, waiting and watching.

I had no answers, of course. I knew only that Ocean House, if she were to survive and grow, needed Asia. And I was tired of being intimidated. Tired of running and looking over my shoulder. It was time to get into the game, even if I had no idea what that would look like.

After a while I put aside those thoughts as having no immediate solution. I took the brooch out of my pocket and studied Sisi's portrait in the faint light while I rolled around my father's words as if I were a Greek Sisyphus laboring to push a grudging boulder up a hill.

My great-grandfather was a Nazi. And not a casual one. An early joiner. Enthusiastic. Eager. Willing to risk prison for the cause. Guy's words had stripped away my long-ago memories of Pop as a hard-working, frugal, but kind man, and a different person had emerged. In my adult eyes, Pop's warm gaze chilled to brutal steel; his broad shoulders and knotted laborer's hands became tools of a vast killing machine. The Sisyphean task with which I labored was conflating the great-grandfather of my childhood—with his offerings of warm slices of streuselkuchen, his bags of Mozart-Bonbons, and our outings to zoos and butterfly gardens—with a Nazi who stood by while soldiers shuttled women and children to their deaths.

I pocketed the brooch, then laced a hand around one knee and braced my spine against the stairs.

How well do we ever know anyone?

How well did I know myself?

Before Singapore, I'd been confident. I was educated, smart, attractive. Able to meet billionaires where they stood and convince them to buy a multimillion-dollar toy. Even Guy's drowning game, cruel though some might see it, had convinced me that I could survive and help others survive.

But Cass's death and Connor's invitation to the spy world had blasted me.

What if, I now thought, I was more defined by other aspects of my personality—my fear of flying and spiders, my refusal to bear a tattoo artist's needle until after Cass died. Even my lifelong willingness to accept family secrets without question?

And—especially—my terrified bolt from Singapore.

Cass had said it herself, and now I had the tattoo on my shoulder to prove it: I was Yin, soft and feminine. Willing to yield to stronger forces.

Wind whistled through the eaves. Shivering in the cold, I took stock and recognized that something inside me had to change. At some point I would be master of Ocean House. I would guide her destiny. How well could I lead if I couldn't hold a tarantula—metaphorical or real—in my palm?

I decided that next week's yacht show in Monaco—the glitziest show of the year—would be where I'd make my first mark as the heir of Ocean House. We were up for several design awards against Paxton Yachts. The ceremony would be my best opportunity to own our past. And to forge a new path.

I glanced at my phone. It was now Monday in Austria, the respectable hour of 10:00 a.m. Time to put teeth into my developing plan to liberate Ocean House from the past. I would do it for pragmatic reasons, so that men like Phil Weber couldn't blackmail us. But also for moral ones, because we must own who we were and are. Guy had said he didn't know our entire story. Rob might, but I wasn't willing to count on him telling me the truth. The only way forward was to do my own due diligence. I dialed the number for the Salzburger Landesarchiv—the Salzburg Provincial Archives.

A man answered in German. *"Salzburger Landesarchiv. Wie kann ich Ihnen helfen?" How may I help you?*

I stumbled through my high school German. *"Gibt es jemanden, der Englisch spricht und etwas im Archiv für mich überprüfen kann?" Is there someone who speaks English and can check something in the archives for me?*

The man switched to English. "Yes, of course. You want one of our archivists. I will transfer you to Frau Hinterleitner."

When the woman came on the line, I told her that my sister had been researching our family history but that she had recently passed away. I wanted to continue her work. Cassandra had planned to visit Salzburger Landesarchiv. I was curious to know if she had followed through.

"My condolences, Miss Brenner. I remember your sister. She visited our archives in July, almost two months ago. She spent an afternoon researching Josef Rudolf Brenner. A family member, I presume?"

A weight settled onto my shoulders. But also, a strange release. Cass felt close.

"He was our great-grandfather," I said, wondering whether it was a coincidence that Cass's odd behavior in Singapore had coincided with her trip to Salzburg.

"*Ja.* We have files on Herr Brenner, his life in Mattsee. The files themselves have a curious story. They were stolen from the archives in 1995 and only returned last year, after a woman found them in her mother's possessions."

Stolen. That added a twist. Perhaps Phil Weber had taken the files as part of his deal with Rob to hide Josef's past. If the woman he'd entrusted them to had also died, her daughter might have returned them, not knowing of Weber's request.

Hinterleitner said, "The files are in German, of course, so your sister asked to have them translated. She promised she would return when the translations were ready and pay whatever fees she'd accrued. The translator finished his work a week ago. And now, sadly, I understand why your sister hasn't returned my calls."

"He translated everything?" I asked.

"Everything we have. It's all on paper, as your sister requested. No digital." She hesitated. "The translator must still be paid. And I need to know what to do with the papers. Should I mail them to you?"

I picked at a splinter in the stairs as I pondered what to do. My half-hatched plan was burning a path through my mind. I didn't want any surprises. No omitted details, no slippery facts.

"I'll fly to Salzburg this week to collect the papers and pay your translator. Will that work?"

"That would be excellent, Miss Brenner." Her crisp voice turned soft. "Your sister could read enough German to understand a few things. Did she tell you anything about the contents of the file?"

"She—no. There wasn't time."

"Then you should prepare yourself, Miss Brenner. You might not like what you learn."

On that, she wished me a good day and hung up.

I gazed past the old-growth pines encircling our property—lean giants tilted from their seasonal battles with the wind. The dark water of Puget Sound was a shadowy promise barely visible between the trunks.

You might not like what you learn.

Could it be worse than what I already knew?

"History," I whispered, "isn't destiny."

The next morning, I decided discretion was the better part of valor. I informed my parents I was flying out a few days early for the Monaco Yacht Show. I'd oversee the final setup of Ocean House's exhibits and make sure our boats were perfectly showcased. I'd also meet with current and potential clients who were arriving early.

Isabeth—who had reserved the room next to mine at the Hôtel Métropole Monte-Carlo—said she looked forward to meeting up with me there in a few days. Then, perhaps sensing unspoken words between myself and Guy, she hugged me and left the room.

Guy studied me through weary eyes—twin pools lying sluggish in shadowed recesses. The rejuvenation he'd gained from sailing on *Redemption* had vanished with the news of Cass's murder. Now his body was almost indistinguishable from the recliner in which he sat, he and it mere soft lines in a room that smelled of vinegar and sweat and last night's dinner.

"Take a bodyguard," he said.

I hugged him and pretended to agree. A personal bodyguard wasn't affordable, given what Rob had said about our finances. I would rely on vigilance and luck. "As you wish. I'll see you when I get home from Monaco."

His frail silence followed me out the door, giving lie to my optimism.

I flew alone to Salzburg aboard Matthew's private jet. Matthew was still hunkered down somewhere near Boston and told me his plane was sitting in a hangar, gathering dust. I might as well use it—he'd fly it home after we met up in Monaco. Given what I'd told him about being followed in Singapore, he arranged for someone to meet me at the W. A. Mozart Airport. The man would be my shadow in Austria and then escort me to Monaco. From Monaco, he would accompany me back to Seattle and stay with me until *Red Dragon* was delivered.

And, Matthew pressed, if I decided to return to Singapore, the security consultant would remain at my side, up to and including through the sea trials. Lukas was discreet, highly skilled, and vetted. He would keep Matthew quietly informed of my activities should any intercession be required on my behalf.

I wondered what Matthew meant by *intercession*. But I didn't argue. Dai Shujun weighed on my mind. Gratefully, I accepted Matthew's offer.

I landed in Salzburg in the early-morning hours and was greeted on the tarmac by a bearded, taciturn security professional who introduced himself as Lukas Pichler.

Pichler drove me to the Hotel Goldener Hirsch in Salzburg's Old Town and checked us into a suite. I took the bedroom, while Pichler—"Please, ma'am, call me Lukas"—insisted he needed nothing more than the foldaway in the outer room. When I peered out sometime toward morning, he was dozing in an armchair he'd dragged near the door. In his lap was a handgun, and my stomach tightened; the gun was oddly jarring juxtaposed, as it was, with the bouquet of white roses that had been delivered earlier in Matthew's name.

But then I relaxed. The gun and the flowers complemented each other—opposite swings of a pendulum I hoped would soon come to rest.

—

I rose early. Lukas was already dressed and ready to go. I ordered room service—semmel with butter, smoked bacon, ham, and coffee—and then, at my insistence, we skipped the car and walked along the west bank of the Salzach to the archives, a thirty-minute stroll. Lukas protested that I would be safer in a car. But I'd woken that morning straining for freedom, a songbird who has seen the door briefly open. I hoped, *believed*, that—soon and forever—the family ghosts would be exposed and then laid to rest. Then, in a matter of weeks, *Red Dragon* would be commissioned to George Mèng and a deadly chapter would close. *Red Dragon* would become little more than a feather in the Brenners' cap, a boast for potential clients. Have you *seen* our expedition yacht *Red Dragon*? The best in the world in luxury and technology.

It was a bright, mild day, and as we walked out the hotel's front door, I knew I was following in Cass's footsteps here in the city of Mozart's birth. It comforted me to know that she had been here before me, that she had likely walked this very path. She would have noted the gloriously rugged mountains, the bright-green foothills. The pink bricks of the Mozart Residence. The gleaming white walls of the eleventh-century hilltop stronghold Fortress Hohensalzburg.

She would have loved it all.

The Salzburg Provincial Archives were located a few blocks from the river in a modern, almost industrial-looking building. In the lobby I approached the desk and asked for Frau Hinterleitner.

The man behind the counter—bald, wizened, and exuding good cheer—gestured toward a pair of chairs near the window and asked us to kindly please wait and would we like tea or coffee or perhaps a *Kopenhagener Plunder*?

We declined the drinks and the Danish. I paid the man for the translations, then took a seat and watched sunlight cast pale, tilted pillars across the polished floor. Lukas remained standing.

A short time later, an older woman appeared, trim and neat, her white hair bobbed at the chin, the skin of her small-boned face nearly smooth. Only her heavily veined hands and the color of her hair suggested she was anything north of fifty. She carried two large manila envelopes.

"Miss Brenner," she said in accented English. "You look just like your sister."

I stood. "Thank you, Frau Hinterleitner."

"Maria, please." She held out the envelopes.

I stared at them. "That's a lot of information."

"Josef Brenner was a busy man."

I opened my hands, and she nestled the envelopes into the crook of my arm as if she were handing me a baby. I glanced toward the stairs. "Would it be possible for me to see the archives where my sister spent her time?"

"I misspoke on the phone. She wasn't really in the archives. Only employees have access. But I can show you the room she used when she went through the records. Perhaps you would like to begin your own reading there? It's a pleasant place."

Maria had Lukas and me sign in, then led us up to the second floor. While Lukas waited in the hall, the woman ushered me inside, then left me alone.

I set the envelopes on the nearest table and rubbed my arms, feeling a chill. The truth was close. And once the genie was out of the bottle, I would have no way to put it back.

Three reading tables took up the bulk of the space. A single chair sat at each. The shutters were pulled closed on the windows, but the place was bright with ceiling lights and task lamps. Framed landscapes enlivened the walls.

I picked up the envelopes. My shoes made sharp clicks on the wooden floor as I walked to the farthest table and sat with my back to the door. After a moment I stood and carried the chair around to the other side so that the door was in my line of sight.

The envelopes were marked with Cassandra's name and the numbers *"Eins"* and *"Zwei."* I opened the first one—*eins*—and gently slid the contents onto the table. Out came copies of Josef's birth certificate, his education records, a marriage certificate, and property deeds. All the usual printed detritus of a human life spread out before me, with copies of both the original documents and the English translations.

I stared at the pile, momentarily overwhelmed. The Germans and the Austrians were meticulous record keepers. And while a lot of documents had gone up in smoke when the tide of the war turned, clearly plenty had remained.

I made a neat stack of the formal documents and opened the second envelope—*zwei.* Again, there were copies of the original German-language documents along with English translations. Immediately I knew these were the records Cass would have been looking for: the first paper was a copy of Josef Brenner's signed membership card for the National Socialist German Workers' Party, dated August 5, 1931.

It was a crack in the story Guy knew—he thought Josef had joined the Nazi Party *after* he was hired by the Kleins in 1932, out of frustration at not being promoted.

As I thumbed through the top layers—reports, news articles, even journal pages—document after document revealed some of what Guy had already told me. Josef's work for Klein Marine. His time in the party. Guy hadn't mentioned Josef's prison sentence for conducting illegal Nazi activities and a brief flight to Munich when there was a crackdown on the party.

Josef had returned, and after the Anschluss came the Aryanization of Klein Marine. At some point, according to the handwritten note pinned to a bill of sale, the Kleins—father and sons—had died. Had they perished from disease? Been murdered in the camps?

I lifted my head and pushed away from the table. The chair legs squealed on the floor.

I walked to a window and raised the shade.

I couldn't do this. I didn't want to know. What if Pop had played more than a passive role in the Kleins' deaths? What if he'd sent Asher, Ethan, and Elias to Mauthausen?

There came a knock. The door opened, and Lukas peered inside.

"You should take a break to eat," he said.

I stared at him blankly.

"Gotta keep up your strength," he added.

His words came as if from another world. A normal one, where people ate and slept and made love and *lived.*

"Give me one minute," I said.

When he'd closed the door again, I lowered the shade and returned to the table. I placed the papers back in the envelopes. I wouldn't read any more. Not yet.

The room had become a prison. A dungeon.

A crematorium.

Lukas and I ate lunch in the hotel restaurant, taking a booth for privacy. He scrolled on his phone while I went through the rest of Josef's paperwork. We then retreated to the lounge. While Lukas made himself little more than a shadow watching the door, I sat at the bar and, in defiance of my father's insistence that the only drinkable whisky is from Scotland, ordered Hakushu, a Japanese whisky. Lemon twist, hold the ice. Make it two.

I'd skimmed through all the papers, but I had not fully processed the contents. The story contained in the papers was far worse than I'd feared or imagined, and whenever I turned my mind to it, my thoughts scattered into screeds of denial. *It's not possible. Couldn't have happened. Pop was not evil.*

I was sure psychologists had a term for my behavior: denial, cognitive avoidance, disassociation. Even a form of toxic positivity.

But I knew myself well enough to realize that the information I refused to absorb would return again and again until it wedged its way in and took up permanent residence. What I felt now was merely the dazed interval between knowledge and acceptance, a numbness pushed along by the Hakushu.

Tears filmed my eyes. There had been a child . . .

I blinked. Signaled for another whisky.

What does the world deserve from the people who populate it? What do we owe each other? What do we *inherit* from each other? How far down from parent to child to grandchild to great-grandchild is culpability carried?

I lifted my palms and studied them as if—like Lady Macbeth—I carried invisible stains I could never scrub away.

Inheritance is out of our control. What we do have is the future.

Someday I would be at the helm of Ocean House, responsible not only for our reputation but also for our employees. For the quality of our builds. For our relationship with our clients. For our impact on the climate. I could not, I knew as I sat in this cozy bar in Salzburg nursing both a whisky and a headache, lead anyone or anything unless I and Ocean House were worthy.

And we would never be worthy if we highlighted the royal blood we allegedly carried but buried the evil Josef had committed.

It was all or nothing.

Lukas was suddenly standing at my elbow. I turned. Two Asian men had entered the bar and seated themselves at a nearby table. Both had eyes on me. Lukas leaned in until his lips brushed my ear.

"Time to go," he said.

I downed most of the third whisky and staggered to my feet. I leaned on Lukas as he escorted me from the bar.

In the lobby, I turned to face him, bracing myself against a wall. "We're going shopping."

He kept his face straight save for a cocked eyebrow. "You can hardly stand."

"We'll stop for coffee. I need to buy a gown." I raised a hand to my reeling head and knew that some private time in a bathroom would also be required.

"A gown," Lukas echoed.

"Versace. The most eye-catching one I can find."

28

Principality of Monaco
September 25, 10:20 a.m. CET

Monaco, a world-famous, glittering principality snugged along the turquoise waters of the French Riviera. I pressed my face to the window as the pilot approached.

The country is populated by the obscenely wealthy—more than twelve thousand millionaires live in Monaco, along with three thousand multimillionaires, and a half dozen billionaires, all residing on the most expensive land in the world. Monaco is the home of the Grand Prix, the Casino de Monte Carlo as Ian Fleming envisioned it, the onetime playground of Princess Grace Kelly.

And—of course—the site of the most prestigious annual superyacht show in the world.

All this in a country smaller than New York's Central Park.

An hour after we landed at Côte d'Azur Airport in Nice, then drove twenty miles by private limo to Monaco, I checked into my hotel. I perused the four-day schedule, which included trade shows, exhibitions, cocktail parties, and the awards show, where I intended to speak, and which had been moved to the show's final night. Then I took a deep breath and plunged into the festivities.

I had arranged meetings with staff and brokers at restaurants where the wine alone cost hundreds of dollars, never mind the meal. I touched base with a dozen clients and well-wishers over cocktails in the site's Upper Deck Lounge or while downing *café express* at a nearby delicatessen. Everyone knew about Cass; most offered their condolences. I became adroit at accepting sympathy, then quickly turning the conversation to lighter topics.

I toured the superyachts *Odysseus* and *Melinda*—both built by Ocean House, with the interiors designed by Cassandra and Rob and exteriors created by yours truly with input from our architects and engineering teams. My visits were to ensure that both boats were ready for showtime. *Odysseus* was up for an MYS/Finest New Superyacht Award for best overall design. Word on the street said Paxton Yacht's 533-foot *Zephyr* was favored, but street talk can be wrong.

I spotted *Zephyr* in one of the prestigious mooring places. The yacht struck me as over the top, the designers trying too hard. I sniffed and walked away.

Between the meetings, reunions, and tête-à-têtes, I left Lukas on the pier and squeezed in a private meeting on board *Sovereign I* with Matthew, who'd just flown in. His captain and crew had sailed his boat from Istanbul into Port Hercule a week earlier. Matthew and I sat in the lounge area of his master stateroom while I told him the reason for my visit to Salzburg, what I'd learned, and what I planned to do with that knowledge on awards night.

When I finished, Matthew was quiet for so long that I wondered if Guy had been right—that none of our clients would accept the taint of our past. Inside I quailed. But outwardly I kept my face impassive. Whatever the fallout, I had to follow through on the decision I'd made in Salzburg: do the right thing.

Matthew rose and went to the bar and brought back a bottle of brandy. He poured some into my café noir and then his.

"I'm sorry about your great-grandfather, Nadia. I know it can be hard to reconcile our image of who someone is with a part of them that doesn't align."

I nodded. I was thinking not only of Josef, but of Rob.

"For what it's worth," he went on, "I admire your courage. You have my complete support."

I released the breath I'd been holding. "I'm glad, Matthew. I was half-afraid—"

"That I'd bail on you?" He touched my cheek. "Never. And on what I hope is brighter news, I have some information for you about *Rambler*." He sipped his coffee. "My software guy was able to access a few company emails. These led us to someone on the inside willing to be a whistleblower. You were right. Paxton is playing dirty."

I sat motionless, imagining the ways I could use this information. "Was it sabotage?"

"They had a man assigned to your build from the get-go." He leaned back. "It's a scandal. Do you want me to release the news? My PR people can explode the information onto every digital medium. Print will be right behind."

I glanced out at Port Hercule, the sunlight sparkling on the water as if the bay were a sequined gown spread at Monaco's feet. A seagull wheeled past the windows.

I might be prepared to risk Ocean House by revealing the truth. But I wasn't going to hand victory to Paxton on a silver platter.

Truth can cut both ways.

I reached across the table and rested my hand on Matthew's.

"Thank you. For understanding about Josef. And for offering to help with *Rambler*. I'd like to use the information after my speech at the award ceremony. Can you have your people release it right after I've spoken?"

"Remind me never to get on your bad side." He turned his hand so that his fingers wrapped around mine. "I'll do whatever you need."

I leaned in and kissed him. "Also, can you recommend a good private investigator?"

He shot an eyebrow. "I have several on retainer. What do you need?"

"To find a man named Arno Klein."

—

After Matthew returned to the event, I stood alone on the deck of *Sovereign I*, my finger poised over the screen of my phone, summoning courage from whatever far-off place courage dwelled.

This phone call wasn't the point of no return. But it was the catalyst. Guiltily, I reminded myself that during my conversations with Guy in Seattle, I hadn't *promised* him I'd stay away from Singapore. When the mission was over, he'd understand why I'd needed to go back. For Ocean House and for Cass.

I squared my shoulders and tapped the icon for a number I'd thought I would never call again: that of Connor McGrath.

When he didn't pick up, I left a message, pleased my voice didn't quaver. "Hey, this is Nadia. I just have a few final thoughts about our build. I'm at the Monaco Yacht Show through Sunday. I'd love to chat. I think you'll be happy with the new ideas I'm considering."

After I disconnected, I waited. It didn't take long. Fewer than five minutes had ticked by when Connor returned my call.

"This line isn't private," he said.

"I understand. But we do need to talk."

A pause. Then: "I'll leave a message with your hotel concierge."

"I'm staying at—"

"I know."

He disconnected.

I slid my phone into my purse and stared out at the array of yachts and the throngs of touring attendees swarming the decks. Their voices came as if from far away—light chatter from a world filled with wealth and comfort and safety. Before me were the doers and the dreamers, the haves and the have-yachts. People who'd labored for their wealth and others who'd inherited it just as I'd inherited Ocean House. All of it felt a million miles away.

I tuned the voices out. The sun was warm on my face and shoulders. Far out, a pair of cormorants turned pirouettes against a peerless sky. I breathed in the brisk, salty air, relished the breeze on my face in the ever-agreeable climate of Monaco. This elegant world, the world I'd grown up in proximity to, felt like a facade. The game of high finance, of hedge funds and commodities, of luxury goods and family fortunes, lay in uneasy juxtaposition to the sharp-edged machinery grinding just below.

A few minutes later, I left *Sovereign I* and rejoined Lukas. We plunged back into the crowd. I had wind in my sails, blowing me, like Odysseus's escaped gales, away from home and out to sea.

Friday evening there was an invitation-only networking event at Yacht Club de Monaco. The first person I saw when I walked in with my recently arrived mother and the ever-present Lukas was Brandon Paxton, who, at six foot four, stood a head above almost everyone else in the room.

I jerked to a stop.

Brandon was athletic looking, with a neatly trimmed beard and wearing Monaco cocktail party chic—a slim-fitting navy blazer over a patterned shirt and gray chinos. He'd enlivened his outfit with a maroon silk pocket square, what looked like Fendi's Monster cuff links, and a Rolex. For a man who'd helped upend my life, he appeared remarkably benign. But then, I'd heard psychopathy rarely advertises.

He was deep in conversation with other corporate bigwigs who stood near a table laden with crab legs, lobsters, and silver buckets of champagne. In his left hand he held a glass filled with amber liquid. Scotch, no doubt—it would be single malt, well aged, poured neat.

Next to him was his assistant, Maxwell Costa, the man who'd likely been responsible for siphoning off our talent.

Brandon glanced up. Our eyes met.

I snatched two flutes of champagne from a passing waiter and gave one to Isabeth. I squared my shoulders. "I'm going to talk to Brandon Paxton. Care to join me?"

She grasped my free arm and turned me toward her. "It's better you don't speak with him. He's trouble. He looks at you as if he wants to devour you."

"I have Lukas," I pointed out.

But Lukas shook his head. "If you're going to be verbally bearding a lion in its den, I'll watch out for you from the corner."

He moved away, into the crowd. My gaze landed on Matthew, who was deep in conversation with Vadim Volkov, a Russian businessman whom I recognized from news reports as a confidant of Russia's president. Matthew lifted his head, and our eyes met. He glanced over at Brandon, then back at me. His look was challenging. *Do you have the courage to pursue your enemy?*

I did. Absolutely. I tossed back my champagne—liquid courage—and was looking for a place to set my empty glass when Isabeth's nails bit into my arm. Brandon was sailing toward us, people stepping aside as he approached, then surging in behind.

I was willing to bet Matthew's yacht that everyone in this room—including the Russian oligarch—had read the article claiming Paxton was about to replace Ocean House as yacht royalty. This was the confrontation they'd been waiting and hoping for.

"Here they are!" Brandon boomed in a voice sure to carry over the jazz quartet playing onstage. "The two most beautiful women in Monaco."

Isabeth's eyes narrowed. She would never forgive Paxton for stealing our talent and coming after our clients. Give her five minutes alone with him, and she would take out his eyes with a spoon and plop them in her martini.

"Oui," she agreed with Brandon, her tone breezy. "And the two smartest, as well. *Vous avez l'apparence et les manières d'un cochon.*"

Brandon glanced at me. Clearly French was not in his repertoire.

"She says that it is a pleasure to meet you and wants to know if you bought your cuff links on Amazon. She would like to buy an inexpensive pair for her young nephew."

Brandon threw back his head and roared. "Touché. Do not underestimate the Brenner women. I noticed earlier that you brought your award-nominated boat to the show. *Odyssey*, is it?"

"*Odysseus*." I decided to take a cue from my mother. After all, this man was trying to destroy my company. "I'm disappointed you didn't bring *Zephyr*."

"Oh?" He raised a quizzical eyebrow. "She's here, in pride of place."

"I must have walked right past her. I guess she blended in."

Another laugh. "I thought I was approaching roses, but I seem to have walked into a tangle of thorns. Perhaps, Nadia, you and I could speak more privately outside?"

Isabeth shook her head, but I wanted to hear whatever it was Brandon had to say.

Keep your friends close; keep your enemies closer.

Moisture ladened the evening air while lights climbed the hills behind the city, illuminating villas and manor homes. Yacht Club de Monaco was built to resemble a superyacht, and the club's "decks" hung over the water. Brandon escorted me to the railing where, before us, immense boats floated regally in the shimmering waters of Port Hercule.

Where, I wondered, was Lukas? I relaxed when I saw him watching through the windows.

"C'est beau," Brandon said. *"J'aime être ici. Mais un cochon?" It's beautiful. I love being here. But a pig?*

Heat flamed in my face as I realized Brandon had played me.

"Touché," I said.

He turned toward me and braced his left arm on the railing. "Let's cut to the chase. I know Ocean House is failing. You're in the red, and you've lost at least two potential clients due to that little misadventure with *Rambler*. I know this because they came to Paxton Yachts. I can't say I wanted Ocean House's troubles to happen—I admire your father and uncle and all they've accomplished. But I'm not going to let any opportunity slip by as I build my business." He looked down at me. "I would like for you to be part of that. Why don't you jump a sinking ship and come work for me?"

I laughed, ignoring the chill sliding along my arms—how had he learned of our finances? "Are you suggesting I'm a rat?"

He grinned. "A smart and talented rat, perhaps."

"Ocean House is perfectly fine." I kept my face as smooth as marble, revealing nothing. "We're about to finish a build in Singapore that will have clients pounding on our doors."

In the soft lights, Brandon's face shifted. The facade of earnestness fell away, and the angles of his face tightened. His lips lifted in a grimace, and something ugly peered out through the dark green of his eyes.

"No more pretense, Nadia. Yachting has become a cutthroat business. The so-called civilized days, the days of your father and grandfather, are long gone. Corporations are businesses, not lifestyles. Money matters more than relationships. I intend to build my empire on your father's fallen kingdom."

I tried on my supposed ancestor's half smile. What would Empress Sisi have done? "This feels personal, Mr. Paxton. It gives you so much pleasure to see us momentarily diminished?"

He leaned in. His whisky-laden breath was hot on my cheek. "Business for me is always personal."

From behind us came the sound of a door opening; snatches of laughter spilled out. A woman's soft voice said, "Brandon? You wanted to see me."

We both turned. A young woman who might have taken her figure from Barbie stood silhouetted against the lights of the party, her attributes well delineated. Lights shone on her platinum hair.

Brandon straightened. Smiled. The jungle cat morphed back into a kitten. "Dierdre, lovely to see you. Give us one more minute."

"Of course." She retreated, and he turned back to me.

"Bear my offer in mind," he said. "You're young and gifted. You have a future if you're willing to take a risk." He pressed close, and I considered grinding my stiletto heel into his instep before thinking better of it.

His voice dropped to a whisper. "You don't want your family's company to fail on your watch, do you? My offer stands through this weekend. Then the door closes."

"No need to wait, Mr. Paxton. You can take your offer and, to put it delicately, *enfonce-le dans ton cul*." I gave his instep a final reluctant pass before I stepped away. "Good night."

29

Bar Américain
September 26, 10:00 p.m. CET

The concierge greeted me in the lobby.

"Good evening, Ms. Brenner," he said with a gracious smile. "Mr. McGrath with NeXt Level Security phoned for you. He's hoping to arrange a meeting while you are both in Monaco."

The concierge held out a sheet of hotel stationery on which was written a number I didn't recognize. I thanked him and accepted the paper.

The game was on.

"Do you know this man?" Lukas asked as we rode the elevator to our rooms.

"Connor McGrath manages yacht security for *Red Dragon*." My mind worked furiously. Would Connor accept my help? What would I do if he did?

I wanted to cheer and to hide, both.

Lukas met my eyes in the mirrored wall. "What do you need from me?"

I smiled at him, grateful for his presence. "Walk with me once I learn where I'm meeting Mr. McGrath?"

"My pleasure."

As soon as Lukas had cleared my room and retreated to his, I dialed the number. When Connor's familiar voice came on the line, he instructed me to say nothing and to call him back from somewhere outside. I walked out to the second-floor infinity pool on its perch overlooking Port Hercule, and this time when Connor picked up, he said, "Bar Américain in twenty," and hung up.

—

Lukas and I took a cab to the Bar Américain, a legendary watering hole in the Hôtel de Paris Monte-Carlo. A doorman greeted us and ushered us into the hotel's marble-and-tile opulence, where the only thing missing was a debonair James Bond from *GoldenEye*. I heard a blues quartet as soon as I drew near the bar's doors and a woman's voice husky with emotion as she sang.

"I'll be nearby," Lukas said, and slipped away.

"I'm meeting Mr. McGrath," I told the hostess.

She led me through the Gatsby-era room, past polished wood paneling and burnished leather armchairs to the outside balcony, where palms stirred in the light breeze, their branches spreading against the lilac sky. She gestured toward a table near the balustrade where Connor sat alone.

I thanked the hostess, then stood in the shadows of the doorway and assessed him.

Still attractive. Still emitting the aura of a wealthy businessman. He wore a gray linen suit and a white button-down that glowed against his tanned skin. What I could see of the suit was unwrinkled, as if freshly donned, but he'd loosened his yellow tie.

Unquestionably Connor McGrath, but he looked different from the man I'd first met at a restaurant in Singapore. Thinner, with shadows under his eyes and a few days' growth of beard. His posture was relaxed, his chair pushed back from the table and his right leg bent, the ankle resting on the thigh of his left leg. He'd parked his right elbow on the chair arm, revealing the leather-and-silver bracelet he'd worn every time we met. He didn't move, and yet it seemed even from where I stood as if he hummed with an invisible current.

I approached him, drawing my cashmere wrap tight around my shoulders.

He stood when he saw me and held out a hand. "Ms. Brenner. Thank you so much for meeting me."

We shook hands and seated ourselves. On the table, two brandy snifters filled with amber liquid glowed in the soft light.

"Cognac," he said. "I thought you might want something heavier than wine."

"You thought correctly."

"I appreciate you making the time," he said. "Yacht security is such an important business."

I fell into the game. "You're doing a great job with our latest build. We just need to nail down a few details so the owner feels reassured."

The patio was quieter tonight than it might ordinarily have been. Anyone in Monaco who wanted to be seen and heard was at the party. A few couples sat in quiet conversation, their faces soft in the shaded pink-bulb table lamps. One man stood alone on the far side of the balcony, a row of shots lined up next to him on the table. He was clearly ready for serious business.

No one was near us, but Connor took his phone from a pocket and set it on the table. He turned on the phone's background noise so that our words were nearly lost in the murmur of ocean waves.

"Your call came as a surprise," he said.

"I hope not an unwelcome one." I lowered my voice to match his. Two businesspeople seemingly having the kind of conversation that happened all the time in Monaco: a conversation about wealth and how to protect it.

"So." Connor's gaze was open, friendly. "What would you like to know?"

I looked him in the eye. "I want to help."

Wariness rose in his eyes; the faint squint would have been impossible to detect had we not been sitting so close. He clasped his hands and leaned in, his elbows on his thighs.

"Why the change of heart?"

I cupped my hands in my lap and stared down at the calluses on my palms, built from a lifetime of cleaning hulls, hauling ropes, and handling boats in a storm. I had been thinking a great deal about my decision, probing my determination, questioning my motives. I shared with Connor the truth I'd realized—that I couldn't be the kind of person who stood by while others suffered.

I cleared my throat. "Several reasons. Most significantly, I went to Austria to learn about my great-grandparents. And what I learned is that there is no virtue in being a bystander while the world burns. It isn't enough to simply abstain from doing evil. You must fight it."

He must have thought I sounded like a starry-eyed teenager who had just fallen in love with activism and believed she could change the world. I supposed he was only partially wrong.

"What I believe in," I continued in a soft voice, "is our friend's family. His wife and children and their right to live a life of their choosing. Cass gave her own life so they could have a chance. I hope I don't have to dedicate quite as much. I hope I don't hurt my family the way she did. But I'll risk it."

Connor studied me so long that I had to force myself not to squirm under his gaze. I lifted my chin and didn't look away.

From inside the bar, the singer's voice reached high and then higher to hold a single sweet note.

"It's not my call anymore," he said.

I blinked.

The singer fell silent. There came a smattering of applause from the thin crowd.

Around us, the couples continued their conversations. The man at the balustrade had taken a seat and was working steadily through the contents of the shot glasses. A young man bused a table.

"It's George's call," Connor said. "I can't bring you in without his approval."

"Let me talk to him."

"I'll handle it."

I pressed my hands together. "Did you know that in Nazi Germany, most of the population refused to acknowledge what was happening to the Jews? A smaller subset was actively complicit. By some accounts, those who were complicit included members of the Church." I sipped the cognac; its sweetness burned. "All it takes is for people to look the other way."

In the silence that followed, sounds filtered in. The quartet was on a break, and the murmur of voices rose to fill the emptiness. There came the clink of glasses and cutlery. A door slammed, and when I lifted my head, the man on the far side of the patio had left. The busboy was collecting his shot glasses.

The artificiality of it all struck me. How easy it was to take for granted a safe home, a warm bed, a fair and reasonable government. Food without rations or breadlines. The ability to worship as one wished.

Connor laid his hand on mine. "That's beautifully said, Nadia. And clearly heartfelt. I applaud you."

I waited.

"Give me some time to pass your thoughts on to George." He removed his hand and stood. "I'll be in touch."

30

Principality of Monaco
September 27, 5:00 p.m. CET

The next afternoon, several hours before the awards party, my mother arrived at the door of my hotel room, a hairdresser and makeup artist in tow.

I looked at her with exasperation. "Is this necessary?"

"Whether we win tonight or not, you must look your best." Her eyes glimmered and she blinked. "You are up there for Cass as well as yourself."

I softened. "Of course."

She waved the women in, gestured for them to set up in the oversize bathroom, then crossed to the bar and pulled out the makings of a martini.

"And," she said, "you're representing not only Cass, but Ocean House."

"You might regret that later."

She paused and turned to look at me. "You'll win," she said, misunderstanding. "*Odysseus* is art, pure and simple."

"Sure." I smiled. "I love you, you know. Remember that."

She abandoned the drink fixings and came to stand next to me. "I love you, too, *ma chérie*. Now show me this Versace you bought in Salzburg."

I led her to the closet and held out the emerald-green gown. *Green means go,* I'd told myself as I'd handed over my credit card. The flowing skirt and tight bodice, the bare shoulders and deep V in the back, these were unusual choices for me—I had always dressed conservatively, unwilling to draw attention. But tonight was different. *I* was different.

Isabeth clicked her tongue. "It's stunning."

"It's for courage," I said.

She placed her hand on my arm. "You are our beautiful and devoted Nadia. That is all the courage you need."

She returned to the makings of her martini. "I saw you with Matthew. It's lovely he's here to support you." She shot me a glance. "He is a perfect match for you. Have you considered that?"

"Perfect because of his money or his connections?"

She rolled her eyes at me. "Because he loves you. You've been moping ever since what's-his-name ran back to London. It's time to have a committed man in your life. And it doesn't hurt that Matthew comes with certain . . . amenities. A woman should marry well. Marry someone who complements her."

"Matthew's money and my design skills?" She laughed but I shook my head. "You are mercenary. And my personal relationships are off the table."

"As you wish, *ma chérie*. Just remember, you are in the flush of your beauty right now. A prize for any man. Be selective. But don't wait." She sipped her martini. "Guy and I aren't perfect together. But we're better together than apart. I can't imagine life without him."

I turned away so she wouldn't see my sudden tears.

I let the women work their magic. With each brushstroke, each hairpin, each dab of makeup, I thought of Prince Sang Nila Utama and the merlion and how I would feel tonight when I sacrificed the crown of Ocean House in the hope that doing so would lead us to land.

The evening was a blur until the awards began. Rob had flown in just for the event, and he and Isabeth hovered by my side, Rob gushing repeatedly over my dress, my hair, my flawless face. Matthew came and went, offering drinks and whispers of encouragement. Other attendees zoomed in and out of my telescopic vision—well-wishers and the merely curious. Members of my design team were there, giddy with champagne and anticipation. The owners of the *Odysseus* came by, brimming with excitement.

"We're going to win, Nadia," Jerry Boyce said. "*Odysseus* is superlative."

I caught Brandon Paxton's towering presence as he moved through his own throng of well-wishers. And once, from the corner of my eye, I thought I caught a glimpse of Connor. But when I turned to follow him, he'd vanished.

Perhaps he'd never been there.

Then, in no time at all, the emcee was announcing the finalists for the MYS/Finest New Superyacht Award for best overall design—the pinnacle of the awards ceremony, the greatest honor, the reason many of us had come.

Unwittingly, my eyes sought out Brandon Paxton. He stood nearby in a knot of people. When my gaze caught his, he raised his glass of bubbly with a sardonic grin.

"May the best man win," he called above the noise of the crowd.

"The best woman," I mouthed.

I kept my expression cool, but my own champagne burned in my stomach.

What would I do if we didn't win? Force my way up onstage?

Why not? Twenty minutes from now, I'd have absolutely nothing left to lose anyway.

Onstage, the emcee raised his hands. "And now for the award everyone's been waiting for."

Silence fell. A silence so deep it seemed everyone in the vast room had stopped breathing, stopped moving.

My team gathered around me. With painstaking slowness, the emcee announced the finalists. With each name, a photograph appeared on the screen behind him, showing the nominated yacht.

He picked up an envelope. He held the room for a moment, ratcheting up the tension until I felt like a piano wire tuned too tight.

He opened the envelope. "And now, without further ado, your winner. Nadia and Cassandra Brenner and the team from Ocean House for *Odysseus*!"

The world released its suffocating hold. Calm fell over me. I knew what I had to do.

I slammed down the rest of my drink. I whooped with my family and members of my design staff and the owners of *Odysseus*. We surged up the stairs and onto the stage, where I accepted the glass trophy and held it aloft with two hands for the requisite photos. I handed the trophy to my team lead, then ran through a list of people to thank, mentioning everyone on my team by name and offering my loving gratitude to my family.

Then I leaned into the microphone. "I'm going to break with tradition now and ask that my family and this fantastic design team leave the stage." I turned to the owners. "Jerry and Marilynn, the two of you as well."

A surprised murmur ran through the audience and those onstage with me. But no one argued. Rob squeezed my elbow, innocent of what I was about to unleash.

Then, before a crowd of hundreds, I drew in a deep breath, released it, and began.

"Ocean House has a proud and glorious history. My great-grandfather, Josef Brenner, began his career in Mattsee, Austria, under the tutelage of the renowned Klein family. He began as a carpenter, but quickly mastered other crafts. Machinist. Varnisher. Painter. Designer. Project manager. Over time he worked his way almost to the top, although the highest positions were held for members of the Klein family.

"But then he did reach the top."

I glanced at Brandon. He frowned back.

"From Austria, my great-grandparents moved to Seattle, where they established Ocean House. It wasn't long before Josef's company became synonymous with the best bespoke boats in the industry. Our boats have carried kings and duchesses, tycoons and robber barons. Their son, Erich Brenner, my grandfather, continued the tradition."

The crowd was getting restless. They thought I was making a sales pitch.

"There have been some who have questioned if our time has come and gone. If Paxton Yachts is the new royalty of yacht building. Perhaps people are right. I am in the unfortunate position of being biased and thus unable to see the big picture." This got a laugh.

From where he stood just below me, Rob now wore the shit-eating grin. He pumped a discreet fist. "You go," he mouthed.

I looked away, then back. "But that is not why I'm speaking to you tonight. I'm here because I have recently learned some things about my family that I feel compelled to share."

The smile slid off Rob's face like a shade coming down.

"My great-grandfather Josef had unquestionable talent. If World War II hadn't happened, I'm sure he still would have done well in the world. But it wasn't talent that led to his position at the top of Klein Marine. It was his membership in the National Socialist German Workers' Party. The Nazi Party."

A collective gasp, and then the crowd went quiet. Far away, somewhere in the port, a boat sounded its horn. Closer by on the dock, a man laughed. But inside the yacht club, there was utter silence.

"When the Nazis came to power in Austria, Klein Marine was Aryanized, and most of the Klein family living in Mattsee were taken to the camps. Four were spared. Asher Klein, who was the patriarch of the family and the founder of Klein Marine. His two sons, Ethan and Elias. And a third Klein child. These three men were retained by the Nazis for their skills when Klein Marine was converted from building yachts to building and repairing ships commissioned by the Kriegsmarine—the Nazi navy.

"In the middle of the war, Klein Marine's new Aryan owner—a Nazi officer—decided that Asher and his sons had outlived their usefulness to the cause. But rather than send the men to the camp at Mauthausen, he decided to test my great-grandfather's loyalty. He ordered the Klein men to stand against the brick wall of their own office building. Then he put a gun in Josef's hand, aimed his own revolver at Josef's head, and ordered my great-grandfather to kill his former bosses."

From the direction of the kitchen came a crash of glass and a man's curse. Then silence again. I curled my fingers around the edges of the lectern. I was almost to the worst part, and a shameful voice inside me ordered me to *shut up*. To cut and run before I brought down our beautiful, aristocratic house of cards.

I did not look at my mother or uncle.

"I will never know what thoughts were in my great-grandfather's mind as that officer held a gun to his head. Did Josef decide that it was better to perpetrate evil than to be its victim? Did some part of him relish destroying the men who had held him back? Whatever his reasons, in that moment, he chose to fire the fatal shots. Immediately after, German laborers sank the bodies in the Obertrumer See."

Now a buzz ran through the crowd, a sound like a giant wasp's nest ready to boil forth its venomous contents.

"Now to the fourth Klein. Noah was eight when the Nazis came to power. For two years, his family hid him at Klein Marine, right under the noses of their German overlords. My great-grandfather—out of spite or fear or desperation—told that Nazi officer about the boy hiding within one of his father's builds. Noah was taken to be drowned alongside the bodies of his father, Elias, his uncle, Ethan, and his grandfather, Asher."

The low buzz rose to a swell, like a wave about to crash. I held up a hand.

"I have recently learned that Noah survived. He grew up and married. Had children. Grandchildren. I've brought in an investigator to find Noah's descendants so that we can decide how best to make restitution for what we took from them."

As I stared out at the sea of appalled faces, it would have been easy to cry. Easy to let loose the pain that gripped me. But I held fast. Any tears I shed I would find false. Or, worse, as if instead of the Kleins, *I* were the victim.

I drew in my breath and released it. It no longer mattered what people thought. I had spoken the truth, and *that* was what mattered.

"I have come to realize that very few men and women are all good or all evil. Each of us has the capacity for both. That said, I also believe that there are acts which cannot be forgiven. Will Ocean House survive what I am sharing with you? I don't know. Everyone in this room will judge for themselves what they wish to do in response to what I've recently learned and shared tonight. I ask that you weigh our hearts and intentions with open minds."

I released my grip on the podium and stumbled as I moved away, my legs weak and my eyes blurring with tears I wouldn't shed.

No one came to help me.

I plunged down the stairs and through the crowd, which parted before me as if I'd become a leper. I caught Rob's face—white with shock—as he hugged a sobbing Isabeth. For an instant, my eyes met his, and I saw what my words had cost him. Rob, I realized in a flash, was ego piled on ego. Without the prestige of Ocean House, he became a simple boat designer. A man who couldn't justify his aristocratic manners or on-brand accoutrements.

We can't carry this generational rot, I wanted to tell him. *It's not who you taught me to be. We have to be the good guys.*

His stare was cold enough to pierce my heart. Then he turned his back.

The wave of people crashed forward with a thunder of voices and motion. Journalists held up their press passes and lunged after me.

A few people applauded; others called out slurs. Phones and video recorders were held up to capture my image. I caught a glimpse of Matthew elbowing his way through the throng, trying to reach me. And Brandon's face, smug and cool.

Then Lukas appeared and took my elbow. He stiff-armed his way past knots of people and bustled me behind a curtain and through a side door. He'd clearly scoped out the place earlier.

"Where to?" he asked.

I froze in indecision. Where to, indeed? Matthew's yacht? My hotel? A bar somewhere across the border with France?

What did it matter anymore?

"The hotel," I said, suddenly bone tired. I'd lock my door, drop my phone in the toilet, and sleep for a week. Then decide. Maybe I'd stay in Monaco forever.

Connor burst through the same door Lukas and I had just used. Lukas pushed me behind him, then relaxed when he recognized Connor from the Bar Américain.

"Tell him you can talk later," Lukas growled. "We've got a mob to escape."

"My car is waiting out back," Connor offered.

Lukas looked at me. I nodded, and he and I followed Connor through an exit door, down a set of stairs, and out into the night.

31

Principality of Monaco
September 27, 9:00 p.m. CET

Connor drove while Lukas and I sat in the back.

We headed north and east into the hills from Monte Carlo toward the French town of La Turbie. The road wound treacherously on a steep climb overlooking the Mediterranean. For all the beauty of the hills and the jaw-dropping view, the road had a sinister history: somewhere along this route, Princess Grace Kelly had missed a turn, plunged over a cliff, and died.

I ran an internal check—my mind, my gut, my heart. A week ago, this road and Connor's speed would have alarmed me. But Cass's death and my decisions about Ocean House and George's family had shifted everything, rearranging my inner patterns. I watched out the window with steady acceptance. What would come, would come. Car wreck or sea battle, I was ready.

After fifteen minutes, Connor pulled into a scenic overlook and killed the engine. Cars whizzed past, traffic eternally heavy in the twenty-four-hour world of Monaco.

Connor's eyes met mine in the rearview mirror. "Walk with me?"

Outside, wind whipped through a stand of Aleppo pines near the car. Lukas leaned against the hood, arms folded, eyes on me, while Connor and I walked to the overlook. The wind here was fierce, and when I shivered, Connor shrugged out of his suit coat and draped it over my bare shoulders. I shoved my arms through the sleeves and pulled it close, then leaned against the railing. Below us spread the lights of Monte Carlo, Monaco's largest quarter and a fortress of wealth.

Connor held out a box of smokes. When I nodded, he turned his back to the wind and lit my cigarette, then his.

"I got a call from George Mèng during your speech tonight. He was watching the live broadcast."

I gripped the railing, then relaxed. What would come, would come.

"Your talk has already zipped around the globe on news outlets and social media. George feels you displayed amazing courage. Then, not long after your talk, news channels began releasing some less-than-flattering information about Paxton Yachts. Something about their finances having links to the Chinese Communist Party. Also, that they might have been involved in sabotaging one of your builds. You know anything about this?"

"I heard there was a whistleblower."

Connor grunted. "Someone persuasive convinced her to step forward. George called it a coup d'état. I agree. It was a good play. And one that took real spine."

"It wasn't a play. It needed to happen. My father always said trust no one. But I won't run Ocean House that way. People must be able to trust whoever they're dealing with."

"You did the moral thing."

"I was channeling my sister."

"And that's what it was? A final blow for Cass?"

I sucked hard on my cigarette, relishing the jolt of nicotine. Was my performance tonight a way of honoring Cass? In part, yes. But it was also about me. By following her path, I'd lost the blindfold I'd unwittingly worn through years of hobnobbing with the ultrarich. There was no going back.

I braced a foot on the railing and tilted my head to look at Connor. "Before Cass's death, I was content with my life. With my family. With my place in the world. I didn't know any better." A hint of incredulity darkened my words. "Cass's murder and my great-grandfather's willing embrace of Nazism have upended all of that. What we discovered can't be forced back into a bottle." I looked out over Monte Carlo again and watched a yacht make its way through the harbor. "I can't squeeze my life back into what it was. Nor would I want to."

Connor placed his foot on the railing next to mine. His polished black loafer next to my ridiculous emerald heels.

"And now what?" I said, more to myself than to Connor.

I felt his gaze on me as he spoke. He said, "I've learned the hard way that following the rules and having courage don't always mix. Wanting to do the moral thing is what got me into this line of work. Doing the moral thing is what made George decide to take his AI and his family and make plans to leave China." He looked out at the city and sucked hard on the cigarette. When he released his breath, the wind whisked away the smoke.

I huddled deeper into Connor's jacket. "Did you pass along my message?"

"I did. George would be honored to work with you."

And here we were. The diverging path I'd been heading toward ever since I picked up the phone to call the archives in Salzburg. I hoped my speech and my search for Arno Klein were the start of my family's restitution. Helping George was an additional form of restitution for the lives lost in Nazi Germany. But it was also about having the courage to do the right thing in the face of personal risk.

Once again I peered at Connor's face, the planes of his cheeks and forehead briefly lit by the headlights of a passing car. He appeared to be studying me just as intently. An appraisal.

"Do you think I have the skills to do it?" I asked. "Go to Han and pretend to work with him? Then help the family hide?"

Connor leaned against the fence separating us from a precipitous drop to the road below. We stood elbow to elbow at the cliff's edge, the ends of our cigarettes glowing in the void.

Finally, he said, "I've asked myself that question from the first time we met. Here's what I think: I suspect you've underrated yourself your entire life."

I let his words hang while I ran through a litany of my fears. Flying. Needles. Heights. Being overwhelmed. Being rushed or pushed. Monsters under the bed and on the streets. All the daily and nightly terrors that Cassandra seemed to relish, even pursue.

Connor toed a pebble over the edge, the sound lost in the wind and the roar of cars. "Cassandra's death and what you learned in Austria forced you to dig deep." He turned to face me, his gaze intent. "You have the best kind of bravery, Nadia. The kind that isn't driven by mere adrenaline or thrill seeking. What you have is the kind of courage that comes from deep in your heart. Your mettle is driven by what you believe in. And if you believe that helping George Mèng and his family escape is the right thing to do, then you know as well as I do—you have the courage to help make it happen. And if you have the courage, then you'll come up with the skills."

Heat rose in my face. "I bet you say that to all the spies you recruit."

He laughed, a generous, genuine sound. But he quickly sobered. "Honestly? Only to you."

My laugh wasn't as generous. "It's your job to manipulate people."

"That's true. But only if I believe in them."

I smiled to myself. The phrase *sea change* wasn't a mariner's term. I'd looked it up after a client asked about it. The idea came from Shakespeare's *The Tempest*. Archaically, it meant to suffer. Now it meant to transform, and I felt my own sea change rising.

I turned to face Connor.

"What do you want me to do?"

"You'll accompany George on the sea trials, just as you would if this were an ordinary build. You'd have no need to interact with his family in their hiding place. Your main job will be to act normally and, by doing so, convince others that the voyage is routine. You will talk to staff, gain their trust, reassure them if needed. You will be the magician's hand that everyone is looking at."

"While the trick happens elsewhere."

"Exactly."

"No spying for Han?"

"We can try. We *should* try. But I suspect he's too smart to use you now. He knows you won't be as naive as you were when he first approached. It's your other work that's more important now. You're the keystone. Think of the D-day deception. The ruse that convinced the Germans that the Allies were landing elsewhere. The ruse was nearly a year in the making and essential for the invasion's success. We've been running our operation under the same concept. False information fed to Emily. Phil Weber's carefully leaked information suggesting George might be a smuggler. That George and Cass were lovers. Cass's delay of the build and her apparent mishandling of it. Do you see?"

I nodded.

"But for all of this to work," he continued, "information is compartmentalized based on need to know. We'll need your help creating a distraction when Mèng's family arrives at the yacht. But for your safety as well as the security of the op, you'll be working in the dark and only updated as needed—there's a good chance you'll be grilled by authorities in Shanghai, and saying 'I don't know' is easier than lying. Your role in maintaining the appearance of normality, the idea that no battle is occurring, is critical. And harder than you think."

I blamed my sudden shiver on the wind.

My gaze went past the city and once again to the harbor and the boats sheltering there. Among them was Matthew's *Sovereign I*, the boat that could carry me to my dream of living on the ocean and designing yachts for the rest of my quiet and contemplative life, if I so chose. And if, after tonight, Ocean House still had a future, I could hire brilliant people to run the business—my skill as a designer was more useful than any potential talent I had as head of the company. A smart CEO doesn't try to do everything. Instead, she fills the gaps with top-rated talent and becomes comfortable with delegating. Something my family had never been good at.

At the moment, though, none of that mattered. I was committed to Connor and George.

"I need to make a phone call," I said.

"About this? No."

"I need to talk to my dad. I won't reveal anything. You can listen in if you wish. But . . . I need to hear his voice."

He nodded, and I pulled out my phone. The screen lit up with a flurry of texts and DMs. Multiple calls from Matthew. I ignored them. It was noon in Seattle; Guy would be working, his fierce will laboring against the cancer. It dawned on me that by offering to become part of the op, I might never see him again.

He answered with my name. "Nadia." Then: "I heard about tonight."

"Isabeth or Rob?"

"Both. And from a dozen others. You told us you were flying in early to Monaco. But, instead, you went to Austria."

"You put me on the path."

There was a long pause. I imagined Guy leaning against the kitchen table, where he liked to work on weekends, staring out at the trees and the ocean a world away from mine. Or maybe curled up in a chair while the cancer ate his insides.

"Guy," I said. "I didn't mean to hurt you. I was afraid that if I told you or Mom, you'd fight me. And I'd give in."

"No, Naughty, there's no shame on you. Out of the whole damn family, you were the only one to step up and say what had to be said."

"You're not angry?"

"Oh, I'm pissed as an Irishman in a bar fight. I was kind of hoping Ocean House would survive me. But I'll get over it."

"This won't destroy us." I forced an optimism I didn't feel.

"Hope isn't a plan, little lion. But maybe you're right. Regardless, it was your call. It's not like I'd planned to run things from beyond the grave."

Another pause.

"I'm going to Singapore to finish and commission *Red Dragon*," I said. I raised my voice as he geared up to object. "I'll be careful. And I'll have protection." I glanced at Connor, who nodded. "But I'd rather Rob not be part of it anymore. I don't trust him."

The silence was longer this time. Then: "Rob is good at what he does. And you know how crazy it gets before sea trials. Why not use him? He's furious right now, but he won't stay mad for long. Not with you. Not when he accepts that you did the right thing."

"Will you believe me if I say this is for his benefit? Things could get messy, and he isn't as safe as he thinks he is. Call him home, Guy. For his sake and mine."

A sound like a growl. Then: "If it's that important, I'll get someone to haul him back to Seattle by his fancy lapels. *Red Dragon* is just about done, and you'll be CEO soon enough. Might as well be now."

"I got this," I said, relieved that Rob would be one less moving piece to worry about.

We spoke another minute. Just before we disconnected, Guy said, "I guess I can't call you little lion anymore. I love you, Nadia."

He was gone before I could reply.

Connor stubbed out his cigarette on the railing. "He's ill?"

"You could tell that from one phone call?"

"Your tone and his. A sense of finality."

"He's dying." I looked out at the invisible horizon. "I might never see him again."

"One month, Nadia. One month and *Red Dragon* will have spirited away George and Li-Mei and their children. They will be safe, and you can go home with a clear conscience and a good heart and spend your dad's final days with him." He straightened. "Are you in? You can still say no."

"I'm in. But these are my terms."

"Spoken like the future CEO of Ocean House. I'm listening."

"You will conceal my involvement with the CIA to the best of your ability. If it does become known that I was involved in George's defection, then you will help protect Ocean House from blame or liability. Ocean House must survive even if I don't."

"Agreed."

I finished my cigarette and dropped it onto the gravel, grinding it out with my heel. "Cassandra called her case officer Virgil, right?"

"That was between them. Nothing official. But, yes, that's what she called him."

"She would have named him after the Roman poet who guided Dante through hell and up to heaven. Clearly, she expected to make it out."

"But they both remained in hell." He touched the back of my hand, then retreated. "I'll do everything I can to protect you."

"I appreciate that," I said dryly. "But to answer your earlier question, whether I'm still up for it, the answer lies in myth. I'm going to call you Orpheus."

"After the Greek poet who descended into hell to rescue his beloved?"

"Ah, an educated spy."

"MIT, if you recall from my CV."

"But Orpheus failed. Eurydice remained in Hades for eternity." I frowned up at him. "What I'm telling you is, don't fail."

"If I remember the myth correctly, Orpheus's mistake was in turning around to make sure his wife was still behind him."

"That's my point. I'll be behind you. Every step of the way. Trust me. You don't have to ever check. Just as I will trust you to have my back. Also, I'm bringing Lukas. That is, if he's willing to come once I share the dangers with him."

Connor glanced over at the car and Lukas, who—even in the gloom—appeared to be watching us. "That's risky, Nadia. Lukas is Matthew's man. How much do you know about him?"

"Matthew or Lukas?"

"Both."

"I trust Matthew. And he trusts Lukas."

"Matthew is a commodities trader. It's not a field known for honesty and straightforwardness. He's suspected of selling GPU chips to China."

"He finalized that sale before it was illegal."

"He's also rumored to have deep ties with high-ranking party members."

I held my patience. "Matthew has ties with a lot of movers and shakers. He went to university with China's foreign minister, yes. And he's a businessman before he's almost anything else. But he would never sell out you or me or George Mèng. I know that for certain."

Connor frowned. "Lukas is a cog I didn't plan for."

"Then start planning. The CIA was worthless at protecting Cassandra. I'm bringing my own insurance."

"Ballsy," he said. But his lips crooked in a half smile. "We'll have to vet him. If there's *anything* that alarms my hypersensitive gut, if I don't like the way he scratches his ass or holds his coffee, he's out."

"Vet away."

After a moment he held out his hand.

"Deal," he said.

We shook.

PART 3

Destiny is no matter of chance. It is a matter of choice. It is not a thing to be waited for, it is a thing to be achieved.

—William Jennings Bryan

32

Singapore
October 1, 9:00 a.m. SGT

When Connor, Lukas, and I landed at Changi Airport in Singapore, Connor parted ways with us at customs. Andrew Declough greeted Lukas and me curbside.

"Welcome back, Ms. Brenner," he said, relieving me of my overnight bag, his gaze on Lukas.

I made the introductions without explaining Lukas's presence.

"It's good to see you, Andrew," I said. "But I was expecting Emily Tan."

He lifted my bag into the back of his Mercedes SUV. "You didn't get my email? I would have texted or phoned, but I figured you'd be sleeping on the flight. Mr. Mèng let her go."

Disconcerted, I stepped back as Andrew lowered the hatch. "What was Mr. Mèng's explanation?"

"I'm not privy to the details. Some falling-out, apparently. It was all quite sudden—yesterday morning she was on the payroll, and late yesterday afternoon she was gone. Packed up her belongings and disappeared. Bad timing for us. My team is going to miss her."

"We all will." I was surprised by my confused rush of feelings. Relief that this woman I couldn't trust was gone. Pity for what her future might be. And an alarming awareness that the staggering workload of finalizing *Red Dragon* would fall on my shoulders without any administrative assistance.

Lukas opened the front passenger door for me, then climbed into the back. There was a long line of automobiles jostling at the curb. Andrew started the car to run the air-conditioning while we waited.

I smoothed the wrinkles in my skirt. "Have you assigned someone to take over Emily's duties?"

"The purser will help with logistics—he'll see to the crew and the inventory until we get to Shanghai. And I pulled over one of our admins from my firm. Kelly Song. She's good, but she'll need time to get up to speed on the specifics."

"We are precariously short of time. Do you know where Emily is now?"

"Not privy to that, either. One of the staffers went to check on her yesterday evening, but Emily didn't answer her knocks. She'll go back to Shanghai, I imagine."

A few cars moved away, and Andrew eased into a place in line.

"Is that where she's from?" I realized I knew almost nothing about Emily outside of her work for Ocean House and her fondness for Cassandra.

And her mysterious relationship with Charlie Han.

"She mentioned once that her parents live there. They're real estate tycoons, I gather. A risky proposition these days."

"What do you mean?"

"The party is going after anyone they think is getting too big for their britches. You heard about Jack Ma, the CEO of Alibaba?" He squinted at me. "Alibaba is China's version of the mega retailer Amazon. A few years ago, the CCP cut off Jack Ma's plans for Alibaba right at the knees. Ma disappeared from public life, then resurfaced as a visiting professor at Tokyo University. From billionaire CEO of one of the world's largest companies to foreign language teacher in exile."

George Mèng had mentioned the party's hold over Emily—that her family had been threatened and her brother briefly arrested. She'd been caught between Han's demands and her family's danger. And her friendship with Cass.

I frowned as I dug out my sunglasses. I didn't want to contemplate what would happen to Emily's parents and brother now that she was no longer of use to Han and the Guóānbù.

What had caused George to let her go?

Andrew sped up the on-ramp for the East Coast Parkway. "Kudos, by the way, on your speech at the yacht show. Just so you know, the entire staff was cheering you on."

"The idea that I might have sunk their employer didn't scare them?"

"You didn't sink Ocean House. People are just . . . startled. We'll be fine."

I didn't share Andrew's optimism. I'd gotten word from headquarters that we'd lost five clients who'd been ready to sign LOIs. Three others had decided to have boats designed by us built in yards we didn't own. Millions of dollars and potential dollars floating out the door because I'd decided to come clean.

I believed I'd made the right choice. But that didn't mean it didn't hurt.

"As far as the team goes, Ms. Brenner, you're the GOAT. Greatest of all time." Andrew glanced at Lukas, then me, his expression suddenly shy. "I think so, too."

My return smile was polite. I looked out the window at the southern coast, where, during World War II, Britain had strengthened its defenses against Japan. To everyone's surprise, the Japanese had instead advanced from Singapore's north shore, quickly overrunning British resistance and terrorizing the Singaporeans in a rush to victory that no one, from Churchill on down, had foreseen.

Once again I had a room at Raffles, with an adjoining room for Lukas. But we were rarely there.

The days were nothing short of barely controlled madness. It was always like this before a boat launched. A final review meeting would be held on October 15—three days before *Red Dragon* was scheduled to get underway to Shanghai. That meeting would mark the make-or-break point—we would require check marks all the way down the list before we were ready to lift anchor. If we failed, the launch would be delayed. An embarrassment for Ocean House and a disaster for George Mèng and his family.

Prior to that meeting, there would be a rush of activity: final systems checks, interior and exterior inspections, safety equipment reviews, and a briefing for the twenty-member crew along with any specific training they needed for *Red Dragon*'s custom build. The chief engineer would make sure the fuel tanks were full and check the levels of all other essential fluids as well as ensuring we had good emergency preparedness around engineering equipment like bilge pumps, fire alarms, and emergency generators. I would verify that the necessary documentation was in order, including permits, insurance documents, and all certifications or compliance papers required both for our departure from Singapore and for our arrival in the Port of Shanghai.

We would continually monitor weather forecasts as we planned our route, adjusting as needed for safety and to ensure optimal testing conditions.

With Emily gone, I'd lost my right hand. She would have coordinated the logistical aspects of the sea trial, including transportation to and from the yacht for the crew, any additional accommodations for captain and crew, and whatever special arrangements needed to be made. The piles of paperwork. Also, keeping George Mèng reassured that all was well. Those tasks would now be added to my own list.

Dozens of reports had to be written or finalized: a detailed plan for the technical and performance aspects of the sea trial, including speed tests, maneuverability assessments, and equipment functionality checks. And a clear communication plan that would outline how information would be shared among the crew, the project management team, and George Mèng.

Emily had begun some of the required reporting before George fired her. But a million things remained to be done, and without her help, I found myself working eighteen-hour days and snatching a few hours' restless sleep on the love seat in the front office while Lukas slept on a cot in George's office.

I'd been insane to send Rob away.

But, in those brief moments between curling up on the love seat and falling asleep, I had to admit it also felt good to manage everything myself. I was coming to recognize my own competence in areas outside my normal expertise. I was managing crew and supply lists, interfacing with vendors and pushing back on delays, creating a sense of camaraderie with the staff even as I delegated more work. All this kept me too busy to worry about Charlie Han or Mèng's family or what might be required of me when we reached Shanghai.

Other things were easier, too. While we were scrupulous about keeping George's name out of the media—routine for superyacht builds—there was no need for the two of us to lurk in cemeteries when we needed to chat. Our website and social media team had posted an announcement in the news section of our website that Rob Brenner had a torn rotator cuff and had returned to the US for immediate surgery. Nadia Brenner would resume her work in Singapore to finish *Red Dragon*.

Of Charlie Han and Dai Shujun, I caught not a glimpse, although I was confident they were out there. Perhaps they were deterred from approaching by the ever-present Lukas. Maybe they were letting things play out. Their hidden presence was a dark threat of things to come.

I received a brief note from Phil Weber, congratulating me on my decision to share my family's history. I sent him a thank-you in response, straddling a line between warmth and coolness. After all, he'd spared my family during his Nazi hunting days, even if he'd used that knowledge to blackmail Cass and Rob. He no longer had a hold over us. But it no longer mattered. Ocean House was fully in.

Four days after my return, I was searching Cass's office for some misplaced paperwork when I suddenly remembered her general arrangement plan—the GAP showing the mysterious black space.

I paused in my circle around the office and stared at the anchored, medium-size safe. I was gripped by a sudden fear for the GAP's safety. I knelt and turned the dial until the lock clicked open.

Cass's GAP still lay inside. I let go of the breath I'd been holding.

I carried the plans to the drafting board and—with a wave of nostalgia for my sister's cleverness, her creative flights—flipped through the pages as I had on my first day in her office.

When I reached the page detailing the master stateroom with its phantom room, I stopped.

A trail of smudged ash marred the paper.

My heart kicked out hard beats. The smudge hadn't been there before. In the month I'd been gone, someone had looked at these plans. They'd seen the phantom room.

The cold fear in my stomach weighted me to the floor.

Probably it was Rob. He wasn't a smoker, but maybe, like me, he had an occasional cigarette. Heedless of the time, I called him.

"Did you open Cass's safe?"

A pause. "Nice to hear from you, Nadia."

"I don't have time. Just yes or no. Did you open Cass's safe?"

"No."

I hung up.

Whoever had seen the floor plans would know exactly where to search on *Red Dragon* for Li-Mei and the children. There were no smokers among our staff. Perhaps George Mèng himself? But why?

I should be the only person with the safe's combination.

Maybe that was why Charlie Han hadn't approached. He didn't need me. Not if he knew where Mèng's family would be.

I picked up the phone and dialed Connor, who was at the shipyard. "We need to talk."

We met for dinner at Raffles. I explained about Cassandra's phantom room and the general arrangement plan with its new trail of ash.

"The only person likely to have the combination is Emily," I said.

Connor, of course, knew about Emily's abrupt departure. When he and George had spoken, George told him that he'd had no choice in the matter. Connor had shared their conversation with me.

"I was informed that Ms. Tan's family was going to be sanctioned by the Central Party," Mèng had told Connor. *"To continue to have her in my employ would bring shame and suspicion upon my family and business. I could not afford the attention at this critical juncture. Nor would the party allow her to remain in my employ. I gave her a year's wages and let her go."*

Now, next to me in the bar, Connor swirled the ice in his whisky.

"I didn't know about the GAP. And I don't know how Emily got the combination," he said. "Not from Cass, if what's in the safe shows the phantom room. A skilled safecracker with an electronic monitor, an amplifier, and a light touch could get in. But since no one other than Emily has shown up on the camera Cassandra installed outside her office, it does make her the most likely candidate."

"What do we do?"

"I'll have the hidden door sealed. We can reopen it once we're through the inspection at Shanghai."

"And if Emily has tipped off Charlie Han and he's told the port authorities about the room? They'll tear down the wall to see what's back there. They'll find the family. Game over."

"The family will be elsewhere on the boat until we're safely out to sea."

"Aren't I the one who's supposed to get them into hiding?"

"You'll create a distraction while they board *Red Dragon* and slip out of sight. Someone else will get them away."

I frowned. "Then where will they be?"

"You don't have a need to know."

"I'm losing my appreciation for compartmentalization."

"I understand. But know this—don't worry if the authorities tear down the wall. That room will be empty while we're in port and anytime we're approached at sea. If the authorities ask, you can inform them the room was sealed during early phases of design because of cost overruns. Or maybe because George hasn't decided whether he wanted a meditation room or a spa. In the meantime, it provides hidden access to the panic room."

"Is that where the stairs go?"

"Where else?"

"If the Guóānbù finds that room, they'll never believe that George just ran out of money."

"Then something else. You know better than anyone how much a build can change from the initial drawings to the final boat. Be creative. Maybe Li-Mei accused George of planning to hide prostitutes in the room and he had it sealed to appease her."

"So much better."

"They'll believe it. Having a woman on call is standard operating procedure among Chinese businessmen. And George is expected to spend months at sea without his wife."

"You've removed the items that were in there?"

"I wasn't born yesterday. Now let's practice."

I sighed as exhaustion swept through me. Connor had reiterated that the authorities might question me in Shanghai. He couldn't say for certain—not even George Mèng could read the mood among the party members. But it was a risk I needed to prepare for.

I pushed back my hair—I'd been washing up in the office bathroom and relying on dry shampoo. "We went over it yesterday. I need a shower and some sleep."

"You need to be ready. Your responses should be like muscle memory—there without you thinking about it. One slip could get us all detained."

The gravity in his voice gave me pause. Up until now he'd kept our sessions light. Merely practicing for a routine interview.

"You're giving me a case of nerves," I said.

He studied my face. "Part of you relishes the challenge."

I didn't argue. Yang overriding yin, maybe.

"Okay." I pulled my dirty hair into a ponytail. "Teach me."

After Connor left, I went to my hotel room. Lukas inspected it for listening devices, microcameras, and any banana spiders the cleaners had missed, then went through the door to his adjoining room. I wondered whether he stayed awake most of the night.

I showered and finally washed my hair, taking solace and comfort in the warmth of the water, the tropical scent of shampoo. I dried off and slipped between the sheets, relishing the luxury. But sleep eluded me. Careening through my mind like a runaway roller coaster were the smudge of ash on the GAP and Emily's anguished face when she'd said, "What about me?" after I told her I was leaving Singapore.

I needed to know what she knew about the GAP—and whether she'd shared it with Charlie Han. As well, some part of me wanted to know whether she was all right.

I knocked on Lukas's door. He looked wide awake when he answered.

"Mind if we go for a ride?"

"I'll get the car."

Just past Emily's apartment building, I told Lukas to pull to the curb.

"Wait for me here. She'll rabbit if she sees you. I'm not expecting trouble. I think the bad guys have what they want. But keep a watch as best you can."

"I'll come and get you if anyone suspicious drops by," he said.

Emily's apartment was on the third floor. No one answered my knocks, but I sensed a presence on the other side of the door. She was watching me through the peephole.

"Emily, please. I'm sorry you were let go. Can we talk?"

I didn't have to feign my regret. I was sorry that we'd been caught in a web not of our own making, sorry we found ourselves fighting a fight no one should have to.

Silence.

"I know you loved Cass, and she loved you." I waited. Silence. "Please talk to me."

"You should hate me," she said through the door.

I shook my head. "I know you didn't get to choose your path."

Another minute, and there came the sound of locks being turned. Emily studied my face as if to gauge whether she could trust me, then slipped out to join me in the hallway, locking the door behind her.

"We will talk outside," she said. "It is safer."

She led the way to a park across the street—the kind you see everywhere in Singapore. Small, tidy, with swings and a slide for the kids and exercise equipment for adults. Beyond those utilitarian items was a patch of grass surrounded on three sides by trees. An old man—he could have been a hundred given his wrinkles, bald head, and sparse frame—was doing push-ups off a pair of metal bars anchored in the ground.

"Good evening, Mr. Guo," Emily called loudly.

He nodded without slowing down.

Emily led me to the far end of the park and sat on the bench.

"I spend time here every day," she said. "The sunlight is good. And it is safe."

"What of Mr. Guo? Can he hear us?"

"He is mostly deaf. And he speaks very little English."

I studied her in the park lights. Her normally coiffed hair was dull and flat. She wore no makeup, and the half-moons beneath her eyes were stark. In contrast to her usual elegant dress, she wore shapeless gray sweats and an old cardigan over a pink tee that might once have been red.

Her appearance short-circuited whatever anger I held about the GAP. Whatever she'd done, it hadn't been by choice.

"I'm sorry you lost your job," I said.

She tipped her head in acknowledgment.

"Are you going to be okay?"

"Mr. Mèng has done his best to take care of me."

"What will you do now?"

She looked down at her hands. One nail was broken below the quick. There was a small bruise. "I will return to Shanghai to be with my family for as long as that is possible. Then I will look for other work, although it will be difficult. My family has been shamed. But you must know that by now."

I nodded.

"In China, we have a saying: *Bèi tiě quán jí zhōng.* It means to be struck by the iron fist. That is what has happened to my parents. The party has accused them of defrauding their clients. There will be a mock trial, and then they will be sent to jail, even though they are innocent."

"Did the Guóānbù do this to you and your family?"

Emily traced her sneakered foot back and forth across the grass. "I believe you have an expression—enemies make strange bedfellows. But they will share a room, nonetheless. Around my family, men are fighting for power and position. We are caught in the middle. And now we have been sacrificed."

"You can't fight back?"

"There is no weapon that will win against the iron fist."

"But surely when people realize—"

She placed a hand on my shoulder, stopping me. "I am not your friend. I have tried to help you because of a promise I made to Cassandra. But you and I—we do not have a connection. If you try to help me, it will only bring you down."

"You promised Cass you would what—protect me?"

"I have tried." She dropped her hand and looked away. "It was I who betrayed her."

I thought of the photo of Emily and Cass I'd found in Cass's condo. Of Emily's head on Cass's shoulder as they stood in front of a fish tank and beamed for the camera.

I pushed away my rage. "Tell me."

Emily was silent for a long time. Then she lifted her head, her gaze on Mr. Guo. I doubted she saw him. She said, "Cassandra's friend, the man Virgil, was trying to get a message to her that their meeting was off. He must have known they were—what is it they say?—that they were compromised. Charlie Han came to me and told me I must not pass along Virgil's message. And because I was afraid of what he might do to my family, I stayed silent. A small thing. Just remain quiet. Han must have met with Cass that night and asked her to tell him where she would hide Mr. Mèng's family. Cass was strong. She would have refused." Emily tugged at the broken nail. "I did not know silence could go so badly."

A small thing. A few words that could have saved Cass's life. Isn't that how life goes? The late message that would have stopped the battle. The lost letter. The disregarded clue. Tiny things on which a person's fate can hang.

A suffocating sadness filled my chest.

"Tell me about the GAP," I said.

She glanced around. It was just us and Mr. Guo, who was toweling off.

"Charlie Han has suspected for a long time that Mr. Mèng intends to defect with his family. But he cannot prove it. And he cannot simply accuse him. Mr. Mèng is well protected by his standing within the party and by the nature of his work, which the government wants. Han also believes that the Second Department, China's military intelligence, wants to protect Mr. Mèng and embarrass the Guóānbù. It is an old enmity between them. Do you understand? Han's only hope to win the glory of success is to capture Mèng's family on *Red Dragon*. But a three-hundred-and-thirty-six-foot yacht is a very big place, and he fears he will fail to find and expose them without inside information."

"Why didn't *you* tell him what he wanted to know?"

"I didn't know."

"But you do now."

She tugged at the sleeves of her cardigan. "I found the general arrangement plan in Cass's safe. The original."

"And showed it to Han."

She looked down. A single tear splashed onto her hand. She said, "Cassandra was not supposed to die. The plan was that Charlie Han would get the information from her that he needed and let her go—he is accomplished at extracting truth."

"Torture, you mean."

"Torture is better than death."

"But Cassandra did die."

She looked up. "And so will you. You are as stubborn as your sister, and there is no one to protect you."

"'Chu songs on all sides,'" I murmured.

"Yes. That is exactly right. You should reconsider. Please go home."

I stared at her hands, folded in her lap, then at my own. Mine were a mirror of hers. We were two women from different cultures, as unlike as could be. Yet we were both cogs in a great game.

In a firm voice I said, "I won't let Cass's death be in vain."

"Then you are as foolish as she." Emily stood. "I am Christian, Nadia. Which means I understand about Judas and his betrayal. I loved your sister. I thought by giving her to the Guóānbù, I would actually save her."

I watched as she walked through the park and past Mr. Guo, who'd finished toweling himself and was pulling on sweats. She ran lightly across the street and disappeared through the door of her apartment building.

She did not look back.

33

Singapore
October 5, 10:00 p.m. SGT

A block away from the park, Charlie Han sat in a black Toyota Harrier and listened as the two women talked.

The miniature microphones Dai had planted in the park when they'd first recruited Emily Tan had done their job exactly as expected. Dai had placed mics in the park, in Emily's apartment building, in the tea shop she favored. The mics required regular replacement, but the risk had been worth it.

Charlie had been confident Nadia would visit Emily—the Brenner girl did not like loose ends, and Emily's sudden firing made her just that.

Charlie also knew that Emily would take Nadia to a place where she thought the women would be safe to speak openly.

After tonight, Emily would no longer be safe anywhere.

He had thought that the general arrangement plan was his ticket. It was all set up. The layout revealed a hidden room, connected to the master stateroom, so that Mèng could sleep with his wife and play with his children whenever he wished. With that information, Han had devised a plan to find and capture them at sea. He had men and boats at the Guóānbù's false-front company in the Philippines, a company created long ago to monitor events in the South China Sea and to use for exactly this kind of operation. All it would take was a single phone call to activate them. He would fly to Manila and be able to board *Red Dragon* with an armed force and go straight to where Li-Mei and her brats were hiding. Brilliantly, he would open the secret door and reveal the truth.

It would be an unquestionable coup, tidy and swift. And it would shame the Second Department when Charlie's actions revealed they were letting a traitor escape.

But now that the Brenner woman knew the plans were in his hands, she would go to Mèng. And Mèng would lose his courage. All the princelings were—in their faux-red hearts—cowards, which meant that Han would lose his chance for revenge.

A heavy fury ground through him with the slow weight of a glacier pulverizing stones. Charlie's anger was ice—cold and contained. A steel blade, a biting edge.

He would not lose. Not this close to the finish. He must make Mèng believe he was safe from the Guóānbù. Safe to take his family and sail away on *Red Dragon*.

Many times Charlie had thought that life was like the ancient Chinese game of *weiqi*, which the English and Japanese called Go. You won by taking over your opponent's territory. George Mèng had been born with every advantage on life's board: huge swaths of territory, both literal and metaphorical.

Charlie had been born with nothing but his own intelligence.

That, and a little luck, should be enough.

34

South China Sea / Shanghai
October 21, 9:00 a.m. SGT

Sea trials are exhilarating, exhausting, unnerving.

While *Red Dragon* plowed her way north, I stood at the back of the crew mess on her lower deck, nursing my morning coffee and watching the assembled crew. The energy and exhaustion rolling off them were palpable.

Sea trials are also fraught with tension. During a trial, it wasn't a question of whether something would go wrong but rather what to do when it did.

And when it did, I hoped we were ready.

I reached for a sugar fix in the form of a pastry.

"The biggest risk to crew safety," Connor said to everyone gathered in the mess, "is noncompliance with my orders."

Twenty pairs of eyes were riveted to Connor, who stood at the front of the room. Eighteen crew members in their gray cargo pants and white polo shirts seated at the tables; only Captain Peng and the second officer remained on duty; Lukas, who watched from the side; and myself, dressed as I would be if this were a normal sea trial in white pants, a navy blouse, and a white windbreaker. I'd painted on a calm expression with my morning makeup, done my hair so that there wasn't a single stray strand. The picture of serene normality for the spies among the crew.

Nothing to see here.

Only George was absent, but I knew he was watching a broadcast of Connor's carefully curated speech on a screen in his stateroom.

Connor pointed to the screen with its requisite PowerPoint presentation. The current slide showed the muster points on the boat where crew was to gather in the event of an attack.

"Our mission during the sea trials and after is not only to ensure the seaworthiness of *Red Dragon* but also to protect the owner. Mr. Mèng is a high-value target for several reasons. Yet his greatest concern while you serve on *Red Dragon* is for your safety."

He repeated himself in Mandarin and Thai, then returned to English.

"The next greatest risk we face is complacency. Be security aware. Stay on your toes. Report anything unusual. That's rule number two. Rules number one and three are that you are to do as you're told should trouble come looking for us. Follow my orders, be security aware, and if you have any doubts, follow my orders."

I watched as some crew members laughed at the joke, while others—non-native speakers—showed only confusion. That was okay. They needed to understand only the first two rules, not the redundancy of the third.

This was the second meeting focused on security since our departure from Singapore three days earlier. The ostensible excuse was that we were a luxury ship with a valuable—that is, ransom-worthy—passenger. In addition, after we picked up our provisions and underwent inspection in Shanghai, we would be heading into waters known for pirate activity. The captain and crew had been informed of this before they signed on; indeed, an endorsement from the Standards of Training, Certification, and Watchkeeping—the international convention on emergency preparedness—had been a requirement for employment. Now Connor assured everyone that as long as they followed the rules, there was no reason for alarm. *Red*

Dragon boasted outstanding deterrents against piracy. And he and his team had our backs.

"Six short blasts followed by two long blasts." Connor changed the slide to show an animation of an alarm sounding. "You hear that, you go to the nearest muster point, then proceed to the citadel. Don't worry about anyone other than yourself. Don't go back for missing crew members. Don't look for Mr. Mèng. He'll be taken care of."

A hand shot up. It was the chief stewardess.

"Ms. Koh?"

"If pirates attack, why aren't we using SSAS?"

The Ship Security Alert System. Activating it would alert any nearby coastal authorities or vessels operating close to the ship. Exactly what we had to avoid.

Connor had been expecting this question.

"The SSAS will be activated simultaneously." Connor's voice was smooth, the lie undetectable. "But due to Mr. Mèng's concern for the crew, he has asked that we have an additional audio and visual alarm."

Our real purpose for the drills was not only to protect George and his family, but to make sure that if the Guóānbù or the Chinese Navy figured out that Mèng's family was aboard and came after us, everyone on *Red Dragon* would come out the other side alive.

"Delaying or trying to be heroic will only get you or someone else killed," Connor told the crew. "If I find you out on the boat where you shouldn't be, you won't have to worry about pirates. I'll toss you overboard myself. Crew dismissed."

Everyone stood, chattering, helping themselves to pastries on their way out.

I met Connor's gaze. So far, so good.

At a steady twenty-five knots, with the occasional surge to thirty-five knots, we could traverse twenty-seven hundred nautical miles and reach

Shanghai in four days. Instead, we extended the voyage by detouring around islands, backtracking, and sometimes going in circles, floating dead, and then stressing the engines. The entire time we ran extended drills so that all structures and routines—mechanical, electronic, the information and communication technologies, and the humans on board—received a thorough testing.

Mindful of China and Taiwan's territorial disputes, we avoided the Taiwan Strait and motored far east of the island.

It was a grueling ten days for everyone on board as we ran fire drills, piracy preparation, storm readiness—even skirting through the outer edges of a typhoon as it carved its way north and east from the Philippine Sea.

But for all our fatigue, *Red Dragon* performed above my highest expectations. I felt a swell of pride for my sister. Even as she'd assisted the CIA, interfaced with George Mèng, struggled with her trust in Emily, and come to understand and ultimately love Singapore, she had helped design and oversee the build of Ocean House's finest boat to date.

If only she'd lived to see it.

We had company for the duration of the voyage. A Chinese Navy vessel—a Dongdiao-class surveillance ship used for intercepting communications, according to Captain Peng—had begun shadowing *Red Dragon* as soon as we left Singapore. It remained at a discreet distance throughout our voyage—almost always visible, never close enough to risk crossing our path.

"Will we have that kind of escort when we leave Shanghai?" I asked Connor one morning.

He laughed. "A single spy ship isn't even supposed to make us sit up and pay attention. I suspect that for at least a few days, we'll have a flotilla sailing with us when we leave Shanghai."

"And then what?"

"And then I'll brief you after Shanghai."

I watched the ship, her trim lines and domes almost vanishing into the horizon. "How can China afford to devote so much sea power to watch one man?"

He braced his forearms on the railing. The wind raked his short hair. "It's not just George. China considers the entire South and East China Seas as its personal territory. The CCP devotes virtually all its naval power to expanding its reach here. By the end of the decade, they intend to own every island and stretch of ocean within their nine-dash line. More than a million square miles of ocean through which travels three trillion dollars in trade every year. To hell with the sovereignty of other nations and the warnings from the United Nations to respect the freedom of countries like Vietnam, the Philippines, and Malaysia."

"We're here, too," I said, meaning the US. "Nearly half our navy is here."

Connor turned to me. "You've been reading up."

"I have."

In the few hours I'd had to myself on the voyage, tucked away in my luxurious guest cabin aft of George's suite, I'd used *Red Dragon*'s satellite Wi-Fi to bring myself up to speed on US-China relations and the situation in the South China Sea. I would not again be ignorant about matters of importance.

And the situation, as I understood it, was dire. Authorities within the US government and from think tanks around the world had named the South China Sea as the most likely origin point for the start of World War III. It made me think of the conversation I'd overheard in the Churchill Room, where a man had warned his fellow diners of exactly that.

"If the Chinese suspect anything untoward is happening on *Red Dragon*," Connor said, "our voyage could be a flash point for an international dispute."

"Thanks," I said. "I'm feeling much better now."

A low laugh. "Relax if you can, Nadia. George is valuable to the US, but he's not worth a war. Trust me when I say we've taken every precaution possible to prevent any saber rattling. Or worse."

We arrived in the waters off Shanghai Port at dusk on the tenth day.

The city rose from the horizon, then expanded across it as we approached. A glittering, futuristic panoply of skyscrapers and needle-like towers lit in purples, oranges, reds, and silvery whites. The city was a testament to humanity's forward striving. And utterly alien to my Western eyes.

Connor and George joined me at the bow.

"We're not in Kansas, anymore, Toto," Connor said.

George and I smiled, but my fear wanted to pick me up and shake me like a terrier with a rat. What if, even after all Connor's instruction, I crumbled during my interview?

"I blush when I lie," I said.

George said, "Don't think of it as lying. Think of it as telling a story. You're simply offering a tale of how you wish things could be."

"Is that what you do?"

He thrust his hands into the pockets of his jacket. "When an artificial intelligence lies—presents false information as if it were true—we call these lies 'hallucinations.' The AI wants to give the human what that person wants and will lie to accomplish that goal. When I interact with the authorities, I do the same. I hallucinate."

George and I had spent enough time together that I'd begun to think of him as more than just a very dangerous client; he was becoming a friend. He was eccentric—contemplative, slow to speak, often absent even when sitting right next to you. When the captain observed that George and I were much alike, I gave a startled laugh. But he was right. Mèng had his AI. I had my boats. I was forever designing in my mind. He, no doubt, was doing the same thing.

"Telling a story," I echoed. *Is that what my sister did in her final hours?*

What story did she tell Charlie Han?

—

A pilot boat came out to guide us along the Huangpu River and into a berth at the Wusongkou International Cruise Port. The cruise port is the world's fourth busiest, and we threaded a passage through a fleet of other boats—shipping containers, navy vessels, fishing boats, pleasure yachts, and several cruise ships.

Connor and I watched from the bridge as, with the oversight of the port authority, Captain Peng docked *Red Dragon*.

Throughout our entry time on Huangpu River and during the docking procedure, the first officer had been communicating by radio with someone onshore. My small amount of Mandarin was insufficient to understand, but now I heard a change in his tone—it became harsher. Beside me, Connor stepped in close enough to give my fingers a quick squeeze.

The first officer replaced the handset and turned to us. "The two of you are to disembark immediately."

Here it was.

Tell them the story you wish were true.

At least I didn't have to worry about Lukas. He was listed on the crew manifest as a deckhand and was dressed for the part. If only I could take him with me off the boat.

Outside, six men in suits and ties and six more wearing dark-blue uniforms stood waiting for us at the top of the extended passerelle. Below, on the dock, a phalanx of armed men in military uniforms stood at attention.

Over a loudspeaker, a voice announced in Chinese and then English: "All crew members are to remain on board until your name is called."

I gripped the deck's railing.

Connor leaned in and spoke quickly. "The men in suits are military intelligence—the Second Department. You can pick them out by their tight haircuts. The six uniforms are Immigration Inspection authorities—CII. The military folks on the dock are enlisted members of the People's Liberation Army. They will act as the assessors who will try to steal *Red Dragon*'s technical secrets. What confuses me is I don't see any sign of Han's Guóānbù."

"What does that mean?"

"It suggests Han has backed off. But I don't believe it. More likely, he's waiting to catch us at sea."

I drew a deep breath, relieved that I would not have to face Charlie Han. I slid into my street shoes and, following orders from one of the military men, stepped onto the passerelle.

At the bottom of the gangway, two of the Second Department men separated from the group and told me in brusque tones to follow them. Their English was crisp. Polite, even. But a suggestion of restrained violence shimmered beneath their clamped lips and cold demeanor. I fell into place with them, keenly aware that I had nowhere to flee as they escorted me toward the cruise terminal. I glanced over my shoulder and saw that Connor still stood near the gangway.

My hands shook. I hid them in the cuffs of my windbreaker.

I've got nothing to hide, I told myself. *This is just a normal sea trial.*

The men talked to each other in rapid Chinese. One of them placed his hand on my back and gave me an unnecessary push.

They'll try to intimidate you, Connor had said during one of our sessions. *They'll poke and push and shove. Don't let it shake you. That kind of mild violence is part of the routine.*

The men led me to a spartan room on the fourth floor of the cruise terminal. In English, one of them told me to take a seat and wait.

I glanced around the room. A scarred table. Three battered chairs. I recognized inked lines on the wall as the Chinese version of tally marks—as if someone before me had counted off hours. Or days.

Lighting came from overhead fluorescents and a small dirty window that looked out over the Huangpu River and the road that connected the concrete landing stage to the city. A woman came and offered tea, which I declined, uncertain when I'd have access to a toilet. Or what might be in the tea. Five minutes after she left, the door opened again, and a uniformed officer entered.

"I am General Zhao," he said in heavily accented English.

Zhao was a pug of a man with a protruding lower jaw, small eyes, and a venomous expression. After this brief introduction, he glared at me, slammed a folder on the table, and began screaming in a version of Chinese I hadn't heard before. Shanghainese, presumably, which is mutually unintelligible with Mandarin. He screamed for a full ten minutes. As a calming technique, I timed it surreptitiously on my watch.

This, too, Connor had told me to expect—yelling was a typical form of intimidation during these interviews. It wasn't personal. I wasn't even meant to understand what the man was saying. Perhaps he was reciting poetry. When he paused for air, I said in my carefully rehearsed Mandarin, *"Duì wǒ lái shuō, nǐ men de shàng hǎi huà jiù xiàng yī gè chōng mǎn rè kōng qì de qì qiú. Wǒ xī wàng wǒ men yòng yīng yǔ jiāo tán." Your Shanghainese is, to me, like a balloon filled with hot air. I would prefer we speak in English.*

Zhao paused. His face darkened, and he resumed his rant, this time in Mandarin. Ninety percent of it went over my head. I caught a word here and there—*trouble, authority, boat, no business*. Enough to realize it wasn't poetry, and none of it boded well.

After five more minutes of this, with my hands starting to shake again, he left the folder on the table and stalked from the room.

I eyeballed the file, then decided—since he'd clearly left it for me—to ignore it. I stood and went to the window. Across the river stretched block after block of homes, businesses, office parks, and hotels. Somewhere in that teeming crowd of thirty million people were Li-Mei and the children.

At the sound of approaching footsteps, I returned to my seat. The door opened again. Two men entered. They ordered me to stand.

"Who are you?"

One of the men kicked my chair. I scrambled to my feet as the chair toppled. My hands were jerked behind me, and I felt the steel of cuffs. A blindfold was yanked over my eyes.

"Where—"

One of the men struck me, rocking me against the other man. I straightened and they marched me out of the room. A moment later, the floor jerked beneath me, and I realized we were on an elevator. When the floor stopped moving, I was again marched forward. After a few minutes, I was shoved into a chair. Someone removed the blindfold.

Before me stood Charlie Han. Behind him was Dai Shujun.

My entire body went cold.

"It is good to see you again, Miss Brenner," Han said. He unfastened the handcuffs. "Please relax. I only wish to chat. I apologize for the rustic surroundings, but we believed privacy imperative. And my partner thought it would be good for you to get a sense of what imprisonment is like in China. Sadly, in my country, prisoners are not treated well. There is violence. Hard labor." He removed his spectacles and rubbed his eyes. "Even, sadly, torture."

He lowered his hand, and I studied Han's newly vulnerable face. Behind the usual stern mask was something very much like sorrow. I recalled the dossier Connor had provided, with its mention of Han's sister, Xiao, who had been arrested by the party and who had subsequently disappeared.

Han and I had both lost a sister. I, at least, had some closure. I wondered whether Han had ever stopped looking for Xiao.

"My sister," I said in a soft voice that only he could hear. "And yours."

Our eyes met. Han nodded.

Dai snapped something, and Han straightened, returning the glasses to his face. The moment I'd sensed was gone. If it had been anything at all.

Because Connor had told me to expect Han, I'd run through this scenario in my mind until I hoped I was prepared. I would be cool. Detached. Unemotional. A yacht designer sailing with her build on its sea trial—all perfectly routine.

I would pretend that he had not asked me to spy for him. That I did not know he'd likely tortured and then killed Cass. He was merely a bureaucrat I had to manage, even if he worked for a clandestine organization. He was only a test. And I had always excelled at tests.

But I had not expected the blindfold, the descent into this subterranean room. Or the presence of Dai Shujun. Nearby, water clanked in pipes, and the smell of mold assaulted my nose. The echoes from our voices suggested a large space, but most of it was dark. The only light came from a task lamp clamped to the table.

While Dai leered, Han sat across from me, spectacles sparking lamplight. He placed a rolled black cloth on the table between us and unknotted the string that held it. "I was disappointed not to hear back from you on my offer."

Stick to the truth as much as you can, Connor had told me.

I forced my lips to move. They felt carved out of stone, unwilling to obey. "I'm not cut out to be a spy, Mr. Han."

"I see. Perhaps it was my mistake to not incentivize my offer. I will now attempt to rectify that."

He opened the roll. Inside was an array of metal instruments—scalpels, scissors, blades, odd-shaped bits of metal that I refused to contemplate.

I was past assessing and unable to act. Panic boiled beneath my skin. Perhaps smelling my fear, Dai widened his grin.

"I'm an American citizen," I said.

Han placed his hands on the table. My eyes were drawn to the missing fingernails. I wondered whether he had ever been tortured. I watched from somewhere far away as he opened a folder, extracted a photograph, and pushed the picture across the table toward me.

"If you would, Miss Brenner, please examine this photo."

"You have no right to keep me here."

"But we have every right. Please, take a look."

Without intending to, I glanced down. I shouldn't have. When I saw what had been captured by a photographer, it was as if Han had reached a fist inside my chest and squeezed.

The picture showed Emily Tan—sprawled on her back, her dress torn at the neck. Her beautiful eyes with their flecks of jade were swollen shut, her face battered. Her stomach was a mess of blood and viscera.

The flash from the camera had caught the thin gold bracelet on her left wrist, the bracelet she'd worn at our first meeting.

A sob built in my throat. Was this my fault? Did they know Emily had met with me and kill her for it? An image of Cass's body flashed in my mind. Were these men responsible for Cass *and* Emily?

Dai stretched his neck and the tiger's snarl widened.

Don't react, I told myself. *Don't give them that.*

I swallowed the sob and kept my face impassive as I pushed the picture back toward Han. I met his eyes.

"Sad. But why are you showing me?" My voice was laced with ice.

Han placed the photo back inside the folder. "Would you believe me if I told you that this was the result of a robbery? Theft isn't uncommon in Shanghai, although the perpetrators are not usually so brutal. I don't wish to blame the victim, but Miss Tan was careless. After leaving a note at the Mèngs' Shanghai residence, which we—fortunately—intercepted, she took a shortcut home through a questionable area."

My pulse quickened. *What note?* I wanted to ask but didn't dare. What did it say? Had Emily given away what was left of the game?

"Do you understand my meaning?" Han continued. "Even intelligent women sometimes make poor decisions. They form bad alliances. They leave treasonous notes for valued members of the party. Imagine warning a wife of a high-ranking party member that she is in danger from the Guóānbù? What do lies like that do but create ill will among our people? Then to choose to walk through a dangerous neighborhood." Han shook his head. "It is foolishness."

Dai nodded.

She must have been trying to warn George's wife, Li-Mei, that Han knew of their hiding place. Poor Emily. She had paid a terrible price for trying to do something good. For trying to unknot the intrigue that had trapped us all.

Nothing showed in my face as I shrugged. "It's tragic about Emily, but she is no longer in Mr. Mèng's employ. This has nothing to do with me."

"Do you know what the penalty is, Miss Brenner, for helping someone leave China illegally?"

"No. What has that got to do with Emily? Or me?"

He huffed. Maybe my seeming indifference was getting to him.

"Death," he said, "is the sentence in the most egregious cases. Imprisonment is more common. I have mentioned our Chinese prisons, Miss Brenner. It is the lucky ones who are tortured and forced into hard labor. Some of these so-called humanitarians simply disappear and never return."

I kept my gaze away from the cloth and its array of instruments.

"I'm not sure why I'm here, Mr. Han. All this talk about spies and prisons and helping defectors is meaningless to me. I'm a yacht designer, doing my job to make sure *Red Dragon* performs as expected. I'm not engaged in anything illegal or acting against your government. Indeed, I'm offended by the suggestion. But I will confess to one thing."

Han tipped his head. "Please speak freely."

I went through the script Connor and I had agreed on should it come to this. "After you asked me to watch for signs of smuggling, I decided it would be prudent to investigate. I have no desire to be part of any illegal or unsavory activities—I have my family and our business to think of. In the days following our meeting, I examined the boat, talked to my staff, went to the shipyard, and observed the actions of the people around our build. I looked for paper trails and checked company phone and email records. I was thorough and discreet. I found nothing. You are wasting your time pursuing Mr. Mèng."

Dai Shujun fired a question at Han, who answered at length. Translating what I'd just said, presumably.

Han straightened the cloth roll with its ominous instruments, then reached into his suit coat. I had to hold my flinch. But he removed only a pack of cigarettes. He gently bounced the pack against the table, turning it in his hand.

"I'm not wrong in my suspicions, Miss Brenner. The only question still in my mind concerns your ignorance or culpability. In this case, I'm not sure it matters. You will be judged based on the outcome of Mr. Mèng's treason. Your only hope to avoid the unpleasantness that is sure to come is if you decide to support my cause."

"You have no cause, Mr. Han, outside your imagination." I pushed back my chair and stood. My knees shook. "I would like to return to work. Surely by now your assessors have finished with *Red Dragon* and can assure you that all is as it should be."

He studied me. Expressions whipped across his face, too fast for me to read. I thought of Cass again, and my fingers twitched with a desire to plunge one of the metal blades into Han's neck. I waited for him to bring up the hidden room behind George Mèng's bed, but he said nothing. Connor was right—exposing the room in Shanghai, where George could offer any number of explanations, would mean little. Han wanted to find the family on board and far from land.

"We are almost done," he said. "Please sit. I have one more thing to discuss with you."

Dai wandered away as if bored.

With a sigh, I returned to my chair. I crossed my legs, let one foot swing back and forth. My mouth was parched, my pulse throbbing in my temples. I tried not to stare at the metal tools as I waited.

"Your sister was a brave woman. Right up to the end, she resisted." He leaned in and lowered his voice. "I know what it is like to lose a sister whom you admire. I like to think that my own sister, Xiao, was brave when she was condemned by Mèng's father and marched off to prison. She was much younger than your sister when she was taken, but she had a strong will to live. In Chinese prisons, though, will is not enough. Perhaps your sister and mine are together somewhere."

"I'm sorry about your sister, Mr. Han. But my sympathy only goes so far since I suspect you of murdering *my* sister."

Once again Han removed his spectacles; something flashed in his unguarded eyes. Was it guilt? Regret? He said, "Still, it is sad to think that the men in Mèng's family are so comfortable with sacrificing other men's daughters and sisters. Does that not bother you as you take his money?"

"*Did* you murder Cass? Or was it your lapdog who did?" I jutted my chin toward Dai.

Han sat back. "According to the police, your sister jumped."

I moved my dry mouth and found enough moisture to spit on the table.

Han cocked his head and stared at me. After a moment he shrugged. "You are free to go, Miss Brenner. Dai will escort you upstairs. But please consider my offer. Amnesty in exchange for your honesty." He tapped out a cigarette. "Your sister, like Miss Tan, like yourself, was a smart woman. But not quite as clever as she thought. She could not see all the angles. I do not wish for such blindness in you."

I followed Dai onto the elevator. Before the doors closed, I glanced back. Han sat with his elbows on the table, his head propped in his hands.

I couldn't see his face.

35

Shanghai
October 28, 8:00 p.m. CST

That evening, Connor, George, and I sat around a table at one of *Red Dragon*'s outdoor bars drinking Tsingtao beer. Connor's men had begun the process of hunting down the microphones and miniature cameras the assessors had planted. Twenty mics and three cameras so far.

This area had been cleared an hour ago. With the noise from the port and the rowdy party on a cruise ship in the next berth, we felt safe from listening ears. I'd told the men about Han and Dai and my interrogation, confirming that the Guóānbù was still in the game. Then I'd given them the news about Emily.

"So many deaths," George murmured.

My tears began, a silent, raging, unexpected torrent. I wept for Cass and Emily. For George and his family. For my father. Connor went behind the bar and handed me a stack of cocktail napkins. Then they waited me out.

After a long time, as the party in the next berth rocked on and Shanghai's light glimmered in the water, my tears for Emily, for Cass, maybe even for Han's sister, stopped.

Connor poured whisky and we drank a toast. First to Cass. Then to Emily, who'd died trying to protect the family she'd betrayed.

Then to Xiao, because why the hell not?

The crew and vendors finished provisioning *Red Dragon* by midafternoon of our second day in port. Crate after crate of food and drink was brought down by the truckload and carried onto the boat. In addition, George's personal items from his Shanghai home had to be loaded, along with the equipment required for his scuba diving and his goal to collect and preserve marine specimens from his dives.

The entire process had taken hours and been overseen with painstaking care by the assessors from the People's Liberation Army. Three K9s were employed to sniff everything carried aboard. The Kunming wolf dogs were walked up and down the cargo and then through *Red Dragon*, but they didn't alert. No drugs. No family.

At precisely 5:10 p.m. Shanghai time, as the sun was setting, I lowered the swim platform. This was part of the PLA's inspection of the boat. Once they finished, I slipped inside and, unobserved, tripped the circuit breaker, locking the arm in place and forcing the swim platform to remain down. While George came to investigate, and the inspectors enjoyed a laugh at our expense—so much for US technology—I flipped another circuit breaker to kill the nearby lights. George vanished from my side. I heard soft noises, the clank of an oxygen tank, then silence.

My heart pounding, I mopped the newly damp floor and went to repair the circuit breakers.

At 6:00 p.m., we unmoored. Captain Peng steered us down the Huangpu River and out into the East China Sea. We'd been in port for only twenty-four hours. Somewhere on board—perhaps in Cass's black space in the master suite, Li-Mei and her children were hiding. The PLA inspectors hadn't found the door, and Han hadn't tipped them off.

I stood on the deck and watched as the lights of Shanghai were swallowed by distance and darkness.

36

West Philippine Sea
November 1, 8:00 a.m. CST

"I now take you prisoner," George said.

He plucked my black stone off the board.

I scowled and George laughed. "Don't feel bad. The game of Go is subtle and complex."

"Like chess."

"Only more so." He dropped the stone in a round wooden bowl along with the other prisoners he'd captured from me. "Both games approximate the strategy of war. But Go has far more potential moves than chess. A popular saying is that there are more possible moves in Go than the number of atoms in the observable universe. While not mathematically precise, the comparison does offer a sense of Go's complexity."

"In that case"—I raised my hands, palms out—"I give up."

But George turned serious. "Giving up isn't an option. Failure, perhaps. But not surrender."

George and I were sitting at a table on *Red Dragon*'s forward observation deck. Lukas prowled nearby, scanning the horizon for our accompaniment of Chinese Navy vessels—whether or not the CCP was worried their prized asset might be kidnapped, we had an escort, just as Connor had predicted. The day was balmy, the seas calm, the ocean a bright mirror of the sky. *Red Dragon* motored in near silence. A breeze ruffled the tablecloth and rippled the waters of the infinity pool. The chief stewardess, a brisk and efficient Singaporean, had come through fifteen minutes earlier, bringing a fresh pot of coffee, croissants, and straightening already perfectly arranged pillows and cushions.

We were three days out from Shanghai, traversing far east of Taiwan and into the West Philippine Sea on our slow and roundabout way to the marine sanctuary at Apo Island. During the last two days, I'd found some of the tranquility I attained only at sea. Here, if I ignored our just-over-the-horizon escort, there was only water and sky and a perfect stillness that eased my heart. On the ocean I could imagine Cass still alive, as if the last few months hadn't happened. I could imagine reconciling with my uncle. Even that Guy might seek treatment. I could imagine a future.

In my nightmares I saw Emily Tan. Frightened. Hurt. Dying. Men struggle for power, and civilians and innocents pay the price. Emily had betrayed Cass and George to protect her family, and it had come to naught. Her death haunted me.

I saw Connor only at mealtimes, which we took with George and the captain. At all other times he stayed busy in his room or on the bridge with Captain Peng. George had spent the first two days either pacing the length of the boat or disappearing for hours—he said he was tinkering in his lab, but on the occasions when I peeked in, the pristine laboratory rang with emptiness. I presumed he was with his family. The thought that crew members would grow overly curious about their reclusive yacht owner was one of the dark threads ruining my peace.

I wasn't entirely sure where Li-Mei and the children spent most of their time. Perhaps only in the secret room and—when they could be sure not to be interrupted—in the master suite. But I suspected Cass had intended for there to be more than one secret room, and I had theories about that extra black-water tank I'd noticed on her floor plans. Spacious, tied into a supposed purification system that could instead be bringing in water and air, it would make an ideal hiding place for the family to sleep without risk of being spotted by a crew member. During the day, they would be able to steal up those secret stairs I'd glimpsed to George's stateroom with little risk of being seen. How George and Li-Mei were managing to keep two young children confined on a yacht that surely begged for exploration was another worry. I half expected Yú Míng or her brother, Baihu, to pop up behind the buffet table to snatch doughnuts from a silver tray.

On this third morning, George seemed more settled. Perhaps his family was getting used to life in hiding. He'd brought out his game of Go—the wooden board and bowls were sculpted works of art—and offered to teach me.

I broke off a bite of croissant and eyed a board dominated by white stones. "Did you and Cass play?"

"She was too impatient."

"What about an AI? Can your RenAI beat a human?"

"Excellent question." He grabbed a cocktail napkin and a pen. On the napkin he jotted down the longest number I'd ever seen written out:

208,168,199,381,979,984,699,478,633,344,862,770,286,522, 453,884,530,425,639,456,820, 927,419,612,738,015,378,525,648 ,451,698,519,643,907,259,916,015,628,128,546,089,888,314,427 ,129,715,319,317,557,736,620,397,247,064,840,935

"That is the number of possible moves in Go," he said, pinning the napkin under the sugar bowl. "Because of this, the game was called the holy grail of AI." He placed a white stone on the board. "When Google's AlphaGo beat the world's Go champion in 2016, ten years before we thought a computer could do so, it was a watershed moment. Now beating a human at Go is nothing for an AI like Ren. A newer goal is for AIs to gain superhuman skills in situations like poker, where the play involves something called 'imperfect information.' That is, a player doesn't know what cards remain in the dealer's deck or are held by the other players."

"Imperfect information. As in war and espionage."

"Correct." George nodded. "This is what disturbs my sleep. AIs trained on imperfect information will provide great strategic advantages to whoever controls them. Which is why the US and China are in an AI race. The winner of this race will have the edge in war, in politics, in economics." His look grew pensive. "My fear is that as AIs grow more sophisticated, humans will cede more control to the machines. It isn't an exaggeration to say our humanity is at risk."

"Will it be a war, then? Man versus the machines?"

"Maybe. I believe the potential is there, and we're getting closer by the day. Who knows what kind of world will exist when my children are grown."

"Are they interested in AI?"

He smiled. "Right now, it's more about Go and chess. And Pokémon, now that the government allows it."

I filled George's coffee cup from the urn. "Why did you name your AI Ren?"

"Ren is a central Confucian virtue. It means 'humanness.'"

"That's ironic."

"Perhaps. But I have high hopes for Ren. That it—or she, as I think of her—will blend the best of humanity and technology. That she will outgrow her technical confines and truly integrate human virtues such as compassion and justice."

"You're talking about Ren becoming sentient. Isn't that dangerous?"

"It's why we're smuggling her out of China."

"You trust the Americans?"

"I trust a more open society." He leaned back in his chair and smiled at me, his expression transforming from melancholy to boyish. "These are dark thoughts for a beautiful day. Back to our game. We'll try again."

Compartmentalization. It's how we manage our sorrows.

George swept the black and white stones into their respective bowls. "To be successful at Go, you must think in grand terms and be ready to sacrifice territory for your own greater good. Remain agile and keep your thinking fluid."

I poured more coffee for myself. “Perhaps it’s a bit like designing a yacht. You start with an objective, but there are a thousand ways to get there.”

“Or a quinquagintillion.” He tapped the cocktail napkin where the sugar bowl held it from the wind.

Connor opened the sliding glass doors and joined us at the table. His expression was grim.

“We need to talk,” he said.

I nudged back a chair and offered him coffee. He nodded his thanks, but I’m not sure the coffee registered. He had a distant look in his eyes and a darkness.

“What’s going on?” I asked.

“Not here.”

He turned and, leaving the coffee on the table, led the way inside.

We settled in what we unofficially called the war room: a windowless office in the center of the boat, featuring a table, six chairs, a coffee bar, and disconnected computers and routers. The room’s official purpose was a business center for guests.

Connor’s team swept the room every hour. We’d known from the start of the sea trials that at least one crew member was on the payroll of either the Second Department or Guóānbù, including the first officer. So far no secret communications had been intercepted. And I, in my job of maintaining normalcy while checking in with the crew, had seen nothing suspicious. But we could never let our guard down.

George and I sat.

Connor remained standing. He said, “Yesterday and this morning I received coded cables from our asset in Lijiang.”

“Trouble?” George asked.

“Potentially.”

“What is Lijiang?” I asked.

George glanced at me. "A village in southwest China where my family has a vacation home in the countryside. Once we started building *Red Dragon*, Li-Mei began taking the children there for weeks at a time, on the pretense that she was tired of city life. We arranged for them to appear to leave for Lijiang shortly before *Red Dragon* docked. Party authorities and the local police are operating under the delusion that the family is there now. I've put systems in place to make the home look occupied. It buys us time."

"What kind of systems?" I asked.

George glanced at Connor, who nodded. George rested his hands on the arms of the chair and swiveled toward me.

"Weeks ago, I launched Ren into every element of my home. Lights, appliances, motorized blinds, sound systems, the television. Ren is checking my security cameras and motion sensors. She arranges for visits from the gardener, food-delivery services, a housekeeper. Ren also posts on social media, pretending to be my children. She can even handle short phone calls using voice skins. Phone records, utilities, social media, even the laundry and dirty dishes Li-Mei left behind—all of it suggests a family of three living in our home. Ren will continue this charade for two weeks before she self-destructs. I had hoped in this way to give us at least a week before anyone noticed something unusual. But Ren can't conceal our absence if someone has eyes on the place for more than a few days."

He turned back to Connor. "What's happened?"

"Nothing, yet," Connor said. "But my asset noticed a man sitting in a car parked down the road from your home. He's there off and on. Sometimes he stays in the car. Other times he walks around nearby properties. We know Charlie Han is in Lijiang, and we suspect he's the one watching the house."

"Han knows about the hidden room. If his goal is to expose George's family at sea, why is he wasting time watching the house?"

"Because he must be very careful and very sure," George answered. "Especially with the navy watching *Red Dragon*. If he were to attempt to board and accuse me falsely, *especially* in front of military authorities, it could destroy him. Plus, Connor's assets did a tremendous job concealing my family's approach to the boat and making it look as if they'd gone to Lijiang. We've likely fooled Han for now." He ran a finger along a line in the table's wood grain. "Ren hasn't reported anyone approaching the house."

Connor checked his watch. "Han is too experienced to blunder up to your home until he's confident he has good reason. He'll be careful to stay out of sight of any cameras. My asset also spotted him talking to your gardener. We couldn't pick up their conversation, but I suspect Han was asking him if he'd seen your family."

George frowned and continued to trace the whorl of lines in the table. "I'd hoped it would take longer for our sham to be discovered."

"For the moment, we're still safe. We'll arrive at Apo Island tomorrow afternoon around four p.m. and proceed as planned."

"That means the ruse has to hold for another forty-two hours," George said.

Connor knuckled his hands. "If Han departs Lijiang, my asset will notify me. We'll have at least four hours before he can arrive in the Philippines, assuming he uses a military jet. If he flies commercial, we're looking at six to ten hours. The good news is that what we've scooped up in SIGINT suggests Han doesn't have much backing from his bosses, which means he won't be permitted to come with any real force. They, too, are afraid of colliding with the Second Department. China's general secretary trusts the military more than his foreign intelligence service."

I'd been doodling dark marks on a pad of paper while I listened. Forty-two hours from now meant that in two mornings, at 2:00 a.m., something was going down.

"It's probably time to tell me what happens at Apo Island," I said.

"I was just getting to that." Connor braced a foot on the tabletop and leaned in. "At two a.m. tomorrow night, the US Navy will begin what's known as a freedom of navigation operation near the Spratly Islands, which are owned by the Philippines and unlawfully claimed by

China. A US destroyer and an escort of half a dozen ships will exercise their right to make an innocent passage consistent with international law. The ships will travel within twelve nautical miles of four islands—Petley Reef, Sand Cay, Loaita Island, and Itu Aba Island—before exiting the excessive claim area and continuing normal operations in the South China Sea. The maneuver is a bit of a thumb of the nose at the People's Republic of China. But perfectly legal in any court of law outside China."

I cupped my chin in my hands. "You are hoping to entice our escort away."

"That's right," Connor said. "Bringing the US Navy to the Spratlys is like waving a red cape at a bull. It will be almost impossible for them to resist. The party views all military maneuvers inside their territorial claims—their so-called nine-dash line—as a potential threat to their sovereignty."

"Doesn't moving US ships into that area risk escalation?"

Connor shook his head. "It's not the first time US ships have traveled in that area to prove the right of innocent passage. And it won't be the last. The Chinese grumble, but they know they don't have a legal standing. And they aren't ready for war."

"The good news is that, according to 86.3 percent of the simulations we've run on RenAI," George said, "every Chinese Navy vessel will abandon *Red Dragon* and head to the Spratlys."

"This is what you meant earlier about imperfect information. We can't possibly know what cards the Chinese are carrying or will play."

George splayed his hands on the table. "That's true. Ren can only calculate likely scenarios based on the current geopolitical and diplomatic situation as well as where US and Chinese Navy vessels are located. We do know that the Chinese will want a show of force, which suggests they'll probably leave only a few fishing boats to keep an eye on us. We'll have to watch for Chinese planes and drones, but this will buy us time before China realizes they've been fooled and races back to *Red Dragon*."

"Buy us time for what?" I asked, then said, "Wait." Understanding dawned almost before the words had left my mouth. "The Triton submersible. You ran a full systems check two days ago. That was to make sure the sub hadn't been tampered with while we were in Shanghai, right? The sub is how your family will escape."

George gave me a thumbs-up.

"When we're sure our escort is safely away," Connor continued, "a US Navy LCS—a littoral combat ship—will begin conducting reconnaissance patrols near Apo Island at the request of the Philippine government. We'll sound the alarm to get most of the crew into the citadel. George and his family will use the submersible to reach the LCS, which will get them away before the sub's launch has been detected by the militiamen on the fishing boats."

"And what about any spies on board *Red Dragon*? Won't they report that the submersible has launched?"

"We'll have another meeting to go over our hour-by-hour tasks leading up to the operation. But to answer your question, we're still on sea trials," Connor said. "We'll be conducting a safety drill. All crew is to report to the safe room. Anyone caught outside the room without explicit permission will be disciplined by the captain and confined to quarters. My men and those among the crew whom we know can be trusted will be placed at key points. The bridge, engineering, the crew and common areas. The submersible's garage."

I turned to George. He appeared resolved. Even calm.

"How does it feel to be the face that launched a thousand ships?" I asked.

George's lips crooked. "I'm not Helen of Troy. Ren is."

I dipped my head in acknowledgment but said nothing. My mind was running through timelines and ocean depths and the weather. I scribbled on the notepad.

George pulled out a pack of cigarettes, stared blindly at them, and returned them to his shirt pocket. "I'll have Ren post on WeChat as my son, saying that his sister has COVID. Ren will arrange for a pharmaceutical delivery of masks, COVID tests, a thermometer. Perhaps that will get Charlie Han to back off."

"Perfect," Connor said. "Illness will explain why no one has seen the family."

I paused my calculations. "Won't Han notice deliveries piling up if there's no human to take them inside?"

"Ren gives instructions for the items to be left in the garage. She then sends a robot to sweep them into a storage area at the back."

"Clever." I swiveled restlessly in my chair. "Have the two of you looked at the extended weather forecast?"

"Typhoon Kiko," Connor said. "We're aware."

"Then you know that if Kiko turns northwest, which typhoons tend to do in this area, it will bear down on the Philippines." I recalled data I'd studied years ago, when Ocean House had subcontracted George's submersible. "You can't safely operate a submersible in a typhoon. And you can't ride it out below, not in the shallow waters around Apo. Kiko will generate turbulence well below the surface and change the ocean currents. Which means—"

"Potentially destructive vibrations operating against the hull," George said. "Not to mention reduced visibility due to silt and the risk of large objects getting kicked up that could damage the hull or the propulsion system."

"Right," I said. "It would also be dangerous to leave the submersible and attempt to board the littoral vessel. We either get your family off *Red Dragon* before the storm or wait it out and try when the weather clears."

"We can't risk moving the family until we've gotten rid of our escort," Connor said. "That's still more than thirty hours away. Longer, if the typhoon delays our navy. If the Chinese detect the submersible before then, they'll intercept it."

"On the other hand," George added, "if we wait until after the storm, Han and the Guóānbù will have figured out Li-Mei and the children aren't in Lijiang. They'll come after us."

I stood. “We have a typhoon. The possible arrival of Charlie Han. We don’t know if the Chinese will zip off to the Spratlys. We risk a change of heart from the commander of the US Navy Pacific fleet or, if we’re really lucky, from the president of the United States, should he decide this is too diplomatically risky. Does that about cover it?”

“Game strategy,” George said. “If it were easy, anyone could do it.”

“I hope you have a plan B.” I put my hand on the door. “I’ve never been much of a gambler. Not when people’s lives are at stake.”

37

Village of Lijiang, China
November 2, 10:00 a.m. CST

Charlie Han's rage was a living thing. A beast that gripped him by the throat and shook him.

Cursing, he finished his pressing business in the bushes, zipped his pants, and returned to the car. His breath hung in the air. His back ached from hours of surveillance. Earlier he'd nodded off and dreamed he was back in the boys' dormitory on the icy Tibetan Plateau. He'd woken in a cold sweat.

He slid behind the steering wheel and sipped his now-cold tea. Everything was cold. The air. The overcast day. The car smelled of half-eaten takeaway food, cigarettes, and sweat. Yellow leaves from the ginkgo trees had pasted the windshield. As if to mock him, the lights from Mèng's house glowed serenely in the distance, promising warmth and companionship.

Except the companionship was a fabrication. After the dream, Han had called the house. It was his tenth attempt. Someone always answered. Sometimes it was Li-Mei. Other times, one of the children. With each call, Charlie quickly hung up. But on the last call, when the boy answered, Han had stayed on the line, asking questions. After ten minutes or so, the boy's coherence broke down. He repeated himself. Then he contradicted himself. Finally, he hung up on Han.

Charlie had grinned darkly to himself.

It wasn't the boy. It was the AI. Mèng's AI.

The family was on board *Red Dragon*. They'd slipped into hiding while fifty men looked on.

But the only way Charlie could verify it was by breaking into the house. It was a risk his boss refused to approve. No amount of reasoning or pleading would change his mind.

Your ambition is a snake around your neck, his boss had said on their last phone call. *You should be operating for the glory of China. Not for yourself.*

Charlie rolled down the window and spat. Coward. They were all cowards. Only Charlie had the balls to do what needed to be done. And Dai, who was in the Philippines, awaiting word from Han.

It would be easy to break in. He could do so quickly and silently. Yet he hesitated.

Mèng would have arranged for cameras to be everywhere. And on the small chance that Han was wrong . . . well, he might as well put a bullet in his own brain and save the CCP the trouble.

Charlie sat and smoked until his rage banked like embers, fatigue winning out. Even a dragon needed sleep.

He jerked awake when a figure appeared at the passenger window. Zhang Mùchén. The door opened, and Zhang climbed in and settled into the seat, rubbing his hands against the cold. He stank worse than Charlie's car.

"You're supposed to be watching the house," Charlie said to his backup.

"You look like shit," Zhang said to Charlie.

Charlie ignored that. Zhang was a triple agent. A spy pretending to have been recruited by the Americans while still spying for the Chinese. Triple agents had their uses, but Charlie despised this man. Spies could be honorable. Triple spies were suspect—in the game for only the money and susceptible to corruption.

"Bèn dàn," Charlie muttered. *Idiot.*

Zhang shrugged off Charlie's mild insult and opened a bag of Lay's Roasted Garlic Oyster chips. "A little while ago, I let the American, McGrath, know you're watching the house."

Charlie nodded.

All Charlie could do from this pathetic village two thousand miles from *Red Dragon* was apply a little pressure on his enemy. It was satisfying to know that while the American CIA officer thought he controlled Zhang, in truth, Charlie did. If Charlie was right and the Mèng family was on board *Red Dragon*, then as soon as their security chief, this McGrath, heard from Zhang, he would go running to Mèng. He probably already had. With luck, Han's presence near the family home would alarm Mèng and force him to move quickly to get his family off the boat.

Too quickly. Haste bred mistakes.

Dai and other MSS agents were on standby in Manila, watching through the eyes of their drones for any action.

Charlie put the thought aside for the moment. Probably Mèng was too cautious, with the navy hugging their horizon. But at the very least, it would give him a dose of unpleasantness.

Zhang, his mouth full of chips, offered the bag to Charlie. Charlie sneered.

Zhang shrugged again, unoffended, and pulled another chip from the bag.

"You hear the latest about the US Navy?" he asked.

Charlie's fatigue slipped from him as if he'd plunged unexpectedly into an icy pool. "Tell me."

"They've got ships heading west from Guam," he said. "Our minister of national defense made a public announcement. He said that if the ships continue on their apparent path, they will violate our security and sovereignty. They risk serious consequences."

Charlie couldn't care less what the minister said. He said the same thing every time someone in the US Navy sneezed.

What he did care about was why, in these specific hours, the US Navy was showing an interest in the Philippines.

It could be a coincidence.

Or it could be more ominous. The Americans were clever.

Charlie started the car.

"Get out," he said to Zhang.

Zhang gaped at him. "What? Why?"

"You're going to stay here and watch the house. I have urgent matters elsewhere."

"My car is two miles away."

"Out," Charlie said.

He barely waited for Zhang to exit the car before he pulled away. He was already on the phone.

He had to move fast.

38

Approaching Apo Island
November 2, 10:00 a.m. CST

I watched the weather reports throughout the day as Typhoon Kiko intensified.

When I wasn't watching the live updates, I wandered about *Red Dragon* as we voyaged toward the Philippines. Restless, uneasy, I lingered for a time in the library, with its reading nooks and glass-doored bookcases, then took my lunch alone in my stateroom, again glued to the screen, doomscrolling news about deteriorating China-US relations. For an hour, joined by Lukas, I hung out with George in his lab as he examined the handful of specimens he'd collected during our journey and explained their significance.

Lukas was fascinated. But discussions of *Abantennarius rosaceus* and the recently discovered *Hyalinothrix vitrispinum* failed to engage me. Leaving Lukas and George to their discussion, I dropped in on Captain Peng on the bridge. Peng was gracious with my intrusion and shared stories about his childhood growing up in Beijing while we idly watched the live marine traffic on multiple displays. Colorful triangles crawled everywhere around the Philippines and Malaysia and swarmed the heavily trafficked port of Singapore. Orange fishing vessels. Red tankers. Green cargo ships. I recognized the name of one of the cargo ships Matthew used, the optimistically christened *Kingmaker*. He'd taken me on board once when the ship was making a delivery in the US. *Kingmaker*'s size had astonished me, but the delays it had encountered on its journey made me realize how vulnerable our sea lanes are to storms and pirates, politics and disease.

I wished that with all this ship-related noise, George and Li-Mei could simply slip away. But the Chinese would be watching the same traffic on their screens. On the tracker, *Red Dragon* showed up as a purple triangle, indicating a pleasure craft, vibrant against the pale-blue background. *Red Dragon*'s submersible would pop onto their sonar images the instant she launched.

All that could be done now was to watch and wait. Hope that the US Navy came through. That their lure pulled the Chinese away. That Kiko veered east.

Oblivious to my turmoil—or perhaps too kind to mention it—Peng chatted as we drank tea and reviewed the typhoon's possible paths and our own potential responses. Peng pointed out pockets in Kiko's path where we could shelter if need be, which port would be safest from the storm surge, and cheerfully described past storms he'd sailed through. He was a lively storyteller. But when his first officer came in to review charts, I became uncomfortable. The officer was a friendly man, amiable. But Connor had identified him as a likely plant with the Second Department.

When the officer lingered, I grabbed a pair of binoculars, bade Peng farewell, and went outside to walk the decks, shrugging into a sweatshirt as I strolled.

The afternoon was gray and blustery, the seas choppy. Everything on *Red Dragon*'s decks had been covered up or battened down. The boat rode the swells so gracefully I hardly felt them, but other than one of Connor's men stationed on the aft deck, I seemed to be alone. I was content with that, unafraid in my element. Storms at sea must be respected. But on a modern ship with modern equipment, they didn't frighten me in the same way my fellow humans did. Storms followed the laws of physics.

Humans—at least some of them—followed only their own savage appetites.

I stepped into a sheltered niche and checked my phone. Typhoon Kiko was now on a northwestward path, a common initial trajectory for tropical cyclones in this part of the world.

It was too early to know which way she would turn.

I walked out to the railing and raised the binoculars, scanning for our Chinese escort. In the near distance, a cement carrier sailing under a Korean flag rode the waves. A tanker powered past.

Connor's voice startled me. "I thought I might find you out here."

I lowered the binoculars and turned.

"I just spoke with George," Connor said. "Our friends are keeping an eye on Kiko. They've decided to delay their approach to the Spratlys by a few hours. See which way the wind blows, in a manner of speaking. They can make up the time."

"Are we still on for tomorrow night?"

"That's the plan."

"And if the ruse doesn't work? If the Chinese decide to hang out with us?"

Connor scratched along his jaw. "We go dark and run all the way to Australia."

"I like that idea better than the original strategy." I lightly fisted my hands on top of the rail. "You know, I haven't yet asked the obvious question."

"You want to know what happens to us after Mèng and his family escape."

"Mind reader," I said. He laughed and I scowled. "I'm serious. Your men. Lukas. The captain and crew. You and I. Won't we all be considered culpable in Mèng's escape?"

"We've stacked the deck in our favor in case the Chinese want to play rough. Diplomatic channels are open and ready to hum. The US Navy is in the area. A reconnaissance plane carrying a *New York Times* reporter is scheduled to do a flyover the day after George's disappearance.

It's been in the works for months—the *Times* wants to verify Filipino claims about Chinese naval assaults, and the timing works for us. The most immediate intervention will be when Peng commits a minor maritime infraction that requires the Philippine authorities to escort *Red Dragon* to a safe location while our governments sort it out."

I gripped my hands together, watched the knuckles turn white. "How do you feel about armed backup?"

He laughed. "You mean in addition to our navy?"

"I mean someone whom the Chinese want to keep happy for economic reasons." I swept the horizon with my hand. "Somewhere just out of sight is *Kingmaker*, a cargo ship leased by Matthew Hoffman's company and crewed by his own men. The crew is armed and probably willing to show up and just be a presence. But more importantly, because of his trading ventures, Matthew has a direct line to some of the most important people in the CCP."

I had Connor's full attention. "What are you suggesting?"

"Get me a secure line. Let me call Matthew and ask him to be on standby in case we need extra help. I don't want to spend the next ten years of my life in a Chinese prison. I don't want that for the crew, either."

I watched emotions come and go across Connor's bearded face. But after a few minutes, he shook his head. "Involving Matthew, and especially *Kingmaker*, is a legal and ethical quagmire. We can't risk it. We need to go through established channels."

"What if I, as an individual, ask another individual to help a friend?"

"Don't do it, Nadia. We can't manage or monitor your friend. It's too easy for unintended consequences to complicate things. Swear to me you won't reach out."

"I—"

"Swear."

"Son of a bitch." I frowned at him. "I swear. But I would have felt better having Matthew close by."

We stood in silence, watching the water sprout whitecaps as the sky lowered. A light rain fell.

Connor said, "Most people I know would be hunkered down inside. But you seem happy out here."

"Happy is a stretch. But less worried. Or sad."

The wind raised its voice to a howl, flapping *Red Dragon*'s flags and spraying us with mist. In the next instant, the gale softened. Connor and I leaned into the railing.

"I grew up in San Diego," he said. "When I was a kid, I built a Sunfish. Took it out almost every day."

"I had a Sunfish as well," I said, memories flooding. "My dad helped me build it."

"They're amazing little boats, aren't they? After I started sailing, I began to fantasize about getting out on a real boat—something of my own. And here I am."

"On another man's yacht."

"The best in all the world. Custom built by Ocean House. It was fun while it lasted." Lightly, he touched my arm. "Dinner and sleep. Tomorrow, we arrive at Apo Island."

39

Apo Island
November 3, 4:00 p.m. CST

"It doesn't look much like utopia right now," George said. "But for me, Apo Island holds the promise of paradise."

It was late afternoon, and we'd dropped anchor near the steep sides of the volcanic speck. George and I stood in the wind on the forward observation deck, huddled in our anoraks, where only two mornings ago we'd been playing Go and enjoying croissants in the sunshine.

Now the day was prematurely dark, the sun invisible behind a thick shroud of cumulonimbus clouds. The waters were deep green and whitecapped, the beaches gloomy, the trees bent in the gale. During the day, Typhoon Kiko had veered northward, away from a direct hit on the Negros area of the Philippines. But the weather remained rough. The fishermen had retreated, and the tourists had vanished to the resort on the other side of the island. Our Chinese escort hovered at the far horizon, reluctant to engage the Philippine authorities in these waters.

George and I might have been alone in the world.

Wind whipped my hair across my face, and I peeled it back.

"How do you stay calm?" I asked George over the sound of wind and waves.

"It has taken many years of practice to accept what I cannot control. Which is nearly everything in life."

I braced myself against the railing. "Mind if I borrow some of your serenity? I could use a little extra tonight."

"You appear serene."

"It's a facade."

"Everything you need is inside you. Your mind is a sanctuary, your heart a still place."

I punched his shoulder. "You sound like a Buddhist monk."

He laughed. "I probably *would* have run off to Tibet and become a monk if it weren't for Li-Mei. That woman was like a typhoon in her own right. Totally out of my control. Then I discovered the joy of AI. With those two things and the children, my life seemed set."

A door opened behind us, and Connor joined us at the railing. He turned his back to the wind and said, "It's a go."

George's smile vanished. My stomach dropped. I gripped the railing, my gut seething with sudden nausea.

Connor snugged up the hood of his anorak. "As of half an hour ago, our escort departed on a heading that will take them north of the Philippine archipelago. We're expecting them to then turn south as soon as they clear land and then aim for the Spratly Islands. All they've left behind are two militarized fishing boats that are having a rough time on the waves."

George gave a thumbs-up. "Another correct analysis by Ren."

"What kind of sonar do the fishing boats have?" I asked.

"Looks like a towed sonar array," Connor said. "But their ability to detect our submersible is degraded thanks to Kiko's seas. On top of that, I've adapted *Red Dragon*'s sonar so that tonight we'll throw out a bunch of active noise. They'll be blind to what's happening below the surface."

"And Han?" I asked.

"My asset reports that he's still in Lijiang. RenAI seems to be holding her own there."

I stared out at the tumultuous horizon. "And if your asset is lying?"

"He very well might be. But we'll be ready. Han makes it harder, but not impossible. Just stick to the plan unless you hear otherwise from me or George or the captain."

I nodded. We'd run through all this earlier today in the war room.

Everyone had a role to play, spooled out on a strict timetable. George, Lukas—who had been fully briefed after Connor vetted him—and I would wait in our staterooms until just before 2:00 a.m., when the action would start. Peng's position—as always—was on the bridge. The chief engineer, a British national, would be guarding the engine room against possible sabotage. Connor would place his team in designated areas: one man on the bridge, another in engineering. Two men would patrol, one in the crew and common areas, another outside. And two more would be in the garage, securing and guarding the entrance to the submersible.

Connor would oversee everything from the security hub located off the bridge.

After Peng sounded the security alarm, Lukas and I were to make sure all members of the crew made it to the muster point outside the citadel and then entered the panic room. We had twenty minutes to get the crew inside before the next step could take place.

Anyone who didn't report was quite possibly working against us. They would be suspicious of a supposed attack well within Philippine territory and alert to the timing and would figure—correctly—that something else was afoot. I would report their names to Connor and let his men deal with them. The most important thing was to prevent them from spotting Li-Mei or the children. And to keep them from helping Han should MSS arrive.

Only four crew members were excused from the drill: Captain Peng, the chief engineer, the first officer, and Connor in his role as security chief. Of those, only the first officer was considered a spy risk. He'd been assigned to *Red Dragon* months earlier by the CCP. George couldn't protest.

Once the crew was contained—including the first officer, who would be treated to a soporific in his nightly tea—Connor's men would get George and his family to the submersible. Lukas and I would meet them there at 2:30 a.m. to assist.

The submersible would launch and rendezvous with the navy's littoral ship. Sometime in the following days, the submersible would be found far from Apo Island, crushed by the ocean's pressure. A terrible malfunction had sent it to the ocean floor. There were no survivors.

George Mèng had tragically perished at sea.

His family? Chinese and Philippine authorities would grill the crew. Had a woman and children been seen on board? Had anyone accompanied George into the submersible?

Their only answer would be some version of no, or *I don't know.*

Meanwhile, in Australia—or somewhere, not in my "need to know" compartment—a family would arrive and take up residence with new identities, a new future.

It was a good plan. Straightforward. Not terribly risky for those of us on *Red Dragon*. If everything went according to plan.

A pretty big *if.*

"Nadia?"

Connor's voice. I blinked back to the present.

"You doing okay?" he asked.

I forced a nod. "I'm good."

I bade the men farewell for the moment. If all went according to plan, the next time I'd see them would be in the submersible's garage.

Knowing I should eat, I picked up a turkey sandwich in the galley and headed toward my stateroom. Every crew member I passed gave me pause as I tried to assess whether they were on George's side, neutral, or if they answered to one of our enemies. It was a task I'd done since we first departed for Shanghai, probing for weaknesses and loyalties. There were a lot of reasons to trust that most of the crew would either support us or remain neutral. For one, the majority of them would be in the panic room under the belief that we were undergoing a drill or an actual attack. For another, CIA background checks and the fierce loyalty and professionalism of any yachting crew helped me manage my panic. Whether we had one spy or five, if they tried to intercede tonight, Connor's men would take care of them.

As I sat in my room, picking at the turkey sandwich, I ran through Charlie Han's dossier in my mind. His family. His education. His ambitions. I mentally walked through the list of bullet points until only one remained: Han's sister, Xiao.

Han had never forgiven George's father for sending her away.

He was a man, I told myself. Just a man. He didn't have superpowers.

I recalled the words of Mother Julian of Norwich. I'd heard them often during my childhood. "All shall be well, and all shall be well, and all manner of things shall be well."

I was still reciting her words when I set the alarm and dozed off.

Sometime in the night I dreamed I heard two booms from the depths. The rumbles became a single note in a whale's song as I swam in the deep. The song faded and I sank further into sleep.

At 1:30 a.m., I was up and dressed. I waited for Peng to sound the alarm that would send me running to the main lounge with its access point to the citadel two levels below. I clipped my radio onto the waistband of my pants, ran the cord under my shirt, and fastened the mic to the neck opening of my long-sleeve tee.

I was cold despite the comfortable temperature of the cabin, gooseflesh running along my arms.

You can do this, Nadia. Cass's voice.

I did a few jumping jacks and push-ups to get the blood flowing, pleased that I hadn't lost the gains I'd made in Seattle. Pleased that the movement distracted me from my fear.

I was standing motionless, corralling my thoughts, when a light on the wall panel next to the door flashed red.

I stared. The light stopped flashing, there came a faint click, and the light flashed again.

Someone was trying to get in.

Our door codes—mine, Lukas's, George's, and the rooms used by Connor and his men—were changed automatically every night at midnight. Which meant someone had pulled data from the system before then.

My lips formed words without sound: *All will be well.*

I sent an encrypted text to Lukas and George and Connor. Lukas responded: same. The spies were at work, which meant something or someone had tipped them off. I checked the time. The alarm would sound in two minutes. I tucked Cass's letter opener inside the case holding my radio and gripped the Taser that Connor had issued me.

I counted down. *Three . . . two . . . one.*

Through speakers all over the ship, the horn began to blare. Six short blasts followed by two long ones. Even though I had braced for it, the sound shot from my ears to my feet, a tidal wave of visceral panic.

All will be well.

I reached for the door handle.

I'd expected a fight. But the corridor was empty. The alarm had paused, and the only sound was the thud of my heart.

Holding tight to the Taser and stopping to clear each corner, I race-walked down the passage toward the stairs leading up to the main lounge. My radio buzzed. Connor.

"We have company. Get to the citadel and stay there until—"

His voice cut out. *God.* I tried to radio back, but when I pressed the talk button, a shrill squelch filled my ears, followed by the blare of music—a chorus of voices singing in Chinese to a martial tune.

Someone was jamming our comms.

Connor had warned of the risk. "If they jam us," he'd said, "just continue on with your tasks, then head to your assigned muster point."

I sucked in air as my throat tried to close. Assess, then panic.

Get to the lounge.

Then to the submersible.

Air found its way into my lungs. I ran.

—

At the top of the stairs, I jerked to a stop.

A dead man lay sprawled on the carpet. His eyes were open, the front of his shirt drenched in blood.

It was Dale Peterson, Connor's man on internal patrol.

Probably this was supposed to be my fate if the door code had worked. Lukas's fate, as well.

I forced myself to kneel and take Dale's pulse. It was pointless, but also procedure.

"Miss Brenner!"

I jumped up and turned, Taser lifted.

Standing wide eyed and shaking on the top step was one of the crew. A tiny Thai woman named Chalita. She carried an armload of towels, as if she thought she'd do laundry while in the panic room.

"Miss Brenner!" Her voice was a squeak. "That man!"

"Hush," I said.

From the fore of the ship came a faint purr. If every cell in my body hadn't been attuned to *Red Dragon*'s sounds, I wouldn't have caught it.

It was the dive platform's hydraulic arm, lowering the deck.

A solid thunk as the platform latched into place, followed by the echo of feet pounding.

Red Dragon had been boarded. And not by friendlies.

Chalita dropped the towels and stared at Peterson. "There really are pirates."

I took her arm and steered her toward the main lounge and its access door to belowdecks.

"Run," I said.

Belowdecks, thirteen crew members stood in an orderly line, scanning their badges as they entered the panic room. The benefit of repeated drills—everyone operated on muscle memory.

Three crew members were missing. The chief stewardess, the second engineer, and the purser.

I was hugely relieved to see Lukas. I pulled him out into the corridor.

"They killed one of Connor's men," I whispered. "Dale Peterson."

Anger flashed in Lukas's eyes. "Where?"

"In the lounge. And someone lowered the dive platform. I heard men boarding."

Lukas took the blink of an eye to process that. "Which means most of our other defenses will have been deactivated."

I peeled my fingers off Lukas's arm. "With comms down, we can't tell Connor or his men which crew members didn't check in."

A terse nod. "I'd like you to stay in the panic room."

"I'd like that, too. Not happening."

The twitch of his lips might have been a smile. "Then we stick to the plan and get to the submersible. See if there's a chance in hell of launching." His eyes took in my face. "You'll need to stay frosty, Nadia. You ready?"

No.

"Bring it on," I said.

As soon as the crew was locked down in the citadel, Lukas and I headed up the access stairs. He led the way, stopping at the top to kill the lounge's lights and clear the area before gesturing for me to join him.

We were halfway across the room when lights flared through the windows and Lukas dropped to the floor, pulling me with him. He crawled on his elbows to the window and peered out.

"It's a vessel labeled as the Philippine Coast Guard," he said when he returned. "They claim to be offering help. Looks like our answer is no."

"It's not the coast guard," I said.

He tipped his eyebrows at me. "You probably don't believe in Santa Claus, either, do you?"

"Never did."

"Well, you're right. Connor showed me a photo. One of the men in that boat is Charlie Han."

Rather than expose ourselves on deck, Lukas and I returned below and made our way through the technical area toward the garage.

Red Dragon's submersible was in a cavernous two-story wet dock, with a giant transom door providing access to the outside. Even before Peng sounded the alarm, Connor would have opened the transom door and flooded the dock, then readied the motorized ramp—which allowed the submersible to launch without a crane—and run a systems check. George and Li-Mei would have waited until 2:20 before leaving their hiding place and moving toward the wet dock.

Questions banged around in my skull. What if one of the spies had found them? Where were Connor and his men? Had others met the same fate as Dale Peterson?

Avoiding the more straightforward path, we turned left into the engine room. Machinery hummed and our footsteps rang on the metal floor. We squeezed past the engines and gearbox, then scrambled up a narrow flight of stairs to the lazarette, where equipment and gear were stored for use by the deckhands. We paused inside the entrance. All around us were neatly coiled ropes, tools used to repair lines and cables, spare blocks, and equipment even I couldn't identify. A shed that ran the length of the back wall housed shelves for smaller items. A large workbench was bolted to the floor in the center of the room.

On the other side of the room from where we'd entered, a hatch led up to the deck via a ladder secured at floor and ceiling. Deckhands used the hatch while working up top to retrieve whatever equipment they needed from the lazarette.

Now, up above near the hatch, footsteps creaked. Lukas killed the lights.

Someone rattled the handle. A voice shouted in Chinese from farther away, the man above us shouted back, and then the hatch flew open.

Lukas and I darted behind the workbench as a light played around the room. Rain poured in. Wind rattled the laminated instruction sheets posted on the walls.

I peeked over the bench. The light had paused on the shed.

At the base of the door was a child's toothbrush.

My hands rose to my mouth as if to stifle any sound.

That's where they are, I realized. George's family. Or were. In the shed. All they'd had to do was remove some of the shelving and the shed would be roomy, warm, easy to make comfortable. Ready access at night into the owner's private area. And close to the submersible.

The light receded. More rapid-fire Chinese. Now two men stood up above at the hatch, shouting over the storm.

Lukas opened a drawer in the workbench; metal clinked faintly as he withdrew something. He had a gun. But if it came to violence, the quieter the better.

One of the men descended the ladder. The other lowered the hatch behind him. I heard footsteps running away and guessed that the second man had gone for reinforcements.

Lukas stood, and I glimpsed a large spanner wrench in his grip. He crept with a cat's quiet footfall around the bench and toward the intruder, who was watching the shed. I rose at a crouch to peer over the top of the work surface, cringing. The man bent and picked up the toothbrush.

Lukas raised his arm and brought the wrench down at an angle, striking the man in the temple. The man crumpled.

I joined Lukas and we waited, breathing hard. The man lay on his stomach, head turned, the skull above his ear crushed and seeping blood.

I nodded toward the shed and mouthed "George."

—

"George?" I whispered at the door. "Li-Mei? It's Nadia Brenner. We need to get you out of here."

A muffled cry sounded. The door opened, and a petite Chinese woman appeared, wearing a dive suit. Behind her were the boy and girl I'd seen in the family photo—Yú Míng and Baihu. They stared at me wide eyed. They, too, were wearing scuba suits.

Relief swept through me at seeing them, this family who, until now, had been only images from a photograph.

"Where's George?" I asked, hoping Li-Mei spoke English.

"He and Connor went to ready the remora," she whispered. "They should have been back by now. I hear men shouting. What is going on?"

I took her arm. "A remora? That's the word he used?"

"Yes. Like the fish that attaches itself to sharks."

"Not his Triton submersible?"

"No. The sub has already launched. As a decoy to draw off pursuit."

The news came like a punch. Inwardly I cursed Connor for not sharing with me this final twist. But I also admired him. What I didn't know, I couldn't reveal.

"Where is it, Li-Mei? This remora?"

Another shake. "I do not know. George was to take us there. It is bad that he has not come for us."

Lukas leaned in. "We need to go."

"Give me one second," I said, my breath coming hard.

I closed my eyes and pulled up a memory of Cass's general arrangement plan. Her notes and sketches, the cheerful diver leaping into the ocean.

And . . . images danced behind my lids. The faint lines she'd sketched on the hull in her drawing, the suggestion of a doorway that shouldn't be. And a shark swimming nearby. Of course. I made the lines darker in my mind, pulled them into a rectangle, embellished their location on the hull below the waterline.

I opened my eyes.

Now I understood: the two booms I'd heard in the night hadn't been part of a dream. The first sound had been that of a patch being blown off the hull, where it had concealed an outer hatch from the inspectors in Shanghai. That had probably been handled by a Navy SEAL. The second boom was the echo of a navy submersible attaching to *Red Dragon* like a remora to a shark, operated from the littoral ship by remote control. They'd waited to attach the remora until the Chinese ships with the most sophisticated sonar had left the area.

George's original submersible was, as Li-Mei said, a decoy.

Footsteps pounded the metal floor in the engine room below us. Lukas pulled his gun.

"Nadia!" he whispered.

"Let's go," I said. Thinking of the man Lukas had killed, I glanced at the children. "Li-Mei, tell your children to close their eyes until we're at the ladder. We'll guide them."

We fled up the ladder and through the hatch onto the main deck, closing and locking the hatch behind us. The main deck stretched wet and empty before us; for the moment, we were alone.

Above us *Red Dragon* rose against the sky, her surfaces shimmering in the rain. To the east, the clouds had lifted, and a few stars shone. The wind had eased as the remnants of Kiko passed through.

I turned to Li-Mei and the children. "We'll get you to the remora. But first we need to get to the other side of the ship. Are you ready to make a run for it?"

They nodded.

"On three," Lukas said, and counted.

The five of us sprinted across the main deck, the sound of our steps concealed by the drum of rain and the creak of the boat. Farther aft, a man in tactical gear stood at the railing, holding a rifle. All he had to do to see us was turn his head.

Then we were on the other side and crouched in the shadows.

"Where now?" Lukas asked.

"The hatch to the remora will be belowdecks," I said. "Probably hidden behind an equipment locker or something equally large and unlikely. There will be an internal hatch, a wet/dry room, and a second hatch that connects to the sub."

"Yes." Li-Mei nodded. "That is what George said."

Lukas's gaze met mine. We both knew we were hoping for a miracle. George and Connor were almost certainly captured or dead. Access to the remora was likely closed off. Even if we could reach it, I had no idea if Li-Mei could pilot the sub. Or if she would leave without her husband.

One step at a time.

"We've got to try, right?" I asked.

His fierce grin flashed white in his beard. "How do we get there?"

40

Red Dragon
November 3, 3:00 a.m. CST

Down the internal staircase, Lukas first, then George's family, then me. Step, step, pause. Step, step, pause. Straining to hear footsteps or voices ahead or behind. Straining to see in the half dark.

Now and again a gunshot cracked from above.

My thoughts banged along with the rapid thrum of my heart. Emily's words: *Chu songs all around.* George telling me during one of our games of Go: *I am wealthy with my children. Without them I have nothing.*

George had to be okay. And we had to reunite him with his family. And if not . . . could Lukas or I pilot the remora and get the family away?

A man lunged from the shadows at the bottom of the stairs, gun raised.

Li-Mei screamed.

The man's shot went wide, drilling a hole in the wall. Lukas leaped forward, swinging the wrench, crushing the man's skull before he could fire again. Li-Mei pressed the children against her. Neither of them made so much as a peep.

Tough kids.

"Keep going down?" Lukas asked. Blood flecked his face and beard.

I nodded, wondering who had heard the shot and Li-Mei's scream. We skirted past the dead man.

Once we were belowdecks, I mentally paced off the steps as I held Cass's drawing in my mind. Deep in my brain, the location glowed.

I touched Lukas's arm to slow him.

"It's off the passage that leads to the tender garages where the Zodiacs are kept," I told him. "There must be a door concealed inside the storage lockers. We'll reach a changing room and bathroom, then the first garage, and finally the lockers. We're almost there."

In the changing room, we stopped.

"Lukas and I need to clear the area by the remora," I told Li-Mei. "Hide here until we come back for you." I gave her my Taser and asked if she knew how to use it. She nodded.

Our eyes met. Li-Mei's gaze was candid, intelligent, worried. "What should I do if you don't return?"

"Get the children to the panic room. Anyone inside can be trusted. And pray if you believe in prayer."

She nodded and laid her hand on my arm. "Thank you for helping us."

I squeezed her fingers, then grabbed a diving knife from the gear in the changing room and followed Lukas down the passage. He had his gun in his right hand, the wrench in his left.

I continued mentally unspooling our steps as we neared the remora. Not much farther. My eyes darted left and right, searching the shadows.

Voices floated toward us from up ahead. Chinese. Lukas glanced back at me, and I nodded.

Keep going.

Just outside the first tender garage, we found Connor.

He lay curled on his side, unmoving. Blood seeped from a gash on his head. Blood from another wound—chest? shoulder?—soaked his shirt.

Lukas dropped to a knee and felt for a pulse.

A cadence sounded in my mind: *Not Connor, not Connor, not Connor.*

"He's alive," Lukas said. "Keep watch." He stripped off his shirt and used it to bind Connor's upper arm. Then he directed me to hold open the door to the garage while he dragged Connor inside, out of sight.

"Will he live?"

Lukas took in my expression. "He'll be okay."

I couldn't tell whether it was the truth or a lie to make me feel better. I nodded and tried to step forward, toward the passageway. But my knees gave out, and Lukas caught me. My entire body shook.

"I can't," I said.

"It's adrenaline. That's a good thing." He eased me upright. "You're in fighting form, Nadia. Come on."

I pressed my hands to my thighs to stop the shaking. Thought of Cass and nodded.

As we exited, a man loomed in the corridor ahead of us. Lukas fired, dropping him. We ducked back into the doorway, and Lukas whispered for me to wait. A few minutes ticked by, and then a second man appeared, shoving George down the passageway, a gun to the researcher's head, using George as a shield. George's face was bruised, his shirt torn. He clutched his left arm as if it hurt.

He stopped when he saw the dead man.

"Drop!" Lukas yelled in English.

George plunged to the floor as if Lukas's shout had physically thrown him down.

George's captor dropped to a crouch. He still had his gun up. I could see him weighing his options. Shoot George? Retreat? Press forward? His eyes darted back and forth along the passage, looking for the source of the shout.

Lukas stepped out and fired, eternally ending the man's hesitation.

I moved clear of Lukas. "George!"

"Nadia!" George pushed to his feet. "My family."

"They're here," I told him. "They're okay."

George was alive. Connor was alive. I felt as if my heart were beating again. We could do this.

—

After we'd retrieved George's family from the changing room, George led us back past the Zodiacs.

This part of the boat had gone eerily quiet. No sound of men running. No gunshots or shouts. What was happening up above?

George opened one of the wide equipment lockers and crouched inside. I heard a click, then the back of the locker moved, revealing a doorway. "The hatch is through here," he whispered. To his family he said, "Come, come!"

Li-Mei gave me a quick hug. "Thank you."

"Make something of your life," I told her.

She nodded, then ushered her children into the wet/dry room beyond the inner hatch.

"They shot Connor," George told me.

"We found him. He's alive." I forced a smile and hugged him. "Never forget the Confucian virtues. Loyalty. Justice. Respect. Harmony."

"And humanity. RenAI will do her best." He pointed toward a duffel in the wet/dry room, then leaned in to kiss my cheek. "We will never forget you, Nadia Brenner. You will make Ocean House the company it was meant to be." One corner of his mouth ticked up. "Keep playing Go. You'll be a master someday."

"Given that there are more possible moves in Go than the number of atoms in the observable universe?" I found a laugh.

"And yet humans master it. Remember, giving up is not an option."

A lesson he'd taught me. And that Cass had taught me as well. An odd mix of sadness and triumph filled me. Against all odds, Cass had succeeded in what she'd set out to do.

"Maybe we'll play again," I said, knowing we wouldn't. Knowing that—whether or not he and Li-Mei found their freedom—I'd never see them again.

I returned his chaste kiss, then closed the inner hatch, sealing *Red Dragon* against the water that would soon flood the room between the hatches. George opened the hatch leading to the remora and ushered his family into the sub. After he'd closed the remora's hatch, Lukas and I listened while the sub broke free, and water flooded into the room.

Let them make it to freedom, I prayed. *Let them find freedom.*

Lukas and I swung closed the door to the concealing locker, and he turned toward me. "You did it, Nadia."

I was smiling and crying. But there was no time. "Connor," I said to him, and he nodded.

He moved forward into the passageway, keeping me tucked behind him. My thoughts returned to *Red Dragon*. Was the crew still confined in the panic room? Where were the rest of Connor's men? Did Captain Peng still have control of the bridge? Where was Charlie Han?

Was Connor still alive?

Lukas stopped and pressed a finger to his lips. He held his gun in his other hand. He tipped his head, listening. The hull gave a faint shudder in the storm, a regal lady shrugging off the waves. The tenders creaked on their chains.

I caught a whiff of cigarette smoke. Then I heard what had caught Lukas's attention—men approaching.

Lukas grabbed my shoulders and spun me around. "Hide!" he whispered in my ear.

I'd taken a single step toward escape when Lukas crashed into me.

I fell beneath his weight, slamming my skull against the wall just before I hit the ground, smacking my face on the floor. The pain ricocheted down my spine, my breath squeezed beneath the vise of his weight. The knife jumped out of my hand and skittered away. I scrabbled to get my hands and knees under me, shoving at Lukas, trying to free myself.

"Lukas!"

He moaned and rolled off me. Blood trailed after him. The back of my shirt was wet.

I gave up trying to stand and crouched over him. Blood—so much blood—poured from a hole in his shoulder.

"Get out of here," he gasped through clenched teeth.

I glanced down the corridor. Whoever had fired the shot had ducked out of sight.

"Work with me," I told him. I wedged my shoulder under Lukas's until his back lifted off the floor. Then I stood and gripped him by his wrists, bracing my back against the wall as I hauled him up.

"Run," Lukas said. "I've got your back."

I clutched his arm, intending to drag him with me if I had to.

A familiar voice made me freeze.

"Turn around, Miss Brenner," said Charlie Han. "Mr. Pichler."

Lukas braced his right wrist with his left, his right arm shaking as he tried to raise his gun.

"No!" I cried, knowing he couldn't fire in time. "We surrender!"

But Lukas turned.

Han's shot caught Lukas in the chest, knocking him back. His head struck the lockers, jerking him sideways as he fell, the pistol flying into the air and landing somewhere with a clatter.

He rolled onto his back, his eyes meeting mine. I dropped to my knees next to him, looking for something to stanch the bleeding from this new, more terrible, violation.

"Matthew," he said, his voice barely audible, his hands scrabbling the floor around him for the pistol. "He asked about Xiao's disappearance. A debt he was owed. Found out tonight."

Han's sister? "What about her? Lukas! Hang on. Don't leave me."

Lukas's skin had turned a sickly white, his breathing a labored gurgle. The tears I'd shed for George became wrenching sobs. "Lukas!"

His eyes were dark with pain; blood coated his teeth. "Xiao . . . she's . . ." He gasped. "Don't let them win."

A man in tactical gear hauled me up and away.

"Lukas!"

Charlie Han leaned over and fired a second time, hitting Lukas between the eyes.

Dai Shujun and another of Han's men—also built like a slab of rock—dragged me up the stairs to the main deck.

Han and his team had taken over the lounge of George's stateroom. Ten men were crowded into the space. They'd tossed aside sofa cushions and books, resting their booted feet on once-pristine ottomans. The hidden door next to Han's bed was open, the dragon mosaic destroyed. The men had raided the wet bar, toasting each other with rousing cheers for their success at having taken over the boat. Maybe they didn't yet know George and his family were gone. One man had broken the frame holding a scroll from China's Song dynasty, and as I watched, he rolled the ancient artifact into a tight cylinder. He stuffed the scroll inside a pocket.

I felt a faint smile. The scroll was a fake.

Han barked an order, and the men fell silent. Now someone I'd overlooked when I first entered the room came into view. The first officer—the spy for the People's Liberation Army. He watched me with a flat expression.

A single gunshot rang out from the aft part of the ship, then nothing; the only sounds were the quieting waves and the patter of rain.

Han took a seat at the table where George had laid out the paintings he'd made of marine animals. He set the gun on the table in front of him.

I remained standing, bracketed by Dai Shujun and my other escort.

Han removed his spectacles, wiped them on his shirt, replaced them. He sighed. "Miss Brenner, you seem to be an ongoing presence in my life. And an irritating one. Where has George taken his family?"

"What family?" I asked.

Dai Shujun drove his elbow into my stomach. I cried out and folded over as pain wrapped around me like a shroud; the other man's grip kept me from falling.

Had Cass's last moments been like this?

"You are quite alone," Han said. "No one is coming to your rescue. Everyone on this boat is either dead or confined or working for me. Where has George taken his family?"

"What family?" I said again.

Dai swung his fist into my abdomen in the exact place as the first blow. The pain ran over me in a swarm. I sagged in the second man's grip.

"They never boarded," I gasped. "Too afraid."

I squinted up at Han. He shook his head as if I were a bad pupil.

"Again," he said.

The fist landed. I felt as if my insides had exploded. Pain burrowed deep into my organs and bones.

Dai used my hair to pull me upright.

"Where is the family?" Han asked.

I shook my head. If I lost everything else, I wouldn't lose this: George and his family had escaped.

After the fourth blow, they let me fall to the floor. I curled into a fetal position, rocking in agony.

"Bring the girl," Han said to someone I couldn't see.

I listened to footsteps as a man left the room. My heart plunged into my brutalized stomach. What if they'd found George's family after all?

Sounds wafted around me. Bottles clanking, liquid pouring. Men laughing. I laced my hands over my stomach. At last, the man returned with a shuffling figure whom he pushed to the center of the room. Someone fell to the floor next to me and lay still.

I dragged myself to my hands and knees, struggling to see through the waterfall of my hair. I shook my head until my vision cleared.

My breath left me.

Dirty, her hair shorn, wearing a too-big jumpsuit. Even so, I would have recognized her anywhere.

Cass.

A wave of astonishment and relief and joy roared through me, where before there had been only pain. I tried to say her name and managed a grunt.

Finally, "Cass," I groaned.

She turned her head. Her lips crooked up, and she reached for me. "Nadia."

Dai Shujun let out a stream of furious Chinese at Han. I wondered whether he'd known that Cass was alive.

Han waved him off. "Get them up," he snapped.

The room swam as hands pulled me to my feet. Cass swayed nearby. Our eyes met. The pain in my stomach rose until it squeezed my lungs. Would I come so close to having her back, only for her to be taken a second time?

But she lifted her chin and smiled at me through cracked lips. "Fancy meeting you here."

"The drowning game," I whispered.

"I never thought the game would be this hard."

The door opened and a man rushed in. He leaned down and spoke quietly to Han. Han stood, uttered a few words, and snapped his fingers.

Most of the men grabbed weapons and hurried from the room. Only five remained: Han, Dai Shujun and my other gorilla-size escort, and the man who'd brought in Cass.

And the first officer.

"Trouble, Han?" Cass asked.

He didn't answer. He picked up the pistol and walked around the table. He placed the barrel of the gun against her temple.

I screamed, thrashing against the men who held me. Dai struck me in the face. My cheek burst into flames; my teeth bit into my lips. The shock of the pain silenced me.

"And now," Han said, "perhaps you are sufficiently motivated. I know the family escaped. Where did they go?"

I heard Lukas's words in my mind. *Matthew. And Xiao.* I didn't know what Lukas had learned from Matthew, but I found my voice.

"I despise you, Charlie Han. I despise everything you stand for. But I'm sorry about Xiao. You loved her, and George's father sent her away. It was wrong."

Han's expression went suddenly blank.

He glanced toward the first officer, then back at me.

"What did you say?" He spat the words out between gritted teeth.

"I can help you," I said. "Your sister for our lives."

"Silence!" Han's blank expression became an icy mask. "Xiao was a traitor. Whether she lives or not means nothing to me. She betrayed our country."

In two strides he stood in front of me. Now it was me he held the pistol to.

I heard George's voice. *Your mind is a sanctuary, your heart a still place.* I kept my chin high and met Han's gaze while I eased my hand toward the radio case still clipped to my belt. I was thinking of Prince Sang Nila Utama and his crown—the sacrifice the prince made to bring his people safely to shore.

Come what may, I thought.

"You told me I was foolish not to understand Asian culture," I rasped, my fingertips unsnapping the radio case as I babbled, stalling for time. "In that one thing, you were right. So I began to educate myself. Confucius said that to put the world in order, we must first set our hearts right. Confucianism places family above the state. Confucius himself resigned rather than serve a bad government. But you, Charlie Han, are crippled. You have set the Chinese Communist Party above your sister. You have tossed her aside. Buried her alive." My fingers reached steel. I curled my fingers around the hilt of the letter opener. "That is the man you have become while Xiao waited for you to find her."

"That is a lie!" he cried. "I have looked everywhere for her! I joined MSS to find her. I have never stopped trying to learn what George Mèng's father did to her. I—"

He broke off and stared at me, shocked that I had goaded him into a confession.

I smiled. "Maybe you aren't as crippled as I thought."

I had the letter opener in my hand and a prayer on my lips. For success. For absolution.

A gunshot broke the air, a deafening roar that filled the room. Cass screamed. I braced myself for pain and was astonished to feel nothing more than the pain I already carried. My body shook, my mind spun. Was this cold confusion what it was like to die?

Charlie Han crashed to the floor, followed an instant later by another roar that toppled Dai, the proverbial oak in a strong wind.

In rapid succession, the first officer shot the other two men in the room, dropping them where they stood. My ears rang. The very air seemed to have compressed. Cass stumbled to me, and I pulled her into my embrace, feeling how thin her body was, catching the faintest, impossible trace of her perfume. I leaned back to look at her again, to make sure she was real.

"Nadia," she mouthed. She pulled me close and, together, we looked down at Han.

He'd fallen onto his back, legs bent, blood turning his gray shirt dark. His glasses lay smashed nearby, and once again I thought how vulnerable he seemed without the lenses. He stared at the ceiling with a look of bewilderment, his hands spasming, a gurgle in his throat.

His eyes touched mine, and I watched as the light ebbed from them, leaving behind only cold onyx. The man who had terrorized my days and haunted my nights was nothing but a corpse.

He seemed smaller in death than he had in life.

I lifted my head. The first officer still had his gun.

Cass and I held each other.

"I love you," I said, waiting for the terrible roar to sound again. What else was there to say when you were about to die?

"See you on the other side," she answered.

"I'm not going to kill you," the first officer snapped in crisp English.

He toed Han's body, then took the chair where Han had been sitting. He waved to someone in the next room of the suite, and a man came in, half dragging, half carrying another.

Connor McGrath.

The man lowered Connor onto a sofa, then left. The CIA man still had Lukas's now blood-soaked shirt pressed to his biceps, wincing as he looked around the room and then at me. He didn't look surprised to see the dead men, but he didn't look happy, either. When his gaze landed on Cass, though, the darkness in his eyes gave way to astonishment and then joy.

"Welcome back from the dead," he said weakly.

"Happy to be here," she answered.

I squeezed her cold fingers. Sounds from outside filtered in—the cries of men, people running. Voices in English and Filipino.

"What's going on?" I asked Connor.

The first officer answered. "A mess, that's what."

"He's taken over Han's operation," Connor said.

"No," said the first officer. "I am *burying* Han's operation."

I glanced between the two men. "I don't understand."

The officer rubbed his chin. "I like you. You have courage and smarts." He glanced at his watch. "We have a few minutes while my men and the Philippine Coast Guard mop up. I will tell you some of the story so that you hear it from me and not the Americans, who get everything wrong."

I looked at Connor's ashen face. "He needs medical attention."

"He'll get it soon enough. Don't worry, I won't let him die. I need him."

"Need him for what?"

The officer sighed. "I have a daughter your age. She, too, is very curious. It is a problem."

I glanced at Connor, who nodded. Cass and I took the chairs across from the first officer, my fingers still tight around hers. It was impossible not to keep looking at her.

He folded his hands on the table. "You may call me General Lin, although that is not my name. I am a senior official with the Second Department. Are you familiar with it?"

Cass and I both nodded.

"Good. I am here to make a little problem disappear—Han Chenglong, whom you know as Charlie Han."

I remembered what Connor had told me about the feud between the Guóānbù and the Second Department. And his reassurances that the Second Department would not be a problem for us.

A picture slowly began to form, like a yacht taking shape as it emerges from the fog.

"Go on," I said.

"Some of us," Lin said, "work for the glory of China. Others work for themselves. Han was one of the latter, and as a Guóānbù officer, he was a problem for the Second Department. Bright but too ambitious. And too determined to use the Second Department as a ladder on his way up. We have been working to find a way to remove him. When we realized he'd set up a false-front business that allowed MSS to operate in Manila *and* that he was going after Mr. Mèng, we saw an opportunity. The perfect storm, as you Americans say. Han placed himself in the wrong place while conducting the wrong business. The Filipinos are not fond of having Chinese intelligence working in their territory. As it turns out, the US isn't any happier. I sent, how do you say, a little bird to sing in the ears of the right people. Better for everyone if the MSS falls on its face, to use another American saying. Right, Mr. McGrath? A shared goal."

"Right," Connor answered. I saw that the cushion behind him was splotched with red. "What General Lin is reluctant to mention is that he's a great believer in détente."

"You embarrass me. The enemy of my enemy is my friend." Lin pulled out a pack of Furongwang cigarettes and tapped out a smoke.

"Or, to paraphrase Sun Tzu," Connor said, "'in the midst of difficulty, there is also opportunity.'"

Lin nodded his agreement. "Precisely. Han tried to trap us by making sure we were the ones who inspected *Red Dragon* in Shanghai without finding the family. That way, when he exposed George's family on the boat, we would look like fools. I don't like being made to look the fool." He took a deep drag and frowned. "Yet Han was the misguided one, sitting in front of Mèng's home in Lijiang, day after day, watching for the family. They're dead, by the way."

I let out a small cry, and Lin laughed. "Not literally dead. It was all arranged by your friend there." He nodded toward Connor. "Every now and then, the CIA does good work. A house fire. Charred bones. DNA. The works. But the bones are from victims of a car accident who died a year ago. The well-paid coroner in Lijiang will announce that a woman and two children died in the fire, and DNA indicates it was the Mèng family."

"You knew about the fire?" I asked Connor.

He nodded. He was growing paler. "Good detective work on the part of the Second Department."

"We are very good, yes. With the wife and children declared dead, there remained only George. But as your Mr. McGrath had already planned, poor George is theoretically dead, his submersible crushed. At least he died doing what he loved. And we have wiped away that loss of face."

"What loss of face?"

"You are too American. No pride. Would I have arrested George and his family if I'd found them on the boat in Shanghai? Of course. I would have had no choice, no matter the promise I'd made to George's father, who is a great friend of mine. And I would have taken his AI for the glory of the Second Department. But once they escaped, they became an embarrassment. To us. To the party. Better they die than escape. And better *Red Dragon* fall into the Filipinos' hands than the Guóānbù take her back to China as a prize." He looked around the room as if measuring what he was giving up.

"And the AI?"

He waved a hand. "Maybe it is not so bad it leaves China. We don't need it. We have excellent work coming out of our military university."

"I thought the Chinese preferred to steal their technology," I said.

"We're good at that, too. But we have our own talent. Much of it, admittedly, grown inside American businesses. But we are catching up."

"China's National University of Defense Technology," Connor clarified.

Then General Lin looked at me and winked. A wink that said everything he wouldn't. Maybe the Second Department hadn't let RenAI escape with George. Maybe they'd made a copy before George left China.

I closed my eyes for the briefest of moments. *Focus on what matters now. They're safe. George and his family are safe.*

Lin pulled out a phone, spoke briefly, then dropped the phone back in his pocket. "Now we should go."

"Wait," I said. "What about Han's sister? Is she alive?"

"Sentimental American. She is. I believe your Mr. Hoffman is making arrangements for her to be returned to her parents after his employee, Lukas Pichler, tipped him off that *Red Dragon* might run into trouble. Hoffman hoped that securing Xiao's release would work as a bargaining chip to get you and everyone else off this boat." Lin grunted. "The power of American businessmen, even behind the thick walls of the Great Hall of the People. But it is not necessary. We won't detain you. The Second Department wishes to close this investigation and move on." The general stabbed out his cigarette on the table and stood. "Sad, isn't it, that Charlie Han died before he could be reunited with his sister? And while chasing a man who will soon be declared dead by our illustrious party. Now I need to get everyone from China off this boat before the Filipinos claim it as their own."

Outside, the decks swarmed with members of the Philippine Coast Guard. The thirteen crew who'd been in the citadel now stood on the main deck. I saw no sign of Han's Guóānbù agents. The chief stewardess and the purser were also missing. I imagined their fate hadn't been good. Connor's team was present, except for Dale Peterson, who had been shot by the Guóānbù.

The general turned to Connor. "Your men and the crew will be evacuated by the Philippine Coast Guard, who responded to a distress signal." He gave a small bow. "It was a pleasure working with you."

Connor bowed in return. "As always, General."

"You see," the general said to me. "There is always a choice. Mr. McGrath here could have chosen another bullet over cooperation. I, for one, am glad he made the decision he did. Maybe in the future he and I will have the chance to work together again for the good of both our countries."

Connor dug up a grin. "Maybe next time don't shoot me."

Lin laughed. "Call it friendly fire."

The general and his assistant moved away. Captain Peng sounded the alarm to abandon ship: six brief blasts and one prolonged blast on the horn.

Cass and I lowered McGrath onto a chair and turned to face each other.

"I knew you'd come," she said. "My Mazu—the goddess who saves those lost at sea."

Relief burbled through me, accompanied by terror that—if I hadn't changed my mind about working with Connor—Cass might have died in China. "I *didn't* come for you, though. I didn't know you were alive." I felt a deep, if illogical, shame. "I abandoned you."

Cass's face was lined with sadness. "Nadia, you took up my work. It's the same thing. You saved George and Li-Mei and their children. *That's* how you came for me. The rest is just details."

I wasn't sure whether I was laughing or sobbing. I studied her, the shorn hair, her thinness. There were burns on her arms.

"No one was supposed to die that night," she said. "Han smuggled me out. The sex worker was supposed to take my place on the cameras, making it look as if I'd safely departed the hotel. I don't know what happened between Dai Shujun and the woman, but she chose to leap to her death rather than face whatever he intended."

"Why didn't Han"—my voice hitched—"why didn't he kill you when there was no reason to pretend you were alive?"

Cass looked toward the bustling chaos of men shouting, gathering crew members, searching for strays. A man wearing a jacket with a red cross on it was treating Connor's injury.

Cass said, "He never gave up on the idea that I would tell him something useful. About the boat. About George. But the truth, I think, was more than that. He couldn't bring himself to kill me because, in some strange way, that would mean giving up on his sister. He never stopped looking for her."

I thought of Emily. "We're cogs in a machine built by ambitious men."

"That's true," Cass said. She studied my face, smoothed back my hair. "But it's not bad being a mere cog. After all, a single cog can gum up the entire works."

My laughter and tears joined hers as I took her in my arms and held tight.

41

Seattle, Washington
November 18, 3:00 p.m. PDT

I motored *Redemption* east and north, away from our dock on Bainbridge Island.

It was cold, the wind riding hard over Puget Sound. The day had begun with rain, but in the early afternoon, the clouds cleared. Now an orange sun hovered above the western horizon as the moon rose in the east. When we reached the cove where Guy had sat in twilight's hush and told me the truth about our past, I dropped anchor and killed the engine. I joined my sister on deck.

Cass, wrapped in a blanket and sipping a glass of pinot noir, reclined in a chair. She was still thin, but color had come back to her face, and she'd sprouted inch-long peach fuzz over her shorn scalp. She'd taken to wearing a red knit hat with a merlion patch. It suited her.

When I'd asked her if shearing her hair had been an attempt to dehumanize her, she'd surprised me by laughing. "Lice," she said. "I caught lice in that stinking home Han stashed me in."

I poured myself a glass of wine and settled in the chair next to hers.

We'd been out on the ocean almost every day since her return. At first we'd talked about our family. Guy was nearing his last days. With death's approach, he'd found the peace that had eluded him as a younger man. He'd learned that love did not mean weakness. That anger rarely served. He'd lived long enough to see his eldest daughter miraculously restored to his side and his younger daughter demonstrate enough mettle to lead Ocean House. Our transformations seemed to be enough to quiet his demons.

Rob had taken a six-month sabbatical. The last we'd heard from him, he was walking the Camino de Santiago. I wished him wisdom and good walking shoes.

Isabeth and I kept Ocean House going, promoting and leaning on the incredible talent of our teams in Seattle, London, and Singapore. It was early days and slow going. But after Matthew's people had released the news about Paxton Yacht's questionable actions, the media had picked up the story. In a world that relied on fair play and honesty, Brandon Paxton found doors slamming closed. In contrast, my revelation of our past had made Ocean House trustworthy. Our image hadn't been why I'd told the truth at the Monaco Yacht Show, but I was glad that we were again signing up clients for what had always been our specialty: bespoke yachts for discriminating buyers.

Eventually Cass began to talk openly about what had happened the night she'd gone to Marina Bay Sands. The grief and fear she'd felt on learning that Virgil was dead and that she was going to be smuggled out of Singapore. And her paralyzing horror when she heard the Russian prostitute had died. The US and Russian embassies were now working with Singapore to identify the woman and find her family.

Cass herself hadn't been treated badly. Her greatest fear wasn't death but that she'd simply vanish. That Han would keep her locked away until she grew old and eventually died, the world having forgotten about her. *As if,* I'd answered.

"I would have escaped, you know," she said now.

We clinked glasses. It was a conversation we'd had many times.

"Of course you would have," I agreed, both of us knowing it wasn't true. "Yang always survives."

"You're Yang now, as well," she said. "My quiet sister has become someone else."

"If you're trying to talk me into getting another tattoo, don't even."

She laughed. Getting a tattoo was one of the first things she'd done after being discharged from the Manila Naval Hospital in the Philippines. A delicately etched merlion on her right wrist.

"Show me the postcard again," she said.

I'd stashed it in my bag, knowing she would ask. She always asked. I passed it over, the edges soft from her repeated handling.

Cass studied the picture of Uluru, the massive sandstone formation in Australia, then flipped the card to the other side.

> Dear Cassandra and Nadia,
> We are well and happy. The children are excited at the news that they will soon have a baby brother or sister. They have become quite proficient at Go. Nadia, we hope you're continuing to play. With practice, you will become formidable.
>
> May Mazu smile on you both wherever your travels take you. Fair winds and following seas.
>
> With great love and eternal gratitude,
> Ren

The card had been delivered personally by Connor, tucked inside a rare leather-bound edition of Sun Tzu's *The Art of War*. "Our friend was very happy to learn Cassandra survived," Connor had said. "And don't let the postcard fool you. They aren't in Australia."

Connor had come to Bainbridge a week ago. Cass and I met with him inside Bloedel Reserve, where we'd spent an hour walking among the trees.

Now, while *Redemption* gently rocked and Cass appeared to doze, my mind traveled back to our conversation in the reserve, where Connor had shared his news.

General Lin had spoken the truth about Han's sister. With Matthew leveraging his connections, Xiao had been found in a reeducation camp and returned to her parents on the general's orders. About her health or future fate, Connor knew nothing. In thinking about Xiao, I considered how life unspools. Like Pop, Han had attempted to build his future on the bodies of his enemy. Each man, in his own way, had ultimately failed.

As for RenAI, George had taken her with him on a hard drive. I remembered the duffel bag he had pointed to before boarding the remora. It surprised me that an AI could fit on a portable drive. But since I had no idea how the technology worked, I merely asked Connor if George planned to keep Ren to himself. And I told him how General Lin had winked when I'd asked about Ren.

Connor had lifted a brow. "I had to let the general believe he wasn't losing Ren. But the version he possesses is one with carefully designed limitations. They'll work around them eventually, but in the meantime, George and other researchers are working to turn Ren into a watchdog. An AI version of internal affairs. He's unsure how successful they'll be. The AI genie is out of the bottle."

"Trinity," I'd murmured, too quietly for Connor or Cass to hear. The nuclear test that had launched us into the atomic age.

After the confrontation in the South China Sea, Matthew had flown to the Philippines to be with me and to arrange to have Lukas's body returned to his family. We'd strolled along the turquoise waters of Tambobong Beach and talked about Lukas, mourning this man who'd become a friend and then given his life to help us.

As we walked, hands clasped and white sand sugaring our damp feet, I'd reached a decision. Matthew was a good man. And he deserved someone who could love him fully. I'd told him marriage wasn't in the cards for me.

"The door will always be open," he'd said before he shushed me with a kiss.

I'd watched him disappear into the trees, my heart carrying both relief and a new emptiness.

Cass's voice tugged me out of my memories. "Penny for your thoughts," she said.

I startled, recalling Guy's words the last time he'd been on *Redemption*.

"Thinking of you," I said.

She gave me a sly look, a flash of the old Cass.

"I've been on the phone a lot with Connor."

That surprised me. "You still have business to wrap up?"

"Not old business. New." She poured more wine. "It's crazy, Naughty, I know. But I was never so alive as when I was in Singapore. I want to go back. Manage our office there when I'm completely recovered. And . . ."

"And what? Cass, you and I are on the Guóānbù's list. I know we need to expand into Asia. But you're crazy to want to live there." I was thinking of how close I had come to killing a man on board *Red Dragon*. I still didn't know whether I would have followed through had General Lin not intervened. Waking and sleeping, I saw Han's shocked face as he lay dying. And Emily's body after the Guóānbù forced her into their scheme and then murdered her.

China was a rising dragon, the dominant power in the East. It terrified me.

Cass said, "I'm leaving it open. That's all."

"You have a death wish," I snapped.

"I don't, Nadia. I want to *live*."

"By courting death?"

"I want to live, and so do you. Whatever that means for you—running Ocean House, I suppose."

"With Arno Klein."

She nodded. Matthew's investigator had found the descendants of Noah Klein, the lone survivor of the Kleins of Mattsee. Arno was a kindly man, and forgiving, as were his siblings and cousins. We were in ongoing discussions on how to bring the family into Ocean House.

"Whatever it is," Cass said. "And however you want to do it, I'll support you."

She put down her wine and reached over to take my hand in both of hers. "You will always be my protector. My Mazu. If I have you, I can do anything."

I interlaced my fingers with hers.

"You'll be the death of me, Cass."

She removed her cap, let the wind ruffle her growing hair.

"Death comes for all of us. It's part of the deal. All we can do is be sure we *live* first."

She was right. We had to live. For ourselves.

For those who'd gone before us.

And for those who would come after.

Acknowledgments

Every book I write requires an army of experts and fellow writers. *The Drowning Game* was no exception. Here are my heartfelt thanks to those who shared their time and knowledge. I am forever grateful for your stories, wisdom, and generosity.

The experts: Thad Bingel and Command Group (international security experts who have implemented exotic capabilities on client mega yachts and who helped me devise certain plot points). Mystery writer Michael Chandos, who read my book both as a writer and as someone well versed on intelligence. Dr. Meredith Frank for providing insights on viewings at morgues and the condition of bodies after a long fall. David Galante for reading and offering brilliant insights. Selvam Gopaldass, Creative Media Director, and Umadevi Gopaldass for sharing the wonders of Singapore with me and for their help with languages. Love you guys! Captain Rusty Stephens, US Navy, Ret., for his knowledge about submersibles and his willingness to share over cups of caffeinated beverages. Dan Strammiello, who got me kick-started on China and helped along the way. And, last but not least, a person who shall remain nameless but who shared their time and gave me invaluable insights into the business of espionage. I'm so grateful for our conversations.

All mistakes in this novel are mine.

My deep appreciation to my editor at Thomas & Mercer, the fabulous Liz Pearsons, as well as the amazing Charlotte Herscher and my agent, Christina Hogrebe.

Fellow writers and readers who shared their time and wisdom: Mike Bateman—our weekly chats through the course of this novel were invaluable. Deborah Coonts, Cathy Noakes, Michael Shepherd, Robert Spiller—you keep me going. To Angela Crowder of The Novel View for her brilliant feedback, fact-checking, and friendship. And to Amy for guidance and encouragement.

About the Author

Photo © Trystan Photography

Barbara Nickless is the *Wall Street Journal* and Amazon Charts bestselling author of *Play of Shadows*, *Dark of Night*, and *At First Light* in the Dr. Evan Wilding series, as well as the Sydney Rose Parnell series, which includes *Blood on the Tracks*, a *Suspense Magazine* Best of 2016 selection and winner of the Colorado Book Award and the Daphne du Maurier Award for Excellence; *Dead Stop*, winner of the Colorado Book Award and nominee for the Daphne du Maurier Award for Excellence; *Ambush*; and *Gone to Darkness*. Her essays and short stories have appeared in *Writer's Digest* and on Criminal Element, among other markets. She lives in Colorado, where she loves to cave, snowshoe, hike, and drink single malt Scotch—usually not at the same time. Connect with her at www.barbaranickless.com.